A Second Chance

Julie,
God's timing is
perfect... Wait for
(Him). Enjoy!
Blessings Dana K. Ray

DANA K. RAY

eLectio Publishing

Little Elm, TX

A Second Chance
By Dana K. Ray

ISBN-13: 978-1-63213-260-4
Published by eLectio Publishing, LLC
Little Elm, Texas
http://www.eLectioPublishing.com

Printed in the United States of America

First Edition.

5 4 3 2 1 eLP 21 20 19 18 17 16

The eLectio Publishing editing team is comprised of: Christine LePorte, Kaitlyn Campbell, Lori Draft, Sheldon James, Court Dudek, and Jim Eccles.

Publisher's Note
The publisher does not have any control over and does not assume any responsibility for author or third-party websites or their content.

This is a work of fiction. Names, characters, places, and incidents either are the product of the author's imagination or are used fictitiously, and any resemblance to actual persons, living or dead, business establishments, events, or locales is entirely coincidental.

Acknowledgments

A special shout out to my husband and four kids for their constant love, encouragement, support and patience over the years when I was engrossed in my writing. They never let me give up my dream. Love ya!

Thanks to my family and all my friends who continually encouraged me in my writing. A huge thank you to fellow authors Linda, Beatrice and Irene. Without their friendship, critiques and inspiration I would've never stepped out of the boat. And to Jesus for giving me the passion, vision, and persistence to write down the *movies* in my head.

A Second Chance

Chapter 1

Raven staggered into her bedroom and fell on the bed. Darkness pressed into her on every side. A shard of light sliced through the room. She tried to focus on the ceiling, but the room spun around her. She slid to the edge of the bed until one foot lay flat on the floor. It was supposed to stop the spinning. It didn't.

Oh, God. If You keep me from puking, I swear, I'll never drink again.

It was an empty promise, as deceiving as the alcohol. The numbness was too short. All too quickly, she'd end up in the same position, praying the same stupid prayer, talking to a God she didn't know.

Teresa appeared. Raven smiled and reached out to her best friend. Teresa came closer. Her face was white and her lips were blue. Raven's smile faded as terror filled her.

"I'm sorry," Raven whispered and blinked away the tears, then gave her head a gentle shake to rid herself of the ghost. Wrong move. Teresa vanished like a vapor, but her stomach churned in protest. She looked back at the ceiling, pushed the thoughts of Teresa out of her mind, and focused on not puking.

Teresa was back with a vengeance, haunting her this time, calling to her...

"Raven."

Raven rolled on her side and pulled the pillow over her head to muffle the girl's voice. The shrink said the memories would fade. They didn't.

"Raven."

Startled, she sat up and tried to focus on something. Her heart pounded as hard as her head did. She must've been dreaming.

"Raven." There was pounding. "Get the door," her sister yelled.

Raven turned. Hailey stood in the doorway of her room. *Is it morning? Did I sleep? Am I still buzzed or hung over?* She sat motionless for a moment. Her head throbbed. *Cotton mouth. I'm hung over.*

"The door?" Raven asked, but Hailey had already disappeared.

Raven crawled across the bed, peeked out the window, and looked down at the front porch. Travis, the preacher boy, pounded on the door again.

"I'll kill him." The doorbell shrilled through the house, intensifying the pounding in her head.

Her mind drifted back to the party. It had been a success except for Travis. Looks-wise, he was a welcome addition to the guest list. Tall, dark, and handsome was an understatement. But he had one flaw, he was a Christian.

Raven wasn't totally against Christians, but Travis always went overboard. Since his conversion, he was known for going to parties—not to party, but to preach. He called it evangelizing. Everyone else called it something even she wouldn't repeat.

She slid off the bed, stumbled, and caught herself on the dresser. She stood for a moment and waited for her equilibrium to stabilize, then started down the stairs. She threw open the front door and was blinded by the unusually bright sun.

"Are you crazy? Do you know what time it is?"

"Yeah, it's nine o'clock." Travis pushed past her and stood in the living room dressed in perfectly creased khakis and an untucked pinstriped shirt. "You going like that?"

Raven looked down at the same clothes she had on the night before. Jeans and a T-shirt with a pizza stain on it. She was sure she had bed head and smeared mascara.

"Where am I going?"

"To church."

Normally, she would jump at the opportunity to go anywhere with Travis. Despite his apparent Jesus freakishness, he was a wrestler with ripples that made her heart pound. But this was nuts.

"Church?" Her head throbbed and she rubbed her temple. "Who said I was going to church?"

"You did. Last night."

"Last night?"

"Don't you remember?"

Raven paced the living room. "I remember having a really good buzz and you asked me to dance."

"Yeah. You remember anything else?"

Hard triceps, wanting smile, and an overwhelming urge to kiss him. "Nope. I don't remember anything else."

"I asked you to church and you said yes."

"I said yes? Are you sure?" Of course he was sure or he wouldn't be standing in her living room at nine a.m. on Sunday morning. Last night's urge to kiss him turned into a deep desire to get him out of her house, preferably with her *not* in his car on the way to church.

"Even if I did say yes, there's no possible way I can go with you. Look at this place." She motioned in the direction of the table littered with pizza boxes, empty beer cans, and crushed chips. "My parents will be home tomorrow. I have to clean this mess."

"You can clean when you get home. I'll even help."

She chewed on her bottom lip. "Church?"

Travis sat on the brown leather couch and smiled. "It's no big deal what you wear. You might want to wash your face and brush your hair before we go."

Heat rose up her neck to her face. She crossed her arms and glared. "I never said I was going."

"Yes, you did, and I'm not leaving here without you. You promised."

"I made that promise so you'd shut up and dance."

He grinned. "So, you do remember."

Vaguely. When he asked her to dance her stomach fluttered and her heart pounded. They had been friends for a long time but he'd never looked at her as anything else. Last night, she thought all that changed. Apparently not. She had been evangelized.

"Do you know how annoying it is to be slow dancing and you start talking about church?" She shifted her weight to her left leg.

"I care about you."

"Yeah, right." She rolled her eyes.

Travis stood, grabbed her shoulders from behind, and led her into the foyer where an oval mirror hung. "Look at yourself and tell me you don't need church."

She stared at her reflection. If he was referring to her uncombed blonde hair and smeared makeup, she could fix that in five minutes. But if he was referring to her lifestyle, he had no right.

She'd admit some bad happened because of her stupid choices. Others were beyond her control. Some things, no matter how hard she tried, would never change. Alcohol was her comfort, her momentary numbness from the pain.

He turned her to face him, his dimples deep. "It's not that I don't like your raccoon eyes, but maybe you could lighten them up."

She pushed his hands away. "Shut up. You just woke me and I've had very little sleep. I don't need your insults."

"I'm not insulting you. I'm just saying…"

"Yeah, I got makeup smeared around my eyes. I get it." She opened the front door. "You can go now."

"Okay." He grabbed her hand and pulled her towards the door. "Let's go."

She yanked her hand from his. "I'm truly flattered that you think I need *saving* so badly, but I'm not going."

"Would you two get outta here so I can sleep?" Hailey stood at the top of the stairs with her hands on her hips.

"He wants me to go to church." Raven knew her sister would back her up. She'd tell him church was stupid and to get out of their house.

"So, go."

Didn't expect that. Raven stared up at her sister with pursed lips. Hailey rolled her eyes and disappeared.

Travis touched her arm. "Go change, I'll wait."

"Fine." Raven stomped upstairs to her bedroom. "If he thinks I'm dressing up or anything…" She grabbed a black V-neck sweater and pulled it on over her T-shirt, covering the pizza stain. "I'm twenty-one years old and still can't do what I want to do." She looked at her reflection in the mirror, licked a cotton swab, and rolled it under her eyes, removing the stray mascara. She powdered her face and tried to hide her pale, tired skin with blush.

She went into the bathroom, brushed her teeth, ran a brush through her long hair, then grabbed a clip and pulled it up. A squirt of clean-smelling perfume and voilà, not bad for a two-minute makeover.

Travis's smile looked painted on as she walked down the stairs into the living room. She wanted to slap him, but sighed instead. "Let's get this over with."

He shook the keys in his hands as they walked to his black Jeep Cherokee. "Sound a little more enthusiastic and you might get lunch outta me."

She forced a smile and slid into the car. "That may make this all worth it. But you're still helping me clean the house."

He laughed, put the Jeep in gear, and took off.

* * *

She followed Travis into the church. He leaned down and whispered, "You'll like this guy. He's not your typical preacher. He's our age, very dynamic."

"Whatever." Did he really think she cared? In an hour this would all be over. Life would return to normal. Well, as normal as it could be.

Travis led her to the second row and sat. She leaned in. "Can you get any closer?"

"Front row is for decisions. You want to sit there?"

That didn't even warrant an answer. She slouched into the pew and pulled out her phone. It was her turn on Words with Friends.

A band came onto the stage, asked them to stand, and started playing the first song. Her eye caught a man walking in. Must be the not so typical preacher. She tried not to look at him, but found herself staring. His short black hair was longer in front and spiked with gel. He was tall and thin, but well built. She guessed his clean-shaven face would be dawning a shadow by noon. *Travis was right. He isn't your typical preacher—more like a Greek god.* That thought made her look away.

The singing and music stopped and the Greek god walked to the front of the church and welcomed the visitors. He looked at her and smiled before looking around at the other people. Heat filled her face. What was that? Did she look odd and out of place? She sighed. Probably.

He pulled out a yellow card and held it up. "If you could take just a few minutes and fill out your attendance cards, when you finish, please pass them to the center aisle where we'll have the ushers pick them up."

He walked back to the front row as the worship service continued. She mouthed the words to the song and glanced back at him. He looked over his shoulder at her. When their eyes met, he smiled and turned away.

When he stood up to preach, she yawned. Greek god or not, she doubted he could say anything she wanted to hear. She pulled out her phone and checked for text messages, filed her nails, and crushed some candy on Candy Crush.

When he asked everyone to stand and sing a hymn of invitation, Travis looked at her and smiled. She rolled her eyes and crossed her arms. *Really? He thinks one sermon would convert me?* After the closing prayer she made her escape to the bathroom. Last thing she wanted was a lecture from Travis or total strangers asking her a bunch of questions.

She came out of the bathroom to find Travis talking to the good-looking preacher. He stood about three inches taller than Travis. She adjusted her purse on her shoulder. Something was up because Travis's grin was deep.

"Matthew, this is Raven."

"Hi." She shook his hand and smiled with little emotion. "Good sermon."

"Thanks."

"I invited Matthew to lunch with us."

"Seriously?" She knew exactly what he was trying to do. Take her to lunch with the preacher so they could gang up on her, condemn her for her lifestyle, and show her the light. Geeze, did he not know her parents had been trying to do the same thing for the last year?

"We can go another time, it's no big deal." Matthew looked at Travis. "I'll call you."

"No, it's okay." Travis grabbed her arm. "He's cool, I promise."

She looked back at Matthew. What an odd statement to say about a preacher. She doubted that was the word to describe him.

"Yeah." Matthew laughed. "I'm cool."

She rested her weight on one leg. "It's not that, it's just..."

Travis nudged her. "What's the big deal?"

Knowing it was an argument she didn't feel comfortable having in front of the Greek god, she shrugged her shoulders. "Whatever."

"How's Mexican sound?" Travis asked.

Raven frowned. "No Mexican. I don't think I could handle it. My stomach's a little upset."

"Are you sick?" Matthew asked.

"Not exactly."

"How about Bistro's? Would Italian bother your stomach?"

"I guess that'd be okay."

Travis pulled his keys from his pocket. "We'll meet you there."

* * *

Matthew ordered cavatelli, Travis ordered ravioli, and Raven ordered a house salad. Raven gazed at Matthew. If she had met him anywhere else, she would have never guessed preacher. Banker. Stock-broker. Model, but not a preacher. Warmth filled her face and she looked away.

"So, you liked my sermon?"

"Yeah." She wondered if Greek gods could preach. Maybe if she'd listened, she'd know. She took the basket he handed her and looked at the warm bread. Her mouth watered, but her stomach churned. She ignored the stomach and took a piece. Maybe small bites with water would help.

"You really liked it?" Matthew slathered butter on his bread. "You looked bored."

"I don't go to church much."

"How come?"

She tore off a small piece of bread and placed it in her mouth. She chewed it, then took a sip of water. If evangelizing was on his mind, she wanted no part of it. Greek god or not, she wasn't in the mood to be converted.

"He doesn't mean anything by it. He's just asking." Travis's gaze shifted to Matthew. "We had this discussion in the car on the way over. She thinks we're going to gang up and try to brainwash her."

"I never said brainwash. I said I didn't want you two trying to convert me, or whatever it is you do."

"I am a preacher. Converting people is my job." Matthew winked, dipped the bread in the marinara sauce, and took a bite. He pushed the food to one side of his mouth. "I usually don't brainwash people the first time I meet them."

The heat was back on her face and she couldn't figure out why. Was he flirting with her? Doubtful, but his eyes were soft and caring. He put her at ease, even though he seemed to see things she desperately tried to hide.

"I went to church when I was younger and was baptized when I was twelve. I don't have much time for it these days."

He seemed content with the answer because he continued eating the bread.

Travis's phone rang. "Excuse me." He got up and left them alone.

Raven glanced around the restaurant until she mustered up the courage to look back at him. His jaw line was strong and distinct. She had been right, his evening shadow was already appearing. Her stomach fluttered, and she couldn't believe she was thinking of him in *that* way. *A preacher and Raven Pennington? Ha. That would be like Heaven and Hell colliding.*

Travis walked back to the table, his hands deep in his pockets. "My mom's car broke down and I've gotta go get her. Matthew can either take you home after lunch or we'll have to go now."

"I can run her home." Matthew leaned back in the chair.

Raven battled a grin. Seemed the Greek god wanted her to stay. "Do I have a say in this?" She raised an eyebrow at both men.

"You can trust Matthew."

"You can." Matthew smiled, his dark eyes inviting.

She chewed on her bottom lip. Trust wasn't the issue, the evangelizing was. But she had to admit, being left with him might be worth the whole evangelism thing. He could say just about anything if she could sit and stare at him for an hour or two. She decided Greek god was an understatement; Calvin Klein underwear model was a closer resemblance.

"We good?" Travis's question brought her back to reality.

"Yeah, whatever."

Travis squatted next to her, his arm around her shoulder. "I'll call you later."

"I won't hold my breath."

Any other day, his words would've stopped her heart but not today. He woke her up and made her go to church. Now he left her with the bill and forgot he was supposed to help clean her parents' house.

A few minutes after Travis left, the waiter set their food on the table.

"I'll pray." Matthew cupped his hands.

Pray? Was he crazy? In public? Someone might see them. Before she could protest he bowed his head, leaned into the table, and spoke out loud.

She bowed her head and hoped no one she knew saw her. Her only saving grace was that he looked like Hercules. The more she thought about it the less worried she became. Any girl in her situation would let him pray, too.

She pushed her salad around on the plate and thought Pepto would be a better choice.

"Seriously, you weren't impressed with my sermon, were you?"

"Does it really matter?"

"I like constructive criticism."

"It had nothing to do with you." She laid her fork down. "I'm just not into listening to a sermon. No offense."

"None taken. So, where have you gone to church in the past?"

"First Christian, years ago. My parents still go there." She sipped her water. "How old are you?"

"Twenty-three. And you?"

"Twenty-one."

"College?" Matthew asked.

"Second year. Working on a business degree. I'd like to run a home for troubled teens." She snuck a small bite of salad. "Did you always want to be a preacher?"

"Yep. I always felt God calling me to preach."

What an odd statement. She had been dragged to church as far back as she could remember, but never once could she say she felt God telling her to do anything. Even if she had, she doubted she would've known it was Him. "What do you mean you felt God calling you?"

Matthew ran the napkin across his mouth. "When I prayed, I knew in my heart that God wanted me to preach."

She shook her head. "Does your father preach?"

"Yeah, and his father before him."

"Maybe it wasn't God. Maybe you felt like you had to preach to follow in the family's footsteps."

The left side of his mouth rose in a grin. "When you know God and pray, you know what He wants you to do." Matthew picked up his fork and took a bite of food. "How did Travis get you to come to church?"

She wanted to lie, but knew she couldn't. He *was* a preacher. "We were at a party. He asked me to dance so he could ask me to church."

"And you said yes?"

"Only to get him to shut up and dance."

"I'm glad you came."

"Yeah. Me, too. You know, you're kinda cool for a preacher. I mean, you figure preachers to be old and stuffy, always telling you the things you're doing wrong."

"I figure you know if you're doing something wrong."

Ouch. He was making her feel guilty without accusing her of anything. How did preachers do that?

"For the record, I don't need converting."

"Okay."

He took another bite. As he chewed, she could see the lines growing deeper on his face. By the slight grin, she figured he didn't believe her about the converting thing. What did she care? After today, she'd never see him again.

"So, this party you were at…"

"Here it comes." She rolled her eyes.

"Here comes what?"

"The lecture. Maybe I spoke too soon about how cool you were." She took another bite of salad. It seemed to be lifting her spirits. It definitely helped her headache.

"I was just going to ask if you go to very many parties."

"I host most of them. Does that count?" She laughed, but he didn't crack a smile. Had she offended him? She gave a mental head shake. Why did she even care?

"Do you drink alcohol?" he asked.

"Can't really have a party without it."

"Why do you drink?"

"What do you mean, why?"

He shrugged. "I've never had a drink, so I don't know what it does for you."

"You what? You've never drank? Ever?"

"Never."

"Not even a glass of wine with dinner? Nothing?"

"Nope."

"I can't remember a time in my life when alcohol wasn't around. My grandparents used to have these really big parties. My sister and I would sit in the bedroom where they put the coats. We'd pick a couple out—big fake furs, and wear them around. We'd get our glass of water, use pencils for cigarettes, and walk around like we were at the party. We thought we were pretty cool."

"And now? You still think it's cool?"

She pushed the half-eaten salad away, took a deep breath, and slowly let it out. "I don't know. I guess."

"What do you mean, you guess?"

"It starts out helping me forget, but it always ends up bad."

Matthew placed his napkin on his plate. His face intense, like he was trying to look deep within her soul. "What are you trying to forget?"

Teresa's pale face flashed into Raven's memory. She could see the room. The bed. The blood. Her stomach roiled. "Things you wouldn't understand." She looked at the time on her phone. "I

15

should be going. If we can get the check?" She waved at the waiter. The last thing she wanted was to remember.

"I'm sorry. Did I say something?"

"No. It's just we come from two different worlds. You don't understand what I've seen and gone through. If you did, you wouldn't condemn me for drinking."

The more she tried to excuse it the more concerned he appeared. An absurd hope grew. Maybe she could talk to him. He seemed sincere. Wasn't there some sort of minister confidentiality thing? Wouldn't he have to keep her secret?

She mentally kicked herself. If three different shrinks couldn't help, she doubted the Greek god could.

"Well, if you ever want to talk, I'm here."

The waiter came back with the check. Matthew glanced at it, pulled out money, and put them both on the table. "This is on me."

"Thanks, I owe you."

"I may collect on that."

* * *

I may collect on that? Did I really just say that? How lame. He started the car and glanced at her before pulling out of the parking lot. Why did he feel such a strange attraction to this girl?

Her face was hard, but her eyes were soft and as blue as the ocean. He knew that even the ocean had under-currents that were dangerous and could easily sweep you away.

She admitted to going to church, but she didn't know Jesus.

He glanced in Raven's direction then back to the road. "You have plans Friday night?"

She turned to him, her forehead wrinkled, her eyes questioning.

16

"Oh, no, I'm not asking you out. Not that I wouldn't... I mean..." *I'm an idiot.* "I have a girlfriend."

"That house, there." She pointed. "Where's she at?"

"She lives in Davenport." How did they get on the subject of Lisa? "About Friday night." He pulled the car into the drive, threw it in park, and turned to her. "A couple times a month we have this thing called Rock the House. Local Christian bands come in and do concerts. I just wondered if you wanted to come."

"Sorry, I can't."

He studied her eyes. Why was she apprehensive? Did she have a party or was she afraid of the whole converting thing? Maybe both.

"What?" she asked.

"Why can't you? Are you going to a party?"

"No."

"Are you throwing a party?" He raised an eyebrow.

"No. I have to work. Thanks for asking. Maybe some other time."

When she reached for the door handle, he grabbed her arm. "Wait, I got it."

He jumped out of the car, jogged around, and opened the door for her. She climbed out, looked up at him, and cocked her head.

"What? You've never seen a guy open the car door for a girl before?"

"Actually, no." She smiled.

"Can I call you sometime?"

"Yeah, I guess." She reached her hand out as if she expected him to hand her something.

His eyebrows wrinkled. "What?"

"Give me your phone and I'll add my number."

He nodded, feeling stupid. He reached in his pocket and pulled out his cell. She took it, punched in her number, snapped a selfie, and handed it back. "I added my photo."

He reached into his pocket and pulled out a business card. "If you ever need anything or just want to talk, give me a call. It's got my cell on there, too."

"Thanks." She tucked the card in her back pocket, pulled her phone out, and clicked a picture. "For your profile." She walked backwards toward the house, gave him a wave, and went inside.

He climbed into his car and took off. There was no denying Raven stirred something in him, something he couldn't explain. He felt drawn to her by an unknown force. A force that would have to identify itself so he'd know how to proceed.

Chapter 2

Raven looked at the alarm on her phone. Five minutes before the deafening beeps would tell her to get up. She couldn't remember the last time she'd set an alarm on a Sunday, let alone woke up before it went off.

The week had dragged on and the only highlights were her all-consuming thoughts of Matthew. She couldn't go to one of the biggest parties of the year because the Greek god got in her conscience. Guilt. It was a new feeling, and she wasn't sure she liked it.

She shut the alarm off, rubbed her eyes, and got out of bed. After flat-ironing her hair, she put on makeup and the little black dress that Vogue said no woman could live without.

She thought for a moment about grabbing a Bible, but had no clue where hers was. She laughed at herself. *You doing this for you, Pennington, or to impress him?* Both, she decided.

Grabbing her purse, she walked downstairs. Her mother's voice came from the kitchen, "Raven, is that you? Do you want coffee?"

Everything changed after the accident. Mom became Irene and rarely did she ask Raven where she was going or who she'd be with. Not because her mom didn't care. She did. Raven just always shut her down. "No, thanks. I'll see you guys later."

Irene walked into the living room. "You look nice."

"I'm going to church. To Calvary."

Hailey walked out of the kitchen and stood next to their mother. "Did I hear you say you're going to church?" She sipped on a cup of coffee. "Why?"

"Why not?" Raven shrugged her shoulders.

"There's gotta be a guy." Hailey smirked.

Raven took a deep breath and wondered how to get out of this. "Can't I just want to go to church?"

"It's Travis." Hailey grinned. "You a Jesus freak, now?"

Irene hit Hailey's arm.

"No. And it's not Travis."

Hailey tipped her head. "Then why?"

"I met the preacher there, okay? His name is Matthew. He's a nice guy and he asked me to come hear him preach."

"The preacher?" Irene's voice rose an octave. "How old is he?"

"Twenty-three. He's a nice guy, just out of Bible College." Raven wished she'd never brought it up. "Maybe I'll find religion." The sarcasm ran thick.

Hailey laughed.

Irene's eyes softened. "You know I'd love nothing more than to have the church help you change your life but—"

"But what? You think I would never do that?" Raven pursed her lips. Anger surged even though she understood the doubts. Nothing her parents tried had helped—group counseling, doctors and their pills, shrinks, the pastor at their church. They all took a shot, but none of them could stop the nightmares. Teresa stayed right there in Raven's head, her dead eyes haunting her. She gave her head a gentle shake; it helped hide the image. "Thanks for the vote of confidence."

"I'm just saying…" Irene reached up to brush Raven's hair out of her eyes. Raven dodged the attempt. Irene crossed her arms. "You can't go to church because of a guy. And if you have some ideas about this preacher and you—"

"I don't." Raven raised her voice. "I'm just going to church. Okay?"

Maybe she should rethink this. Who knew going to church would cause such an uproar? All she wanted to do was listen to Matthew preach. Two weeks ago she was going to a party with a guy who had more tats than you could count, and her mother kissed her cheek and told her to have fun. She goes to church and gets the third degree.

"Whatever." Raven snagged her keys off the table. "I'll see you guys later."

"Will you be home for lunch?"

"Maybe, I don't know. I have to work at one." She hurried out the door.

As she pulled into the church parking lot, she found herself reevaluating the situation. Yes, she wanted to see Matthew. Who wouldn't want to see the Greek god? But there was something else that went beyond his looks. There was something else that drew her to him. Something she couldn't explain.

The tapping on the window startled her. She turned to see Travis smiling. He opened the door. "Don't you look nice all fancied up? You trying to impress someone?"

"Shut up." She climbed out of the car. "I'm trying to decide what I'm doing here."

Travis put his arm around her. "Face it, you can't resist me."

"Yeah, I can." She brushed his arm off. "I just thought I didn't give Matthew a fair shot last week."

"Too hung over." Travis nodded. "You hung over this morning?"

"Nope."

"I didn't think I saw you at Adam's party." He opened the door to the church building.

"You went?" She walked inside. "After work, I hung out with Russ and Irene."

"I'll bet that was weird."

"It was." She smiled at the lady who handed her a bulletin as they walked into the sanctuary. She searched for Matthew. "We watched some lame movie while they quizzed me on why I wasn't out with my friends."

Raven followed Travis to the same pew they'd sat at the week before.

"You'll have to admit, it is kind of unusual that you weren't out partying." He looked over at her. "Why weren't you?"

"Just didn't feel like going."

He grinned, his dimples deep. "Maybe you're feeling guilty? Like there's more to this than you know."

She ignored him. She doubted anything or anyone could take away the pain.

He leaned into her. "I'm glad you're here. Jesus really is the best thing that has happened to me. He can help you."

She gave him a slight nod, still unsure how she would trust Jesus, even if she wanted to. Matthew walked up to the front of the church. His black suit, shirt, and tie looked striking against his dark complexion. When he smiled at her she smiled back, then whispered to Travis. "So, you didn't get anyone to come to church today?"

"Nope. I tried though."

She patted his leg. "Maybe next week."

When Matthew began his sermon, she swore the room emptied. He stood behind the pulpit and talked directly to her. She couldn't remember half of what he said except that she was a sinner, Jesus would forgive her, and He would help her. Only one catch—she had to give her life to Him.

The invitation hymn started. Raven's stomach stirred and she thought she was going to puke. Her heart raced so fast, she knew a heart attack was imminent.

Her mouth felt like cotton, her mind at war with itself. One side wanted to go forward and try Jesus, the other screamed how insane that was. Did she want to be labeled a Jesus freak? Would

Jesus let her down like everyone else had? He hadn't proved too faithful so far.

The singing ended and she sat down. Her heart finally returned to a normal rhythm. She should've stepped forward, but she couldn't. Matthew claimed Jesus could forgive her for anything, but he didn't know what she'd done.

Raven's cell phone vibrated. She looked at the message. *Busted. Come home.*

Raven texted her sister back. *What?*

Mom and dad suspicious about church. Searched room. Found stuff.

She slid the phone back into her pocket and chewed on her thumbnail. She had made the choice to give up drinking and doing drugs so she wasn't quite sure why she didn't throw her stash out. *Stupid.*

Now she'd spend the next hour staring in her parents' disappointed faces, trying to convince them she didn't do that anymore. It might be a hard sell since she was still trying to convince herself.

Travis turned to her as they stood. "You want to do lunch?"

"No, thanks."

Before church, all she could think of was seeing Matthew's godlike bod and listening to the hope he offered. Now, she just wanted to get out of there. Not that she was looking forward to confronting her parents, but talking to Matthew would just remind her of who she really was.

She looked down. No eye contact. Last thing she needed was complete strangers telling her how glad they were to see her.

She pushed on the glass door, walked outside, and ran into Matthew.

"Hi." He smiled. "Glad to see you again. I think Travis and I are grabbing lunch. You want to join us?"

"I can't." The breeze picked up her hair and blew it into her face. She grabbed it and tucked it behind her ears. "I gotta go."

"Hey." He touched her arm as she turned away. "What's wrong?"

She looked into his eyes. How could he be concerned about her? He didn't even know her. If he did, he'd never look at her the same. Maybe that's what she should do. Tell him the truth so she could get him and his Jesus out of her life.

"You really want to know?" She cocked her head.

"Yes."

He seemed sincere. "My sister just informed me that my parents searched my room and found some stuff in it. I've got to get home because Russ and Irene will be ready for this big confrontation and—"

"Stuff?" His eyes narrowed.

Her chin went up in defiance. "Alcohol, drugs. Depends on how hard they looked."

Matthew's soft face disappeared. He said nothing. What had she expected him to say? That he still wanted to do lunch? That he'd call her? By the blank look she knew he didn't want anything to do with her.

She shook her head. "I gotta go."

Her gait quickened to the car. *It doesn't matter. He doesn't matter.* She threw her purse in the passenger seat, started the car, and drove home, leaving behind any ideas of forgiveness and hope.

Tension was thick when she walked into the house. Her parents sat in the living room. Irene's eyes were bloodshot. Russ's were hard.

Her mother motioned for her to sit. "We would like to talk to you."

"I figured."

Raven sat on the edge of the recliner. She knew what was coming, but she was different. This fact posed a problem. No matter what she said, her parents wouldn't believe her. She had told so many lies over the past year, she was having a hard time remembering what the truth was.

Irene lowered her eyes and wrung her hands. "Show her, Russ."

Raven's heart pounded. Her dad placed a large bottle of vodka, pot, a pipe, and some pills on the table. Leftovers from the last party. The party Travis never did help her clean up. She looked at it and wondered why she hadn't thrown it out. Was she that unsure she had changed? Her eyes met her dad's.

"You going to say anything?" Russ's neck was red.

She had been down this same road countless times and it was always the same. They'd yell. She'd yell back, then apologize and promise to never do it again. Only this time, she'd mean it. She hadn't bought into anything Matthew said about Jesus, but she knew that alcohol and drugs were getting her nowhere, fast.

"I quit. I really did." Her shoulders slumped. "I guess I forgot to throw it out."

"Do you know how many times I've heard you say that?" Russ clenched his teeth.

"This time it's true. I promise." At least, she was really trying to quit.

"I thought we raised you better than that." Irene shook her head.

"Yeah, that's right. Turn this back on you. It's all your fault. Go cry to your women's group and tell them what a horrible daughter you have. My problems, well, that should put you on the top of the prayer chain." Raven wondered where the anger was coming from, but she couldn't stop it.

"Don't talk to your mother that way." Russ stood. "This is about you."

"I'm trying to change, okay? That's all I can say." She looked up at her father's doubting eyes. She'd promised she'd quit so many times she couldn't blame him for not believing her.

Russ paced the living room. "I don't know what to do with you anymore. If you want to throw your life away, that's your choice."

"But I've changed, really."

Russ shook his head in disbelief. "I find anything like this again, you're out of here. Got it?"

Tears formed. She tried to blink them away. He'd been mad before, but he'd never threatened to kick her out. Maybe she should move out. Get away from the house, the neighborhood, and the memories.

Russ dropped to the couch. "I hate to be harsh, Raven, but I'm done with all of this."

Irene grabbed Russ's hand and gave it a gentle squeeze. She looked over at Raven, her eyes moist. "Do you have any idea what it's like to lay in bed every night wondering when the police are going to knock on the door and tell me you're dead? Every time the phone rings, I have a panic attack. I can't do it anymore, Raven. I just can't."

"I'm clean, I promise." Raven's pleas were meaningless. She ached for them to believe her, to see that there was something good in her. They couldn't and she didn't blame them. She'd lied to them too many times. "All I can do is try to convince you." She glanced at the time on her phone. She slumped in the chair as silence chilled the room. "I'm sorry, I have to work."

Russ and Irene glanced at each other, then back at her. The nod from her dad assured her the conversation was over and she had permission to leave.

Raven found Hailey at the top of the stairs. Raven's heart pounded. "I go to church and this is what happens?"

"They care about you."

"Maybe they should care more about you. You're the one dropping out of college and marrying Jake. Maybe you could tell them that. Take the heat off me."

"I think you like the heat. 'Cause if you really did quit, you'd have thrown the stuff out." Hailey's eyes pierced through her.

Raven stomped to her room, slammed the door, leaned against it, and slid to the floor. She pulled her knees to her chest, hugged them, and dropped her head. The collision of who she was and who she wanted to be made her feel like she had been sucked up in a tornado. She only wished it would throw her to the ground — at least then, she'd know where she stood.

* * *

Matthew did the preacher thing. Shook hands and talked to the people, even though inside he was in knots. He couldn't deny Raven's confession had shocked him. Only to his surprise, his shock was mixed with repulsion. Not with her, but with himself. Nothing like preaching about love and forgiveness then moments later being judgmental and uncompassionate.

Was he so appalled by her sin that he couldn't offer her one ounce of understanding? How would she know Christ's forgiveness if he couldn't show it to her?

He turned down lunch with Travis and was thankful to have the church to himself. He walked into his office, pulled out his cell, and called Raven.

"Matthew?" He sensed anger in her voice.

"How's it going there?"

"Why do you care?"

Okay, he deserved that. He paced the office. How could he convince her that he really did? "I do." It was all he could think of.

"You could've fooled me."

"I'm sorry. I don't always know the right thing to say." The silence from the other end was deafening. "I really am sorry. I wasn't prepared. I'm an idiot sometimes."

She sighed. "It's okay. I've got to get ready for work."

Matthew rubbed his forehead, trying to figure out how to make this right. "I've just never met anyone like you before."

"It's okay, really." Her voice softened. "I'm not mad. I understand, I guess. I really do have to go."

"Okay, see you later?"

"Bye." She left him with dead air.

He slid his phone in his pocket, locked up the church, and went home.

The house next to the church was his. It wasn't much. It had the essentials, a kitchen table, couch, TV, and no rent. The church owned it.

He tossed his keys on the table, grabbed the remote, and turned on ESPN. He pulled the ringing cell phone from his pocket. It was Lisa.

"Hello." He fell onto the couch.

"Hi, Matthew." Her voice was soft and soothing. "How's it going there? Everything okay at church?"

Matthew gave his hair a quick comb through. His thoughts intense. "I don't know. There's this girl that is really struggling. I want to help her, but she's so closed up, so mad at God."

"How old is she?"

"Twenty-one."

"Did you two go out to lunch?"

Matthew sensed jealously, but wasn't sure about Lisa anymore. At first, he had asked her out to make his father happy. They dated, and at one point, he thought about marrying her. Things had changed over the past year. He wanted more than pleasing his parents and pleasing her. He'd felt restless, like there should be more.

"We went to lunch last week." He stretched out on the couch. "Is that a problem?"

"I was just asking. You made it very plain that you weren't sure about us."

He sighed. Not the conversation he wanted to have. "I don't know about marriage right now and I know that's what you want. I don't know how else to explain it."

"You want to keep dating or you don't. It's not difficult." Her voice dripped with anger or resignation.

"All I said was that I didn't know."

"And now? Are we still dating?"

"Why do I have to define this right now? Seriously, can we not just see where God leads us?" He rubbed his forehead. "This is what I get for being honest."

The silence was deafening. Maybe he should just make a clean break. His new captivation with Raven could be the sign he was looking for.

"I need to go. I love you, Matthew."

"I know." He wanted to return the gesture to make her feel better, but couldn't lie.

Chapter 3

It had been almost a week since Raven had talked to Matthew. They texted a few times. Simple things.

How are you?

Doing okay. U?

Good. What's going on?

Nothing. Just working and school.

Will I see you Sunday?

I'll try. No promises.

Raven thought about giving him a call, but decided against it. Maybe it would be better to forget Matthew and his hope. He was intriguing, but the whole *God thing* wasn't for her. She had already quit drinking and smoking; maybe that'd be enough. She deserved the darkness that consumed her.

She sat in the almost empty sports grill. ESPN played in the background. A few patrons sat scattered throughout the restaurant, which didn't bother her a bit since there were none in her section.

Jenny, another waitress, leaned against the bar next to her. "Your boyfriend's back."

Raven looked up from her chemistry book to see Cody and his three sidekick jocks. Memories tried to surface. She squashed them, refusing to look back.

"He's not my boyfriend. Not anymore."

"You want me to get them?"

"No, I'll go." Raven stood, gave her skirt a quick tug, and wished another inch of fabric would miraculously appear. She walked to their table, gave a forced smile, and laid cardboard coasters around the table. "What'll it be, boys?" She pulled the notepad from the black apron tied around her waist.

Cody slid off his black North Face jacket. The black Under Armour clung to his massive chest and arms. "Four cowboy burgers with rings, and a couple of Dews." He combed his fingers through of his short brown hair, flexing every muscle along the way. "Missed you at the party last night."

Raven smiled even though she knew the only thing he'd missed was the chance to harass her. She tucked the pad and pen into her apron. "I'm trying to keep it clean."

"Oh, yeah. Forgot you were a Jesus freak."

The guys at the table roared with laughter.

He was crazy. Her two appearances at Matthew's church had already labeled her. Maybe she should be thankful that was all he was calling her. He could've called her much worse.

She decided she'd humor him. If she could keep him in a good mood maybe they'd avoid a confrontation. She flashed a flirtatious smile. "By the looks of it, you're still working out."

He grinned and flexed his biceps. "Always."

She forced a smile and walked back to the bar.

Raven punched the order into the computer and walked by the kitchen window where the cook was. "Four boys with rings." She walked back to the dining area and glanced at the door. Travis and Matthew walked in. Her heart pounded so hard, she wondered if they could hear it. She couldn't believe how excited she was to see Matthew when she thought she had decided that it'd be better to forget him.

She laughed at the idea, grabbed four glasses, made the Mountain Dews, and took them to Cody and his friends. "There you go."

"Thanks." Cody peeled the shell off a peanut. "Refill this." He scooted the half empty bowl toward her.

She reached over to a neighboring table, took the full bowl, and set it in front of him. "Anything else?"

"A little volume so we can hear ESPN."

"Sure thing."

"Hey." Cody grabbed her arm and pulled her close. His breath was hot in her ear and for a moment, she remembered a much happier time when Cody's words were full of love—not hate; encouragement—not condemnation. That image vanished with Cody's harsh words. "You ready to talk?" His grip tightened.

She looked into his eyes. "No."

* * *

Matthew's eyes were glued on Raven and narrowed as the young man gripped her arm. Whatever he had said made her cower and her face turn white. She had answered him quickly and it didn't look like it appeased him.

The color returned to her face. She left their table and went to the TV in the corner. Her skirt rose as she reached up to the controls. Heat filled his face and he turned away, ashamed of the feelings she stirred in him.

He'd apologized for how he'd acted the last time he saw her, but wanted to see for himself if she had forgiven him. He gave himself a mental eye roll. Who was he kidding? It was an excuse to see her again.

Raven approached Matthew's table. His heart quickened. She set down two glasses of water and slid in the booth next to Travis. Her hair was pulled back into a pony-tail with a few shorter strands outlining her face.

"How's it going?" she asked Travis before speaking to Matthew. "Nice to see you."

"You, too." Matthew grabbed a menu and avoided her eyes.

"Hey, gorgeous," Cody yelled and held up his empty glass. "How 'bout it?"

She gave him a quick nod, then glanced back at Travis and Matthew. "You two know what you want?"

"Give us a minute," Matthew said.

"Be right back."

Travis looked up at her, his face soft, full of concern. "You okay?"

"Yeah." She smiled at him. "I'll be right back."

Matthew set down the menu as she walked away. "Who's that guy over there?"

Travis took a gulp of his water. "That's Cody. They've known each since they were kids. They dated for a year. Everyone thought they'd be together forever. It ended bad."

Matthew watched Raven make four drinks and walk them back to the table. Cody said something to her, stood, grabbed her arm, and pushed her down a hallway toward the bathrooms.

"Be right back." Matthew followed Cody and Raven.

"You going tonight?" he heard Cody ask.

He stopped and looked around the corner. Cody's neck was red like fire. His face was hard, yet his eyes were soft, and appeared to be filled with love. It was odd.

"Is that a problem?" Her eyes narrowed. She seemed to be picking a fight with him.

"Why can't you just tell me what really happened?" It sounded more like a plea than an order.

Raven shook her head. "I've told you everything."

"Liar."

"Excuse me." Matthew stepped forward, his voice firm. He had no doubt Cody could crush him in a second. He was built like the Hulk. Knowing that fact didn't stop him. He swallowed his insecurity and took another step toward them. "Is everything all right?"

Raven looked over at Matthew. "We're okay."

Matthew's eyes locked with hers. They seemed sincere and unafraid, but the guy's face was hard. "You sure?"

"She *said*..." Cody turned to him.

Raven touched Cody's arm, which brought his attention back to her. "Yes," she said. "We're just talking. I'll be right out."

The red in Cody's face faded.

Matthew nodded, took a step back, and leaned against the wall, his arms crossed. He wasn't about to leave her alone. It wasn't that Matthew wanted to make the guy any angrier, but he'd protect Raven if necessary.

She looked back at Cody, her face soft. "I'm sorry, Cody. I can't tell you anymore."

Cody's face was unchanged as he brushed past Matthew but Raven seemed unable to move. After a moment, she straightened her shoulders and walked toward him. He stood up straight. "You sure you're okay?"

"I'm fine."

"That was intense."

"Cody's always intense."

"Listen..."

"No, you listen." Her voice soft and sorrowful. "You don't know him and you don't know why he acts like that. If you did, you'd be on his side, not mine."

"You're right, I don't know what's going on, but I know you should be treated with respect regardless of anything that happened." He couldn't believe it—he was sticking up for her, even risking a fight, and she was mad at him. He couldn't do anything right around her.

She shook her head and looked at the ground. "I deserve anything he dishes out."

Matthew was about to argue, when she touched his arm. "It's okay. Come on. Let me get your orders."

* * *

Raven took a deep breath and slowly exhaled as Cody throw some money on the table, slid his coat on, and walked out. Fear of her secret being revealed left with him.

Jenny nudged her. "You going to take that food out before it gets cold?"

"Oh, yeah." Raven walked to the window, grabbed the plates, and took them to Matthew and Travis.

"Here you go." She slid their burgers in front of them.

"Can you sit?" Matthew asked.

She looked around at the empty restaurant and laughed. "We're pretty busy." She slid into the booth next to Matthew.

"I'll pray." Matthew lowered his head.

Raven looked around the room. She still wasn't buying into all his talk of church, but lowered her head as Matthew said amen, unsure why she pretended.

When he claimed he was sorry, he seemed sincere. What if he found out about what else she'd done? *He'd never look at me the same.*

Travis took a bite of his burger and pushed the food to the side of his cheek. "You going tonight?"

She shrugged her shoulders. "I guess. Jill wants to." Sitting with a bunch of kids at a wrestling pep rally wasn't really her idea of fun, but she owed Jill.

"Who's Jill?" Matthew squirted ketchup on his plate.

"A friend." Raven hated to admit she was the only one that had stuck by her. Not once did Jill call her crazy or a killer like so many others had.

She glanced over at Travis. "You going?"

"Of course." He scooted his plate to the center of the table. "Unlike you, I like all this college stuff. Making memories."

She rolled her eyes. He could have all his feel good memories. They all could. She'd live without them. She turned to Matthew. "What about you?"

"Travis invited me, so I might stop by. I'd like to see the college ministry at the church grow."

She nodded out of courtesy. What did it matter to her? He could grow the college ministry for all she cared. It wouldn't help her. Nothing would. There wasn't anything he could say that would lift the darkness. She slid out of the booth and set their check down. "Then I guess I might see you guys in a few hours."

Travis laid some money on top of the check. "Yep."

Matthew nodded and gave her a slight grin. "That'd be nice."

Her face flushed. As they walked out, she wondered why a simple grin and kind word from Matthew would make her blush. Maybe it was his innocence. Despite his apparent disgust of her past there was an acceptance about him. He was inviting her to experience something he lived for, something he'd die for.

She shook the thoughts of his faith from her head. She doubted she'd ever feel that way about his religion.

Chapter 4

Raven pulled her red Camry into the gravel parking lot behind the student union. Her heart pounded. This was such a bad idea. It would be like an old high school reunion. All the people she didn't want to see, drug connections, drinking buddies, people she bullied, and Cody.

"Thanks for coming with me." Jill grabbed the gas station Styrofoam cup mixed with vodka.

"Yep." Raven threw the car into park.

"You know what it reminds me of?"

"What?"

"Remember that wrestling match we went and watched—the one right before you and Cody started dating?"

"Districts."

"We were so drunk."

"You were so drunk." Raven grabbed the sheer pink lipstick out of her purse and ran it along her lips. "You were hitting on Sasha's boyfriend. Man, I thought she was going to kill you."

"I got one good kiss out of it." Jill grinned deep. She gulped more of the drink.

"And a black eye." Raven shook her head. The fight had been inevitable and Jill was lucky that's all she walked away with. But she'd been too drunk to care.

"I appreciated the way you stuck up for me."

"Teresa stuck up for you." Raven looked into the mirror, ran her finger along the outside of her lips, and collected the stray color. "I was there for moral support."

"You pulled Sasha off."

"Teresa was the one who got her to calm down." She pointed to the cup. "Dump that before we go in."

Jill pushed the cup toward her. "Why don't you help me finish it?"

Raven shook her head. "I told you, I'm done with it. It's getting me nowhere."

"Yeah, yeah. I've heard it before."

"This time I'm serious." Or at least she was serious about trying. Matthew's question about her drinking only solidified her conviction. The alcohol was not helping her. It only made things worse.

She killed the engine and they climbed out of the car. A group of kids had gathered by the giant bear mascot. Yelling rattled the air as two voices escalated.

"Looks like old times." Jill grabbed the drink and followed Raven.

A chill ran through the air. Raven was glad she had changed into jeans. Her heart pounded harder with each step closer to the crowd. "Sasha's crazy."

Jill grabbed Raven's arm and forced her stop. "Would you think about this for a minute? You can't walk in the middle of it."

"I can't stand by while she pushes herself around, scaring people." She ripped her arm from Jill's and walked to the crowd. The chill was forced out by the heat of the moment.

Jill followed. "This isn't going to be pretty."

Raven pried through people. Sasha was in the girl's face, her finger centimeters from her nose. The other girl said something then stepped back.

Raven's hands shook and her chest pounded. Sasha's face was red, her eyes were bloodshot, and her fists tight. Raven could only imagine what she was on.

"Sasha," Raven yelled, her head held high. "Give it a rest." If she was going to win this battle, Sasha would have to see confidence, not fear.

Sasha tore her eyes from the girl. "You got a problem, Pennington?"

"Yeah, I do. Leave her alone." Raven moved between Sasha and the girl. She pushed up the sleeves on her black jacket. She didn't want to fight but maybe protecting this girl would be a penance of some sort.

"You're out of the loop, Pennington. Don't mess with me." Sasha's stringy, dirty blonde hair fell in her face.

She stared into Sasha's ruthless eyes. She had seen Sasha break noses and loosen teeth. "I may be out of the loop, but I'm tired of you picking on people. Grow up."

Sasha stood motionless and glared at Raven. She reached into her pocket, pulled out a pack of cigarettes, and lit one, then offered it to Raven.

Raven pursed her lips together.

"Oh, yeah." Sasha sucked on the cigarette and let the smoke escape while she talked. "Forgot, you found religion."

"Just because I don't want a smoke doesn't mean I found anything."

Jill burst between them. "Why don't we all just settle down?"

"Shut up," Raven and Sasha shouted in unison. Jill backed away.

Sasha took another drag and blew the smoke in Raven's face. "Why don't you enlighten me? Tell me all about it, Jesus freak."

Raven clenched her fists while the laughter surrounded her like the wave at a football game. Fighting was nothing new. She'd been in plenty, usually doing the exact same thing Sasha was doing now. It was the only way to survive in the world she had made herself part of.

Love your enemies.

What? Where did that come from? Raven tried to shake the thought. A calmness came over her. She took a deep breath, released it, and loosened her fists.

"Just let Cara go. She's done nothing to you."

"Oh, you have no idea." Sasha's eyes widened.

Raven glared at Sasha. She knew staring into her eyes was dangerous, but it didn't stop her.

Sasha laughed, grabbed a large cup from a guy's hand, and threw the liquid on the front of Cara. The crowd laughed. Raven took off her jacket and gave it the shivering girl.

"Thank you," Cara whispered and clutched the size ten jacket over her. She lowered her head and walked away.

"Raven."

Raven turned just in time for Sasha to grab Jill's cup and throw the drink on her. Raven screamed as the cold drink drenched her shirt.

Raven shook the vodka and pop off her arms. "Real mature."

Sasha laughed and grabbed Jill's arm. "Come on." Jill shrugged and walked through the rows of cars toward the student union with Sasha. Raven didn't blame Jill. She had to pick a side and Sasha was the logical choice.

Goose bumps covered Raven's body. She heard someone clear their throat behind her. Probably campus police. "Now what?" she mumbled and rolled her eyes as she turned.

"I saw what you did." Matthew removed his jacket and handed it to Raven. "Here."

Raven couldn't believe the Greek god was standing in front of her decked out in faded jeans and a hooded sweatshirt.

She took his jacket. "Guess you made it, huh?"

"That was pretty awesome."

Raven ignored the comment. The last thing she wanted was to be deemed a martyr.

"I thought I was going to have to jump in and break it up."

"That wouldn't be cool. A preacher in the middle of a fight. Not good for the ol' reputation." Raven walked toward her car.

She wanted to see him and for him to leave. She never pretended, but hated him getting a glimpse into her sordid life. It scared her. Maybe because she respected him or she wished he could respect her. Maybe she was just embarrassed. She didn't know.

"You been in many fights?"

"One is too many." Raven leaned against her car and folded her arms. "My first one was in seventh grade. Bailey. A hood. She kept picking on me. Said she didn't like the way I looked at her. One day a rumor went around that she was going to beat me up after school. I was so scared.

"Teresa and I started walking home the same way we did every day. Bailey and her group of hoods were waiting. Before I knew it Bailey was on top of me and Teresa was on top of Bailey. Bailey finally backed down and Teresa and I were accepted into the crowd. Official hoods."

"Which meant?" Matthew sat on the hood of her car. His legs almost touched the ground.

"No one messed with us. We could stand on the corner, smoke, drink, stupid stuff like that. Man, I thought I was so cool." She paused, memories coming fast and furious. She tried to block them out and focus on the question. "The only thing that got you kicked out was if you got knocked up." She tilted her head. "Pregnant."

"I know what knocked up means."

She nodded. "Last year Teresa got pregnant. Her parents are very strict. I mean, very strict. Not because of religion or anything, they didn't want her messing up her life. They had warned her, one more run-in with trouble and she was gone. They were through with her. She was so scared. She couldn't tell them. Everybody turned on her, even me. I was so mean to her." She paused. The last thing she needed was for him to know the truth, but the words kept coming. "My best friend. The girl who defended me. She stuck by me through everything." Her eyes filled with tears and she tried to blink the memories away.

"It's never too late."

"Trust me. It's too late." Raven kicked the gravel and avoided his eyes. Her chest fluttered and the tears tried to return. She couldn't remember the last time she cried and wasn't about to now. Tears were useless.

"You said you used to go to church. Don't you believe anything the Bible says?"

"I was little when I went." She hardened her heart. "I don't know everything the Bible says. I'm not like you, I don't sit and read it."

"Why not?"

"Like I got the time." *Or the desire.*

"I saw the strength you had back there. You stood up for the right thing and you didn't worry about what it cost you. If you can do that, surely you can go to Teresa and ask for forgiveness."

"You don't understand."

"Then explain it to me."

"Because she's dead." The deep voice came from behind. It was Cody. "Teresa's dead, isn't she, Raven?"

Matthew slid off the car, his stance solid and protective.

Raven turned to Cody and looked into his bloodshot eyes. Drunk. She couldn't blame him. Teresa had been his twin sister. "Yes, she is."

Cody leaned into her. "Tell him why."

Raven looked at Matthew, then back at Cody. Her heart thundered as memories crashed through her. Her eyes rested back on Matthew. She knew the next words out of her mouth would change everything. Any hope he offered would be yanked away.

"Tell him." Cody's voice was firm.

She dropped her eyes and whispered, "Because of me."

Cody leaned into her. "Louder."

She took a deep breath and looked up, past Cody at Matthew. "She's dead because of me."

Cody's lips pursed together as one of his friends grabbed his arm. "Come on, man. She ain't worth it."

Cody scowled, turned, and walked away.

She pulled Matthew's coat tighter around her. "I gotta go."

"Let's go get some coffee and talk."

Matthew didn't look shocked, but she couldn't forget how easily he dismissed her last week. "Why would I talk to you? I hardly know you."

He looked deep into her eyes. "I care about you."

"Why?" Her chin quivered as she fought the tears. "Am I that pathetic?"

"You're not pathetic." His eyes were soft, hypnotizing. "I want to help you."

"Why?"

He ran his hand through his thick black hair and began to pace. "I know this is gonna sound crazy, but I feel a connection between us. I felt it the first time I saw you." He stopped and stared at her. "Am I totally nuts or do you feel it, too?"

She hesitated. She did feel it but if she admitted it, it would expose her. The last thing she wanted was to be vulnerable again with anyone. Yet, he offered her something no one else ever had, a true friendship. A friendship that wasn't based on what she had done or who she hung around with. He was different.

Matthew touched her arm. "Why do you blame yourself for Teresa's death?"

She stared into his caring eyes. For a moment, she wanted to tell him everything. She shook her head, pulled her keys out of her pocket, and opened the car door. "I can't talk about it."

Matthew grabbed the door. "You can trust me. I want to help."

"I can't." She climbed into the car, slammed the door, and sped off.

* * *

Gravel sprayed over Matthew's shoes. He shoved his hands in his pockets. For whatever reason, she blamed herself for Teresa's death. Maybe it was her fault. If it was, would his pastoral skills kick in? They sure didn't help him last week. He shook his head. Maybe he'd pushed her too far.

Travis walked up behind him. "What'd you say to her?"

"Nothing." He pulled out his cell phone.

"You're not going to try and call her, are you? She looked pretty ticked. I'd let her cool off."

"She's got my coat." He put the phone to his ear. "Raven."

"Leave me alone."

"You have my coat."

"I do? Sorry."

"Can we meet somewhere, get some coffee? My treat." Matthew waited a few seconds before adding, "I could get my coat."

"I don't want to talk." Her voice was soft and sounded hurt.

"Okay, no talking." He smiled. "Just coffee."

She sighed. "All right. Kaldi's in thirty minutes. I'm going to stop at home and change."

"Okay, see you then."

He slid the phone in his pocket and looked at Travis. "I got her to meet me. You want to tell me what's going on with her?"

"What happened?" Travis tucked his black hair behind his ears.

They walked toward Matthew's black Pathfinder. "I asked her about Teresa."

"Oh, that would do it." Travis leaned against the car and crossed his arms across his chest. "Teresa committed suicide last year. Raven found her."

"Man." Matthew rubbed the back of his neck. "What happened?" He half expected Travis not to answer since he hadn't offered the info earlier.

"Teresa cut her wrists. I can't imagine what Raven walked into. She never talks about it."

"I can see why." Matthew shook his head. "And Cody?"

"Cody and Teresa were twins. I doubt you can get her to talk. Even if you did, I don't know if it'd do any good. I've heard she's been to shrinks, but none of them helped."

* * *

In her room, Raven pulled off the wet sweatshirt, and replaced it with a pink hoodie. She stood for a moment and stared at the only picture in her room of her and Teresa. *Why* she wanted to scream at it, but didn't. It never gave her the answer she so desperately wanted—the answer she needed. She sighed and pushed the pain deeper inside.

She grabbed her purse and Matthew's coat off her bed and walked downstairs where her mother stood.

"Where are you going?"

47

"Out for coffee with a friend."

"Who's the friend?"

"When has it ever mattered?" Raven tucked her hair behind her ears. "It's just a guy. We're going to Kaldi's."

"Who's the guy?"

Raven put her hands on her hips. "It's Matthew, okay?"

Her mother's eyebrows wrinkled. "The preacher?"

"Yeah, I was at the pep rally for wrestling. This girl spilt a drink all over her so I gave her my coat. Matthew loaned me his and I left with it. I'm just returning it." She wasn't sure why she felt the need to explain.

"What's a twenty-three-year-old preacher doing at a college pep rally?"

"Said he's trying to grow the college ministry." She shrugged her shoulders. "He's friends with Travis." She tucked her hands in her pockets. "I'm just returning his coat and having a cup of coffee. I gotta go."

"Raven?"

Raven turned to her mother. "Mom, please…"

Irene took a deep breath. "I'm not trying to run your life, it's just, I don't want you getting hurt."

She rolled her eyes. "I'm not—"

"Would you listen to me for a minute?"

Raven nodded. Through everything, even in her darkest moments, her mother had always been there for her. She had loved her no matter what. What could another lecture hurt?

"Okay."

Irene stepped closer. "I want you to be careful."

"He's a preacher. He's not going to *do* anything to me."

"That's not what I mean. You've been through so much."

"We're just going for coffee, nothing else."

Irene conceded and gave her a nod. "Don't be too late."

"Okay."

* * *

Raven stood in the foyer of the small coffee shop. The aroma of the different blends floated through the air. She looked around. A man sat with his laptop open, his fingers rapidly striking the keys. A young couple, cozy in the corner. Matthew stood and acknowledged her with a nod. She walked to the table, handed him his coat, and slid into the booth. He slid in on the other side.

They sat in silence until the waitress came. Matthew ordered a black decaf, and Raven ordered a half-caf skinny mocha and a glass of water.

"I spoke to Travis after you left." Matthew folded his hands on the table.

"He told you about Teresa?"

"Yes. He said that she committed suicide and you found her."

Travis couldn't have shared any more if he had wanted to. She never talked about it except that one time to a shrink. The one that swore talking would help. It didn't.

"I'm not here to discuss it. I can't."

The waitress set their drinks down. Matthew waited until the she left. "Why?"

Raven sipped on her coffee, her words mechanical. She'd been through the drill before. "Because it won't help."

"How do you know?"

"I've been to shrinks. I've heard it all, and Teresa is still right there in my head. She'll never leave."

"Why does Cody blame you?"

"For the way I treated her. I should've never..." She slowly spun the cup around, then laughed. "You're good. Maybe you should be a shrink."

One side of his mouth curled into a grin. "And give up trying to convert you? No way."

Raven smiled and sipped more coffee. Matthew's eyes were soft and compassionate. Not like the docs who sat with their notepads and asked questions she refused to answer. She always wondered what they wrote since she never said much. They could've been drawing pictures for all she knew. But they got paid and there she sat, week after week, until she convinced her parents she was okay.

Only she wasn't and she knew it. She couldn't figure out how to get out of the darkness that consumed her. Matthew seemed sincere. Something inside her told her he'd be safe to talk to, so why was she hesitating? She sighed. "You really care?"

"Yeah."

"Why? You hardly know me."

He took a sip of his coffee. "I see a beautiful, young woman who has surrounded herself with this persona of a hard outer shell, but I can tell that deep down it's eating you up inside. Talk to me."

"I didn't believe my shrink when he swore that spilling my guts would help, so why would I tell you anything? I've never told anyone else. Not my parents. Not my sister. Not even Cody, even though he wants me to."

"Maybe it would help him to understand. So he could let it go."

"You don't know what I saw, what was said. It almost landed me in a loony bin."

"No, I don't." Matthew leaned into the table. "But if you told me, I'd have a better idea how to help."

Silence blanketed the table. Maybe he could help. Even if he couldn't, she'd at least know where she stood with him.

Matthew leaned back into the booth. "So, you and Cody dated?"

"Yeah, almost a year. Until Teresa died."

"Is that why you drink?"

"I drank a little bit before. It got worse after, but I haven't had a drink in two weeks."

"Did you find religion or something?" Matthew laughed.

"Or something."

"You gonna tell me what happened? I swear I'll take it to the grave. Just give me a chance."

"Give you a chance?" She cocked her head. "So you can look at me like you did last Sunday when I told you my parents found drugs and alcohol in my room? No, thank you. I'm not in the mood to be judged again."

The lines on his face deepened. He rubbed his forehead then pulled his hand down his face, ending with a sweep of his chin. "I said I was sorry about that. We just come from different worlds. I may not understand everything, but I am a good listener. I'd like to prove I'm not a complete moron."

She hesitated, but there was something about his eyes. They were soft and caring. Coaxing her to talk.

"You'll take it to the grave?"

"Yes."

"Okay. You remember Teresa got pregnant and I wouldn't talk to her. It wasn't just because of the hoods." She looked up at him. "I mean, what do you say to a girl who just totally messed up her life? We both knew her parents would kick her out and she had no place to go. She was in college. She had her whole life ahead of her.

"The guy she was dating was a total loser. He couldn't hold a job, let alone take care of a baby. He did more drugs than he sold.

"We got in a huge fight. I kept going on about how she'd messed everything up. The fight escalated. She started talking about getting an abortion. I hate abortion. I believe it's wrong, but she kept on talking about it being her only choice. I finally told her to go do it, if that's what she really wanted."

She looked up into his eyes and held her breath, waiting for the condemnation. When it didn't come, she let out a sigh. "I don't know why I said it. I don't believe in it. It was more sarcasm than advice, really."

Matthew nodded, his expression calm and caring. "So, did she get the abortion?"

"No. Teresa texted me while I was in class. She asked me to stop by on my way home. Said there were some things of mine she wanted to give back."

"So, you went to her house?"

"Yeah." The story played like a movie in her head. The colors were vivid, and the smell of death made her sick to her stomach.

"When I got to Teresa's, the front door was cracked open, I guess to let me in. I could sense something was wrong. I walked in and called out her name. My heart pounded and I could hardly breathe.

"In Teresa's bedroom was this beautiful white quilt her grandmother made for her. The wedding ring pattern, she called it." Tears flooded Raven's eyes. She tried to blink them away. "I found Teresa laying on it. Blood was everywhere. It was still seeping out of her wrists. Her eyes were wide and I swear they were staring at me—yelling at me that I did this to her. I tried to stop the bleeding, but she was already gone." Her voice softened. "If I could've just been a friend to her." Raven looked away from him and wiped the tears from her cheek. She took deep breaths and forced the image from her mind.

Matthew took her hand. "She committed suicide. It wasn't your fault."

"Yes, it was." Raven pulled her hand from his. She talked mechanically. "I don't need sympathy. I know it was my fault. I know Teresa purposely had me find her to punish me."

"She made the choice to kill herself. She may have wanted you to find her, but maybe not to punish you. Maybe she didn't want her mom or dad to find her, or her brother."

"No." Raven shook her head, detaching herself from the scene. "Believe me, I know."

She reached into her purse and pulled out a small hand-embroidered compact. "This was hers. Her mother thought I'd like to have it." She caressed the silk flowers on top, before carefully opening it. "I keep this in here." She pulled out a small folded paper and handed it to Matthew. "She left me that. I've never let anyone see it. Not Teresa's mom. Not Cody. Not even the police."

Matthew carefully opened it. Light brown spots splattered it. Blood that had faded over the year. The writing was faint, barely legible. He tilted it toward the light.

Raven pointed to the paper. "I have it memorized." She looked at Matthew, who read the letter silently. Her voice shook. "'All I needed was a friend. Would that have been so hard? I hate you for doing this to me. For doing this to my baby.'" Tears filled her eyes; she frantically blinked them away. "See, it was my fault."

"It was not your fault. She may have tried to blame you, but it was her choice. You have to give this to God." He folded the note. "You can't carry something around like this any longer."

"I'm glad you think so highly of God. If He really loved me, He wouldn't have allowed me to see that. He wouldn't have let Teresa do that."

"We don't always understand why God allows things to happen. People change. You've changed. Look what you did for that girl back there."

Raven sipped on her mocha. She pushed the images of Teresa out of her head, burying them deep within her soul. "Oh, yeah. I just delayed the inevitable. Sasha will still get her. Maybe tomorrow or next week."

"Have you prayed about this?"

"Pray? Of course I've prayed, but it's like talking to a wall. If I can't forgive myself, how can God forgive me?"

"But God loves you. You have to believe that." Matthew handed her back the letter, his face lined deeply. "You have to tap into a Jesus that you don't know."

"That's easy for you to say. It's your job."

"It's more than my job. It's my life."

"I know what you're saying. I have to be good and do all the right things."

"No, it's not about what you do. It's about what He did for you and how much He loves you. You have to believe in Him with your whole heart and live for Him."

Raven shook her head. "Maybe I just don't believe the same things you do."

"Promise me you'll pray more about this. That you won't give up."

She gave him an almost unnoticeable nod and sipped on her mocha, allowing the images to fade. "What do you do for fun?"

"What?"

"Is this your idea of fun? To find some poor helpless girl and drag out all her painful memories? Fun—do you know what that is?"

Matthew tapped his finger on the table. "I like basketball."

"Ah, men and their sports."

"In fact, I have an extra ticket to the Iowa State, Nebraska game next Saturday night. Would you like to go?"

"What would your girlfriend think about that?"

He grinned. "I'd tell her a friend and I are going to the game."

"I suppose I'd have to go to church tomorrow."

"I am the coolest preacher you know. And you just might learn something, if you don't file your nails or text."

"Man, can you see everything from up there?"

He laughed. "Only in the first few rows."

"Maybe that's why so many people sit in back." Her face grew serious. "I'm really sorry I did all that. I just wasn't into it."

"You mean you were too hung over?"

"Well," she fought a grin, "that, too."

"I wouldn't smile about it."

She pursed her lips. "Ah, the preacher comes out."

"No, I'm being a friend."

Raven raised her hand to stop the lecture. "I know the Bible says, don't get drunk."

"Then why do you drink?"

"I told you, I haven't had a drink in two weeks, but God and me, we still have issues. If I can't trust Him on one thing, how am I supposed to trust Him on other things?"

"At least you're honest. But for the record," Matthew leaned in, his face serious, "you can trust Him on everything."

"Sure."

"What about the game? I'll pick you up around five."

"Okay, I gotta go." She slid out of the booth. "I'll see you."

"At church tomorrow?"

She grinned. "Guess you'll find out in the morning."

Chapter 5

Raven finished her makeup and went back into her bedroom to slip on a pair of black sandals. They contrasted with the faded blue jeans and matched the black tank top she wore under the white shirt.

Back in the bathroom, she grabbed the flat iron and quickly separated a section of hair. Her mother leaned against the doorframe with her arms crossed. "Where are you going?"

"With Matthew to a basketball game."

"Matthew?" Irene shook her head.

"What's that supposed to mean?"

"Let me see your eyes."

"What?" Raven slammed the flat iron on the counter top. She turned to face her mother. "I haven't been drinking or smoking anything."

"That's what you always say."

Irene went into Raven's bedroom.

Raven followed. "What are you doing?"

Irene bent down, lifted the comforter from the bottom of the bed, and looked under it. "Looking for alcohol or drugs." She slid her hands between the mattress and the box spring.

"There aren't any. Why can't you believe that?"

Irene pulled her hands out and dropped the comforter. "All of a sudden I'm supposed to believe you? How long have you been telling me you don't do that anymore?" She opened dresser drawers and ran her hands through the clothes. "Ever since you met that preacher you've withdrawn from your friends and you've been acting strange. Even your sister has noticed it."

"Maybe I changed for the better."

"I wish I could believe you, but I've heard it a hundred times." Irene spun with her hands on her hips. "Don't you see this is for your own good? I don't want you ending up in the hospital, in jail, or dead."

"What? Mom, I'm better. Really."

Her mother shook her head, tears swelling in her eyes. "What kind of church does this man run?" She slammed the last drawer and walked into the closet, moved clothes around and felt pockets. She looked in shoes and their boxes. "He could be selling you the stuff for all I know. Teresa's boyfriend was supposedly a nice guy working at a bank and he dealt drugs. You've probably come up with this stupid story of him being a preacher thinking I'd believe it." She threw the last shoebox down.

"Oh, please, Mother. He's a preacher."

"No preacher I know would ever…" Irene shook her head and stormed past her. She went through the empty bags that hung on a hook in the corner.

"Here." Raven grabbed her purse, opened it, and dumped it out on the bed. "I'm telling you the truth. You're not going to find anything. And why don't you just say it. No decent man, especially a preacher, would be interested in someone like me. I've ruined my life with alcohol, drugs, and a rap sheet. You wouldn't be telling me anything I haven't already told myself. It's not a date. He's not interested in me *that* way. He's more interested in saving my soul, which is more than I can say for you or Dad."

Irene stopped dead in her tracks. Her neck reddened. "Oh, please. We've tried everything with you. We spent a fortune on counseling and nothing helped, it only pushed you farther away. Now you expect me to believe that you woke up one day—and poof—your life has changed."

"It could happen." Raven's eyes darted to the floor.

Irene crossed her arms. "Well, did it? Has this so-called preacher shown you the way? Have you given your life back over to Christ?"

"Well, no, but he's…"

"Then don't stand there and tell me that I can trust you or this man." Irene walked into the bathroom.

Raven followed. She picked up the flat iron, pulled out a section of hair, and began straightening it. Her mother searched the drawers.

"You honestly believe he's not a preacher?" Raven words dripped with sarcasm. "You're so smart. You figured it out. He's a new age cult leader and he's supplying me with this new drug that makes me calm, rational, and happy."

"Well, is he?" Irene slammed the drawer so hard it rattled the perfume bottles on the counter.

Raven almost burned her fingers. "You're unbelievable. Just get out."

"This is my house. You don't want to be here, you know where the door is."

"If I had the money, Irene, I'd be out of here so fast…" Raven unplugged the straightener. "I've got to get ready, so if you don't mind, you can finish searching everything when I'm gone." She walked from the bathroom into her room and slammed the door.

Raven leaned against the door, closed her eyes, and fought the fluttering in her chest. What was happening to her? She hadn't cried in years and now it seemed the tears were always trying to come out. *No, I won't cry.* She shook her head and hardened her heart. Walking to the bed, she threw her things back in her purse.

* * *

Matthew pulled into the driveway and killed the engine. He pulled the two tickets from his breast pocket and stared at them with a smile. Iowa State versus Nebraska. Courtside. You couldn't get better seats unless you were sitting on the bench.

When he asked Raven to go, he didn't really think about how it might look. He didn't want to. His parents had always warned him about dating outside his faith. But this wasn't a date. He was spending time with her to keep her out of her old lifestyle.

Matthew laid the tickets on the dash and for some reason, his stomach turned. He couldn't remember the last time any girl had made him nervous. He ran his hand through his short black hair, climbed out of the car, walked up the porch steps, and knocked.

Irene opened the door and motioned for him to come in.

Matthew extended his hand. "I'm Matthew Stewart. You must be Raven's mom, Irene."

Irene pursed her lips and glared. "I have one question."

Matthew dropped his hand and continued to smile. "Ask away."

"What exactly are your intentions with my daughter?"

The smile drained from his face. His forehead wrinkled. "Excuse me?"

"Hey." Raven's voice came from the stairs, making him turn. She walked down.

"I think you heard me," Irene snapped, which drew his attention back to her. She folded her arms across her chest.

Raven grabbed Matthew's arm. "Let's go."

"No." He turned back to Irene. "I'm Matthew Stewart, Mrs. Pennington. I preach at Calvary Christian Church."

Irene raised her hand in the air. "I've heard the story. I find it odd that a man who claims to be a preacher is going out with a girl that is definitely not your type."

Matthew stared at Irene's judgmental eyes. He didn't know what to say. How could he explain the feelings he had for Raven when he didn't understand them himself?

"Mother." Raven's eyes narrowed. "Don't start this again."

Irene crossed her arms, spun around, and stormed out of the room.

Raven turned back to Matthew. "Don't worry about it." She grabbed his arm and pulled him out the door.

Matthew followed but was torn. Part of him wanted to leave this woman to her crazy ideas. Courtside seats. The other half told him to stay and try to explain. "You don't understand, I can't just let it be," he said, more for his own benefit than Raven's.

Raven continued to lead him toward the Pathfinder. "I'll explain when we get in the car."

Matthew hesitated, the battle still raging in his mind. He sensed Irene's eyes peering at him. He stopped, looked back at the house, and saw the blinds snap closed. He shook his head, and got into the car, going against every instinct he had.

Matthew drove toward the stadium, glancing at Raven. He wished the darkness hadn't come so fast so he could see her face. "What have you told your mother about me?"

"That you're a preacher. My mom has never cared about anyone I've gone out with. You're the first guy that has ever come to the door to meet her. She must think you're some kind of weirdo." Raven forced a laugh. "Oh, come on. She'll be fine. Just forget it, okay?"

"I can't just forget it."

"Don't worry about it. It has nothing to do with you. She'll be fine."

Matthew tapped his fingers on the steering wheel. "That's not who I am." He pulled out his cell and handed it to her.

"What am I supposed to do with this?"

"Punch in her number."

"What?"

"Call your mom for me." His voice firm and forceful. "I just can't let it go."

* * *

Raven stared out the window while Matthew drove and hugged the phone close to his ear. She wished her mother's accusations were true. She couldn't deny she liked him. His new willingness to accept her, faults and all, made him even more attractive. The closer they got, the more acceptance he handed out. She was even beginning to believe that maybe his God could help her.

Matthew's side of the conversation made her laugh silently and shake her head as the words cult and drugs spilled out of his mouth. She could only imagine what her mom was telling him.

He ended the call and said nothing as he drove. His knuckles turned white from his grip on the steering wheel.

* * *

Heat scaled Matthew's neck. He tried to stay calm, but Irene's comments were making him angrier by the second. He took a couple of deep breaths, hoping his heart would quit pounding.

"You didn't tell me she thought I was a cult leader and that I was keeping you from your friends." Matthew darted a glance toward her. "She even had the nerve to ask if I supplied you drugs."

Raven raised her hand to her mouth as she laughed. "She asked you that?"

"Yeah." Matthew pulled into a gas station. He parked under a light, so he could see her face more clearly. He turned to her and placed his hand on the back of the seat. "Don't act like this is no big deal. This is my life."

"I'm sorry." Raven's voice rose as fast as the redness on her face. "She can't figure out why I don't want to hang out with my friends. She doesn't believe I've changed."

Matthew narrowed his eyes.

"I can't believe you're so worked up about this." Raven breathed a jaded laugh. "Don't you think it's crazy that I was drunk and stoned for the last year, but they never gave me a curfew? I'd stay out all night and not one word from them. But God forbid I should find religion."

This was exactly why Matthew fought his feelings for her. As big as her heart was, Raven had too much baggage. Baggage a new, young minister didn't need. "Your parents think my church is a cult. That's nothing to joke about. Have you told them about my church?"

"It's my mom. I told her it's church. You don't understand. We don't *talk* about anything. I try, but she never listens."

"What about your dad? What does he think?"

Raven shrugged her shoulders. "I don't know, he's out of town most of the time."

"It's not just the cult thing." Matthew rubbed his forehead. "She thinks you and me…she thinks *you* think this is a date. You don't, do you?" Matthew watched Raven closely. He wasn't sure if he'd even be able to tell if she was lying. "I mean, you know this isn't a date, right?"

"Of course." Raven grinned. "You don't think I'd ever date a cult leader that deals in drugs, do you? Who'd be attracted to that?"

Matthew ignored her attempt at humor.

* * *

Raven glanced at Matthew as he stared at the basketball game, his face hard. She knew it was her fault he wasn't having fun. She couldn't believe he got so worked up about what one person thought. It wasn't like her mom even went to his church.

Maybe that wasn't why he was mad. Could he be afraid she thought this was a date? Didn't he understand she knew he'd never look at her that way? Either way, his disinterest was annoying.

She sighed and leaned into him. "I'll be right back." He nodded without making eye contact.

She grabbed some cheese fries and a pop from the concession stand and sat at a table in the commons area. When the fries were about half gone, she dumped them and her drink in the trash. Her cell phone vibrated. It was her mother.

"Yeah." She held it tight to her ear.

"I'm sorry about tonight." Irene's voice sounded sincere. "Your sister told me she dropped out of college and that her and Jake are getting married. You seemed distant and I was worried."

"Hailey told you?" Raven chewed on her thumbnail. "I understand. I know I haven't made things easy for you, but really, Matthew is a great guy. He's helping me more than any of those shrinks did."

"I'm glad. Don't stay out too late." Irene drew in a shuddered breath. "I love you."

"I know you do." She chewed on her thumbnail. "Love you, too."

She slid the phone back in her pocket and stood in the doorway to the stairs and watched Matthew.

He stared at the game for a few moments then turned and looked toward the doorway. She moved out of his sight, waited a few seconds, then looked back to be sure—he was looking for her.

Her phone vibrated. It was a text from Matthew. *You okay?*

She texted back. *Yep.*

She waited a few more minutes then walked down the stairs when the halftime buzzer went off. She slid by and sat down.

"Where'd you disappear to?" He stared straight ahead.

"I got a drink and some cheese fries."

64

"You didn't get me anything?"

She couldn't tell if he was joking or serious. "I'm sorry. I didn't figure you'd want anything. I'll go get you something, if you'd like."

"Naw." His face was soft. "I was kidding. Thanks anyway." They sat. "You know, I could've played ball at one of these Big 12 schools, maybe even a Big 10."

"Really?" She looked at him. "You're not just saying that?"

"You think I'd lie? Don't I look like a ball player?" His chest puffed up.

"I guess. You are tall. What are you, six-two?"

"Six-three."

"So, why didn't you?"

"I wanted to preach."

"Oh, yeah, the whole God-calling-you thing." She smiled. "I didn't mean to make you so mad earlier. There are other things going on at home with Hailey and my mom was just being weird."

"Yeah, she mentioned that."

She nodded.

"And I'm sorry for the way I acted, too. I can't afford people believing things about me that aren't true."

"Then maybe we shouldn't be friends."

"I didn't say that." He rubbed his forehead.

She studied him. "You know, I can't figure you out. You're appalled at me one minute, and accepting the next."

"I'm not appalled by you. Preaching is my life. I don't know what I'd do without it. I can't jeopardize that."

"My mom really didn't believe any of that stuff about you and your church. She's just trying to figure this out." She toyed with the chain around her neck. "It's gotta be hard, you know. Her daughter's best friend commits suicide, causing her daughter to go over the deep end. Then, overnight, she cleans up her act? Not likely."

Matthew ran his hand through his hair. "I should be the one saying that."

"You are the preacher." She playfully hit his arm. "Lighten up, preacher man."

The teams ran in and the crowd roared.

She leaned into him. "You may want to act a little more enthusiastic this half."

He looked over at her and smiled. "Okay, but you have to cheer, too."

"Deal."

By the time the final buzzer went off, he was cheering like nothing had happened. She turned to him. "That was a good game. Thanks for bringing me."

"Glad you could come." He stepped into the aisle and motioned for her to walk up the stairs. When they got to his Pathfinder, Matthew opened the door for her and she climbed in. He jogged around and got into the car.

"Can I show you one of my favorite places?" Raven asked.

"Sure."

"Turn left up here." She pointed.

"Where we going?"

"It sounds kinda silly, but I love the park."

"The park?" He glanced at her with a smile. "Okay."

As soon as he killed the engine, she jumped out of the car and walked to her favorite picnic table. She climbed on the table and rested her feet on the bench, leaned her head back, and stared up at the stars. They appeared brighter than usual. "You know, I've been thinking..."

"That's scary." He laughed and sat next to her.

"It actually is, you know. I've been thinking about what you said about talking to Cody. Maybe I should tell him what he wants to know. At least some of it."

Matthew looked into her eyes, his face soft and caring. "I think it would help him."

"Do you really?" She tucked her hair behind her ears. "He's so angry. He's not the same Cody he used to be. I thought he didn't need to know how horrible it was."

"I don't think it's about what you saw. He wants to know why she did it and he thinks you know."

She turned toward him and pulled her legs into a crisscross position. "I can't tell him about the note."

"But that's not why she did it. It's not about you."

"But he'll see that note and blame me even more."

He took her shaking hands. "It wasn't your fault." Conviction and tenderness warmed his voice.

Raven swallowed. She wanted so much to believe him. Did he know the unyielding ache in her soul? Her best friend's life drained from her arms, and she could do...nothing.

"Raven, you've gotta listen. She didn't kill herself because of you. Not because of something you did or didn't do. You have to believe that."

Her eyes burned. She didn't want him to see her threatening tears, but she needed to see his expression. To see if he really believed what he was saying or if it was all a recitation from a counseling course.

When her eyes met his, the tears finally escaped her eyes. She pulled her hands from his and wiped her cheeks, trying to catch them before they got too far. "I'm trying to believe that. I really am."

"You need to face him knowing that. He may try to blame you. Note or not, he may say things that will rip you up inside. Not out of hate but out of hurt. You have to be ready for that."

She nodded and looked away. There wasn't anything Cody could say that could make her feel worse.

"When are you going to tell him?"

"I don't know." She shrugged. "Friday night?"

"Do you think he'd hurt you? Physically, I mean?" His voice was strong and protective.

She looked back at him. "No, he'd never hurt me. Why would you even ask that?"

"He looked pretty intense at the restaurant the other day."

She shook her head. Cody had been through a lot, but physically hurting anyone except on the wrestling mat was not in his nature. "No, he won't hurt me."

Matthew nodded, but it wasn't convincing. She'd let it go. He didn't know Cody like she did.

She allowed the silence to surround them. Looking at the countless stars, she finally said, "How do you do it?" She shook her head and looked at him.

"Do what?"

"Make me want to change?"

He laughed. "It's not me, it's Him." He pointed up.

She tried not to look in his eyes, they were too easy to get lost in. *Get a grip, Pennington. He's got a girlfriend and even if he didn't, he'd never look at you like that.*

She climbed off the picnic table. "I should probably go. Don't want Irene getting the wrong idea." She half smiled and watched him. His face turned red. She knew there was more between them than even he wanted to admit. She could live with that for now.

"No," he smiled. "We wouldn't want that." He jumped off the picnic table and walked beside her. His pace quickened, and he grabbed the car door for her. "Here."

"Thanks." She stopped, her hand resting on the door. Looking up at him, she raised her eyebrows. "I went to your game tonight, how about you do something with me next Saturday?"

His eyes narrowed, but one side of his mouth curled up in a grin. "Okay, only I want to see you tomorrow."

"Tomorrow? What's tomorrow?"

He laughed. "You show up at church—I go with you next Saturday."

"Deal." She climbed in the car. "I'll tell you how to dress when you get in."

He slammed the door, jogged to the driver's side, and climbed in. "How to dress?"

"Yeah." She buckled up and looked at him as he started up the car. "Wear jeans and comfortable shoes, and bring a pair of shorts."

He turned to her, a puzzled look on his face. "Jeans? Couldn't I just wear the shorts?"

"Wear the jeans. Trust me."

His whole face laughed. "Trust you?"

Chapter 6

Denial was something Raven had gotten used to over the last year—pretending nothing happened and living a numb, lifeless existence. Matthew had somehow made her want to change, but the thought of talking to Cody made her retreat to her shell. She knew she had to tell him, and part of her wanted to, but she dreaded it.

She leaned against Cody's car, silently talking to a God she didn't believe would help her. Her heart pounded. When he came around the corner she could see the hardness on his face. She faintly smiled. "Cody?"

He pushed past her, opened the car door, and tossed his books in the back seat. "What do you want?"

"I wondered if you'd meet me tonight at the park, around eight."

He looked down at her, his face hard. "Why would I do that?"

"Because I want to talk to you."

"I'm right here. Start talking." He crossed his arms, his pecs bursting out of his tight T-shirt.

"This isn't something I can say in five minutes before class." She shook her head. "Maybe this was a mistake."

"Yeah, a big mistake." He stared at her, his eyes hard.

Anger consumed her. For almost a year he'd begged her to talk. Now she offers, and he blows her off. It was just like him. "Fine, if you want to meet me, that'd be great. If not, don't worry about it." She switched her backpack to her other shoulder. "See ya."

She turned and walked away. She could feel his eyes piercing through her. She looked back at him. He continued to glare at her as he climbed into his car and peeled off the campus lot. She didn't know if he'd show up, but at least she'd tried.

After her last class, she pulled her cell phone out to see the missed texts. One from Matthew, and one from Cody. Her heart pounded. She read Cody's first.

She took a deep breath and held it. *Maybe.* She let her breath out and smiled. He'd show.

She read Matthew's next. *Hope your day is going good. Call me later, praying for you.* She grinned, slid her phone in her pocket, and walked to her car.

"Pennington."

She turned to see Cody walking toward her. She leaned against her car. "I got your text. So, maybe?"

He rested his hand against the car next to her. "If I show up, you're really going to talk?"

"Yes."

"No games?"

"No."

His eyes narrowed. "Why not right now?"

"I have to work."

She stared up into his eyes and remembered how she used to get lost in them. "You going to meet me?"

"Cody," a girl yelled.

They both looked over at the cheerleader.

"Come here," she added.

Cody waved and yelled, "Give me a minute." He turned back to Raven.

"I'll see you later?" she asked.

"Maybe." He turned on his heels and strutted over to the blonde bombshell.

* * *

72

Raven sat on the swing drawing circles in the sand with her feet and wondered if Cody would show. She mentally shook her head. He'd show. He wanted answers.

Except for the one streetlight, darkness had blanketed the park. Her stomach growled. She hadn't been able to eat all day. Her nerves were shot. She knew she had to tell Cody her nightmares, only she didn't want to relive it again. Knowing she was going to made her want to puke.

She heard the engine of his car before she saw it. Her heart pounded. He climbed out and walked toward her. She stood and walked to a picnic table and sat down.

"I'm here," he said in his usual *you're wasting my time* sort of way.

Raven took a deep breath and tried to slow down her racing heart. She began to doubt whether or not this would help, but knew she couldn't back down now. "I told you, I'm ready to talk," she said in a soft voice. "To answer some of your questions."

His forehead wrinkled. "I'm supposed to think that now, after all this time, you're going to tell me everything?"

She nodded. "What do you want to know?"

"You're serious?"

"Yes." She picked up a small stick and broke it.

He paced before sitting down across from her. His hands rested on the picnic table. He picked at a piece of wood that stuck out. "Why?" His eyes met hers. "Why did she do it? No letter. No nothing. She would've told you something."

"I showed you the text. What she said in it." She slid her hand in the pocket of her jacket where the compact was. She could show him the note, but she wasn't sure what his reaction would be. Could she take the chance that he'd hate her even more than he already did? Part of her wished she hadn't shown it to Matthew. It was a secret she should've taken to her grave.

"What about the last time you talked to her?" His voice brought her attention back to him. "I know you guys got in a fight."

Raven looked away. She'd have to tell him the truth no matter how bad it hurt. When he grabbed her arm, she looked back, fighting tears. "I told her that she'd ruined her life."

"You told her that?" His voice rose an octave.

"Oh, come on, Cody. It's nothing you didn't say when that Susie girl got pregnant two years ago. You made fun of her in front of Teresa. Heck, Teresa made fun of her."

"But this was my sister. She was your friend."

She looked down. "I know. I wish I hadn't said it. If I could take it back I would, but it won't change anything."

Cody nodded.

She looked up at him. His face was softening. Matthew was right. This was what he needed. He was beginning to look and act like the old Cody. The Cody before Teresa killed herself. The Cody she missed so desperately.

"Tell me what you saw…when you found her."

"Why?" Raven's heart pounded out of her chest. *Why hadn't the shrinks been right? They said it'd get easier. It hadn't. Would it ever go away?*

He took her shaking hands. "I just need to know. I've heard what everyone thinks you saw. I want the truth."

She clung to him. "After I called 911, I held her wrists. I didn't know what to do. Blood was everywhere. I knew it was too late, but I tried anyway. I found a scarf on the floor. I tied it around one of her wrists to see if I could stop the bleeding."

"Had she been cutting herself?"

She looked up at him, the tears streaming down her face. "No, I don't know who started that rumor."

"Was she on my grandmother's quilt?"

"Yes."

"Did she say anything before she died?"

"She was already dead when I got there. She must've just been so sad, so devastated. You know Jack had dumped her. Maybe she was scared. I don't know."

Cody stood up and walked around the picnic table, his hands deep in his pockets. He sat down next to her. "Why did you break up with me?"

She looked away from him, ashamed. She knew her excuse would sound lame even though it was real to her. How would he understand? It was the same excuse she'd heard people say his father gave when he left them.

His voice drew her back to him. "When I needed you the most, you walked out. Do you know how I felt? What it looked like? Like you thought I was as crazy as she was."

"But that's not why I broke up with you. I just couldn't..."

"Couldn't what?"

"You reminded me of her, of the pain, of what I saw."

"Same crap my dad said." He shook his head.

Raven had to get away from him now, like she had so many months ago. She hadn't expected him to understand. This was a mistake. She stood and walked toward the trees.

He followed, grabbed her arm, and forced her back around. "You called me, remember? I'm sick of being full of anger and hate. I want to get over this. You're not walking away, not now."

She covered her face in her hands and fell to her knees. The tears flowed freely.

Show him the note.

The voice inside her head was soft but firm. Show him the note? That was crazy. He'd have all the ammunition he needed. It would prove it really was her fault.

Show him the note. The voice was softer, almost assuring her that it'd be okay.

She looked up at him. "Cody, it was my fault."

His forehead wrinkled. "What?"

She dug into her pocket and pulled out the small embroidered compact. Her hands shook as she held it out.

He took it and rubbed it with his fingers. "This was my grandma's. She gave it to Teresa. How'd you get it?"

"Your mom gave it to me after the funeral."

"What did you mean it was your fault?"

She clutched her arms around her stomach, which brought him to his knees in front of her. "What haven't you told me?"

"Open the compact."

He opened it, pulled out the faded blood-splattered note, unfolded it, and read it to himself.

Tears fell from her eyes. "I'm so sorry."

He looked at her. His face was soft, gentle, not at all what she had expected. "Why didn't you show me this? Why didn't you show it to my mom or to the police?"

"I couldn't. They already blamed me. You blamed me. That would just prove it." She began to cry. "It was my fault. I can't make it stop. It won't stop. I see it every day. I see *her* everyday laying on the white quilt. The blood. The smell. It won't stop." She sobbed. "God, I just want it to stop."

Cody pulled her close. His strong arms held her shaking body. "The note doesn't prove it's your fault, but it does help me understand how messed up my sister was. She was sick." His arms tightened around her. "I'm sorry you had to see that and for what she put you through."

"I'm sorry." Her chest heaved and the tears wouldn't stop. "I should've been more of a friend. I never thought she'd do anything like that."

"None of us did."

She rested in Cody's strong arms for a long time. The Cody she remembered. Her friend. The one from childhood was back. Matthew was right, it did help him. Her body started to relax. Wiping her eyes, she pulled away from him. "I hate you hating me."

"It doesn't feel good to me, either." He smiled down at her. "And I don't hate you."

When she looked up, he took her face in his hands and kissed her forehead. He backed away and they stared at each other for a long while. It was closure. Just knowing Cody didn't hate her lifted some of the heaviness from her chest.

"Thank you for telling me." He folded the note. "Why have you kept it?" He handed it to her, along with the compact.

She replaced the note and slid the compact into her pocket.

"I don't know." She lied. She knew why she kept it. It was her penance—to remember the part she'd played in Teresa's death. If she hadn't been so self-absorbed in her own life, she'd have seen how much pain Teresa had been in. She should've been a better friend.

"I'm sorry it took so long for me to talk to you and show you that." She gave a small smile which forced more tears down her cheek. "Can we be friends?"

He nodded and rubbed her arms. "I'd like that."

"Thanks."

He stood and reached down to help her up. He took her hand and walked her to his car.

"I'm sorry for blaming you for what Teresa did." He rubbed his thumb on her hand. "It wasn't your fault."

"I'm trying to believe that. I guess it's something I'll struggle with for a long time." She found comfort in his strength and held tight to his hand. She was saddened over the friendship they'd lost over the last year, but thankful that they could start again.

Cody pulled her close. "You know that Matthew guy is over there watching us."

"What?" Raven started to turn her head.

"Don't look."

Too late. She turned anyway. There he sat in his black Pathfinder. She smiled, wondering what it meant. She looked back at Cody. "I didn't know he was here," she whispered, more to herself than to Cody.

"What'd he think I'd do—hurt you?" He grunted a laugh. "I could snap him in half."

She looked into his eyes. They were soft. It was like the old Cody had never left. "I know you'd never hurt me."

"I know you do."

He played with her hand. It felt good, but not in a boyfriend-girlfriend sort of way. They had been friends from as far back as she could remember and now he was back. If felt right. No one could ever take Teresa's place, but he was as close as she'd ever get.

"So, what's with you and that guy? How old is he, anyway?"

"Matthew? He's twenty-three. Preaches at Calvary."

Cody raised his eyebrows. "A preacher?"

"We're just friends."

"There's more to it than that. The guy is jealous."

"Jealous? No way."

Cody smiled. "Has he asked you out?"

"We've hung out a couple of times, that's it."

Cody grinned. The dimples reappeared on his cheeks. It'd been a long time since she'd seen them. He glanced back at

Matthew. "I kinda like making him jealous." He cupped her face in his hands. "Maybe I should give you a real kiss."

"He's really jealous?"

Cody gave a subtle nod. "Say the word and I'll plant one on you. Let's do it. See what he does."

Her grin deepened. It was tempting. She'd love to see how Matthew would react. She pulled his hands from her face. "That wouldn't be nice." She giggled.

"You like him, too. Look at you acting like you did when we first started dating."

Her face flushed. She had forgotten how well he knew her. "Shut up and get out of here."

He pulled her into a hug. "I missed you." He gave her a wink, got in the car, and left.

She watched him drive away before turning to Matthew's car. Matthew jealous? What did it matter? Even if Matthew did think of her that way, they could never be together. She still wasn't buying into everything he believed about his God, and he'd already mentioned he'd never date outside his faith.

He got out of the car and leaned against it while she walked toward him.

"Are you spying on me?" She fought a grin. She tried to look angry by crossing her arms.

"Not spying. Protecting."

"And you thought you could take Cody down? He's got more wrestling medals than you could count."

Matthew ran his hand through his hair. "Oh, I knew I couldn't take him down. But I would've tried." He grinned. "I really wanted to be here, in case you needed me."

"Thanks. I'm glad you came." She leaned against his car.

"So, you and Cody...you looked pretty close."

"No." Heat filled her face. "We're just friends."

Matthew rubbed her arm. "Are you okay? I know this wasn't easy."

"I'm good. For the first time in months I think I'm really good."

"I'm glad." He stared down at her, and for a moment, she thought he'd kiss her. "So," he said, "I guess I'd better go study for my sermon since I don't know what time I'll be home tomorrow night."

"I won't keep you out that late."

"Still won't tell me where we're going?"

"Nope. I'll pick you up around nine."

He pulled his keys from his pocket. "Not even a hint?"

"Nope. Go study." Her eyes flashed. "Maybe I will keep you out late."

This time, his face turned red. "I'll see you tomorrow."

"Bye." She walked to her car, a smile on her face. He did have feelings for her, but could it ever work? She knew it never would, if she wasn't willing to believe in his God. And she wasn't ready to do that.

Chapter 7

Raven tapped her fingers on the stirring wheel. The day with Matthew was going to be fun. It was as if he'd given up on the converting and had become a friend. It was nice to have someone who knew her secrets and liked her anyway.

He walked out of his house carrying a pair of shorts and sandals, climbed into her car, and buckled up.

"Good morning." He tossed his things into the back seat.

"You study last night?"

"Yeah. Why?"

"Just wondering how long we had." She grinned as she put the car in drive and took off.

"Still not gonna tell me where we're going?"

"Nope." She liked having some control. Normally, he held all the cards because she was so messed up. This was her turf and she couldn't wait for him to experience it the way she had so many times.

They drove to the north edge of town then turned off the highway and headed down a two-lane road. When the city had almost disappeared behind them, she turned onto a gravel road and dodged some deep potholes before it came to an end.

"We're here." Raven threw the car in park and killed the engine.

"Where exactly is here? Is this private property? Are we breaking the law?"

Raven laughed and climbed out of the car. "Private property, yes, but they know we're here so we're not breaking the law." She popped the trunk, grabbed two backpacks, and tossed him one. "You can put your stuff in it. Here." She handed him a couple jugs of water.

"We're going hiking? Shorts would be better, don't you think?" He stuffed the water, shorts, and sandals into the backpack. He zipped it up and put it on.

Raven gave him a smile. "Trust me." She flung the backpack over her shoulders and took a deep breath. "Smell that? Fresh Iowa air. Intoxicating, isn't it?" She gave his arm a smack. "Let's go."

They walked to the edge of the road. The old field was now overgrown with weeds, some hitting them at their waists. Lone corn tassels tried to reach over the wild plants, but were being choked out.

"We've got some pretty tall brush to go through, so jeans work better. We'll change once we get there."

"Change?" His eyebrows wrinkled.

"Don't worry, I won't look." She laughed, parted the weeds with her hands, and began walking through them. He followed. They made a flattened path as they headed toward what appeared to be a small cluster of trees.

* * *

They hiked for half an hour. Raven turned back every once in a while and looked at him. "You doing okay?"

"Yeah." He wiped the sweat that appeared on his forehead. It wasn't that he was out of shape, he just hadn't prepared for a hike. If he'd known, he'd have been drinking water all morning to stay hydrated. He dropped the backpack and unzipped it enough to grab a water bottle. After taking a drink, he swung it around and put it on.

He loved the country air. The chirping of the crickets. The squawks of birds. It was freeing. When she finally stopped, the small group of trees now showed themselves as more of a small forest.

"We're almost there." She tucked her hair behind her ears.

Matthew took a gulp of the water. "Good."

They left the tall weeds to enter the trees. The heat and sunlight were shadowed, and the breeze was refreshing.

The trees filled the sky with branches and leaves. Sunlight peeked through, giving off shards of light. The ground underneath was scattered with brown leaves. Green moss covered the bottom of the trees. Birds and crickets chirped like a chorus.

"Beautiful, isn't it?" She looked up and pointed.

"Yeah."

"You ain't seen nothin' yet."

Her pace quickened as she walked into the clearing and turned to him. "Come on."

Matthew followed her through and stopped. His heart quickened. "Wow." The small, but magnificent cascading waterfall was as breathtaking as it was soothing. Huge silver-gray rocks surrounded half of a large pond filled with sparkling water. A huge weeping willow stood proudly on the other side of the pond, draping gloriously over a sandy beach. "This is amazing."

"That's the usual response." She pointed to the stream. "It goes through the trees on the other side. Not sure where it ends up."

"This is so cool." He slid the backpack to the ground. "How did you ever find it?"

"A friend of mine. His grandparents own it. We used to come here when we were in high school. His grandma lets me come out whenever I want."

Matthew didn't ask what she used to do here. He wasn't sure he wanted to know. "Can you drive in?"

"Nope, you can only hike. I've heard Grams say that's the first thing those darned kids of hers are going to do when she dies."

She tossed the backpack on the ground, unzipped it, and pulled out her shorts. "I'm going to get out of these." She looked down at her jeans. They had attracted almost every thistle, thorn, and sticky leaf.

She walked over to the trees. Tucked behind one was a blue and white pinstriped beach tent. She disappeared inside it.

He turned with his back to her as heat filled his face. "You've done this before?" He kicked at a root on the ground. He wasn't seeing or doing anything wrong, so why did he feel guilty?

"Yeah." She tossed her jeans on the ground and walked toward him in shorts. "No big deal. Go ahead."

He hesitated. He'd assumed they would be changing at a restaurant or gas station bathroom—not in the middle of nowhere, and definitely not in front of her.

"It's a tent. It's safe. I won't look, not that I could see anything anyway." She grabbed her backpack and climbed barefoot up on top of the first rock, oblivious to the conflict in his mind.

He took a deep breath. The argument in his head continued. He sighed, rubbing the back of his neck. He knew they'd have to walk out. He'd have to change again. *Nope.* He couldn't do it. He started pulling the thistles and sticky leaves off and flicked them to the ground.

"That's going to take you forever."

He shook a thistle off his fingers. "Guess you'll just have to wait."

She laughed and took a gulp of water. "Come up when you're done." She perched high on a rock. "It's so much prettier up here."

"I can't imagine that." With most of the thistles still stuck to his pants, he gave up, grabbed the rock with his large hands and hoisted himself up. Getting his footing, he walked over to where she was. "This is quite a view." He stared at the waterfall. The reflection of the sun shot rainbow colors everywhere.

"Sit." She patted the spot next to her.

It was a defined area and almost as comfortable as an easy chair. It had a straight view of the waterfall. It wasn't huge but big enough to show its power. The overflowing water glistened in the sunlight, and the constant flow was soothing. "This is beautiful."

"Yeah." She pulled another jug of water out of her backpack and handed it to him. "I didn't think you were going to make it there at the end."

"What?" He grinned, thankful she had water. He had left his by the trees. "Why didn't you think I'd make it?"

"You were breathing pretty hard."

"You were walking fast."

"I thought since you played basketball you'd be in better shape." She nudged him.

He laughed. "You and me on the court any day."

She sipped on the water. "Tell me what it was like growing up in the Stewart home."

"Hard." He turned toward her. "At least I thought so until I met you." He grinned and gulped the water.

She looked at the waterfall. "How was it hard?"

He relaxed against the rock. "Well, it was like living in a fish bowl. My dad was the preacher of this big church and people expected me to be perfect."

"I can picture you perfect."

"I wasn't."

She laughed. "Tell me the worst thing you've ever done."

"People are judgmental. For example, if anyone knew I was here with you, alone, it wouldn't look good."

"Why, we're not doing anything wrong?"

"Whether it's right or wrong isn't the point. It's the perception." He doubted she'd really understand. It was hard to understand the pressure unless you lived it.

"That's stupid." She turned to him. "Do you feel like you're doing something wrong? Did you want to leave?"

"No," he said quickly, probably too quickly. "This is great. I like talking to you." The heat returned to his face and he hoped she didn't see it. He wasn't ready to admit his feelings to her, especially because he wasn't sure of them himself.

"Tell me about your mom."

"My mom." His smile deepened. "She's the best. Fun and easy to talk to. She'd be talking about God one minute, and playing the latest video games with me the next—even beat me sometimes. Like most moms, she gave up new clothes and new things so I could have the latest basketball shoes. She told me I could do anything, and I believed it. I still believe it. She's great."

"And Lisa? When did you two start dating?"

"About two years ago. It was kinda expected. I was on the basketball team—she was a cheerleader. Her dad preaches at a big church like my dad. Knows my family. Almost like they'd planned it from birth."

"That didn't bother you?"

"At first, yeah." He stared at the flowing water. "Until I got to know her. She'll make a great preacher's wife someday."

Raven turned to him, her eyebrows wrinkled. "What do you mean?"

"My dad always said that it takes a special person to be a preacher's wife. She has to possess certain qualities."

"Sinless?"

"No. That's impossible for anyone. But she will be looked at through that glass bowl, so she'd better…"

"Be able to hide her sins well?"

He laughed. Raven saw things very clearly for someone who didn't go to church. "Something like that." He took the last gulp from his water bottle. "How about you? What was it like in the Pennington house before all your drinking started?"

"Good, I guess." She shrugged her shoulders.

"What made you start drinking?"

"At first, it was because I wanted to look cool, to fit in." She finished the last of her water and tapped the plastic bottle on the rock.

"And Cody? When did you two start dating?"

She took a deep breath and slowly let it out. "I really don't know. Cody, Teresa, and I were inseparable. Then one day, we were dating. Teresa started dating Jack, and before I knew it, Teresa was pregnant, and everything went downhill from there."

She stood up, flung the backpack over her shoulder, and motioned with her hand. "Come on."

He guessed it was her way of ending the conversation. He followed her over the rocks, down to the water. She crossed in front of the waterfall over a pathway of rocks. He rolled his pant legs up, stood, and dipped his foot into the water. "Oh, man, this is cold."

She turned back to him, rolled her eyes, and grabbed his hand. She pulled him along, laughing. Before he knew it they had crossed and were walking on the sandy side of the shore. She talked, still holding his hand, and pulled him along.

"This sand was brought in by the truck loads. Took a good couple of years before the weeds grew up enough to cover the crushed path."

Her voice was soft and sounded like music on the wind with the waterfall playing in the background. He stopped listening to the words, getting lost in her touch. It was warm and refreshing. She hadn't been shy about whether or not to take his hand. He knew he should let go of it, because he didn't want her to get the wrong idea, but instead of letting go, he found himself holding tighter, following her every move.

"Hey." She stopped.

He looked up from her hand and smiled. "What? I'm sorry. What did you say?"

She dropped his hand, tossed her backpack on the ground, and pushed him toward the water.

"Hey," he said, resisting. "What was that for?"

"You weren't even listening to me, ya big putz." She shoved harder.

"Putz? Did you just say putz? Is that even a word?" He held her back with one hand and bent over and splashed her with water. She squealed, pulled away from his grip, and pushed him, again. They both lost their balance and fell into the water, laughing.

She crawled onto the beach and rolled on her back. He followed and lay on his side, his head resting up on his elbow. "What were you saying?" He ran his hand through his wet hair and shook the water on her.

She tried to catch her breath. "I asked you a question, but if you want to just tune me out, that's fine. Don't worry about it."

He grinned. "I didn't mean to, I just was thinking about something."

"About what?"

His grin deepened and the heat filled his face. "Nothing." He looked down at her. His breath quickened. He wanted to take her in his arms and kiss her.

Her face softened. Her hand touched his arm. "You can tell me. I've told you my darkest secrets. It might be nice to know one of yours."

Matthew took a deep breath and stared into her eyes. They appeared inviting, like she felt the same way. His heart pounded so fast he knew she could hear it.

No. I can't do this. As much as I want to, I won't. Even if Lisa were completely out of the picture, Raven hasn't given her life to Jesus. I can't date someone who doesn't believe like I do. It could ruin my ministry.

As if sensing his inner turmoil, she reached for his arm and pushed him off his elbow. She sat up, grabbed her backpack, and pulled it to her lap. "You hungry?"

"Sure." He was thankful she changed the subject. "Did you bring something?"

She pulled out a sandwich and handed it to him as he sat up. "It's ham and cheese." She tossed him a bag of chips.

"What? No dessert?"

"Of course there's dessert. I'm assuming you're going to pray for this?"

"Sure."

* * *

Raven watched him as he prayed. A moment ago, she'd thought for sure he was going to kiss her, that he had looked at her with love.

When she had grabbed his hand, she hadn't even thought about it. It felt like the right thing to do, like they were meant for each other, but knew that wouldn't happen. He had just told her all the things his girlfriend would have to be, and she was none of them.

When he said amen, she pulled her sandwich from her baggie and began eating. "So, preacher man, tell me the worst thing you've ever done."

"I could never tell you that."

"Okay, how about something you did that was bad, and you had to be a teenager or older when you did it."

"And I was going to tell you about when I took a cookie before dinner."

She smacked his arm. "Confess one."

"Okay. Okay." He put his hands up in defeat. "Last year, in college, I snuck out of the dorms to grab some coffee with a friend."

"A girl." Her eyes widened.

His face turned red.

She laughed. "You blush so easily." He turned redder. "Okay, seriously." She composed herself but fought the grin. "You snuck out with a girl. Was it Lisa? Were you two dating?"

"Man, if you tell anyone, I'll be so embarrassed."

"Who am I going to tell?"

His eyes narrowed. "Lisa and I were dating, and it wasn't Lisa."

"Was it a date? You went out on Lisa?"

"No." His face turned serious. "I'd never do that. That would be wrong. It was an old friend from high school. She came into town later than curfew, and I wanted to see her."

"So, the only thing you did wrong was sneak out."

"Would you be happier if I'd gone out on Lisa?"

"No, it's just, *sneaking out*? That's the worst thing you've done wrong? I mean, I can't hold that over your head now, can I?"

Not that she wanted something to hang over his head, but it would be nice to know that he had done something wrong at least once in his life. It might make her feel less tainted.

After finishing the sandwich, she pulled her knees to her chest and rested her arms on them and stared at the waterfall. "I came here all the time after Teresa died. Did some praying to your God." She looked at him. "It didn't do me a lot of good. I still feel this heaviness in my chest, like I could lose it at any moment."

He turned to her and stared into her eyes. Was he trying to see things she still kept hidden? The thought forced her to look away.

"You have to keep praying." His voice drew her attention back. "He will help you."

"I know you really believe that, and part of me wants to, but I don't know." She shook her head.

He scooted over to her and took her hands. "Can I pray for you right now?"

She shrugged. Maybe this time it would work. Surely God would listen to him since it appeared He never listened to her.

She closed her eyes. Matthew started out quiet and with reverence, then pleaded with God to take away her pain. Tears seeped through her closed eyes, and she tried to control the tightness of her chest. The pain overtook her, and the tears fell freely. The more she tried to control it, the more her chest convulsed.

He pulled her into a hug and continued to pray. She wasn't sure when he said amen. She clung to him and wept.

Matthew's arms tightened around her. She could hear him whispering something, maybe another prayer. Her body started to relax, and the crying began to ease up. She felt some relief. The heaviness was a little lighter.

She pulled away from him and wiped away the tears. "I'm sorry. Wow. I don't know where that came from."

"I do." He pushed her hair out of her eyes. "God can help you overcome this, if you let Him."

She nodded and stared into his eyes. They shone love and forgiveness. Could she somehow draw from that?

"God wants to help." He held her hands. "I want to help, but you have to completely surrender to Him."

She nodded.

* * *

Her nod looked like more of an affirmation than a willingness to give her life back to Christ, but Matthew knew she felt His power. He would be patient and let Christ win her back.

Matthew stared into her eyes and couldn't understand how they could be so filled with pain, yet still so beautiful. She clung to his hands and he let her. He smiled at her as the thoughts of what could be popped into his head.

Ashamed, he looked down. What kind of person was he? To pray over her with such fierceness, then want to take her in his arms and kiss her? Why were those desires so strong? Was the devil trying to sidetrack him so she wouldn't turn back to Christ?

All he knew was he had to get some distance between them, or he would succumb to his desires. He gave her hands a gentle squeeze, released them, and turned back to the water.

"Thank you," she whispered.

"Anytime. You know, I think this was better than the basketball game."

"The problem at the game was you were mad at me."

"I wasn't mad at you."

"Yes, you were." She nudged him.

He looked over at her, his grin deep. "Okay. I was."

She reached into her backpack and pulled out a plastic baggie. "Here, your dessert."

"Ah." He pulled the chocolate brownie out. "You make these?"

"Irene."

He took a bite. "Mm, tell your mom they're perfect."

"Coming from a cult-leader-slash-drug-dealer, she'll be impressed."

He laughed and shoved the last of the brownie in his mouth. He looked at his watch, then stood. "We'd better get going. I do have to study a little bit tonight. And we have to hike out."

Raven nodded. He reached down. She grabbed his hand and pulled herself up. Picked up her jeans and walked inside the tent. He turned with his back to her.

She reappeared in her thistle-covered jeans and shoved the shorts in her backpack.

They walked to the car in silence. She tossed him the keys. "You want to drive?"

"Sure."

She settled into the passenger seat, laid her head back, and closed her eyes.

Matthew started the car and drove, glancing at her every so often, wondering why he felt so strongly about her. Raven was everything he didn't want in a girl. She didn't believe in God. She had baggage even she couldn't deal with. She could ruin everything he'd worked for all his life—yet, he wanted her with his entire being.

He shook his head and focused on the road. Maybe it was Lisa who he needed for his ministry. She was the better choice. He sighed. It was a hard sell, even for him.

They pulled into his driveway. Raven opened her eyes, sipped on her water, and waited. He jogged around and opened the car door for her. She climbed out of the car and looked up at him. He stared deep in her eyes and for a moment, he thought about kissing her. One kiss. Would it really hurt anything?

Yes. It would hurt his ministry.

"I guess I'll see you in the morning?" She smiled.

"Good. And lunch afterwards?"

"Sure."

He walked into the house and heard the chirping of his cell phone. He looked down at the dresser. The phone lay right where he'd left it. He grabbed it and put it to his ear. "Lisa?"

"I've been trying to reach you all day. Is anything wrong?"

"No. I left my phone at home. Sorry. What's up?"

"I just wanted to talk."

"Hold on a sec." He dropped the phone on the bed, peeled off his partially wet jeans and shirt, slid on a pair of shorts, and put the phone back up to his ear while he walked into the closet. "I'm sorry I haven't called. I've been busy."

"I was thinking of driving up next weekend. We could hang out like old times, talk."

"Next weekend? I don't know. I've got a couple of pretty busy weeks coming up." He pulled a T-shirt off a hanger in the closet. "I've been asked to speak at a city-wide men's lunch next Saturday, and I've got to prepare for it. I'm swamped right now."

Matthew slid the shirt over his head and pictured Lisa. Maybe she should come up. It might get his mind off Raven. He walked into the living room and sat down on the couch. "Next month, I promise. I'll check my calendar and let you know a definite weekend. How's it going there?"

He closed his eyes and laid his head back on the couch and listened to her talk.

Chapter 8

Raven helped close the restaurant, shifted the trash bag to her other hand, and looked at her watch. Eleven. She yawned. The night manager gave his horn a honk. She waved at him as he pulled out, then tossed the trash bag in the large metal dumpster. When she turned to her car, she looked closely at one of her tires. *What? Flat?*

She looked up and shielded her eyes from the headlights of a car pulling in. Sasha climbed out. Raven's heart pounded. "What do you want?"

"Having car trouble?"

"Yeah. I wonder who would've flattened one of my tires."

"Crazy people around here. Get in." Sasha pointed to her car. "I'll give you a ride."

"No, thanks."

"Why?" Sasha jiggled the keys in her hand.

"Besides the fact you've always wanted to beat the crap out of me, I don't know what you've smoked, drank, or taken tonight. There's no way I'm risking my life in that car with you."

"I don't always want to beat the crap out of you. Just most of the time."

"Why is that? Give me one good reason why you hate me, and I'll think about letting you give me a ride."

Sasha's eyes narrowed. "You have everything. Parents, a house, college, but it was never enough. You had to come slum it, acting like you're doing us a favor. It's sickening. Even Teresa thought so."

"You keep her out of this."

"Oh, she's all over this. She always knew you'd ditch her someday. You always thought you were better than her."

"I did not." Raven pulled her phone out and called Cody. "Can you help me out? I've got a flat. I'm at work. Thanks." She ended the call and slid the phone in her pocket. "Cody's on his way."

"Cody? Really?" Sasha's laugh was pure evil. "He's forgiven you for killing his sister?"

"I didn't kill her." Raven's heart pounded.

"Yeah? Who you trying to convince?" Sasha turned to leave. Raven grabbed her arm and pulled her back around. "I didn't."

"You didn't do much to help her, did you?" Sasha had a slight grin on her face.

Raven's eyes teared up. "I didn't kill Teresa."

"Even her mom blames you."

Raven's forehead wrinkled. "What?"

Sasha laughed and turned back to her car. Raven grabbed her arm again. "What did you say?"

"Get your hands off me." Sasha gave Raven a shove. Raven lost her balance and fell back. A small explosion went off in her head as it hit the corner of the dumpster. She felt a warm rush flow through her hair. Her head pounded. She reached up and felt the blood.

* * *

Sasha ran to her. "Oh, no." She leaned over Raven. A stream of cuss words spilled from her mouth. She pulled her jacket off and laid it under Raven's head.

Raven looked up at her. "Hand me my phone, then get out of here."

Sasha's hands shook as she held her jacket tightly against Raven's head, using her other hand to search Raven's pockets. She handed her the phone.

Raven looked at her. "I said get out of here. I'll call 911."

96

"I didn't mean…"

"Go." Raven hit 911 and put the phone to her ear. "I'm at Sports Grill and I fell. My head's bleeding pretty bad and I can't drive." She laid the phone against her chest and whispered to Sasha, "Go. Now."

Sasha gently laid Raven's head down on the ground, ran to her car, got in, and took off. She drove around for a while, wiping her bloody hands on her pants before driving home. Her mother was passed out on the couch.

She took two stairs at a time to her bedroom in the basement, went into the bathroom, put her hands under the running water, and watched the blood run down the drain. More cuss words came. She clutched the side of the sink and held back a scream.

Sasha walked back into her room, grabbed a cigarette, and lit it. She knew why Raven told her to go. One more run-in with the law and she'd be in an orange jumpsuit sitting in the county jail. But why would Raven be nice after what she'd said to her? After what she'd done to her over the years? It didn't make sense.

* * *

Cody pulled into the parking lot and threw the car into park. He heard the sirens and looked around. His heart pounded. He ran around the car to find Raven on the ground. He grabbed the blood-soaked jacket and pressed it against her head.

"Raven." He nudged her, but there was no response. "Come on. Raven."

The ambulance pulled in and blinded him with their headlights. Two EMTs jumped out. One of them yelled, "What happened?"

"I don't know. She had a flat. I found her like this."

"Step back," he said.

Cody scooted away, his hands covered in blood. The EMTs removed the jacket and replaced it with gauze. They moved her on the stretcher, rolled it to the ambulance, and lifted her inside.

"Where you taking her?" Cody wiped his hands on his jeans.

"Mercy North," the EMT shouted as he placed the stethoscope back on her chest and listened.

The other one slammed the door shut. "You know her parents?"

"Yes, I'll call them."

The EMT nodded, jogged around to the front, and climbed in.

Cody watched them drive out of sight before bending down to pick up the jacket. His eyes narrowed. It was Sasha's. He threw it into his car and took off. He grabbed his phone and called Russ and Irene.

* * *

Matthew was making rounds at the hospital when he saw the ambulance pull in. He watched the EMTs roll the gurney into a room. He was chatting with one of the nurses when Cody ran in.

Matthew hurried to him. "What's going on?"

"Did you see where they took Raven?"

"What?"

"An ambulance just came in. Raven was in it." Cody tried to catch his breath. "She called because she had a flat tire. When I got there her head was split open and she was unconscious. Where is she?"

"I can find out." Matthew leaned over the counter to the nurse. "Julie, can you tell me what's going on with the girl they just brought in. Raven Pennington. She attends my church."

Julie nodded and disappeared.

"How'd you do that?" Cody asked.

Matthew pulled out a clergy ID card. "It lets me go places others can't go."

Julie walked up to them. "Are her parents on their way?"

Matthew looked over at Cody, who nodded.

"She's still unconscious and lost a lot of blood." Julia pointed toward the waiting area. "They're ordering a CT scan. The trauma nurse will be out in a minute. She can tell you more when her parents arrive."

Matthew nodded. "Thanks."

"It looked bad." Cody stared at his blood-covered hands.

"You should go clean up."

Cody walked into the bathroom.

Matthew began pacing and praying. Everything about her told him to run and run fast. But underneath her apparent bad choices was a fragile young woman. He couldn't give up on her.

Another nurse emerged from the room and approached Matthew.

"How is she?"

"Pastor Stewart." She led him to a quiet end of the hall. "They're still waiting on the CT scan. Are her parents here yet?"

"No. It's serious, isn't it?" He knew she couldn't tell him anything, but her expression was easy to read.

She gave him a sad smile. "Do you want to pray with her?"

That answered his question. "Yes."

"Come on."

Matthew opened the door to the hospital room. Raven lay lifeless, a white bandage wrapped around her head. Machines played quiet beeping sounds, assuring him she was alive. "Thanks." The nurse backed out of the room and shut the door.

Each step closer to Raven made his heart pound harder. He pulled a chair up to the bed, picked up her hand, held it, and laid his other hand gently on her head. He closed his eyes. "Lord, You know how this girl has captivated me. I know she loves You, she's just afraid to admit it. Heal her, Father. Give her the chance to live for You. I know this is strange to say, but I don't think I could live without her. You have to heal her. Please, Lord, heal her body and her mind. Help her wake up so—"

Matthew heard a noise. He opened his eyes. A man stood in the doorway. He figured it was Raven's father. Matthew stood. "I was praying."

"I heard," Russ said.

Irene pushed past her husband and rushed to Raven's bedside. She leaned over her daughter, whispered something in her ear, and began to cry. A transporter came in. "I'm Nancy. I'm going to take her to get a CT scan."

Russ nodded and they followed the young woman who pushed the bed and Raven into the hallway. "You'll have to wait here." Nancy and Raven disappeared into the restricted area.

When the doors closed, Matthew reached out his hand to Russ, who shook it. "I'm Matthew Stewart. It's nice to finally meet you, Mr. Pennington." Russ nodded. Matthew backed away and mentally kicked himself for not praying silently.

* * *

Raven opened her eyes. The room was dark. She tried to lift her head but it was heavy, like a rock, and pounded like a jack-hammer. She looked around, trying to get her bearings. As she took a deep breath, the smell of antiseptic tickled her nose. She was at the hospital.

It all came rushing back. Sasha. The fight. Hitting her head. She lifted it slightly to see her mom and dad sleeping in chairs. Her eyes met Matthew's.

He came to her, took her hand, and whispered, "How are you feeling?"

"Head hurts. How long have I been out?"

"About six hours. I'll wake your parents. They've been so worried."

He turned to walk away, but she held tightly to his hand. It brought him back around to her. He leaned over. "You need something?"

"Thanks for being here."

"Of course." He grinned.

Matthew walked over to Irene and tapped her shoulder. "Raven's awake." He then turned to Russ and gave his forearm a gentle shake. "Mr. Pennington, Raven's awake."

Irene rushed to Raven's side. Her eyes filled with tears. "Are you okay? How are you feeling?" She turned to Russ. "Get the nurse. They wanted to know when she woke up."

Matthew nodded. "I'll go tell her."

"I'm okay, Mom." Raven touched the bandage. "Head hurts a little."

The nurse walked in with Matthew and Cody behind her. She looked down at her. "I'm Jan. Glad to see you're awake. Do you need pain meds?"

"Please."

"Can you tell me what day it is?"

"Thursday."

"Can you tell me what happened?"

"Yeah, I was at work, taking out the trash. My car had a flat and I called Cody..." She looked past everyone, into Cody's eyes. "I must've tripped and fell against the trash bin."

Jan nodded. "That would explain the twenty-some staples in your head."

"And the headache." Raven looked over at her parents. "You two should go home for a while. I'll be fine."

Russ stepped forward. His face looked as unconvinced of the story as Cody's. Irene and Matthew were the only ones who bought what she said.

"Maybe in a little bit," Irene said. "I would like a shower."

Jan stopped typing on the computer and looked over at them. "She's awake and alert. The worst is over. The doctor won't be in before ten, so you have time." She handed Raven a paper cup with a pill. Irene handed Raven a glass of water.

Raven took the pill and the water.

Russ looked over at Irene. "Why don't you go grab Raven some crackers and juice out of the visitors' lounge."

Jan checked her vitals, then turned to Irene. "I'll show you where the lounge is."

Irene nodded and followed her out. Russ looked back at Raven. "That's what really happened? You fell and hit your head."

"Yeah."

"You hit your head pretty hard for just falling."

"I fell. Okay?"

"Why don't I believe you?" Russ shook his head.

Matthew grabbed Cody's arm. "Maybe we should step outside."

"Cody?" Russ's voice was hard. He glared at him. "You have anything to do with this?"

"No, sir." Cody's eyes narrowed. "She called about a flat tire. I went to help."

Russ dismissed them with a nod. Raven knew Cody would interrogate her as soon as her father left. She looked back at her dad. "I know you don't believe me."

"I don't. I'm not stupid. Was it a drug deal gone bad? A drunk friend?"

"No." She stared into her father's eyes. The disappointment she saw cut through her. "I told you, I'm through with that lifestyle."

Russ pursed his lips together, his neck now a solid red. "Do you know how many times I've heard that? You say you'll change, and then you don't. Had you been drinking?"

"No."

"Were you fighting? Are you bound and determined to wreck your life?"

"No. I changed, Dad. I promise, I have."

"Yeah, that's what you said a month ago." He ran his hand over his face. "You said you'd prove to us that you were different. Is this your proof? Almost getting yourself killed?"

"What do you want me to say?"

"The truth." He was almost shouting. "For once in your life, tell me the truth."

A single tear rolled down her cheek. She forced the words out. "I can't."

Russ nodded. "I'm taking your mother home for a shower. We'll be back before the doctor gets here. Get some rest." He leaned over and gave her a kiss on her forehead.

"I love you, Dad."

"I love you, too. I just don't understand you."

"I know." She turned away from him and closed her eyes until she heard the door close.

There was a soft tap, and Matthew peeked his head in. "Care if I come in?"

"Please." She wiped her eyes.

"Your dad looked pretty ticked." Matthew sat down. "You okay?"

"Yeah." Raven raised the bed. "He thinks it was a drug deal gone bad."

"Was it?" Matthew pulled the chair closer to her bedside.

"Would you hate me if it was?"

"Not hate." The left side of his mouth turned up in a grin. "But I would have to reassess our friendship."

"It wasn't." She smiled. "Cody still out there?"

"Yeah, he's talking to your mom. He should be in any minute with your crackers."

Cody came in, set down a couple packages of saltines and Sasha's blood-soaked coat. "You lose this?"

His face was hard and his eyes pierced through her. She glanced over at Matthew as he stood. "Should I go?"

"No, it's okay." She looked over at Cody. "Where'd you find that?"

"Wrapped on your head." Cody pulled up a chair on the opposite side of the bed. He and Matthew both sat down.

"I know it's Sasha's. You want to tell me what really happened?"

"Don't worry about it, okay?"

"Let me guess. You and Sasha were fighting and she pushed you into the dumpster."

"No." She glanced at Cody, then at Matthew. "Okay, we were arguing. She said some stuff and I got mad."

Matthew cocked his head. "So, you hit her?"

"I grabbed her and she shoved me. I fell—she didn't mean it."

"She never means it." Cody gave a deep eye roll.

Raven looked over at Matthew. She couldn't care less what Cody thought. He already knew all about her. It was Matthew she was worried about. It would be a glimpse into a part of her life that she was ashamed of.

She looked back over at Cody. "Stay out of it. It was an accident."

"Whatever." Cody stood. "I gotta go. Glad you're okay."

* * *

Sasha stood in the shadows of the parking lot inhaling deeply on the cigarette. She watched Raven's parents leave, but until Cody drove off, it wouldn't be safe. She tossed the cigarette to the ground and walked through the entrance.

A woman sitting at the information desk looked up and smiled at her. "Raven Pennington's room?" Sasha asked.

The lady took a piece of paper out with a map of the hospital on it and wrote a number down then handed it to her. "Thirty-four-fifteen, but visiting hours don't start until eight a.m."

"Yeah, thanks." Sasha took the paper, slipped it into her pocket, and walked toward the elevator.

* * *

Raven heard a soft tap on the door. "Come in."

Sasha came into the room. Their eyes locked and Sasha stepped closer to the bed. "You okay?"

"Yeah. How'd you get in here?"

"I waited until your parents and Cody were gone. I figured Cody would want to kill me."

"You figured right." Raven raised the head part of the bed. "You been out there this whole time?"

"Yeah. You sure you're okay?"

Matthew stood, his forehead wrinkled. "Are you Sasha?"

Sasha gave him a nod, then turned back to Raven. "I didn't mean to, you just made me so mad."

"Maybe you shouldn't be in here." Matthew walked around the bed until he stood in front of her.

"She's okay." Raven waved him back. "Come sit back down. It's all right." It took a minute before Matthew moved. She knew he was trying to decide if he should trust Sasha or not. But he knew nothing about the past or the loyalty she had for Sasha, regardless of what she'd done.

When Matthew sat, Sasha grabbed the other chair and sat. "You tell your parents? They gonna call the cops?"

"No. You're in the clear."

"What about Cody?"

"Cody won't say anything. If he does, I won't back him up."

Sasha's eyes narrowed. "Why would you do that?"

"You'd do it for me," Raven said with a smile.

Sasha remained emotionless.

Raven sighed. "I did it because you've been in juvie five times already. You're an adult now. It's real jail. You want to go to there?"

"Not particularly."

"I didn't think so."

Sasha's chin jerked up. "What do I gotta do for you?"

Raven gave her head a gentle shake. "You always think there's a catch. There's not." Raven handed Sasha her coat. "Hopefully the blood will come out."

Sasha took it. "Thanks."

"You're welcome." One side of Raven's mouth turned up into a smile. She gave Sasha an almost unnoticeable nod. It felt good to be her friend regardless of how she acted, or the turmoil it put her family in.

Matthew waited until Sasha left the room. "You think that was smart? She could've killed you."

"It wasn't all her fault. I grabbed her. She just pushed me back, I lost my footing and fell."

They sat in silence for a long time. Matthew rubbed his hands together. "It was neat the way you forgave her."

"She'd do it for me." Raven shrugged her shoulders.

"I'm not sure she would. The way you forgave her is amazing. Maybe you're beginning to see how Jesus can change your life."

"You think I'm buying into this religion stuff? Don't you wish." She reached out and took his hand without even thinking. "Thanks for being here."

She fought the heaviness in her eyes. She was thankful he stuck around, and that he didn't appear repulsed by the fight, or her sordid life.

"Anytime." He held tight to her hand.

Chapter 9

Matthew drove to Kaldi's, his mind reeling with thoughts of Raven. The idea of looking at her as only a friend seemed impossible, but it was something he knew he had to do. Spending all his extra time at the hospital the past couple of days didn't help, but he found he couldn't stay away.

Confronting Raven's father might just shake him into reality. That's why he had called Russ. In a few minutes, Russ would tell him all the reasons why he shouldn't be with Raven. He would agree, apologize for his words in the prayer, and promise to only be her friend. At least that's how he hoped it would play out.

He parked, jumped out of the car, and walked in. The scents of the different brews danced in the air. Russ sat in a corner booth. Matthew ordered himself an espresso and walked to where Russ waited.

"Thanks for meeting me, Mr. Pennington." Matthew extended his hand before he sat in the seat across from him.

"Sure. Call me Russ." Russ took a gulp of his coffee. "What can I do for you?"

Get your daughter out of my head. "Something has been bothering me about that night at the hospital."

"The prayer?" Russ raised an eyebrow.

Matthew clasped his hands on the table. "I wanted you to understand something. I have never been inappropriate towards Raven. She doesn't even know how I feel. I haven't told her because I know it isn't the right time. I just wanted you to know that."

"I appreciate the honesty." Russ gave his cup a slow spin. "You seem like a good man, but Raven has some serious problems. She's had to deal with more than most people. I'm proud she's gotten through these last two years of college. If she can get her life straight, she still has a couple more years of college left, and I don't want her giving it up for some guy. I need you to respect that."

"I understand." Matthew looked up as the barista set down a cup. "Thanks," he said to her, then looked back at Russ.

"I want you to be careful." Russ sipped his coffee. "Irene seems to think Raven has feelings for you. I don't want her getting attached, because if something happens it could break her."

Matthew nodded.

"Raven keeps insisting you have a girlfriend. Do you?"

"Not really. Well, kinda." He rubbed his forehead. "I don't know. She's ready to get married, but I told her, before I even met Raven, that I wasn't sure. Now I'm really not sure."

"Because of Raven?"

He looked into Russ's eyes and gave him a nod. Matthew sipped his coffee. "Can I ask you something?"

"Sure."

"And I ask this because I'm really trying to understand my feelings. If Raven has changed and was following Christ, do you think it wouldn't work because I'm a minister?"

"Look at her background. I'm not knocking my own daughter. I love her very much, and if a minister would make her happy, then I'd be all for it. If you were that man, I'd be all for that, too. I know about your family. You have a very good reputation, but she's been into drugs, fights, suspended from school, arrested. She's not the type you'd be proud to take home to your father, is she?"

"Arrested?"

"Yeah. At fourteen. Picked up for illegal possession of beer. No juvenile hall or anything, but she did have to appear in court. That no-good Cody. I should've never let her go out with him, but at the time he seemed nice enough and Irene loves him."

"I thought Raven and Cody only dated for a year."

"They did, but they've been friends forever. They seemed to get in more trouble than I care to mention. The things I've caught them doing…" Russ shook his head.

Matthew could imagine what that meant. Sex. That answered another nagging question. He was proud he had saved himself for his wife, and he had always hoped the girl he dated and married would have the same commitment.

"Well…" A sadness weighed on Matthew's heart. "I don't want to keep you. Thank you for understanding."

"Sure thing." Russ stood, laid a couple of bills on the table, and left.

Matthew got into his car and dialed Lisa's number. "Hey, how about you come down this weekend?"

"Are you serious? You know I'd love to." Lisa's voice danced. "I could leave Friday."

"That would be great." Matthew forced a smile and hoped he sounded convincing.

"Will you make arrangements so I can stay with the Greens?"

"Yes, I'll work it all out."

"Thanks. I love you," Lisa said.

"See you Friday."

He hung up, his heart heavy. Maybe he should completely break it off with Lisa, but that wouldn't solve these feelings for Raven. Asking her to come visit just might be the right thing to do. Maybe it would help him decide.

Matthew drove back to the hospital. He knew he couldn't walk out on their friendship. Raven finally trusted him. He wouldn't blow his witness, but he had to get her out of his head.

"Where'd you run off too?" She laid the remote call intercom down on the bed. "The Feud is getting ready to start."

"Didn't we watch that one already this morning? Remember, I won the twenty grand."

She shook the remote at him. "It's the Game Show Network."

He laughed and sat down. He looked up at the TV. "Lisa is coming to town this weekend."

"Really?"

He wanted to look at her face—to see her expression—but he didn't. He stared blankly at the TV. "Yeah, I'd like you to meet her."

"Me too. She's got to be someone special to be with you."

That made him turn, but she stared at the TV. She gave him no chance to guess her thoughts. She didn't look too concerned. If she only looked at him as a friend, meeting Lisa wouldn't bother her. Either he was an idiot for thinking he felt something special between them, or she was a great actress. Either option was plausible.

"They say I should be getting out of here this afternoon." She turned to look at him. "Can I meet you and Lisa for dinner Friday night?"

"Sure, do you want to bring Travis or Cody?" He held his breath and felt stupid. Jealous over a woman he couldn't have.

"No. I'd like to go by myself, if that's all right. It won't be awkward, will it?"

"No, that'll be fine."

"Did you tell her about the fight I got into?"

"No, did you want me to? I could call her back." He smiled.

"No." Her eyes wide. "It's pretty embarrassing. Not an impression I'd like to give to someone I'm just meeting."

He looked over at her. "What'd you hear about school?"

"Finals start Monday. All my professors will let me turn my papers in late."

He leaned back in the chair, brought his leg up, and rested it over his knee. "Then shouldn't you be studying?"

"I am. You don't think knowing the top five answers to *name a famous Michael* is going to be on a final?"

He laughed and yelled out, "Jackson, Keaton, Landon."

She smacked his arm. "No fair."

He playfully raised his eyebrows and stared up at the TV.

Chapter 10

Raven sat in the Mexican restaurant and sipped her Diet Coke. The waiter approached her again. "Are you sure I can't get you something while you wait?"

Raven shook her head. "No, they should be here soon."

"Okay, let me know."

Her heart raced when she saw Matthew's car pull in. It always did. She thought being attracted to your preacher was about as dumb as being in love with your professor, but she couldn't help it. And as awkward as that was, in a few minutes, she'd be sitting with him and his girlfriend. Her biggest fear was that she'd like her.

Raven stood as they approached the table. Lisa was just as Matthew had described her, tanned and dainty in a beautiful sort of way. She held tightly to Matthew's hand and Raven wondered if Lisa was nervous or marking her territory. It made her smile.

She walked around the table and gave Lisa a hug. She wasn't sure why. Was it to make her feel welcome or to keep an enemy close? She'd have to examine that one later.

"It's so nice to finally meet you." Raven smiled. "Matthew has told me so much about you."

It wasn't a lie. After Matthew had said Lisa was beautiful, Raven had pretty much tuned him out. It made her feel threatened, not because Raven was in love with Matthew, but she needed his friendship. She wasn't about to give it up for anyone. "You had a good trip?"

"Yes, thank you."

"Matthew says you teach."

"Yes." Lisa picked up the menu that already sat on the table. "At a private school. Fourth grade."

"That's neat. I'd like to work with kids, too. I've got my eyes on the troubled ones."

"That would be good. You could use some of your own experiences." Lisa looked over the menu.

Matthew's eyebrows wrinkled as Raven's face became somber. "I don't think she meant that the way it sounded."

"Oh, no," Lisa stammered. "I just meant..."

"I understand, really, I do." Raven looked in her eyes and they genuinely appeared sorry. Sometimes the truth hurt. And she might be right. Experience was sometimes the best teaching tool.

Raven took a long sip of her pop. "Would you guys eat some queso if I ordered it?"

"No, thank you," Lisa said.

"I'd love some." Matthew smiled deep. His arm rested on the back of Lisa's chair.

When the waiter brought the queso, Matthew passed out small plates. "Mmmmm. That looks awesome. Thanks, Raven. I'll pray, so we can feast."

After amen, Raven looked at him and smiled, then reached for the chips and cheese dip.

"Raven?" Lisa sipped on her water. "How do you like college?"

Raven finished chewing, then swallowed. "It's okay, I guess. I'll be glad when it's over."

"You plan on staying here after you graduate?"

"Yep." Raven looked at Lisa. "I'm a great challenge for Matthew. He's been trying real hard to convert me." She looked over at Matthew. "You couldn't live with yourself if you failed to do that, could you?" She raised her eyebrows at him and smiled.

"Nope." Matthew reached for Lisa's hand and gave it a squeeze.

Lisa smiled. "Matthew said you were in an accident recently?"

"Yes."

"What happened?"

"Fell at work. Split my head open."

"Was it bad?"

"She spent some time in the hospital." Matthew took a drink of his water.

"Got out a couple of days ago." Raven pushed the small plate off to the side. "I'll get the staples out next week."

The waiter set their food down. Raven thought now was as good a time as any to see just where Matthew and Lisa really stood. "Why are you in Davenport?" Raven picked up her fork. "Why not find a school to teach at here?"

Matthew's eyes widened and Raven thought shock was a good way to describe his face, but he spoke without missing a beat. "We both agreed when we graduated last year that we would go where the Lord led us. Lisa's family is there and she felt led back home. I came here. We have to wait for God's timing, don't we?"

Lisa appeared to agree with a nod, but her shoulders slouched.

For the first time, Raven felt sorry for her. She looked awkward and out of place. "Lisa, what do you do for fun?"

"I play some golf, and I love to take pictures."

"What kind of stuff do you take pictures of?"

"All sorts of things, but I guess my favorite is people."

"Did you bring your camera?"

"Yes."

"Matthew will have to take you to downtown. You should be able to get some wonderful shots. There are some pretty cool old churches down there, too."

"That would be wonderful. Maybe we could do that tomorrow."

"Yeah, we could do that after my basketball game."

Raven scooted her plate toward the center of the table, her beef burrito half eaten. "I shouldn't have eaten so much queso. You want some of this? I can't finish it."

"It was good, though." Matthew cut into her burrito and took a bite. "We all going to a movie?"

"I can't. Russ gave me a curfew. I almost argued. Twenty-one and a curfew, give me a break." Raven rolled her eyes. "But I'll do what he says because I know it's what God wants me to do."

"Raven…" Matthew's tone was both authoritative and loving. The room appeared to clear out, like it did so many times when he talked to her about the Lord.

She stared into his eyes as he spoke, hypnotized by the love that came with each word.

"You know you can't earn God's love. He loves you no matter what. You just have to accept Him."

"I'm just not sure." Her voice was soft, coated with honesty. "I know it's not enough for Him, but it's all I have right now, you know that."

He reached out and grabbed her hand. "I know." He gave it a gentle squeeze and stared into her eyes.

Lisa cleared her throat. Matthew quickly released Raven's hand. He looked over at Lisa and smiled. "I'm going to get her to turn back to Christ sooner or later."

Lisa pursed her lips. Raven tried her best to cover, even though she could feel the heat from her own face. "Yeah, preacher man. Someday."

Matthew put his arm around Lisa, but Raven saw her body stiffen.

"Well, I gotta go." Raven pulled money from her purse and pointed at Matthew. "I insist."

Matthew nodded. "I got the tip."

"Fair enough. Lisa, it was nice to finally meet you. See you both Sunday."

Raven drove straight home, talked to her mom and dad for a few minutes before heading up to bed. As she lay with the covers pulled up to her chin, she thought about her relationship with Matthew. She had always felt something between them, much more than friendship, but had decided it was pointless. There was no denying the moment at dinner when they connected in a way they hadn't before. Matthew's quick jolt back to reality made her wonder if he'd ever admit it.

* * *

Matthew pulled into the Greens' driveway, put the car in park, and turned to Lisa. He knew a confrontation was coming. She hadn't spoken since the restaurant.

"Matthew, I know there's something going on between you and Raven. You can tell me."

What could he say? *I'm attracted to another woman, but I can't date her.* It was so unfair. He did love Lisa, but enough to marry her or even date her? He wasn't sure. And Raven had too much baggage. She would hurt his ministry.

"I don't know." It seemed easier.

She took his hand and scooted closer. "Maybe if I moved here it would help. You know that's what I want to do."

He turned to her. "Yes, but have you prayed about it?"

"Have I prayed about it? All I want is to be with you, to start our life together."

He looked away. "I'm not ready for that."

"Why not?"

"I don't know."

"You really don't know? Or are you just saying that?"

He looked into her eyes. "I really don't know."

It was the truth. He knew all the reasons he couldn't be with Raven and all the reasons he should be with Lisa, but it didn't feel right. He didn't know why.

Lisa sighed. "I think something is going on, and I want you to tell me."

Matthew looked out the front window of the car.

"I know it has something to do with Raven. I can tell. I saw it at dinner. Talk to me, Matthew. You owe me that much."

He did owe her the truth, but he hated hurting her.

Her jaw tightened. "Are you attracted to her?"

He looked over and said nothing.

"Okay, I know the answer to that one." Her chest shuddered. "Do you want to go out with her?"

He shifted his body to face her. If his feelings were changing, she deserved to know it. "Yes."

She crossed her arms and slumped against the passenger door.

"I do have feelings for her and I know they're not right."

Lisa's eyes filled with tears. "Do you love her?"

"Yes, but it's different. It's hard to explain."

"Well, try."

There was no way to even begin to, because he didn't understand it himself. Instead, he stayed silent.

"Do you want to ask her out?" she asked.

"No...I don't know." The lines on his face grew intense. "I can't."

"But you want to?"

"I'd be lying if I said no. Part of me wants to. I know I can't. I won't. I'm with you right now because I want to be. If I didn't think this was right, I wouldn't be here."

"You want to date her, but can't? What exactly does that mean?"

Matthew sighed. The pain he caused her was eating away at his heart. He could think of only one way to make it completely go away—ask to marry him. It would make his father happy. It would make Lisa happy, but he wasn't convinced it'd make him happy.

Instead, he exhaled and chose his words carefully. "From the moment I saw her, I was drawn to her. I believe that was so I could lead her back to Christ."

"You've done that."

"No, I haven't. You heard her tonight. But she's close."

"She can't follow Christ because of you. You have to let her go."

"I can't," he said.

"Can't or won't?"

"It's not that simple. She still has a long way to go. She has lived through more in the last three years than you and I will probably live through in our entire lives. I'm in awe of how God has changed her. She's gone from picking fights to breaking them up. Forgiving people when even I'd have a hard time forgiving them. She just blows me away." Matthew looked at Lisa. Her eyes were tearing up and her chin quivered. Why was she getting so upset? "What'd I say?"

"It's not what you said. Your face...nothing." Lisa took a deep breath and slowly let it out. "Let me ask you this. If we never saw each other again, would you ask her out?"

"No."

She nodded. "She's in love with you."

"No, she's not."

"Yes, she is. And you need to tell her there is no future. And if there is still going to be an 'us'—you and me—you have to stop seeing her."

He nodded. He wasn't sure why.

"I trust you. I expect you to tell me if things change."

Matthew hugged her.

"I'm leaving in the morning. You need to talk to her tomorrow."

"You drove all this way. Spend the weekend. I can talk to her next week." He wasn't sure he wanted Lisa to stay, but he knew he didn't want to tell Raven anything about his feelings.

"No." Lisa's voice was firm. "The sooner you talk to her, the sooner we can get on with our lives. I love you, you know that, but I want you to be sure." There was an awkward pause. "I should go, Mrs. Green will wonder what we're doing out here."

Matthew got out of the car, walked around, and opened her door. When she climbed out, he gave a sad smile. "Drive careful tomorrow, and text me when you get home."

She leaned into him. He knew she wanted a kiss, some reassurance that he still had some feelings for her, but he couldn't. Instead, he gave her another hug.

"Thanks. I will."

Matthew drove like a zombie, walked into his house, and threw his keys on the table. He sat on the couch, lowered his head, and prayed out loud. "Lord, what a mess. Is Lisa right? Should I tell Raven? How do I explain something I don't understand myself? I can't date her, even if—or when—she turns her life over to You. Even though I do love her."

Why?

"Her past has too much baggage. Arrested. Alcohol. Sex. I can't. No way."

He waited to hear from God.

"Is Raven really in love with me? Irene saw it. Lisa saw it. Is that a sign maybe we should be together?"

Now you're listening.

He slid his jacket off, grabbed his cell, and called Raven. "Hey." His voice soft, just in case he woke her. Not that she would care. They spent many nights talking well into the morning. They'd discuss everything, from changing the world to the last *Survivor* episode.

"How'd it go with your dad when you got home? You weren't late, were you?"

"No. I played the perfect daughter. Visited with them for a few minutes then went to my room. Been staring at my phone."

Matthew lay on the couch, holding the phone with his shoulder. He threw the basketball in the air and caught it. His feet rested on the arm rest, making his Sperrys look larger than the size thirteen they were. "Sounds fun for you. Don't quite understand how you can stay on social media that long."

"I don't know, just can." There was silence, then she said, "Can I ask you something?"

"Sure." His heart pounded. Was she going to confront him, too?

"Cody called. He wanted to know about going to a movie, just as friends, he says."

"What are you thinking?" He silently prayed he could offer sound advice, even though the jealousy was overwhelming.

"I was kinda thinking it wasn't a good idea. Because of our past."

"I would agree." Matthew felt foolish. Jealousy was an emotion he hated, so to have it over a girl he couldn't have? That was just plain stupid.

"But then, it's not like we're getting married. We'd just be going to a movie."

"Yeah, but you should never date anyone you wouldn't marry."

"Why?"

"You were in love with him once, weren't you?"

"Yes, or at least I thought I was."

"You may fall in love with him again. Love can lead to marriage before you know it."

"Except in your case." She giggled.

He laughed and lost his concentration. The basketball fell to the end table and knocked over the small iron candelabrum that Lisa had bought for him. The only feminine thing in the house. "I am the exception. I'm sure Lisa wishes I would make up my mind." He had to get off this subject.

"Why don't you ask her?"

"I'm not ready for marriage." There, he'd blame it on marriage itself. It would have fewer follow-up questions.

"That's the only reason?"

"Yes." He sat up. "Why?" He rubbed his forehead. Maybe she could see his feelings like Lisa had. Maybe he'd asked one too many questions.

"Just wondered. I should be going."

"You coming to my game tomorrow?"

"I don't know."

"I'll miss my only cheerleading section."

"You'll have Lisa. Doesn't she cheer?"

"Not as loud as you." He hesitated. "Anyway, she's leaving in the morning."

"She is? Why?"

"Something came up. How about my game? Can you come?"

"I don't think I can. I'm supposed to help Hailey get her things packed. She gets married next week and she's trying to get all her stuff to Jake's."

"Okay." He was neutral. He still wasn't sold on the whole idea of telling Raven anything. "I'd better let you go. Good night."

"Night."

Chapter 11

Raven headed to the church to do the maid of honor things for her sister. She walked down the aisle in the black taffeta dress before Hailey did. As she stood in front of the church, she couldn't help but think about her life and wonder how hers might end up. Would she find happiness like her sister had?

She handed Hailey back the bouquet as the preacher pronounced them man and wife. The small group of friends and family clapped.

Raven took the best man's extended arm and they followed behind the bride and groom. She hugged her sister. "It was beautiful."

"Thanks." Hailey grinned. "You staying for cake?"

"Of course."

Raven stood in the reception hall of the church and put her last bite of wedding cake in her mouth when her dad walked up. "Big plans tonight?"

He looked handsome in his black tux. "I'm heading over to the church, if that's still okay. A Christian band is playing."

"What time will it end?"

"Probably ten."

"And what are you doing after that?"

"Coming straight home." She knew her father hadn't bought into the fact that she'd changed. She'd do anything to prove it, even come home early.

"Will you be seeing Matthew?"

"Yes. He'll be speaking between sets."

"You can stay out later, but I want no drinking and no trouble. Do you hear me?" His voice was both loving and stern.

"Daddy, I told you that life was over."

He nodded, his eyes still disapproving. Raven wondered if he'd ever trust her again. In the changing room, she pulled on jeans and a T-shirt, slipped on a pair of sandals, checked her makeup, and then drove to Matthew's church.

* * *

The night air had a slight breeze that helped cool off the unusually hot May temperatures. Raven walked across the church's parking lot. She could hear the bass escaping from the building. Christian rock was a strange concept to her, but she had to admit the bands Matthew had introduced her to were pretty good.

She walked into the church and moved her head to the music. Not bad. She smiled at Travis who was on the stage doing the thing he loved most next to evangelism, playing drums.

She clapped to the beat and sang along to the songs she knew. Colored lights flashed and smoke machines blew fog.

After about thirty minutes, Matthew walked to the stage while the crowd went wild. He was dressed in black jeans, T-shirt, and jacket. He grabbed a microphone, thanked the band, and began his twenty-minute sermon.

Travis pushed his way through the crowd. She hugged him and whispered, "You guys were awesome."

"Thanks. I gotta get backstage. Just wanted to say hi."

She looked up at Matthew as he spoke. He was hypnotizing. His eyes locked with hers as he paced the stage, his Bible open, his voice intense. She heard the same thing he always said. It's not enough to be a good person. You have to give your life over to Jesus. It made her heart pound and her palms sweat.

She knew what she had to do. The same thing she did when she was younger; repent, pray for forgiveness, and allow Jesus to be Lord of her life. She closed her eyes and prayed. A rush of coolness came over her. A cleansing. A new hope. Tears filled her eyes and she smiled.

Jesus.

She knew that He had been there all along, helping her, keeping her safe. Now, she had given her life back over to Him.

She opened her eyes and felt like she was going to explode with happiness. Trumpets didn't blare. The crowd didn't cheer, but she could picture God and Jesus throwing a party for her in heaven.

Finally, I knew you'd come back to Us.

"Thank you," Raven whispered to Him as she looked up at the ceiling.

Travis slid next to her and leaned in, "We're all going to grab something to eat when we're done. You want to come?"

"No, but thanks anyway." As excited as she was about her decision, Travis wasn't the first person she wanted to share the news with. "I should go straight home."

"Okay, thanks for coming. I'd better get going, he's about to close."

The band entered the stage and the crowd roared as they sang another set of songs. She didn't see Matthew leave, but found herself looking for him, anxious to tell him about her decision.

Matthew stood in the middle of a crowd of college students. Her heart dropped. She wanted so badly to tell him her decision but knew now wasn't the right time. She'd wait. She smiled and gave him a wave as she walked by.

"Hey," Matthew yelled. "Are you joining us for a late dinner?"

"No." The people crowded closer to him. "I'm not hungry. I'll see you later."

He nodded and turned his attention back to the students.

Raven drove to the park. Her dad had lifted her curfew and she was not only free from his rules, but from all the bondage from the last few years. It was invigorating.

She jumped on a swing and grabbed the metal chains. They were cold against her skin. She leaned back, stretched out her legs, and began to pump. The faster she swung the farther back she leaned her head. The stars grew closer, then farther away, then closer again. The wind picked up and the breeze flew through her hair, forcing it away from her face then back into it. She laughed. Her breathing quickened as her pumping increased.

When she got as high as she could go she relaxed and allowed the swing to do all the work. She couldn't believe how happy she felt. Was it real? A twinge of doubt crept into her thoughts. Who did she think she was, really? She had spent so much of her life trying to forget about Christ, even persecuted those who believed in Him. Now, all of a sudden, she had changed?

She took a deep breath and asked Jesus to help her clear her mind. As crazy as it sounded she felt different. She felt clean. New. Forgiven. It was real. It had to be. Matthew would never lie. But could she ever live up to what God wanted her to be? What Matthew would expect her to be?

A verse Matthew had told her popped into her mind. It said something about forgetting what was behind and pressing on. How do you forget the past? The drinking. Standing in court. Teresa. How could she do anything for God with that lingering in her head?

God, help me forgive myself.

The swing stopped and Raven dragged her toes in the sand, then spun herself in small circles.

* * *

Russ Pennington rubbed his forehead. He yawned, reached over, and grabbed Irene's hand. "The wedding was beautiful. You did good."

"Yes, she was a beautiful bride. It's still crazy she didn't want a big reception."

"The cake was good, though." Russ pulled onto Interstate 80 and began the twenty-mile drive home. He popped in the new Taylor Swift CD and gently tapped his fingers to the beat.

"You think I've been too hard on Raven?" He glanced at his wife.

"No, you let her go out tonight." Irene gave his hand a squeeze.

"I don't want her to ruin her life."

"I know."

After listening to his favorite song, he reached over and fumbled through the stuff in the console, looking for another CD. He glanced away for a moment, then looked up and noticed the two bright lights coming straight at them. He swerved too late.

The loud crashing burst into his ears. Metal crumbled under him like aluminum foil. He heard Irene scream. The dash of the car pressed against his knees as the steering wheel pressed into his chest. Blood trickled down his face. He stared at the spider web that had become his windshield. In an instant he saw the brightest light. He silently prayed before gasping twice. His head fell forward and everything went black.

* * *

Matthew killed the engine to his car and saw Raven. She sat on the swing. Her hair hung over her face as she spun. She looked beautiful.

He had politely visited with the group of students after the concert when all he really wanted to do was talk to Raven. When she waved at him earlier, there was something different and he wasn't sure what it meant.

His heart pounded. She had made him nervous before, but this felt different and he wasn't sure why. He took a deep breath, grabbed the door handle, climbed out of the car, and walked toward her.

She looked up and tucked her hair behind her ears. "What are you doing here?"

"I noticed your car on the way back from the restaurant. Have you been here the whole time?"

"Yeah." She stood. "I didn't feel like going home."

They walked over to a picnic table and sat down. Matthew ran his hand through his hair. "Why didn't you come with us? Travis was so pumped."

"I don't know." She rubbed her hands together, her face subdued. "I just didn't want to be in a crowd."

His eyebrows wrinkled. "What's going on?"

She turned toward him and grinned. "I gave my life back to Christ tonight."

His eyes widened. "You did?"

"Yes."

He smiled, grabbed her and pulled her into a hug. "I knew you would." He closed his eyes and held her. She felt good. Her new life had begun, but did that change things? Could he date her now? She was just beginning her walk with Christ. Would she be strong enough? Could he take the chance?

She pulled away from him. He brushed her hair away from her eyes. Her face had lost its smile and looked somber. He mentally kicked himself. *She shares the most life-changing news, and all I can think about is myself.*

"What's wrong?" he asked.

"I don't know. I've just been thinking about my past, and my future. My dad is still so sure I haven't changed, and sometimes I wonder—I mean, how do you throw away all the garbage you've learned?" She shook her head and moved away from him. "I don't know. I guess I'm scared I'll fall back into my default. Drinking, drugs, lying to my parents, getting in fights. Am I just fooling myself?"

"No, you're not fooling yourself. I see the change in you. You're the most passionate person I know and now you're living your life for Christ."

"But I'm so stupid. I don't understand half of what I read in the Bible. You're like this spiritual giant and I'm this little speck of…I don't know what."

"I'm not a spiritual giant."

"Yes, you are. You're amazing. You can stand up there preaching to those students. Half of them would rather be out getting drunk, but you have this awesome way of reaching them. I spend my day just trying not to mess my life up any worse than I already have." A single tear escaped down her cheek. "I will never be able to be a witness for Christ."

"You already have. You showed Christ to Sasha, and you didn't even know you were doing it."

"I was just trying to keep her out of jail."

"Why? Two months ago, would you have cared if she went to jail?"

She shrugged her shoulders and stared at the ground.

"Raven." Matthew placed his hand under her chin and raised her head. "That's the Spirit working in your life." He looked into her eyes and brushed away the tear with his fingers. Her face was soft.

He cupped the back of her neck and pulled her to him, gently kissing her lips. He released her. She smiled and leaned into him again. He kissed her more passionately.

"We shouldn't…" he whispered, but she drew him back to her. He obeyed, cupped the back of her head, his fingers tangled in her soft hair, and pulled her into his very being.

After a few minutes he forced himself to back away. He stared at her for a moment, then stood and began to pace. He stopped and ran his hand through his hair. "I can't believe I just did that. I should not have done that."

"What? Why?" She took his hand.

He caressed her thumb. What could he say to her? *I think I love you but you could destroy everything I've worked for?* He sat next to her. "We can't. You and me, it would never work."

"What are you talking about?"

Matthew released her hand, rested his elbows on his knees, and detached himself from the situation.

This girl will ruin your ministry.

"Talk to me," she whispered.

He took a deep breath and wondered how to answer without hurting her.

She leaned into him. "I'm glad you kissed me."

He looked at her with a faint smile.

"I've always had feelings for you and I felt terrible about it," she said. "I mean, really, being attracted to your preacher." When he looked over at her, she smiled. "How creepy is that?"

He was forced to laugh.

A breeze started up and blew hair into her face. She grabbed her hair, pulled it into a pony-tail, and twisted it a couple of times. "So, you and me, it would never work?"

"I have feelings for you, but I can't date you."

"Why? Is it Lisa?"

"No."

"Why'd she leave so suddenly last weekend?"

Their eyes met and he looked away. He rubbed his hands together. "She saw something between us and questioned me about it. I told her how I felt."

"And how do you feel?"

"I told her I was attracted to you, but I would never date you."

"Back to that again. I don't get it."

They sat in silence for a few minutes.

"I'm going to lose you before you even give us a chance," she said.

"We never had a chance." Matthew stood and shook his head. Why had he let his emotions take control? "I'm sorry. I shouldn't have kissed you."

* * *

Raven's heart pounded. *He does have feelings for me. There is a possibility of us being together.* It was a dream she'd dared not think about until tonight. *I guess I have to deal with this 'no dating thing,' whatever that means.* But in her heart she knew how he felt, and it was real. She'd be satisfied with that, for now.

"I really need to go." Matthew ran his hand through his hair. "Are you staying?"

"No, I guess I should go, too."

He held the car door open and looked down at her. "This was a good night."

She put her hand on his, grinning. "Yes, it was."

He pulled his hand from hers. "I meant your decision for Christ."

"Me, too." Her grin deepened. "What'd you think I meant?" Her phone chirped. She ignored it and stared in his eyes; they were easy to get lost in.

"You better get that."

"What?"

"Your phone."

"Oh." She slid her hand into her pocket and pulled out her phone. She looked at the caller ID before answering it. "Hailey? You're supposed to be on your honeymoon."

"There was a car accident. I don't know how to tell you this."

"Oh, no. Jake?" Her heart pounded and she raked her hand through her hair. "I'm so sorry. Is he okay?"

"Jake's fine. It's Mom and Dad. Mom's okay. She has a concussion. She's at home. It's Daddy. He's..." Hailey's voice jerked. "He's dead."

Raven rolled her eyes. "Not funny, Hailey."

"Raven, it's true. He's gone."

"No." She shook her head. "I don't believe you."

Raven ended the call and threw her phone in the car seat, ignoring the chirping sound. Her body began to shake as she pushed the thoughts out of her head. *No way. Dad is not dead. No.* She wouldn't believe it.

"What was that about?" Matthew said as his cell phone rang.

"Some sick joke of Hailey's." Her head reeled and her heart pounded. "Um, I should go. I have to go." Her hands shook as she pulled her keys from her pocket, climbed into the car, and tried to put the key in the ignition.

Matthew pulled out his phone and put it to his ear. "Hello, Hailey. Oh. I'm so sorry."

"Tell her I'm on my way." Raven tried to slam the door but Matthew grabbed it.

"Wait." He slid his cell phone in his pocket.

"Let go of my door." She pulled harder until he let go. She started the car, backed out, and took off, fighting the tears. *No. I won't believe it. I can't.* She sniffed hard and shook her head. *I won't cry. This is not true.*

Her phone chirped. It was Matthew. She ignored it and concentrated on driving. She wasn't about to have a total mental breakdown; at least, not yet.

Chapter 12

Raven pulled into the driveway and looked at the cars: her mom's, Hailey's, and her Aunt Jean's. *Aunt Jean? What's she doing here?* She looked for her dad's but couldn't find it. Her heart pounded. Maybe it was true. Who was she kidding, she knew it was true. Hailey would never joke about something like that.

She got out of the car. Her stomach churned and she hugged it. Darkness blanketed her like it had when she found Teresa. Her chest felt heavy and made her fall against the car. She leaned over and the tears seeped out. *Lord, how could You allow this to happen?* Raven cried. *I'm not strong enough to go through this. Help me, please.*

She felt Matthew's hands and he drew her to him. He held her as her body convulsed and the tears fell freely.

"Sh… It's going to be okay," he whispered.

She tried to draw from his strength. A strength she wished she possessed.

"I'm so sorry." He held her tightly. "You'll get through this. I promise." He pulled her away and wiped the tears from her face. "God is faithful. He's there for you."

Anger overcame her. She sniffed hard and wiped the remaining tears. She looked up at him. "I can't imagine how I'll make it through this."

"We don't always understand why things happen, but God gives you the strength you need."

"That's so easy for you to say, isn't it? The right words roll off your tongue because you're a preacher. They don't mean anything to me."

"I know you're angry, and that's okay, but you have to trust the Lord."

"And this coming from a man who probably hasn't lost more than a goldfish in his entire life." Raven began pacing, fighting the urges that were running through her. A cigarette would make her feel better. A drink to take the edge off.

"I have struggled all my life," she almost yelled. "*All* my life. Nothing comes easy for me. It never has. I have struggled every day and when I finally decide to give my life back over to Him, this is what I get?"

"Nothing I say will make you feel better, but I'm here for you."

She continued to pace, making fists with her hands, releasing them, then clenching again. "Man, I want a drink so bad."

"You really think that will help?"

She stopped, her lips pursed together. "I don't know. Maybe." Raven's eyes filled with tears. "No."

"Then don't think like that."

She hugged her arms tightly over her stomach and cried. "I'm just so angry."

"Your father just died. You have a right to be." He turned one side of his mouth up into a faint grin. "You can vent on me anytime." He took her hand. "You ready to go inside?"

"I guess."

They went into the house. It appeared the same but Raven knew it never would be. Hailey emerged from the kitchen. They hugged. "Where's Mom?"

"She's in the bedroom. She has a concussion. Aunt Jean was great. She was barking orders like the ER belonged to her. I've never seen people move so fast. It's nice to have a doctor in the family. Jean said she'd stay a week or two. Depends on Mom."

Raven and Matthew sat on the couch next to Hailey.

"On your wedding day." Raven looked at Hailey. "I'm so sorry."

Hailey wiped her eyes. "At least Daddy got to walk me down the aisle."

They both cried and hugged again.

Raven wiped her eyes. "Did they say what happened?"

"Cops said it was a head-on collision." Hailey's voice quivered. "It looks like the other car crossed the center line. Dad tried to swerve. They said that he probably died instantly."

"Was it a drunk driver?"

"No. They said the driver…" Hailey swallowed hard. "You're not going to believe this. He fell asleep."

Raven's eyes widened. "What? How stupid." She stood and paced. "Fell asleep? That's the dumbest thing I've ever heard."

"Right now, that doesn't really matter, does it?" Matthew asked.

Raven turned to him and tried to calm down. "I guess not." This incredible anger kept popping up. With Teresa she believed it was her punishment. She deserved the darkness that engulfed her. This was different. She hadn't done anything to deserve it.

Jake walked out from the kitchen. He gave Raven a hug. "I'm sorry."

"Thanks."

"Mom's asleep." Hailey stood and took Jake's hand. "Jean said she'd stay in there with her. I think we'll go home and try to get some sleep."

"Okay." She hugged Hailey. "Night. Love you."

"I love you, too."

Jake gave her arm a rub. "Hang in there."

Matthew stood. "Can I pray with you guys?"

"Sure."

They made a circle and held hands as Matthew prayed.

Raven squeezed Matthew's hand. "Thanks. I'm going to check on my mom. Can you stay a little bit longer? I mean, if you don't mind?"

"Sure. I don't mind at all."

Raven walked up the stairs to her parents' bedroom. She slowly opened the door and saw her mother sleeping. Raven snuck in and gently gave her a kiss on the cheek.

Aunt Jean opened her eyes and gave her a faint smile.

"Go back to sleep," Raven whispered. "We'll talk in the morning."

Jean nodded. Raven closed the door and made her way back down the stairs.

Matthew came out of the kitchen with two cups of coffee. He looked up at Raven as he set down the cups. "It's decaf. Can I get you anything else?"

"No. Thanks." Raven picked up the coffee and took a small sip. "I never dreamed something like this would happen."

"I don't think anyone is ever prepared for death. How can you be?"

"Why would God allow this?"

"You'll probably never know."

"But why now? I keep thinking of all of the things I never said to him. He still didn't trust me. I never got to prove to him that I had changed."

"He knew."

Raven laid her head back on the couch. "What a terrible way to end a beautiful evening. I can't imagine how Mom feels." She began to cry. "I can't believe he's gone." She buried her face in her hands and prayed the nightmare would end.

Matthew took her in his arms. "I'm so sorry."

Raven melted. The soft touch of his hands caressing her hair made her think of her father. She closed her eyes and tried to picture his face. Tears seeped through no matter how hard she tried to stop them. She silently prayed for strength, but the Lord saw another, more important thing she needed. Sleep. Her body began to relax and her breathing deepened.

Hours later Raven felt movement under her head. When she opened her eyes, they burned. She quickly rubbed them before she realized it was Matthew's chest she was lying on. For a moment, she thought she was dreaming. She put her hand on his chest and forced herself to raise her head.

Matthew opened his eyes. "Hey." He smiled. "How you doing?" Matthew sat up and gently moved her off of him.

"Thank you for being here. Staying all night went way beyond your pastoral duties."

Matthew took a sip of his cold coffee. "I do this for all the people in the church. You don't think I did this for Mrs. Mason when Johnny died?"

"Hmmm, I'm having a hard time picturing it." Raven forced a smile at the thought of a ninety-year-old woman sleeping in Matthew's arms. "Can I get you some real coffee?"

Matthew stood. "I can't believe I fell asleep." He looked at his watch. "It's almost seven and I've got a meeting at nine. I really need to be going."

Raven walked with him to his car.

Matthew shook the keys in his hand. "I'll call you later. Hang in there."

"Thanks." She looked into his eyes. They were so loving and strong. She hugged him one more time.

As she looked up at him, he gave her a small smile, pushing her hair behind her ears. "You're going to get through this."

She nodded. Her father had just been killed, and all she could think about was Matthew kissing her again. He didn't. He got in his car and left.

Chapter 13

Raven retreated to the deck, praying for strength and comfort, but knew it wouldn't come, at least not for a while. She remembered Teresa's funeral. People told her it would take time to grieve and to heal. How much time? A month? A year? Would she ever? She'd barely recovered from Teresa's death. She doubted she'd ever recover from her father's.

The thought of being in this mechanical state for any length of time scared her. She prayed, but feared her prayers fell on deaf ears. Why would God listen to her now? All she had done was say she'd live for Him. She hadn't proved it. Was this her test? If it was, how on earth did He expect her to pass?

The ringing of the phone drew her back inside. She grabbed it. "Hello?"

"This is Philip from Larson-Muse Funeral Home. We are so sorry for your loss."

"Thank you."

"We're handling your father's service and wanted to let you know that you and your family can come by anytime today to tell us your wishes on the arrangements. We are here to help you in any way we can."

"Today? Oh, okay. Someone will be down later. Thank you."

She hung up the phone and walked to the bathroom and stared at herself in the mirror. Her eyes were bloodshot and her cheeks were streaked with tears. She sluggishly ran a brush through her hair, pulled it back, and tied it with a band.

She took a deep breath and walked into her mother's room. "Mom?"

Irene sat on the chaise lounge reading a book. Not a hair on her head was out of place and her makeup had been applied flawlessly. The aroma of gardenias made Raven smile. Her mother's favorite perfume.

Irene looked up and smiled. "Raven, you're up early. Do you have plans today?"

Raven glanced at her mother, then at Aunt Jean. Her heart raced. "Um...do you have plans for today?"

"Jean said she decided to stay a few days so I'm going to spend the day with her." Irene walked to Raven and touched the end of her ponytail. "You really should clean up. You don't look good. Are you ill? You didn't go out drinking last night, did you?"

Raven forced herself to smile. "No, of course not. I told you that lifestyle is over. I'm fine." She fought the tears. "I just didn't get much sleep last night."

"Why don't you go jump in the shower? It'll make you feel better. I'll start some breakfast. Your father should be home shortly. He got up early, had some work to finish at the office. He'll be home soon and we'll eat out on the deck. How does that sound?"

A single tear rolled down Raven's face. "I can't. I've got to be somewhere." She wiped it away and blinked to stop the others. "Aunt Jean, can I talk to you?"

"Certainly."

Jean helped Irene back into the chaise lounge, whispered something to her, then covered her with a quilt. "I'll be right back. You rest."

Raven leaned against the doorway with her arms crossed. Jean touched her arm, guided her out of the room, and closed the door. She motioned for Raven to go downstairs. Raven turned while Jean was still on the last stair. "What was that all about?"

"She has amnesia. It's from the concussion. She's lost her memory of the car accident. They did a CT scan last night, and there were no lesions on her brain. It's trauma. I already called the hospital, and we've scheduled another scan."

Raven followed Jean into the kitchen. "When will she remember?"

"No way of knowing." Jean poured herself a cup of coffee. She reached for the sugar, then began opening and shutting cupboards.

"What are you looking for?"

"The creamer." Jean slapped her hand on the counter. "Do you have any or should I use milk?"

"Here." Raven opened the refrigerator and grabbed a bottle of Coffee-mate.

Jean stirred the coffee. The spoon clicked loudly against the University of Iowa coffee mug. "I'm sorry about your dad. He was a good man."

"Thank you."

"Your mother…" Jean hesitated. She appeared to be searching for the right words. "It may take time."

"But she has to go to the funeral home and make the arrangements. They called."

"You'll have to do it. She thinks your father is at the office."

Raven shuddered. She shook her head. Her stomach ached. There was no way she could pick out a casket. "I can't do it."

"Then what about Hailey?"

"Oh, come on," Raven said. "She just got married. She's supposed to be on her honeymoon."

"Then who?" Jean asked. "You want me to? I will, but you'll have to stay with your mother and pretend your father's still alive."

Raven closed her eyes and turned away. Pretend her father was alive? What a morbid thing to have to do. She needed her mother, the one who was strong, not the stranger upstairs who had slipped into a mental straight-jacket.

"All right. I'll do it." Raven grabbed her purse and put on her sunglasses.

"Are you going like that?"

Raven swung around to face her aunt. Her fight between sorrow and anger overtook her, and anger won. "You got a problem with the way I'm dressed? It's not like I'm going to a fashion show. I'm going to pick out a casket for my dead father. I don't think they'll care what I look like." Raven stormed out of the house and drove to the funeral home.

She threw the car in park when her cell phone rang. Looking at the caller ID, she saw it was Matthew. Seeing his name brought some renewed strength.

"Hey."

"How're you doing?" he asked.

"Okay. I'm sitting outside the funeral home. I guess I'm in charge of making the arrangements."

"What about your mom?"

"She has some sort of amnesia. She forgot about the accident and thinks dad is at work." Her chest shuddered and she fought the tears. "Life just keeps getting better."

There was a long pause. "You know if you need me to do anything for the funeral, let me know."

Odd. He sounded distant, almost as mechanical as she felt. "Yeah, okay. Thanks for staying last night."

"I feel really stupid about that. I've never done that before. I'm sorry."

"Why are you apologizing?"

"It wasn't appropriate."

"For who?" She rolled her eyes. "Nobody even knows about it."

"That doesn't matter. You don't understand." She could hear irritation in his voice.

"Explain it, then," she snapped back.

"I wish…" He sighed. "Nothing."

"You wish what?" Tears escaped her eyes. "That the kiss didn't happen? That you didn't fall asleep at my house? That you didn't have feelings for me? You know what, I'm beginning to wish the same thing."

She silently prayed he would tell her it wasn't a mistake. That he was glad he kissed her. That he loved her. But he didn't. His silence was more cutting than any words he could've said. "I gotta go," she choked out.

"If I can help…do you want me to come over there?"

"No, I'll be fine."

She ended the call and cried. She'd lost Teresa, her father, and now Matthew. Over something as stupid as a kiss. She took a deep breath. "Get it under control, Pennington," she said out loud. "You can do this." She slipped the phone into her pocket, wiped her eyes, grabbed the keys, and went inside.

The funeral home was cozy, homey, and weird. Soft, soothing music played over the sound system and it smelled of sweet florals. Guess it was better than organ music and formaldehyde. She approached a middle-aged man in a three-piece suit. "I'm Raven Pennington. You, um, have my father."

"Yes, Ms. Pennington. I'm Philip Muse. This way, please." He led her into a small office, offering her a seat. "Coffee?"

"No." Raven removed her sunglasses. "I'd really just like to get this over with."

"I understand." Philip pulled a catalogue from his desk. He opened the pages, exposing multiple pictures of coffins. "If you'd like to look through these."

Raven stared at him, her face emotionless. "Not really. Something brown, I guess. It doesn't have to be fancy. Cream-colored lining, with a pillow."

Philip nodded and flipped the pages of the book. "How about this?"

Raven glanced at the picture, then quickly looked away. "That'll work." Did this strange man really think she wanted to leaf through a book of coffins? Did he really think she cared how many strings were in the silk or the filling contents of a pillow? His words became mumbled jargon, and she tuned him out as he scribbled on the notepad.

"Where will he be laid to rest?"

Raven stared blankly at him, the words bringing her back to reality. "Excuse me?"

"A burial plot. Did he have one already?"

"No, I mean, I don't think so. He never mentioned it. It wasn't something we discussed at dinner." She had no idea about any plans he might have had or wanted. There were no relatives buried around here, so it probably wouldn't matter. The only cemetery she knew of was next to Matthew's church. It was where Teresa was. "Does Hillside have any…spots?"

"Yes. Would you like to purchase two so that in the future your mother can be laid to rest next to her husband?"

Raven took a deep breath. *Lord, do I have to think about this?* "Can I speak to my mother and get back to you?" Her voice turned sarcastic as her face filled with heat. Anger seemed a much better emotion than crying. "I mean, will they sell the spot next to him in the next day or two?"

"You can let me know." Phillip scribbled something on the notepad. "When you speak to the minister, set a date and time, and then get back to me."

"Do you need clothes?"

"We're recommending a closed casket. We have what he was wearing, and that will work. Unless you want something else?"

"No." She shook her head. "What he was wearing is fine."

He handed her an envelope. "Here are his personal belongings. His wedding ring, wallet, watch, and money."

The tears rolled down her face. She brushed them away and took the envelope.

"We need to discuss payment."

Raven got out her checkbook. "Can I give you a down payment or something?"

"Yes, that would be fine." He handed her a statement.

Ravens eyes widened. "Eight thousand dollars?"

He pointed with his ink pen. "This is what we need now."

She pulled out her checkbook but knew she'd have to have her mother sign a check to cover this one. "I'll get you the rest in a couple of days." She ripped the check from the book and looked at Philip. "I want to see him."

"You understand…he was in a car accident."

"I'm aware of the way he died."

"Then I have to tell you that I think you should remember your father as he was."

"Are you telling me I can't see him?" Raven stood, arms crossed in defiance. Who was this man to tell her she couldn't see her own father?

"No, I'm saying I don't think you should."

"Well, you're not me. No one is going to lay my father in a casket or in the ground without me seeing his body. Please, I have to see him."

Philip placed both hands on his desk and pushed himself up. "All right. Give me a few minutes."

Raven sat in the outer office. The glare from the sun shining into the large glass windows made her head pound. She put her sunglasses back on.

Philip finally emerged. "This way." He led her through the hallway into a back room. A red curtain hung in the doorway. Philip turned to her. "You have to understand, his color, I mean we don't normally..."

"I understand." Anger still teetered above her sorrow. "He's going to look terrible. He's dead. It can't get much worse than that."

Philip nodded, raised the corner of the curtain, and allowed Raven to enter the small room. Soothing religious music played.

She stood at the corner and stared at the opened coffin. She could see the tip of her father's nose and his hands above the side of the coffin. Her heart raced but she had to do this. She had to see him, to prove he was really gone.

With her eyes on the floor, Raven clenched her purse and made her way to the casket in slow motion. She raised her head, gasped, and threw her hand over her mouth as tears flooded her face. She couldn't look away. She stretched out her hand and gently touched her father's cold, purple cheek, avoiding the gashes that covered his face. She ran her hand down his chest until it rested on his scarred hands.

After wiping the stream of tears that ran down her face, she touched the large, grapefruit-sized knot on his forehead. "Oh, Daddy."

"Excuse me," Philip said.

"Yes." Raven didn't turn around.

"It's the death certificate. The coroner reported that he passed away from an internal brain hemorrhage." Philip pointed to the bump on the head.

Her hands trembled as she took the paper.

"I'll leave you alone." Philip touched her shoulder and left the room.

Raven stood for a long time, staring at her father's lifeless face. The hollowed eyes made him look like a mask from a horror movie, but it didn't make her sick like she thought it might. It was an image now engraved in her mind, one to sit next to Teresa's.

She leaned over and gave her father a kiss, shuddering at the hard, cold cheek. "Good-bye, Daddy. I love you."

* * *

Raven threw her keys on the counter. "Hailey?"

Hailey knocked on the French doors and motioned for Raven to come outside on the deck. Raven went out and sat next to her.

"Jean says you've been down to the funeral home."

"Yes." Raven motioned with her head at Hailey's cigarette. "When did you start smoking?"

"I didn't. Just needed one."

"Oh." Raven looked away and forced herself to resist the temptation, praying silently for strength.

"I'm glad you went." Hailey let the smoke escape while she talked. "I couldn't have."

"How's Mom?"

"Oh, Mom." Hailey flicked the cigarette over the deck. "While you were down hanging at the funeral home, I'm here dealing with her. I should be on my honeymoon."

"Wait a minute." Raven's neck filled with heat. She shouldn't have been surprised by her sister's attitude. Selfishness was nothing new for Hailey, but for some reason, she was. "Let me get this straight. You're actually mad at me? You want to know what I did? I had to pick out a casket. I bought a burial plot, and I saw Dad's body. Why don't you just leave, go on your honeymoon." Raven stood. "I don't care."

Hailey grabbed her arm and tears filled her eyes. "I'm sorry."

Raven bit her lip, looked at her sister, and sat back down.

Hailey's eyes widened. "You saw his body?"

"Yes. He didn't look as bad as I thought he would."

"They said he was pretty cut up."

"Yeah. His head had this big knot. I guess he hit the windshield pretty hard. Hard enough to kill him." She closed her eyes. "I guess it was just something I had to see. To make it real."

Hailey squeezed her hand. "This is supposed to be such a happy time for me."

"I know."

Hailey sniffed. "While you were gone, Mom freaked out."

"What happened?"

Hailey stared straight ahead. "Aunt Jean called. I could hear Mom in the background. I rushed right over. She kept screaming, 'No, it can't be true.' Then she'd cover her ears and start shaking her head. Finally, Jean gave her some sedative. I think she's lost her mind."

"She has a concussion. She'll be fine. We have to give her time." Raven chewed on her thumb nail.

"Travis called, and Cody a couple of times."

"Yeah, they called my cell."

"You blowing them off?"

Raven rubbed her forehead. "I guess. I don't feel like talking to them right now."

"Are all your finals done?"

"All but one, and I'm skipping it. I'll still pull a C out of the class." Her emotions were too raw to face a class of students. Half of them hated her, the other half didn't even know her. All of them would offer condolences, reminding her of her new normal. Something she didn't need.

Raven chewed on the inside of her cheek. "Do you have any idea how to access Mom or Dad's account?"

"No. Why?"

"I just wrote a check for eight hundred bucks, and they need another seven grand to cover the funeral costs."

"It costs that much?"

"Yeah, and we still have to decide on flowers."

Hailey stood. "Let's start in Dad's desk. He's got to have something written down somewhere. If not, we'll call his lawyer. What's his name?"

"Sayer, I think. You start with Daddy's desk. I'm going to check in on Mom."

Chapter 14

Raven and Hailey sat in front of the casket under a green tent. Mourners surrounded her and her sister. Aunt Jean had stayed home with their mother.

The weather seemed appropriate. Dark and drizzly with a chill in the May air that seemed to rip through her skin.

Pastor Chartier, from her parents' church, spoke, but Raven couldn't have told you anything he said except amen. She stood up, placed a single rose on the casket, and walked a few feet away, glancing around at the small crowd.

Travis came up to her and gave her a hug. "I've been trying to call you."

"I know. I've been...I can't."

He nodded. "I understand. If you need me, I'm here."

"Thanks."

Men shook her hands, women gave her hugs. Many were complete strangers.

Matthew walked toward her, his hands deep in his pockets. "You doing okay?"

"I guess."

"I've been praying for you."

"Thanks." She gave him a faint smile. He smiled back and turned to walk away. "Hey." When he turned back to her she asked, "You coming over to the house?"

"I'd like to, if you don't mind."

She shrugged her shoulders. "I don't mind." She wanted to say so much more, but she didn't have the energy.

"I'll see you in a bit." He turned and left.

Raven's eyes widened when she saw Sasha. She grinned and walked over to her. Sasha leaned in and gave her a hug.

"Sasha. I'm so glad to see you."

"I was so sorry to read about your father."

Raven took Sasha's arm and they walked through the graveyard. "You look good."

"Thanks." Sasha tucked her hair behind her ears. "I wanted to let you know that I'm clean and I got a job at the hospital. They said if I work for three years, they'll help pay for college."

"That's wonderful."

Sasha looked down. "I'm so ashamed of what I did."

"Don't worry, it's in the past."

"When you kept quiet...it blew me away. Thank you." Tears flooded her eyes. "I was thinking about checking out your church someday."

"That would be cool." Raven smiled. "You want to come over to the house, help me sort through all the casserole dishes? I'll never get them returned to their rightful owners."

"I really need to get back to work. I've only been there for a few weeks. They let me off for a couple of hours to come."

"It was so good to see you."

"You too. I'll call you sometime." Sasha waved as she walked off.

A breeze blew and rustled the trees above Raven's head. A shudder ran through her body. She stood for a moment before looking down at the headstone. It brought her to her knees. She read it out loud. "Teresa Marie Anderson. How in the world?" She leaned over it and wiped the grass clippings away. "Blessed daughter taken away from us on the wings of angels."

Cody's deep voice came from behind. "Funny how it's so close to your dad's, huh?"

Raven stood and turned to him as he wrapped his arms around her. "I'd never seen it. It's very pretty."

"For a tombstone, I guess."

They stood in silence. *Why, Lord? Why are you letting this happen to me? Why flood my memory of my best friend committing suicide? Do I have to see her face again? Does it have to be next to my father's? You expect me to stay faithful after all this pain heaped on me?*

Be faithful, even to the point of death, and I will give you the crown of life.

I'd rather be dead. It'd be easier.

You don't mean that.

She sat down next to the tombstone and leaned her back against it. "What's next?" She looked up at Cody. "I've seen my best friend kill herself, my father died, and now my mom has amnesia. What do you think? Is God punishing me?"

Cody sat next to her. "Maybe you should ask your preacher boyfriend about that."

She ignored the boyfriend comment. "Why did he have to die?"

Cody shrugged his shoulders, but the Voice kept talking.

Death is not final, My beloved one. I raised My Son from the dead, and I can restore your life but you must stand firm and believe.

"I don't know. I just don't know." Tears fell freely.

Cody took her hand and gently caressed it. She had forgotten he was there. She squeezed his hand. "I'm sorry. I guess I should go. They'll be waiting for me at the house." She wiped her face. "You coming over?"

"Sure, let's go."

"Give me a few more minutes. I'll be right there."

He nodded and disappeared.

When she heard his car rev up and drive away, she lowered her head and cried. She missed her dad. She missed Teresa. Her chest shuddered. She missed Matthew.

Her cell phone vibrated. She looked at the text. It was from Hailey. *Where are you? Get home, now. I'm not doing this alone.*

She texted back. *Okay.*

She sighed, stood, and headed home.

* * *

"It's about time you got here," Hailey whispered, as she walked into the house. "Where have you been?"

"Cemetery. I just needed some time alone."

"It help?"

"Yeah, a little." Raven looked around at the house filled with guests. Last thing she wanted was to try and make some sort of civil conversation with complete strangers.

Aunt Jean walked up to them. "Would you go get some coffee and start refilling cups?"

Raven stared at her for a moment before shaking her head. "No."

"No?" Aunt Jean looked bewildered. "There are over fifty people out there, they need to be tended to."

"Maybe in your day you tended people, but my dad just died. I'm not becoming a hostess. They should be getting me coffee, asking me if I need anything." Raven stormed out of the house onto the deck. She wiped her hand across the wood, flinging a few stray water droplets into the air, then sat down.

Hailey followed. "Way to go, sis." She sat next to her. "I hate the idea of all these people coming over. I know they want to help but it's like we're supposed to entertain them."

Raven closed her eyes and tried to drink in the smell of the fresh air, hoping it would be cleansing. Her stomach growled. She looked over at Hailey. "I really am kinda hungry."

Hailey laughed. "Me, too."

"Yeah?" Raven nudged her sister. "Let's wait until some of the people clear out. Where's Mom?"

"Aunt Jean gave her some kind of pill so she'd sleep through all this."

Raven nodded. She hated the idea of sedatives, but sleeping through this was probably better for everyone. A lot fewer questions to answer.

"We need to clean out Daddy's office." Hailey stood and did a quick pace of the deck. "I'd like to do it tomorrow. Then I think Jake and I are going to get out of here for a few days. Try to salvage some of our honeymoon."

"Okay."

"I'll pick you up?"

"Sure."

Matthew appeared in the doorway and opened the sliding glass door. Hailey patted Raven's arm. "I'm going to go make a plate. You want me to bring you something?"

"No, thanks."

Hailey nodded at Matthew as she walked by.

Matthew looked down at Raven. "Can I sit?"

"Sure." Raven stared straight ahead. She wanted so badly to lean on him. To draw from his strength. But he was acting like a minister, not a friend. She believed it had to do more with the kiss than the death of her father. *How could someone get all worked up over one kiss?*

One kiss. The best and worst thing that happened to her. Matthew's words echoed in her mind, *I shouldn't have done that.*

You and me, it'll never work. The only thing the kiss did was ruin their friendship, and right now, that's what she needed.

"You doing okay?" he asked.

"I guess."

"You disappeared for a while. We were worried."

"Yeah." Raven fought the tears. "I just needed some time."

"I'm sorry for not being around more, it's just…"

"Hey, it's okay." She stood up. She wasn't in the mood to hear his excuses. "I guess I should go in there. Thanks for stopping by."

"Raven?" He stood. When she turned back to him, he took her arms and pulled her into a hug. "If I can do anything, please let me know."

She forced herself to smile. "Thanks."

She went inside.

* * *

Matthew had hugged her but she was stiff, unresponsive. His embarrassment for kissing her was only increasing. He hated himself for being self-absorbed as he watched her walk mechanically into the house. He had overstepped his boundaries. His pride and shame had overtaken. He couldn't even be the friend she needed him to be.

He walked through the house and stopped in the living room. He watched her nod as Cody talked. A twinge of jealousy flew through his body. He wished he could take her away, to hold her, comfort her, and even to kiss her again, but he couldn't—he wouldn't. His ministry was on the line, and he wouldn't let it suffer, no matter how bad it hurt him or her.

He lowered his head and walked out the front door.

* * *

Raven looked up at Cody.

"How come you haven't been returning my calls or texts?" he asked.

"I don't know. It's been hard."

"I'm here for you." He caressed her arm. "How's your mom?"

"She doesn't remember anything." Someone handed Raven a glass of water. She smiled at them. "Thanks." She turned back to Cody. "She thinks Daddy's away on a business trip. The doctor said it's from the concussion."

"That must be weird."

"Tell me about it." Raven sipped on the water, wishing he'd go away. She wanted everyone to go away.

"Do you want to do something tomorrow? Maybe go out to eat, see a movie?"

"No, I've got to clean out Daddy's office. Hailey's going to help before they leave on their honeymoon. I don't know how much fun they'll have, but they're going to try." She touched his arm. "Thanks for stopping by. I'd better go mingle before my aunt gets mad at me."

She walked away from Cody and went into her father's study, closed the door, and slid into her father's chair. She closed her eyes and silently prayed for the house to empty.

Chapter 15

Raven woke to another dreaded day. It seemed every day got a little bit worse. The funeral home, her mother's amnesia, the funeral, and now she had to go to her father's office and clean it out. She was thankful Hailey was coming with her. It was something she couldn't do by herself. The burden of her family had been thrown on her and she didn't know how much more she could take.

Her friends meant well, but they couldn't stop the pain or do the things she was expected to do. Raven felt more lost than ever. She tried to pray and read her Bible, but nothing seemed to comfort her. The pain was unbearable. She shared it with nobody. But something forced her to go on.

Raven stared out the window, waiting for Hailey. She hoped she'd keep her promise and come. The thoughts of her mother's condition overwhelmed her. Aunt Jean was constantly taking care of her and pretending. Eventually, Jean would leave. Raven wasn't sure if she could take care of her mother, even though she knew she'd have to.

Raven's thoughts were interrupted by the honk of a horn. She walked out the door and jumped into Hailey's car. Hailey handed Raven an oversized convenience store cup. "I brought you a pop."

"Thanks." Raven cautiously looked at her sister. "What is it?"

"Our drink." Hailey glanced over and lit a cigarette. "I thought it might help. I don't think you'll go to hell for one little spiked drink."

Without the strength to fight with her for trying to drag her down, Raven set the drink in the cup holder. "I can't drink that. Let's just get this over with."

Hailey rolled her eyes and drove on. "If we're lucky, his secretary will have things boxed up for us. Mom should be doing this. I can't believe she's flipped."

"Mom has a right to be upset," Raven snapped.

Hailey glanced at Raven as she drove. "Upset, yes, but she's gone bonkers. When is she going to snap out of it and remember?"

"I don't know."

Hailey pulled into the office parking lot and shut off the car. "As much as I love Mom, I can't take care of her. I don't want to. Maybe we should put her in a hospital."

"No. I'll take care of her. She's not going in some loony bin." Raven paused, waiting for any advice from her older sister, but none came. Why did she expect Hailey's insight, anyway? Her lack of depth on most situations had always been apparent.

"It's your life." Hailey slapped Raven's leg. "Let's go. I really want to get this over with."

They walked into the building. Raven could feel their father's colleagues staring at them. Once inside their dad's office, Hailey shut the door.

Raven sighed, relieved to be hidden behind the walls. The smell of their dad's musky cologne clung to the walls. Raven walked over to the chair and felt the cold black leather on the palm of her hand. She slowly turned it toward her and sat. The leather squeaked beneath her.

Hailey set the drink on the desk, threw an empty box on the floor, pulled a pack of cigarettes out of her purse, and lit one. "Come on." The smoke escaped while she talked.

"I don't think you can smoke in here."

Hailey rolled her eyes and snuffed out the cigarette in a coffee cup. "Let's pack it up and get out of here. This is giving me the creeps."

Raven nodded, opened the top drawer, and began boxing things up. The first person who stopped by the office offering condolences wasn't bad, but soon a steady stream of strangers found their way in.

Hailey began tossing things in boxes and quit acknowledging them. She stood. "I've got to get out of here. I can't do this. I won't."

"Hailey, you're not leaving me here. It's daddy's stuff. Can't you finish helping me with this?"

"No, I can't. I don't want to. I want to forget this happened. I want to move on with my life. I want to go on my honeymoon. I can't spend the next few hours looking blankly at these strangers' faces. I don't want to go through his things. I know you think I'm selfish—but...well, I'm not. He's dead. I've accepted it and I'm moving on."

"You're going to leave me stranded?"

Hailey threw a twenty at her. "For a cab. Sorry, sis." Tears filled Hailey's eyes. "I just can't."

"Keep your money." Raven threw the twenty back at her. "I'll get a ride. This is just like you. Whenever something gets tough, you run off."

Hailey glared at Raven before storming out.

Figures. Raven's chest fluttered but she refused to cry. She punched Matthew's number in her phone and held her breath for a moment before letting it out. Her voice was calm when he finally answered.

"I hate to bother you, but my sister stranded me at my dad's office. We were supposed to pack things up, and I guess it was too hard for her. Is there any way you could come and get me in about an hour?"

There was a long silence. "Well..."

Raven's heart dropped. She was sorry she called. "Never mind. You're busy. It's all right. I can find someone else."

Matthew hesitated. "I'm kind of with someone right now. How long will you be there?"

Raven fought back the tears. "Really, it's okay. Sorry I bothered you. I'll call someone else. I'll talk to you later." She hung up the phone, tears streaming down her face.

* * *

Matthew slid his phone in his pocket. Every instinct told him to go to her, but he sat motionless. Ever since he kissed her, life was in an uproar. His feelings twisted. The night she fell asleep in his arms was a night he never wanted to end. He wanted to comfort her. He wanted to be her pillar of strength.

Lisa interrupted his thoughts. "Who was that?"

"Raven. She needs help."

"Let her be. We talked about this. She needs to get her strength from God, not you."

Matthew stared at Lisa and wondered if that came from her heart or from her jealousy. "Her father just died. She's reaching out to me. She needs help." He stood, angry at himself for acting so childish. "I've got to go to her."

Lisa grabbed Matthew's hand as he walked by her. "You asked me to come."

Yeah, he had asked her—out of desperation to get Raven out of his head, but it wasn't working. All he wanted was Lisa out of his life and Raven in it.

"If you go over there, it's over."

Matthew's eyes narrowed. "Did you just give me an ultimatum? You're telling me if I go help a friend our relationship is over?"

Lisa's chin lifted in defiance. "I'm telling you if you leave me and go running to a woman you have feelings for…then, yes, it's over."

He slipped his hands deep in his pocket. His face hard. "Drive careful." He jogged out to his car.

* * *

Raven sank into her father's chair. She laid her head on the desk and cried. "I can't do this. Why did You leave me, God?"

Never will I leave you; never will I forsake you.

The words echoed in her head. She raised her head and looked aimlessly at the ceiling. "You did leave me. You're gone. Why do I feel so empty? I can't get out of this dark tunnel. I'm stuck. Help me, please."

She noticed the drink. It was still there. Hailey had carried it in and left it. Raven was hypnotized by it.

It will help. It'll get you through. It has before.

Her hands shook as she reached for it, then stopped. She took a deep breath, closed her eyes, and pulled her hands back.

With a heavy sigh, she grabbed her cell phone and dialed Cody's number. "Hey, could you come to my dad's office? Hailey and I were cleaning it out, but she ran off and I don't have a car."

"Sure thing. I'll be right over."

"Thanks, Cody."

Sitting for a long time, she stared at the boxes and the last reminders of her dad's job, avoiding the drink that sat on the corner. She couldn't even throw it away. It was too powerful to touch.

Finally, she stood up and began putting folders in boxes.

Woodsy cologne drifted in, making her smile before looking up. Cody leaned against the doorframe, arms crossed over his chest showing off his huge muscles in his tight white Under Armour shirt and baggy shorts.

"What up?" He grinned and cocked his head.

"Thanks for coming. I don't know what Hailey's problem is."

"Hailey's Hailey. She's a bit preoccupied, you know. Just getting married and all." Two steps and he stood next to her. He picked up the drink and took a long sip through the straw. "You need to mix your alcohol with something other than diet."

Her eyes narrowed. "It's not mine. Hailey left it." His joking, carefree attitude was intoxicating. She couldn't believe her silence for all those months had made him so angry and how easily he let the pain go. "And if you drink any more of it I'll be driving."

"Nobody drives my Mustang."

"Then put it down. Grab that box and start filling."

He obeyed. After filling the box, he stood. "I gotta find a real pop, that stuff was nasty. They got machines anywhere?"

"Yeah, I think you have to go left and down the hall. You can ask someone."

"You want something?"

"No, thanks."

Silence blanketed the room until she heard a quiet tapping on the doorframe. "I got here as soon as I could." Matthew looked around at the room. "Looks like you still have a ways to go."

Raven stood with mixed emotions. Maybe he had realized how idiotic he was being. "I wish you'd called. I got someone else to come."

Matthew nodded, his face unreadable. "I texted you."

"You did?" She reached in her pocket for her phone but couldn't feel it. Her forehead wrinkled as she searched on top of the desk, finally locating her purse. After digging for a few seconds, she pulled it out and looked at it. "Yeah, I guess you did. Sorry."

Matthew stepped closer to the desk, looking down at a coffee cup where the crushed cigarette was. He picked up the drink, took the lid off, and smelled it. The lines on his face hardened. "I'm sorry I couldn't come when you called, it's just that Lisa is here…and, well, I guess if you've got another ride I should go. I'll call you later."

"Yeah. Whatever." Sarcasm dripped from her words. She began throwing things in boxes.

"What's with you?" Matthew slid a hand in his pocket.

"Nothing."

He pointed to the drink. "You're drinking and smoking again?"

"You just assume they're mine?" she blasted at him. "What if I had a drink and smoked a cigarette. I don't have a right?"

"You know how easily it would be to get sucked back into your old lifestyle. Is that what you want?"

"My father was just killed and my mom is crazy. Give me a break." She closed the box and ran the packing tape across the top.

"And that's a reason to go back to your old life-style? You know the only way to get through this is by leaning on Christ."

"Yeah, I know. You can quit lecturing me and go. Be with your precious Lisa."

"Where is all of this coming from?"

Raven glared at him. Her neck felt like it was on fire. "I'm angry, okay? My dad is dead and my mother has lost her mind."

"And the alcohol? Does that help?" Matthew stared at her, his face red.

Raven stood and glared at him, her hands on her hips. "It's not..." She looked deep into his eyes and figured it was a lost cause. "Just forget it."

He took a step toward her, his face softening. "I'm here for you...but you can't..."

"No, you're not." Her hands began to shake. "You look at me like I've got the plague. I'm tainted because of my past, so who could blame me for drinking? That's the way you see me anyway."

"I do not."

"You do, too. You said you wouldn't date me. Why? Because of my past?" She grunted. "You can preach about forgiveness but you can't dish it out. Well, you know what? I'm moving on because that's what I have to do. So please go. I wouldn't want to keep you." Raven crossed her arms.

Matthew stared at her. "You don't understand."

"I do." Raven eyes fell to the floor, her shoulders drooped. "All too well. I'm not good enough for you and I never will be, so please, just go."

"Hey, so get this." Cody's voice entered the room before he did. "I found…" He looked at Raven then over at Matthew. His chest filled as his stance changed with the hardness of his face. The same look he had right before heading into a wrestling match. "What are you doing here?" He glared at Matthew.

Matthew stared at Raven. She could see jealousy or sadness, she couldn't tell which.

"I was just leaving."

* * *

Go back in there. She needs you.

Matthew ran his fingers through his hair. *I can't. She's been drinking and smells like cigarettes. You know I love her. I just proved it by letting Lisa walk out of my life.*

He climbed in his car and sat. *I just let Lisa walk out of my life. For what? For a girl I will never have because she's choosing a path I refuse to follow.*

Help her.

As much as I love her, Lord, I can't stand to be around her. She will ruin my ministry, my life. I'm sorry.

You should be.

* * *

168

Raven looked down, fighting the growing tears in her eyes. She threw things in boxes.

Cody tossed her a chocolate caramel candy bar. "Some guy was selling them for his kid."

Raven grabbed the candy bar, ripped one end open, and broke off a section. She threw a piece in her mouth and sighed as the chocolate brought her some comfort. Looking up at him, she faintly grinned. A tear slid out of the corner of her eye. She wiped it away, scooted to the wall, and leaned against it. "You want a piece?"

Cody popped open the soda and took a sip. "No thanks." He sat against the wall next to her. "What was going on with you and the preacher man?"

"He thinks the drink and cigarette were mine." She broke off another piece and ate it.

"Did you tell him it wasn't?"

"No. He wouldn't have believed me."

"You know the guy really likes you."

She pushed some of the chocolate to the side of her mouth. "How do you know that?"

"It's so obvious." He pulled his knees to his chest and rested his arms on them. "That first day I saw him at the restaurant, when he was acting like he was going to protect you. Like he could take me out." Cody laughed. "Then he was all ready to defend you again, the night at the pep rally. I'd a laid him flat."

"He's just protective. He'd stick up for anyone like that." She put another piece of chocolate caramel in her mouth.

"How about the time he was jealous when we met at the park, or the fact that anytime you're around he stares at you like he owns you. And we won't even mention the way he acted at the hospital."

She swallowed. "How'd he act at the hospital?"

"All 'I'm her preacher' just so he could get into the room with you when no one else could."

She laughed. "He was worried. It's his job."

"Has he ever kissed you?"

Heat filled her face and she threw the last two pieces of chocolate in her mouth.

Cody leaned into her, jokingly elbowing her. "He has, hasn't he?"

"I never kiss and tell."

"Oh my gosh. The preacher man kissed you."

"Despite the preacher part, he is a man." She tried to clean the caramel from her teeth. Grabbing his pop, she took a gulp.

"Hey, you have your own." He took the can from her and pointed to the cup on the desk.

She smiled and felt, for the first time since her father died, that her chest wasn't going to cave in. "Let's get this stuff boxed up so we can get out of here."

Cody got to his feet and carried a box to the bookshelf. "All these go?"

"Yes."

Chapter 16

Screeching tires, the two cars flew together in slow motion. Sheets of metal flew through the air...screaming... her father's mangled body lying in the middle of the destruction, blood everywhere...

Raven sat straight up in bed, panting. A horrible dream followed by an awful headache. She sunk back into the bed and tried to relax when she heard the scream again. This time, it wasn't a dream. She was awake. She ran to her mother's room.

Jean was shaking her sister. "Irene, wake up." Jean looked up at Raven. "I can't get her to wake up."

Raven ran to the bed. "Mom. Wake up. It's me, Raven."

Irene finally opened her eyes and looked at Raven. "It's not true, is it? He's not really gone, is he?"

Raven's and Jean's eyes met. Raven looked down at her mother. "Yes, Mom. Dad's gone." Her mother began to cry. Raven hugged her and cried with her.

Jean bent over and handed Irene a pill and a glass of water. "This will help."

Irene's hands shook, but she took the pill and water before lying back down. Raven rubbed her back until she dozed off. She walked to the door, motioning for Jean. Raven whispered, "A pill? Really? Shouldn't we let her face it?"

"She was clearly out of control. It wasn't that strong and it will help her stay calm."

"But she'll never deal with this if she's comatose all the time." Raven turned. Her head pounded. She went to the kitchen to take some Tylenol.

She grabbed a cup of coffee and went out on the deck. Her cell phone rang.

Cody was on the other end. "You doing okay?"

Raven rubbed her temples. "Yes. Thanks for coming yesterday. You were a life-saver."

"How are things at the house?"

Raven wished the Tylenol would kick in. "Mom's not doing very well."

"I thought I'd come by and see her today."

"She'd like that. Come by anytime. We'll be here."

"I'll see you soon."

Raven hung up the phone, went in, and made more coffee. She prayed for strength to get through this and to apologize to Matthew for acting like a complete jerk.

She was leaning against the counter when Jean walked into the kitchen.

"Raven." Jean's red lipstick was perfectly applied and not a hair out of place, like her mother's always was. "I'm going to have to leave in a day or two. We need to talk about what to do with your mother."

"Not now," she whispered. *God, how much more do You think I can take?*

"What, dear?"

"What do you mean *do* with my mother? She'll be fine." Raven wasn't in the mood for a confrontation.

"We can't leave her here alone, honey. Maybe a hospital…"

Raven raised her hand. "Hold everything, Aunt Jean. She's not going anywhere. She'll be fine."

"She's my sister, you know. You think I like talking about a hospital? But the fact of the matter is there is no other way. Who's going to watch her?"

"Me."

"You think you can handle that?"

"I'm going to have to."

"Will you promise me something?"

"Maybe," Raven said.

"If she's not better by August, you need to find her other help. I know how important college is. You need to finish."

"I plan on going back to college." Raven began wiping the counter top where some coffee had spilled. "And Mother will be better by then."

Jean nodded and left her alone.

The morning dragged on. Raven's headache had subsided and she felt like she could finally eat something. She was standing over the counter, spreading mayonnaise on two slices of bread, when Cody peeked in.

"Your aunt let me in."

"Just in time for lunch, as always." She forced a smile. "You want me to make you something?"

He nodded and squeezed her arm. "How's your mom?"

"Better, I guess." She pulled out two more slices of bread. "Why don't you go up and see her. I'll finish these. You want mayo?"

"Of course. Be right back."

Raven sat at the table making imaginary circles with her finger. Cody burst into the kitchen, pulled out a chair, and sat down. He tapped his fingers on the table. "Your mom is pretty out of it, but I had a nice chat with your aunt."

"Aunt Jean?" Raven whispered. "She's getting on my nerves." Raven stood and placed the sandwich in front of Cody, along with a bag of chips and a drink.

"How much longer is she staying?"

"A couple more days."

"So maybe we could go out tonight. Dinner or a movie. I think a change of scenery might do you some good." He began to devour the sandwich.

Raven stared at her plate. She had no appetite. She tossed it in the trash and carried the plate to the sink.

Cody stuck the last bite of the sandwich in his mouth and washed it down with a big drink of pop. "So, what do you think?"

She took his plate. "You want more?" He shook his head. Raven ran water on the plate.

"So…how about it? You and me tonight?"

Raven narrowed her eyes. "I can't start something with you."

Cody threw his balled up napkin at her. "I'm asking as a friend. Nothing hot and heavy. Promise."

She chewed on the inside of her cheek. Part of her wanted to say yes. To let him pamper her. To forget about the past week and her new reality, but the other part of her didn't think she could. How could she enjoy herself when her father was dead and her mother was still so out of it?

The left side of Cody's mouth rose into a grin, his dimple deep. "What? You afraid you can't keep your hands off of me?"

Raven turned to the sink. Her mouth turned up into a grin and she immediately felt guilty about it. She rinsed the dishes off. "Believe me, I can resist you."

Cody walked up behind her and whispered in her ear. "You've rinsed those twice now."

The heat from Cody's breath sent a chill down her spine. She closed her eyes and tried to fight off the same old feelings he used to stir in her.

The phone rang. She slid away from him and grabbed it. "Hello."

"Hey," Matthew said. "I wondered if you'd like to grab a bite to eat tonight. I think we need to talk."

"Is Lisa still in town?"

"No. She left yesterday. I really have some things I want to talk to you about."

"You mean lecture me about?"

"I'll pretend you didn't say that." He didn't sound mad. "What about dinner tonight?"

"I can't tonight. I've got plans." She felt Cody's breath on her neck. She turned to see him leaning over her, eavesdropping on her conversation. He whispered, "You talking about me?"

She pushed him back.

"Tell him you're going out with me tonight."

She covered the phone. "It's not a date."

"Just tell him. It'll make him jealous." There was a definite edge to his voice.

"Go and sit down," she whispered.

"I'm sorry, did I interrupt something?" Matthew's voice drew her attention back to the phone.

"Cody is here." She shot him a severe glare.

"Is that who you have plans with?"

She sensed jealousy in his voice but quickly dismissed it. "Yes." Matthew was silent. "You still there?"

"Yes, sorry. How about tomorrow night?"

"Yeah, that'll work."

She hung up the phone.

Cody had refreshed their pops and handed her a glass. "What was that all about?"

Raven sipped on the pop then placed it on the table. "He wanted to go to dinner tonight to talk about some things."

"Like what?"

"Things, I don't know." She began to stand but Cody grabbed her hand.

"You know I've always loved you, even when I hated you after Teresa died. If Matthew's too stupid to admit his feelings for you, then give us another chance."

"A date?" She couldn't deny the love she once had for Cody but she wanted Matthew. She shook her head. "You said as friends."

"If there's no you and Matthew, why not?"

"That's just it. I don't know if there is me and Matthew."

"Go to dinner with him and find out. If he's willing to give you a chance, we're still friends. If he's not, we try again." He raised his eyebrows at her.

Raven stared at him for a moment and chewed on her lower lip, afraid of the emotions he was stirring in her. "You're serious?"

"Yeah. You and me. How about it?"

Raven shook her head. It was too tempting. Not so much because she used to love him, but she thought maybe he could offer her the strength she needed to get through this. "I don't know how I feel about you. I'm pretty messed up right now."

"I know you like Matthew. I'm not walking into this blindly, but if he's not willing to fight for you, is he really worth it?"

She stood. "It's not just Matthew, it's…nothing." Even if her feelings for Matthew were gone, she knew that Cody didn't share her newfound faith, and that could drag her down. "Can we just be friends?"

Cody looked into her eyes. "Okay, friends."

She nodded.

"I'll pick you up at six."

Chapter 17

Matthew sat at his desk. He was trying to write out a sermon outline, but all he could think about was Raven. He went from anger to forgiveness then back to anger. He wanted to be with her but he was afraid she'd hurt his ministry. She had proved she hadn't really changed the other day by drinking and smoking.

He rubbed his forehead when he heard a pound on the doorframe. He looked up to see Cody already taking a seat in the chair in front of his desk. "Got a minute?"

"Sure." Matthew sat back in his chair and tossed his pencil on the notepad. "Did you and Raven go out last night?"

"Yeah, to a movie."

Matthew nodded. "What can I do for you?"

"I think the way you're treating her is crap."

Matthew frowned. "Did she tell you that?"

"She didn't have to. I can see it. You used to spend every minute you could with her and at the worst time of her life, you're blowing her off. You can't even be her friend. Either you're the worst preacher I've ever seen, or you have feelings for her, and for some dumb reason you think you can't pursue them."

"What?"

Cody brought his leg up and rested it on his other knee. "Raven lost her father. Why haven't you tried to help her? Or even talk to her? You've abandoned her."

"Is that what she said?" He knew he had backed away, but thought it would be better than leading her on. Who was he kidding, he backed off because every time he was around her all he thought about was being with her, holding her and kissing her. "I wish—"

"Wish what? She took care of everything for the funeral. Her mother's got some sort of amnesia and her sister won't help. And where have you been?"

"I've been here for her. She knows she can call me anytime." The heat rose up Matthew's neck. He didn't have to explain himself to Cody.

"Oh, come on, preacher man. You've been avoiding her because you have feelings for her."

Matthew's eyes narrowed. "Who said I have feelings for her?"

Cody stared him square in the eyes. "I can tell by the way you look at her, the way you watch her. I confronted Raven and…"

"She told you what?"

Cody gave him a fierce look. "You kissed her. You showed her how you feel and now you're blowing her off."

Matthew looked away from him, angry because he was right. He clasped his hands together. "I'm not going to sit here and argue with you. If I led Raven on, I'll apologize to her. I never meant to."

"I want another chance with her but it will never happen unless you cut her loose." Cody stood.

Matthew looked up at him. "I don't know what else you think I should do."

Cody leaned over the desk. "Just be honest with yourself and with her."

* * *

Matthew sat across from Raven. Her hair was piled on top of her head with a few strands gently falling around her face, which enhanced her high cheek bones. *Lord, why does she look so beautiful? This is going to be harder than I thought.*

"How's your mother doing?" he asked.

178

"Still doesn't remember. Aunt Jean is leaving tomorrow so I'm going to take care of her. Hopefully, she'll be okay so I can go back to college in the fall."

"She will be." He took a long drink from the pop. "I had a visit from Cody this afternoon." He avoided her large brown eyes. There was something alluring about them. He had decided, no matter how he felt, he couldn't date her. She wasn't right for his ministry.

"Cody came by? What'd he want?"

"A chance with you."

She shook her head. "I told him we were only friends."

His demeanor changed. He sat tall, serious. "He wants more than a friendship with you."

"He told you that? Why would he tell you that?"

"Because he thinks we're in love with each other." He watched her eyes widen. The lines in his face grew serious. "I assured him we're not."

She nodded, taking a sip from her glass. "So, that's why you're here? To remind me that we're not in love with each other?"

"Raven..." He slowly spun his glass on the table. "I should've never kissed you. I was wrong."

"Okay." She leaned back in her chair, her face soft. "I understand it was a mistake. You can never date me. It was an impulse. Believe me, I understand."

"I don't think you do."

"You don't think I know what it's like to have feelings for someone, knowing it'll never work, and trying to move on?" She rolled her eyes. "Walking away from Cody after Teresa died was one of the hardest things I've ever done, but it was what I had to do."

"Did you ever think about marrying him?"

Raven looked at the table before raising her eyes slowly to his. "I guess. I mean, I couldn't imagine my life without him. Why? You thinking about asking Lisa to marry you?"

Matthew shrugged his shoulders. Maybe if Raven thought he was moving on it would make it easier. "It would make our families happy. She's a preacher's kid. She knows my hours are long and what's expected of me."

"Sounds more like a job description. You never mention love when it comes to Lisa. Do you love her?"

Matthew quickly replied, "Well, I thought so, until…"

"You met me?"

Heat filled his face. "Yeah, but we're destined to be nothing more than friends."

Raven looked up at the waitress. "I'm not really that hungry."

Matthew set the menu down. "I'll take the Reuben, chips, and iced tea. Thanks."

Raven waited until the waitress walked away. "What's the big hurry? Is your biological clock ticking?"

That brought a smile to his face. "No." He wasn't about to tell her that Lisa was gone for good. "What about you and Cody?"

She sighed and tucked her hair behind her ears. "I'm not sure. He stirs up old feelings—what it was like before everything went bad—and that scares me."

"I think you need to be very careful. You're trying to walk with the Lord now, and he's not. I don't want to see you fall back into your old lifestyle."

She frowned. "And you think I would?"

You already have, he wanted to say but he kept silent.

"This is about the drink at my dad's office, isn't it?" Raven gave a sarcastic laugh. "I think I get it. It's not just about my past. You're afraid I might not act like a Christian. Is that it?" Her eyes narrowed. "I sin like the next person, but mine are worse than Lisa's or yours? Is that why you can't date me?"

He ignored her sarcasm, his face serious. "Let's say we're dating and you have a cigarette or a drink when you think no one is looking. But someone sees you or smells you. At that point, it's not just you, it's the preacher's girlfriend. Do you understand? All I've ever wanted to do was preach. I come from a long line of preachers. My father always told me that a good woman would help build a church but a bad one would destroy it. I'm not saying this to be mean, really."

"I understand, Matthew. Really, I do." She frantically tried to blink away the tears. "Because of my past, I will never be good enough for you." She sniffed. "I can only do the best I can. I didn't think my sins were unforgivable. I'm sorry if that makes you love me less."

"Raven, please." He touched her hand. *God, I messed this up. Help me make it right.* "I do have feelings for you. I would've never kissed you if I didn't, but I don't know if I should. I've fought the way I feel because I just don't know if I can take the chance. I see that you love the Lord, but you've only just given your life back over to Him. You still have a long way to go."

She pulled her hand from his and crossed her arms over her chest. "And I may not stay with Christ."

"I didn't say that."

Raven shook her head and held out her shaking hands. "Can I have the keys, please? I'll meet you in the car."

"Wait…"

She stood and snapped her fingers at him. "The keys."

When he dropped the keys in her hand, she clutched them and stormed out. He had his sandwich wrapped to go and paid the check.

She sat in the car with the door open, her feet on the concrete. Her head bowed and hands cupping her face. "Why now God? After everything I've lost, You have to take him, too."

Matthew laid his hand on her back and squatted down. Taking both her hands, he stared into her eyes. "You're not losing me. I'll always be here for you, no matter what."

She wiped the tears from her face. "It's not the same. Forget it."

"Tell me."

Her chin quivered. "We'll never get past this, will we?"

"I think we can. We have to. I don't want to lose our friendship." He wiped the tears from her cheeks. "I haven't been a very good friend lately, have I?"

"No, you haven't."

"I'm sorry. I'm an idiot sometimes, you know that. But I'll do better, I promise."

She pulled her hands from his and swung her legs into the car. "I should go."

Matthew shut the door and watched her stare straight ahead. They drove to her place in silence. He killed the engine and turned to her, his arm rested on the back of the car seat. "I really am sorry. I want to be there for you."

Raven tilted her head. "As friends."

He nodded.

"Okay." She leaned over and gave him a hug. "I'm going to hold you to it. No more blowing me off."

He wrapped his arms around her, closed his eyes, and soaked her in. "Never again. No matter what. I promise."

She pulled away from him and smiled through her tears. "Thanks."

Matthew watched her walk into the house. He wanted to go after her, tell her he wanted more, but he couldn't. He wouldn't.

Chapter 18

Raven woke. Survival mode kicked in and she would mechanically do the things she had to. Her aunt bustled in the kitchen, making more noise than normal. *Must be Jean's way of waking me up.* Raven dragged her feet all the way to the kitchen, stood in the doorway, and ran her fingers through her uncombed hair. "Morning."

"Good morning, dear. How was your date last night?" Jean poured Raven a cup of coffee and scooted it to her.

"It wasn't a date. He's a friend." She grabbed a single ice cube from the freezer and dropped it in her coffee. "What time you leaving?"

"I'm all packed. I'll get Irene some breakfast and I'll be out of your hair."

Jean talked while she cooked. Raven nodded, but didn't listen. She wanted her life back. She loved her aunt but was ready to start a new normal and she couldn't do that with Jean running the house.

Raven found herself saying "uh-huh" when there was a lull in her aunt's conversation, continuing to sip on her coffee. Jean picked up the breakfast tray and headed upstairs. Raven refilled her coffee as her cell phone rang.

"Hey, friend."

"Matthew?" Raven smiled. Just his voice gave her strength. "Hello."

"Are you okay?"

"I am. I don't have time to talk right now. My aunt is getting ready to leave, can I call you back?"

"Sure."

Raven slid the phone back in her pocket and smiled. Maybe they really could be friends.

"Your mom said she was going to rest a while longer." Jean pulled her keys from her purse. "Call me if you need me."

"Thanks for everything you've done." They hugged. "I love you. Drive careful."

Raven stood at the door and waved. She peeked in on her mother, who was sleeping. Good. It'd give her a chance to shower. The water beat against her as the past two weeks spun in her head. She begged God to make it better. She relaxed, closed her eyes, took a deep breath, and let it out.

A scream echoed through the house.

She shut off the water, grabbed her robe, and listened. It was quiet. Stepping out of the shower, she cracked the bathroom door and listened again. Nothing. With a shrug of her shoulders, she grabbed a brush and pulled it through her hair. The scream came again.

The brush fell to the counter and she ran into her mother's room. Irene sat on the bed. "Where is he? Where is he?"

Raven took her mother by the arms and tried to shake her into reality. "Mom, it's me. Raven. Daddy's not here. Calm down."

Irene stopped yelling and looked at Raven with an innocence in her eyes that reminded Raven of a small child. "Where did he go? Did he say when he'd get back?"

Raven's heart raced. "He wanted me to tell you that he loves you. Maybe you could rest a while and I'll get dressed. How about we go for a walk?"

"That would be nice. I'll just wait for you." Irene laid her head back down on the pillow and closed her eyes, her body shaking.

Raven watched her for a moment before climbing off the bed. The doorbell rang. She peeked out her bedroom window. It was Matthew. Grabbing her phone, she shot him a text. *Give me a minute.*

K.

She threw on an old sweatshirt and a pair of jeans, went downstairs, and opened the door. "I'm sorry, I was just getting ready."

"I came by to see your mother. Do you mind?"

"No, not at all. Come in."

"Raven?" Irene yelled.

Raven and Matthew ran up the stairs. "Mom?"

Irene sat on the edge of the bed, crying. "I can't remember where your dad said he was going. Why can't I remember?"

Raven held her mother and rocked her. She stroked her hair. "You'll remember. It won't always be like this, I promise."

Wiping her eyes, Irene looked up at Matthew. "It's your friend. He's the doctor. No...preacher."

"Yes." Raven looked up at Matthew and smiled. "It's Matthew. He came to see you."

Irene looked down at her pajamas. "I'm not dressed for visitors."

Matthew gently shook her hand. "You look beautiful, Irene. Can I get you some coffee or tea?"

"Tea sounds wonderful." Irene smiled and Matthew helped her to the chaise lounge.

Raven watched as he poured her some tea from the carafe that Jean had left. He sat with her and they began talking. It brought a tear to Raven's eyes.

Matthew looked up at her. "We'll be fine. Why don't you go finish getting ready?"

Raven nodded and went to her room. Combed through her wet hair and put on some makeup. She sat on the floor outside her mother's room and listened to Matthew talk about the things God was doing at the church. He never mentioned the death of her dad. She heard her mother tell him she was getting tired.

He walked out of the room and looked down at her. He held out his hand. She grabbed it and he pulled her up.

"She's lying down." Matthew smiled. They went downstairs. "Can I get you a pop?" he asked.

"You've done plenty. Sit and I'll get us something. Thank you for coming to see her."

Matthew sat on the couch. "I thought you might need some help since your aunt left. I never really thought about how tough it must be to pretend your dad is still alive."

"Yeah." She handed him a can of pop and sat next to him, tucking her legs up under her. "I'm going to play along until she remembers. Doctor said it could be anytime."

Matthew took a small sip, set the can down on the table, and looked at her. "You've taken on a big responsibility. You sure you can handle it?"

"Yeah, I think so."

He smiled at her. "You can." He took her hand and gave it a gentle squeeze. "We good?"

"Yeah, we're good." She felt herself move closer to him, drawn to him like a magnet. He gave her an inviting smile. "Friends?" she asked.

"Yes," he whispered, touching her face.

She leaned in to kiss him.

He stopped her, their faces inches apart. "We can't do this."

"Because of Lisa?"

"No."

"Because of my sins?"

"No." His grin deep.

"Oh, yeah…friends."

Their eyes locked and for a moment, she thought he'd throw the whole friends argument out the window and kiss her anyway, but her cell phone rang. She reached over him and grabbed it off the end table.

"Hello?" She rested against him, breathing in his crisp clean cologne. "Eleven? That would be great. Thank you so much. Okay, see you then. Good-bye." Raven hung up the phone, settling in close to Matthew. She knew it would only last a few moments. "That was Cody. He's coming by later. I have to meet with the attorney at eleven-thirty."

"You could've asked me. I would've stayed."

She tucked her hair behind her ear and smiled. "Cody was here when the attorney called the other day."

Matthew stood, his hands deep in his pockets. "I need to go."

"Need to or have to?"

"Both."

She laughed and followed him to the door. He turned to her. "Let me know if you need anything."

"Okay."

They hugged. "Call me later."

She nodded, feeling safe in his arms. She knew he was still attracted to her. All she could do was pray that he'd change his mind and give her a chance.

* * *

Raven walked into the house and tossed her purse on the couch.

Cody trotted down the stairs. "Your mom just fell asleep. How was your meeting?"

"Financially, great." She followed him into the kitchen. "Thanks for watching my mom while I was gone."

"Not a problem." Cody started making sandwiches. "She told me you guys were going out for a walk later. Can I join you?"

"Sure, but I thought you had your physical today."

"I do, I have time." He set a plate in front of her. "Your mom also told me Matthew came by."

"Yeah, so?"

"I just wondered how that went."

Raven sat, running her hands over her face. "Good. We talked. We're friends." She thought about that moment—almost kissing again—and smiled.

"Who are you trying to convince?"

"Ha. Ha. Quit worrying about Matthew and me." She bit into the sandwich, trying hard to eat it, but food still tasted like cardboard.

Cody walked over and began massaging her shoulders. He leaned over and whispered in her ear, "I worry about you and Matthew because I want you all to myself."

"You are so full of yourself."

He playfully smacked her upper arm. "Thanks a lot for the vote of confidence."

She pushed the sandwich to the center of the table, got up, and walked toward the living room. "You shouldn't just assume I'll take you back. What Matthew does has nothing to do with us."

Cody grabbed her and turned her around to face him. "You drive me crazy." He firmly grasped the back of her neck, pulled her close, and tried to kiss her.

She dodged it.

Cody brushed her hair away from her face. "Let's not play games. I told you I loved you and I meant it."

She brought her eyes to meet his. "I'm not playing games. I just don't know about us."

She hated it but it was hard to fight the feeling of someone holding her, someone that was strong. Someone she could lean on and who'd keep her safe. But the lingering doubt hung over her like a cloud. Not just because of Matthew but because Cody didn't believe in Jesus the way she did.

He pulled her close and tried to kiss her a second time but she turned away again. He released her. "All right, I get the hint. Let's take your mom for that walk. After that I'm off to my physical."

* * *

Matthew walked down the corridor of the hospital to the waiting room. He peeked in, like he always did, to see if there were any families he could pray with. Cody sat in a wheelchair in front of a window dressed in a hospital gown.

"Cody?"

When Cody looked up, his eyes were bloodshot. Crying, Matthew guessed.

"What are you doing here?" Matthew sat. "What's going on?"

Cody's cockiness was reduced to a whisper. "I've got leukemia. I just found out."

"I'm so sorry. Where are your parents?"

Cody stared out the window. "Dad left after Teresa killed herself. I'm not sure where he is, Florida I think. I told Mom to leave me alone for a while. I couldn't stand to hear her cry anymore."

Matthew rested his elbows on his legs. "How'd they find it?"

"Had to get a physical for my wrestling scholarship. They did some blood work and here I am." His chest shuddered. "College is gone. Wrestling is over. Life stinks." Cody looked over at Matthew. "You know the worst part is my mom. I die and she's got nothing, nobody. Maybe you could share some of that Jesus stuff with her, you know, just in case." He rubbed his eyes.

"How about I share it with you?" Matthew grabbed his forearm. It was a solid piece of muscle. "You know Jesus loves you, too."

"Yeah, that's what Raven keeps saying." He rubbed his forehead. "I'm afraid of what this will do to her."

"You think she'll start drinking again?"

"I don't know what she'll do." Cody readjusted the blanket over his legs, his face softening. "I don't know how I'm going to tell her I'm sick." His eyes swelled with tears and he looked away.

"You want me to tell her?"

"Yeah, if you don't mind." He looked at Matthew. "Can you do me a favor?"

"Yeah, anything."

"I can't believe I'm asking you this." His face hardened. "They're moving me up to Mayo. She'll want to come see me and I don't want her driving that far alone, not after she just found out I'm sick." His lips pursed together. "Would you drive her up there for me?"

"Yes." Matthew saw defeat in Cody's eyes and he knew that if Cody was going to fight this disease, he needed Raven. "Raven and I are only friends." When he saw Cody's face soften, he asked. "How long are you going to be here?"

"They're keeping me for the next few days, then moving me up there next week. Maybe you could tell her tonight. I'd like to see her tomorrow before they start chemo."

Matthew clutched tighter to the small leather Bible. "I'll go tell her now. Can I pray with you?"

Cody shrugged his shoulders. "Sure, I guess."

* * *

Raven sat on the couch, her legs curled up beneath her. She had finally gotten her mom to go to up to her room.

There was a knock on the door. She peeked out the window and saw Matthew, his face serious. She pulled the door open. Her heart pounded. "What's wrong?"

"It's Cody."

She shook all over and backed away from him. "No, not an accident. I can't go through it again."

"No, it's not an accident." Matthew ran his hand through his hair, then down his face. "I just saw him, he asked me to come here and talk to you." Matthew hesitated. "Can I come in?"

"What? You saw him with another girl?" She stared at Matthew's emotionless face. "Well, it wasn't like we were dating or anything. We were only friends."

"No, he wasn't with another girl. I was at the hospital making some calls. He's sick."

"Sick? What do you mean, sick?"

Matthew looked into her eyes. "He's got leukemia."

There was silence. Raven began to chuckle. "He's got what? Leukemia? You're kidding, right?" The world closed in on her. The dark cloud reemerging. "No, that's cancer. That's a childhood disease, isn't it?" She stared at Matthew. "This *cannot* be happening."

"He's in the hospital. He'd like you to go see him tomorrow. They're going to start chemo. I'll stay with Irene."

Raven was numb. Darkness fell over her like a blanket. She became mechanical. "Yeah, okay. I'll go see him tomorrow." She walked to the door and opened it. "Thanks for coming by."

Matthew walked toward her, his forehead wrinkled with troubled thoughts. "You sure you want me to go?"

"Yeah. I'll be fine." She tried to laugh but the sarcasm showed through. "I mean, it can't get any worse, can it?"

"I don't think I should leave you."

"Why? You think I'm going to get drunk?"

"I didn't say that."

"But it's what you're thinking." She rolled her eyes. "I'm fine, really."

He grabbed her arms. "Look at me." When she obeyed, his grip loosened. "What are you thinking?"

"I don't know."

"Yes, you do. Tell me."

She looked away, ashamed. "I don't understand how God could do this to me…again."

"He's not doing this to you."

She pulled away from his grip and sat on the couch. "You know, part of me understands that." She looked up at him. "I do. I know this is not about God punishing me or even about me. It's about Cody." Her chest fluttered. "Cody." She sighed, tears flooded her eyes. "He's gonna need me to be strong."

She wiped the tears. "Really, I'm okay. You can go."

"You sure?"

"Yes." She walked to the door. "I'm fine. Go." She pushed him out the door.

Matthew walked slowly to the car. She waited until he was in it before closing the front door. She peeked through the blinds. He still sat. She knew he didn't want to leave, but she wanted to be alone.

After a few minutes, he pulled out of the drive. She walked into the kitchen and made herself a soda. The tears started and she couldn't control them. She threw the glass across the room. It shattered while Raven fell to her knees. "Why?" she screamed. "Have I not gone through enough?"

She looked up, searching for God. "Do You want me to fail? How much do You think I can handle?" She began to cry as she scrunched into a ball on the floor and rocked back and forth. "I can't do this anymore. Why? I just want to understand."

She felt the hand on her back. Raven looked up while the tears continued to stream down her face. The light glowed behind her head and she could hardly make out the face.

Irene took Raven in her arms and whispered, "It's going to be okay, sweetie. Mommy's here."

Raven melted in her mother's arms.

Chapter 19

The cancer floor. The smell of disease ambushed Raven's nose, almost making her sick. She closed her eyes and took short quick breaths as she fought the tears. She walked down the hall, pushing the image of Teresa out of her mind. Her palms were sweaty and her heart raced. At the nurses' station, a young woman looked up at her. "Can I help you?"

"Cody Anderson's room please."

She took a moment before pointing Raven in the direction of his room. "Do you have a cold or have you been ill?"

"No."

"Don't forget to use the hand sanitizer before you go in."

"Thanks." Raven took a deep breath before pushing the door open. "Cody?" She tried to smile, but tears came instead.

"Hey, gorgeous." Cody reached for her. "I'm so glad you're here."

Raven walked toward his bed. "When did you find out?"

Cody took her hand as she sat down. "Yesterday. I came for my physical. They did some tests and voilà, cancer."

She stared at him, forced the tears away, and tried to be strong. "What happens now, I mean, chemo?"

"They're starting chemo right away. I'll be in the hospital for a couple of days then they're moving me to Mayo. The doctors are confident that I can fight it and get it into remission. How's your mother?"

"How can you be so calm?"

"Hey, I don't plan on dying. Who would take care of you?"

She shook her head and looked away. "You have confidence? I don't know anymore."

"What don't you know about?"

"God and His plan. Matthew keeps insisting He has reasons for everything, but look what has happened in a month."

"You know me, I'm not sure about this whole God thing, but I did some soul searching last night, and I think we can't blow off God so quickly."

She cocked her head. Who was this guy? Not the Cody she knew. "Did Matthew convert you last night?"

He laughed. "No, but I'm not an atheist. How's your mom?"

Raven wiped the tears that had escaped. "She really surprised me. Last night after Matthew left, I kinda lost it for a moment, and she came down the stairs and, well, she was my mom again." Her whole face grinned. "It was wonderful. I've missed her."

"See, something good has come out of this already." Cody squeezed her hand.

"I can't stay very long. Matthew is watching her."

"I understand. Don't feel like you have to come up all the time. You've got your hands full."

The room fell silent. Raven sat and held his hand, gently stroking it. Every time the thought of him having cancer seeped into her mind, her head spun. The walls felt like they were closing in. *I'm not going to have a panic attack.* She stood and did a quick pace of the room, finally landing on the edge of the bed.

He grabbed her hand and pulled her to him.

She wrapped her arms around him. "If you die...I don't know what I'll do." Her tears soaked his hospital gown.

He rubbed her back then cupped her face in his hands. "I'm not going to die. They caught it early."

Raven nodded, turned her head, and kissed his large hands before lying down on his chest. He cleared his throat. "I asked Matthew to drive you up to Mayo next week. Will you come see me?"

She sniffed. "Of course."

Cody touched her cheek. "You should go. Call me later, you know, if you need someone to talk to."

"You, too. I'll be home." She leaned over and gave him a kiss on the cheek.

He smiled. "Come here." He pulled her close and gave her a peck on the lips. She let him. How could she deny him that when he was beginning a battle for his life? He stroked her hair then gently touched her cheek again. His eyes filled with tears. "Don't worry about me."

"I'll try not to. You're going to be fine?"

"Of course." Cody wiped his eyes and laughed. "If you'll quit making me cry like a baby. It's not very manly."

"I'm sorry." She leaned in and hugged him.

"I love you," he whispered.

* * *

Raven laid her purse down on the dining cart. She glanced between Matthew and Irene. "So, how are you two?"

Irene laid the remote on the coffee table. "We've just been watching some TV. How's Cody?"

"He looked better than I thought he would. Can I get you some pop?"

Matthew stood. "Sure."

"No, thank you." Irene stood and stretched. "I think I'll go upstairs and rest. I want to be fresh when your father gets home."

"That's a good idea." She was beginning to get used to the charade. She grabbed two sodas.

Matthew sat back down. "I thought I might go back and see Cody. You think he'd care?"

"He seemed a pillar of strength, but I wonder how much of it was an act for me." She sipped on her Diet Coke. Cody knew how to lie and he could do it well. "I can't believe the impression you made on him. He's up there talking about God and that I should have faith."

"That wasn't me." Matthew opened the can of pop she had brought him. "There's something about looking death in the face that makes you think about God."

"Yeah, well, he has more faith than me right now. I'm on the fence, teetering." She paced the room, her fists tight. "I'm just having a hard time believing He's really up there." She stared at him, waiting. "I thought for sure I'd hear an *'I told you so.'*"

"Why would I say that?"

"Because of what you said to me. About my faith or lack of it."

Matthew shook his head. "I never intended you to think I didn't believe in you. I didn't mean that I didn't think you would make it as a Christian. I just meant that you've got a long road ahead of you. We all do."

"Yeah, well, why does my road have so many obstacles in it?"

"I don't know, but you have to believe that everything works together for the good. You have to lean on your faith."

She shook her head.

"What?"

"It's so easy to say, isn't it? But you've been raised in a Christian home, went to Christian schools, even graduated from Bible College. Your biggest decision is whether or not to marry Lisa. I've seen my best friend kill herself, planned my father's funeral, I'm taking care of my mother, and now one of my best friends may die from leukemia."

If Matthew was shocked at her bluntness, he kept it to himself. "God never said it'd be easy."

"Yeah, well why is it easier for some?"

"I don't know. You just have to stand firm, no matter what's thrown at you."

"I've said it to myself a thousand times. I keep praying for strength, but feel like I'm just getting weaker. I just don't think I can do it."

Matthew stood. "You are stronger than you think, more than anyone else I know. Just hang in there."

Raven nodded. Not because she agreed but to appease him. She wanted to know why God was making her go through this. She sighed. "Thanks for staying with Mom and listening to me babble."

"Anytime. Hang in there." He squeezed her shoulder. "Call me if you need to talk. Promise?"

"I promise."

Chapter 20

Raven killed the engine and climbed out of the car. Matthew walked out of his house with a duffel bag. "I really can go alone." Raven leaned against the car. "Rochester isn't that far."

"I promised Cody." He tossed his bag in the backseat. "You want me to drive?"

"No, but thanks." They climbed in and took off.

"Is Hailey staying with your mom?"

"Yep. It worked out good. Jake had to go out of town on business." She glanced over at him. "So, how's Lisa? You ever gonna ask her to marry you?"

"Lisa, um, no. Guess my biological clock isn't ticking so loudly."

She laughed.

"Actually, we're not dating anymore. She couldn't deal with certain things."

"What do you mean?"

"My feelings for you."

Raven could feel his stare. She glanced over at him, then settled her eyes on the road. "You mean the feelings you had for me."

"Yeah, had. The feelings I had for you, you know, because you're with Cody now."

"I'm not with Cody." She gripped the steering wheel tighter. "And we're friends, so what's to deal with?"

"Yes, friends." Matthew pretended he was playing the drums on his legs.

Raven laughed. "You're so strange. I can't believe you're a preacher sometimes."

"Why?"

"It's just hard to picture a preacher doing that." She pointed to his drum solo. "Jamming to music."

"We are human, you know. You don't like it when I do this?" He slapped on his legs faster and harder.

"You play them very well. I use to do the same thing, but I was sixteen and drunk."

Matthew nudged her arm. "This is great."

"What?" She was thankful she was driving so she had a distraction.

"This. You and me."

She nodded.

The car became silent except for the music she played on her iPhone.

"Raven?"

"Yeah?"

"How are you doing, financially? Are you and your mother okay? I don't mean to be nosy, but do you need money?"

"We're fine. In fact, better than fine. It seems Daddy made sure we'd all be financially okay if—when he died. His attorney is handling all the details." She glanced over at him. "Thanks for asking."

There was silence again. Familiar landmarks flashed by the windows. They made her smile.

"What are you thinking about?" he asked.

"My dad used to bring us up here fishing. I was little, maybe ten years old. We had so much fun." She scratched her head then let her hair fall through her fingers. "I miss him. I guess that will never go away."

"It won't, but it'll get easier."

"I hear you've been talking to Cody's mom."

"Yeah, she's amazing. A Christian. Did you know that?"

"No. It's hard for me to see her. It makes me too sad." She readjusted her hands on the steering wheel. "Do you think Cody will live?"

"It sounds promising. If they can get him in remission they say he can live a full life."

"It scares me."

"You mean because he might die?"

"Yeah. With Teresa, Daddy, and now Cody, it really makes you realize how short life can be. You have to cherish every moment as if it were the last. At the hospital, he was acting like Cody, cocky and arrogant. He told me he loved me. I feel bad because I didn't tell him I loved him back."

"But do you?"

"Yes, but not in the same way. It's just…Cody acts like he can't get enough of me. It's like he soaks up every minute we share together. It's hard to explain. He's intense and so sure of his love. I, on the other hand, wanted something else." She glanced at Matthew.

He nodded. "Go on."

"I just haven't looked at him that way for so long. Now, it's all different."

"Because of me or the cancer?"

"I think both. I can't remember life before Cody. Before Teresa died I was madly in love with him. I would've done anything for him."

She pulled off at a rest stop. They walked around to stretch their legs. She tossed him the keys. "Will you drive?"

"Sure." They took off, both absorbed in thoughts.

Matthew sighed before he finally broke the silence, "I think you need to be careful and not allow Cody's sickness to guilt you into a relationship."

She cocked her head. "Would it be so bad if I could help him?"

"You can't help him that way. Just be his friend."

"And what if it turns into more?"

He glanced at her then back at the road. "I thought you said you didn't love him."

"Not in that way, not now, but..." She watched his grip tighten on the steering wheel. "Would it bother you if Cody and I were dating?"

"Yes." He shook his head. "I mean no."

"Why do you do that?" There was a hint of laughter in her voice.

"Do what?"

She pulled a jug of water out of her purse and took a drink. "I don't think you do it intentionally."

"What?"

"Lead me on."

"What?" His voice rose an octave. "I'm not..."

She raised her hands in defense. "I said, you don't do it intentionally. You can't sit and tell me you broke up with Lisa because you have feelings for me then try and brush it off. Now you're questioning me about my feelings about Cody. It's just confusing."

He stared straight ahead.

"Maybe it's just me. I guess I read more into that kiss than there really was." She picked at her fingernails. "I didn't think you would do that unless there was something really there." When he didn't answer, she turned and tried to read his face, but couldn't. She looked back out the window. *I shouldn't have said anything.*

They drove in silence the last thirty miles. Matthew pulled into the hospital parking lot. "Looks like we're here. You ready to go in?"

Raven nodded.

Outside Cody's room, she tapped on the door. "Cody?" She peeked around the door. A nurse caught her and whispered, "You need to wash your hands and wear this mask."

Raven and Matthew nodded and washed their hands. She peeked around the corner and got a glimpse of Cody. He looked pale and thin. She placed the mask on and turned to the nurse. "Can I touch him?"

"Yes, now that you've washed your hands. We just can't take the chance of him getting any germs. He's got almost no immune system with all the chemo. He sleeps a lot, but he'll be glad to see you. You're Raven, right?"

Raven nodded.

The nurse smiled and squeezed her arm. "He's told me all about you. He's doing good."

"Thanks." Raven walked to Cody's bed. She sat and tried not to disturb him.

Matthew whispered, "I'll be back in a little bit."

Raven nodded. She concentrated on being strong, focused on Cody.

Cody opened his eyes and smiled. "What I surprise. I was just dreaming about you."

"Liar." She smiled, even though he couldn't see it through the mask.

"You look good in that." He tried to sit up.

She reached for him. "Can I help? What can I do?"

"I'm fine. Just rearranging. Did you meet Angie, my nurse? She's been an angel." He coughed. He tried to bring his hand up to cover his mouth, but didn't make it in time. Every movement was in slow motion.

Angie walked into the room. Cody weakly grinned. "Speak of the devil."

She smiled at Raven, then turned to Cody. "Don't give me any grief. I'm just here to take your vitals. You can keep talking."

Cody's speech was drawn out. "We were talking about you." He winked.

Angie looked at Raven. "Don't believe everything he says."

Raven held his hand, fought the tears, and laughed. "I learned *that* a long time ago."

"What happened to your friend?"

"He stepped out for a bit." She squeezed Cody's hand. "You know I could've driven myself."

"I just wanted to make sure. Besides, I knew he would jump at the chance to spend some time with you. You two a thing yet?"

"No."

"Good." He swallowed a couple of times and tried to lick his lips. "I wanted you to have company, but honestly, I don't like it when you two are together."

Raven poured him water and brought the straw to his mouth. "You don't have anything to worry about, we're just friends, really."

Raven returned the glass to the table. He took her hand, brought it up to his mouth, and kissed it. "I'm really glad he came. I'm glad you had the company."

"Angie said that you're responding well to the chemo. Hopefully you won't be here very much longer. I wish they hadn't moved you so far away."

"The doctors say they may let me go home in a couple of weeks. I can do the rest of my chemo as an outpatient."

She held his hand as he scooted farther down in the bed and stared at the ceiling. Cancer frightened her, but she didn't want him to know it. The silence was deafening.

Matthew came around the corner and shook Cody's hand. "How you doing?"

"Pretty good." Cody smiled. "Where've you been? Flirting with the nurses?"

"Ha-ha." Matthew sat. "Talking to your mom."

"Thanks. I know she appreciates it." Cody turned back to Raven. "Sorry if I fall asleep on you guys. I'm getting tired."

"Where is your mom?" Raven wasn't sure she wanted to talk to her. It was bad enough to deal with Cody's sickness, but she didn't think she could rehash Teresa's death too.

"She went down to the cafeteria. Said she'd talk to you later." Matthew gave Raven a nod.

"She's been staying in the room with me." Cody pointed to the folded up cot. "She's a trouper."

Raven stood and stretched. "I think we should go before they kick us out. Let you get some rest. We'll come back in the morning."

"I'm not going anywhere."

Raven bent over and gave him a hug. "Hang in there." She touched the side of his face.

He took her hand and kissed it. "I'll see you later."

Matthew patted his leg. "Get some rest."

Chapter 21

Matthew set Raven's bag outside the hotel room door and handed her the key. She took it and slid the plastic key into the lock. When the green light flickered, she grabbed her bag, opened the door, and walked in.

"I've got to straighten something out." Matthew left his suitcase in the hallway and followed Raven into the room. Her words ate at him. Who was she to imply he had led her on? He'd made a mistake by kissing her, he knew that. His feelings had overtaken common sense.

"Sure, come on in." Raven kicked her shoes off, pulled the pillows out from under the covers, and piled them on the bed before lying on them.

Matthew rubbed his forehead and silently prayed for the right words. "When I kissed you, it *was* important to me, but I did that in haste. I'm sorry. I didn't mean to ever lead you on."

He stared at Raven, who said nothing. What did he expect her to say? Her silence was more maddening than any hateful words she could've thrown at him. "Well?"

"Well, what?"

"Aren't you going to say anything?"

"What do you want me to say?" Raven chewed on her bottom lip. Her eyes met his. "You kissed me and I kissed you back. Now we're friends."

He stared into her brown eyes. It made his heart ache. His desire for her was overwhelming, and he questioned God for allowing it to be there.

Raven sat up and pulled a pillow on her lap. She looked down and tugged on a small string that hung free from the dainty stitching. "What else is there to say that we haven't already said?"

Matthew knelt down, placed his hands on the bed by her legs, and tried to look into her eyes. "You have to believe me. I kissed you because I wanted to, but I was wrong. I should've controlled myself." When she raised her eyes to look at him he lost his concentration. Her warm breath was soft on his face and his desire to kiss her was overwhelming. "I can't explain this."

"Then quit trying." She looked into his eyes. "It was wonderful and I will never forget it. In a moment, my dream came true. God answered my prayer. Don't belittle it by trying to explain it away."

He forced himself to look away so she wouldn't see the tears. "That was the nicest thing anyone has ever said to me." He turned back and gently touched her cheek. He fought the urge to take her in his arms and to tell her how he really felt. "I should go. I have to go." He stood and began to walk out.

"This is what drives me crazy," she shouted. "We have this beautiful, innocent moment and you run off. Why do you do that?"

Matthew stopped and turned to her. He pursed his lips. "Because...I...nothing." He shook his head and walked out. He was tired of fighting the temptations, the sinful thoughts, when it was pointless.

* * *

Matthew stood in the bathroom of his hotel room brushing his teeth. Why had he allowed himself to get in this position? He should've never come with her. It was only causing more trouble.

There was a soft tap on the door. He opened it with the toothbrush hanging out of his mouth. "Raven?"

She walked past him and sat on the bed.

"What are you doing?" He walked into the bathroom, spit the remaining toothpaste out, dropped the toothbrush, and wiped his mouth.

Raven folded her arms. She wore a T-shirt that hung mid-thigh. "We're going to finish this conversation if it takes all night. Do you want to know what I think?"

Matthew threw a pair of his shorts at her. "I'd feel better if you put those on." He turned away.

"I want some answers." She obliged and sat back down with the shorts on. "This thing, whatever it is, seems to be hanging over our heads. It's preventing us from moving forward. Sit down and start talking. Let's get it all out. Whatever we say doesn't leave this room."

"This is ridiculous." He paced the small room. His hands were clammy and his heart raced.

"If it's so ridiculous, then why are you acting so strangely?"

"Because you're half-naked in my hotel room."

"Oh, please." She rolled her eyes. "I'm not half-naked." She grabbed his hand, which stopped his continuous circling of the room.

"All right." He pulled his hand from hers. "First, I am a preacher. I should not be here, right now, alone with you in a hotel room. It's just not proper."

"For who, the little old ladies of the church? We aren't doing anything wrong. We're two adults talking. So, let's talk."

"All right. You want answers?" He paused and turned toward her. "The truth is, I do have feelings for you." The anger from his own words burned through him. "There. Are you happy? I've admitted it."

She sat in silence.

Matthew sighed, turned, and sat on the small red couch. "I've never had such strong feelings about anyone before."

"There's nothing wrong with those feelings."

"Yes, there is." He looked at her. "You don't know what I struggle with. Some days you drive me crazy. I have thoughts about you that shouldn't be there." He stood and paced again. "I'm supposed to be a man of God, but I stand before you, wanting to take you in my arms. I want to hold you. I want to kiss you. I want to…" He rubbed his hands over his face then ran them on the back of his neck.

"God made you and gave you certain desires."

"Don't try and reason this away. I know myself, and I know what's right and wrong. I should not be feeling this way about you. My thoughts are sinful." He continued to stare at her. "There, now I've confessed to you my deep dark secret."

Raven's face softened. "Well, Matthew Stewart, you are human."

He sat down and rested his head in his hands. "This is not a joke."

"I'm sorry. I'm trying to lighten the mood. Why are you beating yourself up over this? You've never acted like anything but a gentleman around me."

"You can sin inwardly even if you don't act on them."

Raven turned to him. "Listen, I'm not asking you to date me. I just want to know why you never even gave us a chance. Was it really because you thought I wasn't a strong enough Christian?"

"Partly." He looked down. "It was also because I don't know if *I'm* a strong enough Christian."

"You really think I would let anything happen?"

He stood up and threw his arms in the air. "Don't you see? That's the problem. I'm the preacher. I'm supposed to be a man of God. If I don't think I can control myself on a date, then I can't take you out." He shook his head and looked at her. "Don't you get it? I don't know if what I feel for you is love or lust." He ran his hand through his hair. "Man, I can't believe I'm telling you this." He shook his head. "I can't take the chance of pulling you down. I won't allow it."

"Do you think God may have put these desires in you for a reason?"

"It doesn't matter. You and me, it would never work." He sat back down on the small red couch.

"Oh, yeah. I forgot. Because of my Christianity or lack of it."

Matthew's eyes widened.

Raven quickly held her hand up in defense. "I understand, really. I'm not trying to be sarcastic, but it's because of my weaknesses, my sins. You're a preacher, you can't have a girlfriend that sins."

She shook her head. "Wait. I didn't mean it that way." She walked over to the couch and sat next to him, tucking her legs up under her. She looped her arm through his and rested her head on his shoulder. "I just want to get past this."

"I want to, too." He grabbed her hand. He knew he should push her away, but instead he entwined his fingers with hers and held on tight. He lowered his head in defeat. "This is my problem, not yours."

Raven leaned into him. "I don't think it's a problem." When he was about to protest, she tightened her grip. "Let me finish."

He conceded.

"I understand that we may not be right for each other. I mean, we're total opposites, but doesn't this feel right?"

He knew if he denied it, he'd be lying. How could he fight this? He never wanted the moment to end. "It's not enough, I'm sorry. I don't mean to hurt you, but I can't take the chance with my ministry. It's my life."

"I understand. Really, I do. Thank you for telling me." She gave his hand a squeeze, then stood up.

"This isn't easy for me." He looked up at her. "Friends?"

"Of course. I'll give you these in the morning." She pointed down at his shorts.

He forced a smile as she left.

* * *

Matthew fell to his knees. "God, forgive me for my sinful thoughts. Forgive me for my weakness. Tell me how to handle this situation, please. I need the guidance only You can provide." Tears rolled down his cheeks. "Forgive me for my sins. I am so unworthy of Your forgiveness, yet I continually ask for it. I know what Raven could do to my ministry—Your ministry. She could ruin it."

She could help it.

"She could backslide."

All have sinned and fallen short.

"No. Maybe I should get back together with Lisa. She is patient, she is loving."

So is Raven.

"Raven is hot-headed."

She is passionate.

"Lisa knows what I expect of her."

Raven is independent, with her own desires to further My kingdom.

"No. I can't take the chance. The ministry is my life. Raven could ruin it in one action. Her mistake would ruin my life. I can't take the chance. I won't take that chance. Take these desires away, please. Doesn't Your Word say that charm is deceptive and beauty is fleeting?"

But a woman who fears the Lord is to be praised.

"If Raven feared you, she wouldn't have taken that drink."

Is that sin greater than any other sin?

"Not in Your eyes, but in the world's eyes, it is. It not only blows her witness, but mine also."

What about love? It burns like a blazing fire, like a mighty flame. Many waters cannot quench love; rivers cannot wash it away.

"But will that last? I can't take that chance. Lord, tell me what to do."

I have.

"Lead me to follow Your will and not my own. Help me to make my decision and to be content in it. Amen."

Matthew sat up, exhausted. He leaned against the bed, resting his head in his hands. He would seek the advice of the man he respected above all men. His hero. His mentor. He pulled out his cell phone and called his father.

"Hey, Dad?"

"Matthew? I just tried to call you. Did you get my message?"

"No, I'm in Minnesota visiting Cody."

"The young man with cancer."

"Yes. He's hanging in there. Dad, I need your help."

"Okay."

"It's about Raven."

"I thought this was settled."

"I thought it was, too. So why do I have still have these feelings for her?"

"Are you thinking about pursuing a relationship with her?"

"I don't know." Matthew combed his fingers through his hair. "I'm afraid she's not far enough along in her Christian walk. She's not a strong Christian yet, but I know she will be."

"Are you willing to put your ministry on the line?"

"No."

"Then I believe you answered your own question. I don't care who you date or marry, just remember whoever you marry must have certain qualities. Not every woman possesses the characteristics needed when taking on the role of a minister's wife."

"But if it's not right for us to be together, why can't I shake these feelings?"

"I don't know, you have to figure that out." He paused. "Do you feel like she has to prove her Christianity to you?"

"Yeah. I know it sounds bad, but I guess I want to see the change. I *have* to see the change."

"How long do you think it will take for her to convince you?"

"I don't know."

"Are you willing to wait?"

"Maybe...I don't know if I can."

"What do you mean?"

"Nothing." Matthew shook his head. It was bad enough he admitted his desires to Raven, he didn't want to tell his dad too.

"I think I understand." John grunted. "Your mother used to drive me crazy like that."

"So, you think it's God telling me I should be with her?"

"I can't answer that. You have to be sure she is going to stay true to Christ. Until then, I'd wait. Only you will know when the timing is right. Keep praying."

"Thank you, Dad." Matthew rubbed his forehead. "I appreciate it."

"Your mom and I are praying for you. Follow God. He will never lead you down the wrong path, but you must listen and find His will."

"I know. I just wish I could see it."

"You will, if you keep seeking. God bless."

"Good-bye."

I've shown you My will, Matthew, but you refuse to see it.

Chapter 22

Matthew stood at the end of Cody's bed. He glanced between Cody and Raven, who talked non-stop, hand in hand. Cody smiled, nodded, and laughed at Raven's endless walk down memory lane. Matthew could see the love Cody felt for her. It showed in his eyes. The thoughts that ran through Matthew's head made him unable to decipher which was worse, his anger or his jealousy. Both feelings made his stomach turn in disgust at himself.

Lord, this young man has cancer and could die, why are these thoughts of Raven bombarding me? I have no right to be jealous. Forgive me. Matthew dropped his head and quietly slipped out of the room.

* * *

Cody had noticed a change in Matthew and Raven the minute they came in. They both appeared melancholy and by the lines on Matthew's forehead, he was jealous to see Raven pour attention on him.

Cody feared he'd never have Raven's whole heart, but right now, that didn't matter. He needed her strength to help him fight this disease.

He squeezed her hand. "You going to tell me what happened last night between you and Matthew?"

"We talked."

"It must have been one heavy conversation. He's been eyeballing me all morning."

"There were some things I had to say and things I needed to hear from him." She grinned through the obvious pain. "It was good. We finally cleared the air, and for the first time in weeks, I feel pretty good about our relationship."

"He didn't ask you out, did he?"

"No."

"Good. That means I can still try to win your heart."

"You've got to get out of this hospital first."

The nurse came in. "I'm sorry to have to break this up, but we really have to get him started on these tests."

"Five more minutes." Cody looked up at her. "Come on, they can wait that long."

"You want me to tell the *doctors* to wait?" Angie stared at Cody then looked over at Raven. "Five minutes."

Raven nodded.

"I'll write and call you." Raven took his hand as tears swelled in her eyes. "I'm going to miss you." She laid her head on his chest.

The sweet aroma of strawberries floated from her hair. He closed his eyes and pushed out the thought that this could be the last time he saw her. He didn't want to think about what might happen. He wasn't afraid of death; he'd already made peace with that. It wasn't even his mother that concerned him because she seemed stronger than ever.

It was Raven he was worried about. He knew his death could throw her right back into the lion's den. A den he wasn't sure she'd make it out of a second time. He stroked her hair. "I'll be home before you know it."

Raven looked up at him. "I'm counting on it."

Cody pulled her close and in one quick motion, grabbed her mask, pulled it down, and gave her a peck on the lips.

She pushed away from him and pulled up her mask up. "Cody, if you catch something from me…"

"I won't. I love you."

"I know you do."

He'd hoped for a different answer but knew Raven wouldn't lie. He'd have to wait to hear those words from her. "Tell Matthew I want to say goodbye."

She nodded and waved as she walked out.

Matthew went to the sink, washed his hands, and put on his mask. "Raven said they were kicking us out."

"Yeah, I got some tests to take. Thanks for driving up here with her."

"No problem."

"I want to talk to you about something." Cody took a deep breath and wondered if his request would do any good.

"Raven?"

Cody nodded. "If something happens to me, I'm afraid she won't make it. She's been through so much already."

"Have the doctors said something you're not telling us?"

"No, and I'm not planning on dying, but if I do—forgive me for my bluntness—put aside your pompous holier-than-thou attitude and be there for her, no matter what she does. Do you understand? She's going to need a friend, not a judge."

"Did I really treat her that badly after her father died?"

"Yeah, you did. You don't come from where we come from. We're used to dealing with hurt and bitterness with alcohol, not prayer, meditation, or whatever it is you do. I'm afraid she might fall so far back into that world, she may never get out."

"I'll be there for her." Matthew nodded. "I promise."

Cody stared at Matthew. *Lord, I hope he can put aside his disgust for sin and look at Raven for who she is.* He grunted. Was he really praying?

* * *

Raven stared out the window while Matthew drove. Her mind swirled with thoughts of Cody while she silently prayed for him.

She didn't pray for God's will, although she knew she should. Instead, it was selfish. *God, You can't let Cody die.*

She could feel Matthew glancing over at her. For miles, she tried to ignore it, but when he did it again, she turned to him. "What?"

"Nothing."

"Then why do you keep staring at me?"

"I'm just wondering what you're thinking about."

Raven laid her head back on the seat. "Don't be paranoid." She patted his hand. "I wasn't thinking about you."

He ran his hand through his hair then tightened his grip on the steering wheel. "I knew I shouldn't have said anything to you last night."

"Calm down. I didn't mean anything by that. I was thinking about Cody. Actually, praying for him." She stared back out the window before looking back at him. "I told you nothing left that room. I don't think any less of you because of what you said. We're friends and I would never do anything to jeopardize that."

"I'm sorry. It's just I've never shared anything like that before, with anyone. I'm a little embarrassed."

"Don't be. Everything's fine."

Matthew tapped his fingers. "Can I ask you something? Do you feel like I abandoned you when your father died?"

"I felt abandoned by everyone, but I understand that your life didn't stop because mine did."

"I should've made more time for you."

"It's no problem. I survived. I think there were some things God meant for me to work out myself. I'm the first to admit that I didn't handle it very well."

"I'm sure you did your best."

"No, I didn't." Raven stared out the window. "I didn't rely on God. My faith wavered so much. I was angry with God, but I understand things happen and I have to trust God and draw from His strength."

"I should've been there to help you."

"I would've just gotten angrier and resented you." Which could've caused her to plummet into destructive behavior. It was her reaction the first time her father confronted her when he found alcohol in her room. The idea of her room being searched didn't bother her as much as him ordering her to never touch the stuff again. She did what any normal teenager would do—rebel.

"You do have a temper." He grinned.

"I do, don't I?"

The emotional strain of the last few days had worn her out. Peace was settling in until they pulled into Matthew's driveway, where Lisa's car sat. "I thought you two weren't seeing each other."

His eyebrows wrinkled. He sighed and rubbed his forehead. "We're not. I don't know what she's doing here."

The relief was overwhelming. It wasn't because she thought she had a chance with Matthew. He'd made it clear they'd only be friends. So, why was it so hard to accept? She mentally shook the thoughts of him away, climbed out of the car, and stretched. "Thanks for going with me. It was nice to have the company."

Matthew reached into the backseat and got his black duffel bag out and flung it over his shoulder. "Sure."

She climbed back into the car behind the wheel this time. He turned and waved at her before going into the church. Her thoughts went to Matthew and what he said the night before, but she quickly thwarted it off. How could she secretly still want Matthew when Cody was so sick? No, Matthew would never be more than a friend. Her future was with Cody.

* * *

Matthew dropped his bag on the floor in front of Lisa. "Hi. I didn't know you were coming."

"I heard you went on a trip with Raven. How is she?"

"She's fine. I drove her up to see a friend of hers. He's got cancer."

"How is he?"

"Pretty sick." Matthew took a deep breath then released it slowly. She was the last person he wanted to deal with right now. He needed time to think, to sort things out. "I guess you want to go grab some dinner?"

"If you don't mind."

"Can you give me about an hour?"

"Sure." She smiled and patted his arm. "I'll head over to the Greens. You'll pick me up there?"

"Yes. I'll see you in a few."

Matthew walked to his house. He fell on to the couch, laid his head back, and closed his eyes. He regretted ever telling Raven his true feelings. But despite his confession and the fact he wasn't dating Lisa, she still looked at Cody with love. He was losing her. What was he thinking? How could he lose something he didn't have? Regardless, it hurt.

* * *

"Mom? Hailey? I'm home." Raven set her suitcase at the bottom of the stairs. Her mother emerged from the kitchen with a tattered blue apron over her clothes. The same apron she'd worn since as far back as Raven could remember. Raven hugged her. "Smells like cookies."

"I'll get you one."

Hailey walked out of the kitchen, wiped her flour-covered hands with the towel and sat down next to Raven. "How's Cody?"

"The same, only sleepier. It seems that not even cancer can keep him down. You know Cody, flirting with the nurses every chance he gets. How's Mom?"

"I'm amazed, sis. She's almost back to Mom, except for…it's hard to hear her talk about Daddy like he's going to walk through that door. I don't know how you can pretend he's alive every day."

"It gets tiring." *So frustrating sometimes I want to scream.*

"What's that new doctor think?"

"Dr. Lars says she'll remember. He just doesn't know when. He said it could happen anytime."

"Dr. Lars, huh? How did you find him?"

"He goes to my church. He's a good man, and most importantly, he makes house calls. We just pretend he's coming for coffee and she's never the wiser. I think she'll remember soon." Truth was, Raven *hoped* she'd remember soon. The charade was wearing thin.

"Have you spent any of Daddy's money?" Hailey asked.

"I paid off my car and opened up a couple IRAs. The rest is still sitting in the bank." This was the one area Raven was proud of herself. Her first desire was to go shopping and buy all the things she'd always wanted, but she didn't. She decided to save it, at least for now.

"Not me. I went out and bought new clothes, paid some bills, and bought new furniture. You'll have to stop by and see the house."

"I will soon, I promise."

"Yeah, that's what you always say." Hailey twirled the dish towel and snapped it at Raven. "I've gotta go."

"Thanks, Hailey."

Raven heard cupboards slam in the kitchen. She hurried in. "What are you looking for?"

"I don't know." Irene's hands began to shake.

"Sit down. I'll get you something to drink." Raven set an iced tea in front of her. "What's going on?"

"I don't know. Your sister, I guess." She took a sip of the tea. "I never realized until today how much maintenance Hailey is."

"Mother." Raven laughed. "I can't believe you just said that."

"Well, it's true. She just kept going on and on about your father."

Raven eyes widened. She wondered if Hailey spending the night had caused more harm than good. "What about Daddy?"

Irene stood and began cleaning the dishes from the afternoon of baking. "I'm the first to admit your father's been gone a long time, and it's not like him to not call, but he'll be back. He's never let us down." Irene threw the dish rag into the sink. Her head hung low.

"Mom?"

Irene slowly turned around, "There's something going on, and I just can't figure it out. It's about to drive me crazy."

Raven stood and rubbed her mother's back. "It'll be okay." Raven prayed her mother would remember soon.

* * *

Matthew sat in the deli with Lisa. She looked beautiful. She always did, only this time his heart didn't flutter or even jump a little. She was like a loose string that needed to be cut. "I was surprised to see you. Haven't talked to you since you left a few weeks ago."

"You gave me no choice."

"Choice?" Heat surged through his veins. "You gave me an ultimatum and I will not live like that. Raven is my friend and she needed me."

Lisa rolled her eyes. "A friend you're in love with."

Matthew pursed his lips together as the waitress walked up. "You two ready to order?"

"Yes." Matthew looked up. "I'll take the special. Lisa?"

"A Caesar salad, dressing on the side."

Matthew waited for the waitress to get out of ear-shot. "I can't believe I was honest with you, and now you're throwing it back in my face. Raven is my friend. Her dad had just died. Give me a break."

"Are you still in love with her?" Lisa asked in a need-to-know sort of way.

"Why do you care?" His eyes narrowed. "Why would it even matter to you?"

Her eyes softened. "Because I was wrong. I should've trusted you and I didn't. I'm sorry. I just needed to come, to see if there's still a chance for us, or if my leaving opened the door for you and Raven."

The waitress set their food down. He prayed, then took a bite of the sandwich.

She picked at her salad. "Is it too late for us?"

"Yes, and it has nothing to do with Raven."

She gave a derogatory laugh and crossed her arms. "Now you're lying to both of us."

He set the sandwich down. "No, I'm not. I saw something in you that I didn't like. You wanted me to desert someone I cared about because you were jealous."

"I had a reason to be jealous."

"Did you know she had given her life back over to Christ the same day her father was killed? She could have easily fallen away and you would've allowed it."

"That wasn't my intention. You know that."

"Regardless, it could've happened."

Lisa shook her head, her eyes moist with tears. "You told me you were attracted to her. How was I supposed to feel when she calls you and you drop everything, even me, to run to her side? Can't you even understand how I felt?"

Matthew sighed. "Okay, I can understand that."

"So, maybe we can try again?"

He lowered his eyes.

"Have your feelings for Raven changed?"

"I'm not going to talk to you about Raven." He bit into his sandwich and took a big gulp of his soda.

"Is there a chance, however small, for us, or should I just leave tonight?"

"You can't drive home tonight, it's too late."

She blinked away the tears that swelled in her eyes. "Will it bother you if I go to church tomorrow? I'm staying with the Greens. I don't want to have to answer a lot of questions."

Matthew nodded. "You can come. You can join us for lunch, if you'd like, before you head back."

"Who is 'us'?"

"Whoever wants to go. Usually me, Raven, Travis, any number of people."

"I'd like that."

He pushed the plate to the center of the table. "I need to study. You about done?"

"Yeah."

Matthew threw some money on the table and drove Lisa to the Greens' house. He understood about not wanting the questions. Lunch after church would be good. It would keep people from asking. Then he'd get her in the car and on her way out of his life.

Chapter 23

Raven and Irene sat in church. Raven was out of sorts. She felt like the weather outside. Dark and drizzly. *Why?* Maybe the whole ordeal with Matthew, her father, and Cody had taken its toll. Her defenses were at an all-time low. It was even hard for her to get out of bed.

Lisa made her way to her seat, glanced at Raven, and Raven swore she looked like she was gloating. Maybe Lisa had a right to gloat. She and Matthew could've made up.

Raven's heart dropped. What did it matter? Matthew was very adamant they would be friends only. She'd have to live with that and move on with her life.

The music minister began the service. Raven went through the motions. Stood when told, sang without paying attention to the words, passed the offering plate…it all seemed meaningless. She was preoccupied with thoughts of Cody and his illness, and Matthew, what might have been, and what would never be.

Irene fumbled in her purse. Raven leaned into her, "What do you need?"

"A Kleenex," Irene whispered.

"I've got one. Here." Raven handed it to her. Irene's hands shook and she started to cry. Raven put her arm around her. "What's wrong?"

Irene stood and hurried out.

Matthew glanced Raven's way as he continued to preach. She grabbed her things, got up, and went into the foyer. "Mom. Where are you?"

An usher approached her. "I saw her go out the front doors."

Raven nodded, her heart racing as she hurried outside. "Mom?"

The man followed her. "She's over here." He pointed.

Raven hurried to the side of the church lawn and spotted her mother walking to the cemetery. "Thanks. Could you please get Dr. Lars and send him out here?"

Raven ran as fast as her high-heeled shoes would allow. "Mom, please stop." Irene collapsed. Raven knelt beside her and clutched her shoulders. "Are you okay? What's going on?"

Her mother cried. "I remember…he's dead…your father is dead."

"Sh, sh, sh." Raven held her. "It's okay."

"It's not okay," Irene yelled. "Your father is gone."

Dr. Lars walked to them and dropped to one knee. "Irene? You're going to be fine." He looked at Raven. "She's going to be fine. Let's help her back to the car so you can take her home."

Irene brushed Raven's hands off and stared at Dr. Lars. "There was a car accident. Russ was killed. I hit the windshield." She touched her head. "I remember he died." She looked at Raven then back at Dr. Lars. "I don't remember the funeral. I don't understand. How long has it been?"

Dr. Lars squeezed her shoulder. "It was a few months ago."

"A few months?" Irene put her hand on Raven's face and wiped the tears away. "You poor thing. I'm so sorry about your daddy. He was a good man."

Raven cried with her. "I know, Mom. I know." They held each other for a long time. Raven finally felt comforted. Closure was imminent now.

Irene pulled away from her and looked around. "We must look pretty silly sitting out here."

Raven laughed. "Who cares." She watched her mother transform before her eyes. Her hands quit shaking and she stood confidently. Reaching down, she helped Raven up and put her arm around her. "Will you take me to the grave?"

"Yes. In fact, it's not too far." Raven told her about the arrangements, the service, and all the people that showed up. Raven stopped before a gray marble tombstone.

Irene knelt and touched the etched letters of her husband's name. "It's a nice tombstone. You pick this out, too?" She hesitated then looked up at Raven. "Did you see him?"

"Yes." The picture of Raven's father came fast, but she pushed the sight of him out of her head. She needed to keep her thoughts straight so she could be there for her mother.

"How bad did he look?"

"Pretty bad. They said he died instantly, no suffering. I had to see for myself. I couldn't imagine someone just telling me he was in the casket. I had to know he was really gone."

"I understand. I wish I could've been there for you." Irene stood and tucked her daughter's blonde hair behind her ears.

"It's okay, Mom. Really. Let's go home."

* * *

Raven sat with Irene at the kitchen table. Her mother had stopped crying and appeared dazed. Raven wasn't sure what to say. She knew the grieving process for her had begun, but Raven was tired of crying.

Raven's cell phone rang. "Hey, Hailey. You got my message?"

"I got it," Hailey's voice shot at her. "I'm glad. Now she can get on with her life."

Raven turned away and walked toward the sliding door. "You coming over?"

"Why would I? I don't want to hear the crying. I'm moving on. Call me when she has."

"I hate you sometimes."

"Why? For being honest? I'll bet you're thinking the same thing only you'd never admit it."

"Bye." Raven ended the call and slid her phone in her pocket.

"What'd Hailey say?" Irene asked.

"She said she might stop by later." It wasn't a lie. Later could be a week or a month, right?

Irene sighed. "I'm going up to my room."

"Mom, if you need anything let me know."

"I will, honey. Thank you." Irene squeezed Raven's hand.

Raven went outside to the back deck and lay on the wooden bench. She stared up at the clouds. Car doors slammed followed by footsteps. She lifted her head to see Matthew and Lisa walk toward her. She sat up, unsure if she wanted company, especially Lisa with Matthew.

"I spoke with Dr. Lars." Matthew slid his hands into his pockets.

"Is there anything I can do to help?" Lisa asked.

Raven stared at her, dumbfounded. The fact that Lisa was at her house shocked her beyond words. Did she really have to be hostess to her arch-enemy?

Matthew must've sensed the awkwardness. He turned to Lisa. "Could you make us a couple of sodas?" He pointed to the kitchen. "The glasses are in the first cupboard."

Lisa walked into the kitchen and began her pastor's-wife-like duties. Raven ran her fingers through her hair. She glanced at him. "You two together?"

"No."

She nodded, relieved. "You guys didn't have to come."

Matthew sat down next to her; his arms touched hers. "I wanted to, and I promised Lisa lunch. She's heading home after that. How's your mother? Dr. Lars said she remembered everything."

"Yeah. She's okay, but to her, Daddy just died."

"I'll go see her in a minute."

"Thanks. She'll like that." Raven took the drink that Lisa handed her and watched her sit down across from them. "You know what the hardest thing is? I have to relive this. Only there won't be any of her friends or relatives coming around like they did when he first died. Everybody has gone on with their lives. It's just me."

Matthew took her hand. "You're not alone. Remember that."

"I know, but I feel bad because I don't want to do this again. Am I terrible?" She stared into his sympathetic and loving eyes.

"No. You're human. Just be there for her, that's all you can do. And you know I'll be here for you both."

"Thanks, Matthew." Raven glanced at Lisa's staring eyes then pulled her hand out of Matthew's. "Why don't you go check on her?"

"Sure."

Raven leaned forward and rested her forearms on her legs. They sat in silence. She glanced at Lisa a couple of times.

Lisa broke the silence. "I'm sure Matthew has told you about us?"

"That you're not dating anymore, yes."

"Are you in love with him?"

Raven raised her eyebrows. "It doesn't matter how I feel. Matthew will never date me."

Lisa sat up a little straighter, as if the statement gave her a glimmer of hope.

Matthew walked out on the deck. "She's resting. We talked and prayed. I think she's going to be fine. She's strong, like you."

"Thank you." Raven set her drink on the table. "I'm sure you two have things to do. Don't let me keep you."

Lisa stood, ready to go. Matthew looked back at Raven. "How about we pick up lunch and bring it back?"

Matthew was either eager to be there for her or hated the idea of lunch alone with Lisa. Probably both.

"Okay," Raven said. "Only we can eat here. I have food. That is, if Lisa doesn't mind."

Lisa shrugged. "Sure, whatever you want."

"I have stuff to make sandwiches. Come on inside."

Raven set the lunch meat on the counter. Her cell phone rang. She motioned for them to continue as she grabbed it and put it to her ear.

Cody's voice came fast. "They're letting me go. I'll be home next week."

"Are you serious? Does this mean you're in remission?" Raven watched Matthew stare at her. She wondered if Lisa saw the same inkling of jealousy in his eyes that she did. "When will you be here?" Raven asked Cody.

"Those tests they were running when you guys left showed I'm in remission, and if all goes well, I'll be home on Wednesday. I should prepare you, though. I lost all of my hair; well, I had them shave it off."

"You did? How's it look?" Raven laughed and pointed to her hair, mouthing *he lost it* to Matthew. "Mom remembered about Daddy being killed today."

"She did?" Cody asked. "How's she doing?"

"She's doing good. Matthew came by to talk with her."

"He still there?"

"Yeah. I was getting ready to make them some lunch."

"Who's they? Matthew and your mom?"

"And Lisa."

"Oh, I wish I was there," Cody said with a hint of humor in his voice. "I'll bet it's quite a little gathering. You're not being too hard on her, are you?"

"No." Raven laughed. Lisa readjusted herself in her seat, as if sensing they were talking about her. "Call me and let me know what time you'll be home. I want to be there."

"I want you to be there. I'm planning on you being there."

"I'll see you soon then?"

"Hey, Raven."

"Yeah?"

"I love you."

"Good-bye, Cody."

Raven hung up the phone and sat down. Matthew prayed and they began to eat. Matthew pushed his chair away from the table and sat back. "So, he's coming home. What's that mean?"

"He said he's in remission. From my understanding he'll still do some chemo, but he can do it here." Her heart was filled with contentment. Cody was well.

Matthew smiled. "We should get going. Your mom will be awake soon and you'll probably have a lot to talk about."

"Thanks for staying for lunch." She turned to Lisa. "And thanks for coming."

Lisa nodded. Matthew opened the front door for Lisa. "I'll be right out." He waited until she walked to the car, then turned to Raven. "Can I call you later?"

"I'm counting on it." She reached around and hugged him tightly.

He smiled, then walked to the car, got in, and drove away.

* * *

Raven stretched out on the couch and dozed off. She awoke to sounds coming from the kitchen. Her mother must be cleaning, something she always did when she was stressed. Raven walked up, gave her a hug, then grabbed a dish rag and helped her finish wiping down the counter tops.

Irene sat. "Raven. You said that your father took care of everything. I want to know what you meant by that."

"I'll be right back." Raven went into her father's office and emerged with a folder. She spread the papers on the table. "These are the accounts and the amount of money in each one. The house was paid off by the accidental death insurance, and there's an annuity for you. Mr. Sayer and I have gone over the figures and there is plenty of money, Mom. You're set financially, for the rest of your life."

Irene shuffled through the papers. "What about you? Hailey's got Jake, she'll be fine. What about money for college?"

"One of Daddy's life insurance policies came to Hailey and me, over a hundred thousand each. That will be plenty of money to pay for my college."

"Can we drive back to the cemetery now?"

Raven wrinkled her eyebrows. "Sure. We were out there this morning. Do you remember?"

"Of course I remember. I'd just like to go back."

"Okay."

Raven stayed by the car and watched her mother stand at her father's grave. She cried and talked to him like he was there. She said her good-byes and turned away. Raven walked up to her mother and took her hand.

Irene stood tall. "Hon, I can't thank you enough for all you did. Making all the arrangements and going through this by yourself."

"I wasn't by myself. I had Matthew and Cody and more importantly, I had the Lord. He got me through. He can get you through it, too."

"I know. And I'm so relieved you are leaning on Him."

A tear came to Raven's eyes.

Irene took her hand. "Let's go home."

"Okay." She squeezed her mother's hand. "I love you."

"I love you, too."

Chapter 24

Raven chewed on her thumbnail as she sat on the steps outside Cody's house. It wasn't the same house they lived in when Teresa was alive or when their dad lived with them. That house had long been sold.

Her stomach was in knots and she wasn't sure why. Were her feelings for Cody deepening? If they were, was it because he got sick? Or was she ready to face the fact that she and Matthew could never be anything but friends?

There was still a part of her that hoped there was a chance with Matthew. She prayed about it, then pushed the thoughts away, trying to forget. She knew Cody needed her. She would not leave him for a fantasy.

Raven stood when she saw the car come down the street. She grinned and walked to Cody as his mother helped him out. His body was still sculpted like a state champion wrestler even though he was thinner and bald. Raven hugged him.

"Hey, you're going to knock me over." He laughed.

"Sorry." She wrapped her arms around him. "Hello, Mrs. Anderson."

"Hello, Raven." Martha turned to Cody. "The doctor said to put you right to bed. It was a long trip and you need your rest."

Cody had a wicked look in his eyes. "Only if Raven comes with me."

She laughed, smacking him. "How about if I help?"

"Agreed."

Once Martha saw to it that he was situated, she left them alone. Cody took Raven's hand, caressing her soft ivory skin. "You haven't said anything about the hair."

"Or lack of it?" She smiled and ran her hand over the baby soft skin on his head. "You look better than you did that time you got the Mohawk junior year. I'm just so relieved you're home." She kissed his hand.

"You can do better than that." He grabbed the back of her neck and pulled her close, her hair falling between his fingers. "I want a real kiss."

"You need to rest." She avoided his eyes.

"Come on. You know I love you. I want you all for myself. You haven't figured that out yet?"

"You are so full of it."

Cody sat up, pulled her close, and cupped her face in his hands. "I'm serious. Forget about Matthew. Give us a chance."

What could she say? *I'm trying to forget about Matthew but can't figure out how?* Cody was offering her everything Matthew was not. It was obvious how much Cody loved her. She nodded. She'd try to love Cody, but wondered if her attempt would be enough to satisfy him.

Cody pulled her down and she lay next to him. "Will you stay for a little bit?"

Raven rested her hand on his chest. "Yes. If you promise to rest."

He closed his eyes and held her tight. "I will. I promise."

When his breathing slowed and deepened, she slid out from under his arm and walked into the kitchen where Martha was.

"Hello, Mrs. Anderson."

"It's Martha, Raven. You know that."

"I'm sorry for not getting a chance to talk to you at the hospital. It just seemed every time I left the room, you were gone."

"Just giving you some space. I know I make you uncomfortable." Martha pulled a mug from the cupboard and began to fill it with water. "You want tea?"

"No, thanks." Raven sat at the kitchen table. "I'm sorry it's that obvious. I wish I didn't."

"Why, exactly, do I make you feel that way? And why are you back in Cody's life?"

Raven looked away, staring through the window to the trees outside. "I thought Cody would've told you about us, explained things."

"He said that you dumped him because he reminded you of Teresa." She put the mug in the microwave and hit one minute.

"Yeah." Raven stared back at her. "At the time, when I looked at him, I saw Teresa. What she did. How I found her."

Martha nodded. "You sound like George. That's the same excuse he used for leaving us. I think that's a cop-out."

Raven chewed on her bottom lip. She understood how he must have felt. When the pain is fresh and the wound still deep, it's hard to be around people who have that same excruciating emptiness.

"I didn't mean to hurt Cody like I did. I really was just trying to deal with it."

"And now you've dealt with it?"

Raven frowned, unsure where Martha was going with the conversation. "Yes, I think so."

"I just don't want to see my son hurt like that again. With what happened to Teresa and now his sickness, I won't allow it."

"I can understand that."

She pulled the cup of water from the microwave and dropped the tea bag in it. "It just seems like he likes you more than you like him."

Raven had no idea anyone else could see it. Admitting it seemed the right thing to do. "It's true."

Martha's lips pursed and her eyebrows wrinkled.

"He knows how I feel. I've been totally honest with him. I just don't know if I can love him as deeply as he appears to love me." Tears filled Raven's eyes. "He scares me. I don't want to hurt him again."

Martha nodded and lifted the tea bag out. She squeezed it against the cup with her spoon then set it aside before she took a small sip. "I'm glad you've been honest with him. You know you're both still very young."

"And life is short." Cody's voice came from behind her.

Martha smiled. "What can I do for you, hon? Something to eat or to drink?"

"You can quit giving Raven the third degree and stay out of my life." He walked to Raven, rested his hand on her shoulder, and gave it a gentle squeeze.

Raven looked up at him. "She's not giving me the third degree. We were just talking."

"About me and you. It's none of her business." He glared at his mother. "I told you, I'll take whatever Raven can give me right now. That's enough. If you can't deal with it, then I need to move out."

"And go where?" Martha snapped.

"Wait a minute." Raven stood and turned to Cody. "You are not going anywhere except back to bed. I can handle a talk with your mother." Cody stared at his mom. Raven touched his arm. "Go, I'll be right there."

Raven smiled when he finally nodded, turned, and left. "Sorry about that."

"Don't worry about it. Thank you for being honest. Just be careful. I don't want to see him hurt anymore. You see how he is about you. If things go bad like last time, I don't know what he'll do."

"I understand."

She really did. The drinking, anger, and hatred they had for each other—to hide the pain of Teresa's suicide—was one of the worst times of her life. She never wanted either one of them to be in that place again.

She walked into Cody's room. He sat on the bed and rubbed his hands together. He looked up and smiled. "Shut the door."

She obeyed and walked to the bed. "The doctor said you need to rest."

He lay down and pulled her next to him. "I meant what I said. I will take whatever you can give me."

"I know."

He kissed the top of her head. "I need you with me right now. Do you understand that?"

"Yes."

"Life is too short."

She looked up at him. "You're in remission, right?"

"Yes, why?"

"You sound like you're not telling me something."

His arm tightened around her. "I've seen what death can do, and I've come too close to mess around anymore. I'm not kidding myself; remission or not, I'm still recovering from cancer, and I've got to get my strength back. It may be slow, it may be fast, but I'm not going to waste any time. It's too precious. I need you to help me through this."

"I won't leave you, not now."

He squeezed her hand and kissed her head. "Thank you. Now, would you let me get some rest? No more disappearing."

"Okay."

"I love you."

She smiled. "Go to sleep."

"Is that all you've got to say?" he whispered.

"It's all I can give you right now."

"I know. I'll take it. Now, let me sleep."

Chapter 25

Cody sat in the wing of the hospital, waiting for the nurse to hook the bag to the port in his chest. It would pump chemo into his veins. Maintenance, they called it. Cody's heart pounded when the doctor walked in and sat down. "Don't usually see you in here, Doc. What's up?"

"Your white count." The doctor stared over his John Lennon glasses.

Cody's face hardened. "You mean the cancer's back?"

"I'm afraid so."

Cody pursed his lips together. He fought the tightening of his chest and the tears that wanted to form in his eyes. The chemo was supposed to be keeping the cancer away. The poison was supposed to be fighting for him. His heart raced at the thought of trying to go up against this disease again. "Now what?"

"You've only been in remission for eight weeks." The doctor closed the folder. "That's not a good sign. You need to return to Mayo. We'll get you back into remission, then talk about a stem cell transplant."

"I could die from that. Are you saying it's that bad?"

"There is always that possibility, but you're a strong young man. Let's get you back in remission and go for it."

"Okay." His heart pounded. Disgusted that his own cells didn't fight back. Angry that this God he was trying to trust—the One that Raven and Matthew carried on about—would give him hope, then so quickly yank it away.

It wasn't that he was totally buying into Christianity, but he sat by Raven's side every Sunday and Wednesday. If nothing else, it made Matthew jealous.

"We'll get your mom tested." The doctor's voice jarred him back to his new reality. "Make sure we have a match. We may need to get in touch with your dad. If you could get me his number." The doctor removed his glasses and slid them into the front pocket of his shirt. "I want you at Mayo tomorrow. I'll order an ambulance."

"No. My mother will drive me. I'm not having some nurse sticking me with needles while I ride six hours to Minnesota." His voice was hard, full of contempt.

"Fair enough. I'll call your mother—"

"No. I'll tell her."

"All right. I want you in Mayo tomorrow."

"I'll be there on Monday."

The doctor stared down at him. Cody glanced away. He'd lose this argument if he didn't do something. "Come on, Doc. You were young once. Give me one more weekend. It's only two days."

"Tomorrow." The doctor's voice was firm. "If you're not there, I'll call your mother and you'll get an ambulance with the meanest nurse I can find."

* * *

Raven walked down the aisle of the auditorium.

Matthew waved. "We're sitting down front." He took her arm and led her to the row of seats. "Thanks for coming."

"No problem. I'm excited to hear your dad preach." She looked around at the crowd. "I had no idea he was this famous."

"Famous?" Matthew laughed. "He's just a guy that loves the Lord."

"And preaches to thousands," she guessed. The auditorium held at least that many, and by the looks of the people who still streamed in, it was going to be full.

"Couldn't get Cody to come?"

"No. He had chemo today."

Matthew nodded. A man walked up to them. Matthew turned to talk. Raven greeted some of the people from their church. They filled the first few rows. She saw a few empty chairs by a beautiful woman. Immaculate makeup, and hair that appeared naturally blonde was piled high on her head with multiple strands falling freely around her face.

"Mom," Matthew turned back to Raven, "this is Raven."

Raven forced a smile even though her heart felt like it would pound out of her chest. This was his mom? She looked more like a runway model. She smiled deep and lovingly, Christ radiating from her very being.

Raven went to shake her hand but Matthew's mother pulled her into a deep hug. "Raven, it's so nice to finally meet you." Her voice was soft and inviting. "I'm Fran."

Raven smiled, even though she felt like a peasant in the presence of royalty.

"Nice to meet you, too."

"We're sitting here." Fran motioned to the empty chairs.

Raven nodded. "I'll just grab a spot back with…" She looked over the first few rows and saw no empty chairs.

"Best seats in the house," Matthew said from behind her.

She hesitated, but there was something about Fran's inviting smile that made her feet move toward her and sit down. Fran leaned in. "Are you joining us for dinner?"

"Um…" Raven was caught off guard. "I don't know." She looked up at Matthew, but he was busy talking to someone. "Matthew didn't say anything about it."

Fran gently touched Raven's arm. "Then you'll come."

Raven nodded, readjusting her Bible on her lap. When Matthew walked toward them, she stood and moved over a seat so he could sit next to his mother.

She leaned into Matthew. "Your mom invited me to dinner."

He smiled at her. "Can you go?"

"I don't know if I should." Dinner with the parents was a pretty big deal in her world. Her heart fluttered. Maybe Matthew was ready to throw out the idea that they couldn't date. But even if he did, could she leave Cody? She didn't think so. Not until she was satisfied he was better.

"Why not?" Matthew interrupted the argument in her mind.

"They're your parents." Trying to remind him of who they were and what it meant.

"So, we're friends." Matthew gave her a shoulder shrug. "If you don't want to go, I guess I can understand. It might be awkward." He leaned in close. "But you get to tell my mother." He raised an eyebrow and smiled.

Raven leaned around him and looked at Fran. She smiled perfectly as she listened to another woman talk to her. There was no way she'd be able to tell her no.

"It'll be okay. It's no big deal. Lots of people have met my parents."

"Have you told them about me?"

"A little."

"Like what?" She wondered if he was changing his mind. Maybe dinner with his parents was what she should do. What could it hurt?

"When I first met you, I asked them to pray for you."

"You told them about my past?"

"Only that you needed to find your way back to Christ."

The lights began to dim, and the band came on stage. "These guys are really good. You'll like them." Everyone stood and the music started.

She loved the band. They led the crowd in both contemporary worship songs and some old hymns that helped her respond to God's glory in ways she never had. Lifting her hands, she felt as though she couldn't get them high enough to honor Him. She felt His Spirit surround and fill the place.

After worship and a time of prayer, John Stewart was introduced and took center stage. He delivered a powerful and genuine message. Raven's heart grew heavy. Listening to this Godly man, she knew Matthew was right. They could never be together. She would never fit in with his life and his family.

Raven touched Matthew's arm as the closing song ended. "I'll meet you in the back."

"Hey." Matthew tried to grab her, but she brushed him off and left.

She walked down the aisle toward the exit, pushing herself through the crowd. When she was finally out of the auditorium, she felt her phone vibrate. It was a text from Matthew. *U okay?*

She texted back. *I'm fine. I'll meet you in back.*

Raven crowded her way toward the resource table and saw stacks of books. She picked one up. It was written by Fran. "Wow."

"That's a great book. One of her best," the young woman behind the table said.

"Fiction?"

"Yeah."

"I'll take it." Raven paid for it, slid it into her purse, and eyeballed the other stacks of books written by Fran. There were at least six. Not only was her husband an amazing preacher, but Fran was a famous author.

Raven pushed her way out of the crowd, leaned against the wall, and wondered why she had ever thought she and Matthew had a chance. Seeing where he came from made her feel unworthy to even be friends with him.

Matthew was right. He couldn't take a chance on her. She could ruin his ministry. Not his current ministry of preaching at a two-hundred-member church. He was destined for greatness. He was being called to a world she could never be a part of.

His touch made her jump. "Oh, you scared me."

Matthew smiled. "Mom and Dad will meet us at the restaurant. Is your car here?"

"No, it's at the church. I rode with the Greens. I don't think I should go. I can get a ride."

"Why? You're not intimidated, are you? He's just a guy."

"Who preaches to thousands and your mom is a famous author. Yeah, nothing to be intimidated by."

Matthew's grin deepened. "I don't think I've ever seen you shy away from anything, let alone two people. Come on."

* * *

John and Fran Stewart sat on opposite sides of the booth of the small Italian bistro. John's voice was deep, which fit his slightly overweight body. "Raven?" He held his hand out to shake hers. "Nice to meet you."

"Your sermon was great." She smiled at the perfect-looking evangelist, as she scooted into the booth next to Fran.

"Thanks." John smiled. He ran his hand through his short gray hair. "It felt good—Spirit-led."

"How's your mother doing?" Fran asked.

Raven took a sip of her water. "Matthew told you she had a concussion and amnesia?" When they nodded, she continued, "She remembered a couple of months ago and is actually doing really well."

"Was your father a Christian?" John asked.

"Yes, but that fact doesn't seem to make his death any easier to accept." Raven looked down, avoiding eye contact.

"It must be very hard." Fran had a sweetness in her voice that reassured Raven of her sincerity.

Matthew handed her a menu. "Okay, change of subject."

"Matthew mentioned that you recently turned your life back over to Christ?" Fran asked.

"*Mother.*"

"That's a fair question." Raven took a sip of her water. "I mean, if I was sitting here with my son and some strange woman,

I'd like to know all about her. I don't have a problem discussing my past."

Matthew placed his hand over his eyes and nudged her leg under the table.

Raven leaned into him, a grin on her face. "Did you just kick me?"

Matthew leaned into the table. "Don't do it."

"Do what?" Raven teased. "Are you ashamed of my past? Wasn't it you who said my slate was clean? They're just interested in where I come from." She put two fingers up and made quotation marks in the air. "My personal testimony."

Matthew rolled his eyes. "Oh, no. Here we go."

Raven laughed. The last time someone asked her to give her personal testimony, it was a disaster. She had gone overboard. Instead of telling about the wonderful things Christ had done for her, she shocked them with the horrible things she used to do. "What? I really don't mind."

Fran tapped Matthew on the hand. "What's wrong, honey? We're just talking. How else are we supposed to get to know your girlfriend?" Fran patted Raven's hand. "He's never spoken so highly of a girl before. In fact, I believe you're only the second girl he's dated that we've ever met."

Raven almost choked on her drink. Did she call her his girlfriend? A month ago, she would've jumped at the idea of them thinking of her that way. But now she knew she was wrong for Matthew, no matter how she felt.

"Mr. and Mrs. Stewart, I'm not Matthew's girlfriend. We're friends. My past is scarred with alcohol, drugs, and a lot of stupid things I've done. I'm doing my best to stay true to the Lord, and your son has been my rock. He's shown me a side of Christ I had forgotten about."

Matthew stared at Raven. "You don't have to rehash your past."

Raven leaned into him, lowering her voice. "What? These are your parents. I have no problem telling them anything they want to know."

"Then why don't you tell them *everything*," Matthew snapped, sitting back in the booth, his arms folded.

"What do you mean?" Raven tilted her head. "I'm not embarrassed about my past. I'm just glad I'm not a part of that world anymore."

"As of a couple of months ago," Matthew muttered.

Raven's heart pounded and her eyes teared up as the betrayal sank in. "You don't even know what you're talking about. Excuse me." She got up and walked to the bathroom.

* * *

Matthew rubbed his forehead.

Fran stood, her eyes piercing. "You're acting like a two-year-old." She followed Raven to the bathroom.

Matthew stood and slid into the booth opposite his father. "I just hate it when she uses her past as an excuse."

"I didn't think she was using it as an excuse. She's got to learn from it. She can't do that unless she looks back."

"You don't know." He shook his head. "She uses it. Anyway, I'm sorry."

"I think you should be apologizing to her, not me." John took a drink of his iced tea. "She seems very nice, and looks like she's sincere about loving the Lord."

"She is. She's very passionate. More understanding than most."

"That's because she's gone through more than most. You'll probably find her more forgiving, too."

"She is." Matthew smiled. "I sure made a mess of dinner."

"Your mom will bring her out. I will say this, I can see the spark between you two. Something I never saw with you and Lisa."

Matthew nodded. "I just don't know if that's enough."

"What happened a couple of months ago?"

"She had to clean out her father's office. I caught her with a drink."

"Alcohol?"

"Yeah." Matthew shook his head. "She called and needed my help. I had just broken up with Lisa over her, and I caught her drinking. Then she actually got mad at me about it."

John's forehead wrinkled. "That sounds odd."

The waitress came over and John ordered them all food. He handed the menus back to the waitress and turned to Matthew. "You know, you need to be patient with her. You're used to being around people who have known Christ all their lives. She's different, and that makes her special. She could actually take your ministry to new heights. Reaching people you could never reach."

"So, you think I should just ignore the drinking?"

"I didn't say that, but you need to be patient with her and let God work this out."

Matthew nodded, more confused than ever. It was obvious his father saw something between them. It was the same thing Matthew felt.

Chapter 26

Raven sat on the small couch in the bathroom, trying hard not to cry. She looked up when Fran walked in.

"I'll say this..." Fran sat down next to her. "You fight like you're a couple."

Raven grunted out a laugh. "He won't date me because of my past. I used to think that was stupid until tonight. Now that I met you guys, I think I finally agree with him."

"Why because of us?" Fran gently rubbed her back as if she were a longtime friend. "You can't base your relationship on who we are."

"You can't be serious." Raven smiled, which forced a single tear out. "I say this with all honesty. I'm not a good choice for your son. Like I said, I come from a background of alcohol and drugs. I was in court when I was fourteen. The day I gave my life back to Christ, my father died. I doubted God's love for me. I questioned everything about Jesus and what He was doing. Matthew can't date someone like that. Not if he wants to preach like his dad."

"You're right, he can't. But the Lord can help you stay true to Him." The lines on Fran's forehead deepened. "What did Matthew mean when he said as of a couple months ago? Did something happen?"

"No, well...Matthew thinks so." Raven wiped her nose. "I was cleaning out my father's office. My sister is not a Christian and she brought in a drink mixed with alcohol. She forgot the drink when she left. Matthew came in and thought it was mine, but I swear, I never touched it."

"Did you tell him that?"

"No. He was so angry. He would've just thought I was lying."

"You need to tell him the truth."

"I know, but it never seems to come up."

"Well," Fran handed her another tissue. "We should go back out there. You ready?"

"Yeah." Raven took a deep breath and let it out slowly.

Matthew stood as they approached the booth. Fran slid in next to her husband. Raven slid in. Matthew sat and leaned into her. "I'm sorry, I didn't mean—"

"It's no problem." Raven smiled at the waitress as she set their plates down. The last thing she wanted was a bigger scene in front of his parents. "So, Fran, I bought one of your books."

"Which one?" Fran repositioned her plate.

After John prayed, Raven pulled the book out of her purse and held it up.

"That's my newest one. You didn't have to buy it. I would've given you one."

"That's okay. I don't mind." Raven took a bite of her pasta. "What's this called? It's very good."

"Chicken and spinach manicotti," John said. "I hope you don't mind that I ordered when you gals were in the bathroom."

"Not at all." Raven felt her phone vibrate. She glanced at it. It was from Cody. *U still with him?*

She typed, *yeah.*

"Everything okay?" Matthew asked.

"Yep." She slid the phone into her pocket. "It was Cody."

"Cody?" John scooted his half empty plate away. "He's the boy with cancer?"

"Leukemia." Raven took a sip of her water.

Matthew swallowed a bite of garlic bread. "He's in remission and seems to be doing well." He turned to Raven, who nodded.

The conversation lulled and the only sounds coming from the table were the clinking of their forks on the plates. Finally, John waved at their waitress to get the check. "We should be going. I'm beat."

John paid the check, and they walked to the car. "It was so nice meeting you both." Raven shook John's hand.

Fran pulled her into a hug. "I'm sure we'll see you again."

"Thanks."

Matthew opened the car door for Raven. She slid in and he closed the door. The Stewart family talked and hugged. Her phone vibrated. Cody again.

She texted back, *be home soon, I'll call.*

Matthew climbed into the car, started it, and began to drive. "I want to say I'm sorry."

"For what?" It was an honest question. Raven wondered if he even knew why she was upset.

"For making you mad. I just didn't want you to go into this long explanation of your past. You have a tendency of trying to scare people off."

"That wasn't what I was mad about. It's all your talk of my sins being forgiven and before I know it you throw them back in my face."

He glanced at her as he drove. "I'm sorry. That's not what I meant. My mom said I acted terrible. You were making me angry. It was like you were trying to make my parents hate you."

"I was not. I just won't lie about my past."

"Who asked you to?" He pulled into the church parking lot, next to her car. He turned and rested his arm on the seat behind her. "I didn't want you to lie, but your past is also something I see you use as a crutch. It's like you try to give people a reason not to trust you, or even to not like you."

"I do not, at least not intentionally."

"What are you so scared of?"

She looked at him. "Maybe I want to know up front if someone is going to look at me the way you do."

"What?"

She felt her phone vibrate and knew it'd be Cody. "Forget it. I should go."

He grabbed her arm. "You can't accuse me of something like that and just leave."

She sighed. "Maybe you don't do it on purpose, but you're very judgmental. I just feel like I can't live up to what you want me to be."

He shook his head and sighed. "I don't mean to come across that way. I'm sorry."

"It's okay. Really. I gotta go."

Matthew jumped out of the car and jogged around to open the door for her. "I really am sorry. I'll try not to act that way anymore."

She looked up at him, feeling another text. "Really, it's okay. I'll see you later."

She walked to her car and pulled the keys out of her purse. Matthew drove to his house next to the church. She watched him pull the car into the garage and moments later the bluish glow from the TV shone through the drapes of the living room window.

The headlights from another car made her turn. She recognized Alan's Honda. She walked over and leaned into the opened window on the passenger's side. Cody smiled at her.

"I was about to text you," she said.

Cody stumbled out of the car and almost fell over, but caught himself on the door. "Thanks, Alan. I'll have Raven take me home."

Alan took off. Raven shook her head. "You had chemo today and you're drunk?" She walked to her car and got in. "Get in. I'll take you home."

Cody caught the driver's side door, climbed in next to her, and grabbed the keys. "I'll be fine and we're not going anywhere. I want to talk to you. No, I don't want to talk." He began kissing her.

Raven pushed him away. "Come on, Cody. Stop it."

He grinned foolishly and tried to kiss her again. She pushed him back away. "Why are you acting like this?"

"I'm in love." He laughed, grabbed her, and pulled her to him.

"Get away from me." She smacked him. He backed off and laughed. She glared at him. "Give me the keys."

He opened the door, threw the keys in the grass, then slammed the door. "I'm sorry. Come here." He pulled her to him. He whispered in her ear. "I love you, you know that."

She studied his face and wondered if this was more than jealousy. "Why are you drunk? Are you sick? Is the cancer back?"

"You know, the only thing I ever wanted was you."

"You have me."

"No, I don't. Not really."

She stared into his eyes. "I'm sorry I can't give you more."

"Why can't you get him out of your head?"

"What are you talking about?" She struggled but his grip tightened.

"Matthew. You'd rather be with him."

"No, I wouldn't."

He cupped her head in his large hands. "Yes, you would."

Raven's heart raced, her eyes wide. "You're starting to scare me. Please let me go."

They stared at each other for a moment and he released her. She got out of the car and began to shake. She had to find her keys. She walked into the grass, got down on her knees, and used her cell phone as a flashlight.

Cody climbed out of the car and leaned against it. "You'll never find them."

"Keep your voice down."

Cody brought his finger to his mouth. "Sh, sh, sh, don't want Matthew to hear." Cody staggered over and fell to the ground next to her. "I'll help you look."

"I don't think you can, you're too drunk."

Cody grabbed her. They rolled to the ground and he lay over her. His strong arms held her down. She struggled to free herself but he kissed her.

"Get off of me," she yelled.

"Come on, babe."

Raven pretended to relax, which made Cody's grip loosen. She waited a moment before shoving him with all her might, knocking him to the ground. "I said get off of me."

Cody laughed. She hurried to Matthew's house and pounded on the back door, glancing back to see if he was following her.

He yelled as he pushed himself up to a sitting position. "Run to Matthew." He laughed. "He'll save you."

* * *

Matthew opened the door. "Raven?"

"Can I come in?"

He looked into the darkness. A man started to stand but fell over, then tried to stand again. This time he succeeded but swayed. "Is that Cody?"

"Yes. Can I come in? He's drunk, he..." She swallowed, her breathing fast.

Matthew shook his head. This was one of the many reasons he tried to get her out of his head. What would people think if they saw this? He could feel the heat rising up his neck. "I can't have this going on outside my house or the church."

Raven glared at Matthew. "Okay. Next time I'll just let him attack me in your backyard."

"I did not *attack* you. Geeze," Cody yelled.

"Yeah, well what would you call it?" Raven crossed her arms and clutched her stomach.

"I *love* you." He laughed.

When Raven moved into the light, Matthew saw she'd lost all color in her face. His heart pounded, his hands in fists. "Did he hurt you?"

"He threw my keys in the yard. If you have a flashlight I could borrow…"

"Go inside." Matthew held the door for her, then let it slam as he walked out into the yard. He'd never been in a fight but found himself wanting to beat the crap out of Cody. With his sickness taking away half his body mass, Matthew thought he just might win.

He shook the thoughts of fighting him out of his head, grabbed Cody's arm, and pulled him into his house, past the kitchen where Raven was standing. "Stay there," he ordered her. He yanked Cody into the living room then pulled out his phone. "I'm calling you a cab."

Cody waved his hand at Matthew. "Whatever, big preacher man."

Matthew shook his head. "What's your problem?"

"You. Now get out of my face."

"Sit down." Matthew gave Cody a shove which landed him on the couch. "I don't know why you're acting like this, but I wouldn't blame Raven if she never talked to you again."

"Oh, you'd like that, wouldn't you?"

"I feel sorry for you." Matthew paced. "You're trying to hold onto her, but pulling a stunt like this will drive her away."

"It's no big secret why I won't have her." Cody stared at Matthew, emotionless. "It's because of you she won't love me."

"You're crazy." Matthew stood up when the head-lights of the cab shone through the front window. "Your ride is here. Do you need money?"

"I wouldn't take a thing from you."

Matthew watched Cody stagger to the cab. After they pulled away he walked into the kitchen.

Raven looked up at him. "Is he gone?"

Matthew nodded, his hands still in fists. He couldn't believe any guy would try to hurt someone, but for Cody to try to hurt Raven made him even angrier.

Raven stood up. "If you have a flashlight I'll go look for my keys."

"Stay here," he growled. "I'll go look."

"Don't do me any favors." She stood and slid her shaking hands into her pockets.

"Did he try to…" He couldn't even finish the question.

"Cody's never scared me before. I've never seen him like that."

Matthew didn't really want to pursue it. It would only make him madder. "Stay here. I'll find your keys." He could tell she was hesitant. He pulled a flashlight out of the drawer. "I'll be right back."

She nodded.

Matthew returned a few minutes later. He tossed the keys on the table, still fighting the anger stewing in the pit of his stomach.

"Thanks." She looked at him. "What's that look for?"

"What look?" He knew the look. He wasn't very good at hiding his feelings.

"Like you're disgusted with me." Raven's eyes teared up. "I didn't do anything. This is not my fault."

Matthew sighed, giving his hair a quick comb-through. "I know, I'm not blaming you." At least he was trying not to. *Cody thinks Raven loves me and he knew she was meeting my parents. It had to make him crazy with jealousy.*

He leaned against the counter. "Do you want to call the police?"

"No." She shook her head. "He was drunk."

"Why do you think he's acting like that?"

"I don't know."

"Do you think the cancer is back?"

She shrugged her shoulders.

"You have to understand. I can't have this kind of stuff going on."

Her chin quivered as she spoke. "I'm sorry. It wasn't like I invited him to come here, drunk."

Raven grabbed the keys from the table, but Matthew grabbed her hand. "I didn't mean it like that." How did he always mess things up? He tried to sound nice and loving, but he was still fighting his anger. He wanted to punch something.

Raven stood. "I'll just leave."

"No." He went against everything his head told him and followed his heart. He pulled her into a hug. "I'm sorry. I'm glad you're okay." He held her tightly until she stopped shaking. "Are you really okay?" When he felt her nod, he pulled away. "Why don't you sit down? I'll make you something to drink." She continued to stand. He looked into her eyes and smiled. "Please sit down."

She sat and took a deep breath. She looked around his kitchen. "I've never been in here before."

"That's not unusual." He grabbed two cans of pop out of the fridge and made a cup of ice. "I don't usually entertain girls. It doesn't look good."

"I'm sorry. I didn't think about that. I'm fine. I don't want to cause any more trouble."

His smile deepened. "You're not going anywhere. We're not doing anything wrong." He set a glass of ice and pop in front of her. "That's what *you* always say, isn't it?" He raised an eyebrow.

She tucked her hair behind her ears. "Cody still has this crazy idea about you and me." She poured the pop in the cup.

Matthew sat down. He wondered if she could still see how he fought his feelings for her, like Cody could. "He insinuated that to me when we were in the living room. I can't believe he tried to hurt you. I'm sorry."

"This is how he acted after Teresa died. I mean, he never forced himself on anyone because he didn't have to." Their eyes met and she continued. "He's Cody, every girl's dream guy. He's not used to being turned down. But that's something I'm saving for my husband."

Matthew tipped his head to the side. He pursed his lips together to fight the smile. His heart pounded, and he silently prayed that this was the one time he could hide his feelings.

Raven grunted out a laugh. "You didn't think I was a virgin, did you?"

"Umm, no, I mean..." His face turned red, now embarrassed that she even knew he had thought about it. "I just figured with all the drinking and drugs that sex just went with it."

"There's that judgmental attitude again." She shook her head. "Anyway, I can't imagine what's going on with Cody."

"What are you going to do?"

"I don't know."

"I can try to talk to him. See what I can find out." That was the pastoral side of him; the man side still wanted to beat the crap out of him.

She gave an almost unnoticeable nod. "Thanks, I should go."

Matthew walked her to her car and opened the door. "You sure you're okay?"

"Yeah."

He stared at her for a moment. She was so innocent. So beautiful. He wanted to throw out all his arguments and take her in his arms and kiss her. He practically had his father's blessing, and he knew his mother approved. She already thought they were a couple.

But could he take a chance on her when just a couple of months ago she was drinking? *No.* He had to wait. Somehow, she had to prove to him she had completely walked away from that lifestyle.

"Text me when you get home." He closed the door and watched her pull away.

Chapter 27

Matthew sat in his office and waited for Cody. He had reluctantly agreed to come by and talk. Matthew jotted down some things he wanted to say; it was the preacher in him. The flesh still wanted to punch him.

He sensed someone in the room and looked up as Cody sat.

"Okay, boss," Cody snapped. "Which lecture you want to start with? Drinking? Or how to treat women?"

Matthew raised his eyebrows. "Which do you want me to start with?"

Cody shook his head and gave Matthew a deep eye roll. "You want to know why I was drunk? The reason is you. You claim to be just friends with Raven when you really love her. You're just too chicken or too stupid to admit it. I can't figure out which."

"Raven, now that's another story." Cody leaned in. "She's been honest with me from day one. I just thought I could make her love me instead of you. But until you deal with it, I'll never have a chance with her. It drives me crazy."

Cody looked away for a moment, clenching his jaw before locking his glare on Matthew. "You want to know something that's really sick? I was actually glad when I got cancer. I thought it would make her realize she couldn't live without me. To get her mind off of you for five minutes and see how much I love her."

Matthew's heart raced, but he stayed calm. He figured Cody would blame him for everything. He twirled the pencil in his fingers. "You want to know what I think?"

"Ah, yes. Let the *man of God* have his say."

"You're using me as an excuse. Your troubles with Raven have nothing to do with me. Despite what you think, I care about you. Drinking will not make you happy. Raven will not make you happy. Only God can."

Cody clapped his hands. "Good speech. The only thing is you're missing the whole point." He leaned forward and rested his arm on the desk. "I'll make a deal with you. Admit your feelings, not to me, but to yourself. Then deal with them—I don't know how, but do it. After I see you quit stringing Raven along, we can talk about straightening out *my* life. As much as I want Raven, I can't make her happy when you continue to put ideas in her head."

"I don't put ideas in her head." At least not on purpose.

"Whatever." Cody shook his head and stormed out.

Matthew tossed the pencil, leaned back, and rubbed his forehead. Cody's words hung in the air. He was trying to deal with it. *God, I never meant to drive Cody to this, or to hurt Raven.* "Okay," he looked up and whispered. "Cody is right. I am in love with Raven. I have been since the day she walked into the church. I admit it." He threw his hands up, surrendering. "What do *You* want me to do about it?"

His phone vibrated. It was a text from Raven. *You talk to him?*

He texted back. *I'm heading that way.* He grabbed his keys and left.

* * *

Matthew stood outside Raven's door. His heart pounded and he wasn't sure what he was going to say. All he knew was he had to tell her the truth. He tapped on the door and slid his sweating hands into his pockets.

Raven opened the door. "Come in. Did you talk to Cody?"

He nodded and sat on the couch. "Yeah, we had quite the little chat. It seems he's still blaming this all on me."

"On you? Why?"

"Well, not just me, but both of us. He says we have unresolved feelings for each other and that's why you won't give him a chance." Matthew rested his forearms on his legs, rubbed his hands together, and prayed for a clue that Raven still felt the same about him. When she said nothing, doubt crept in. He thought her feelings hadn't changed, but maybe they had. Maybe she loved Cody.

He stood as Irene walked down the stairs. "Hello, Irene."

Irene smiled. "Don't get up. I've got a meeting. I'll see you both later."

"Bye, Mom." Raven turned back to Matthew. "I really don't know what to say. I thought we said it all in Minnesota."

"Cody seems to think it's still not resolved." He sat back down and rubbed his forehead. "What do you think?"

"I think if you had changed your mind about us, you would've said something."

Matthew ran his hand through his hair. He said nothing. Not because he didn't know what to say, he wasn't sure if he should admit it.

"Then I take it you didn't get through to him." She sat. "Did he look like he'd been drinking?"

Matthew shook his head and closed his eyes for a moment, mustering up the courage to be totally honest. "Cody is right."

She cocked her head. "Right? About what?"

"I don't know how I feel. I thought I could get you out of my head, but I can't. When I'm around you, I feel alive and excited. I just need time to think and pray about this." He looked into her eyes. They looked like they still loved him, but she said nothing. His heart pounded. Was he too late? Had she fallen back in love with Cody? "Aren't you going to say anything?"

"Hey." She smiled. "I've been down this road before and never liked the outcome. I'm keeping my mouth shut."

"But how do you feel about me?" Now, all he wanted was a glimmer of hope. That he might have a chance with her. How could he want someone so much, yet still be unsure? It was driving him crazy.

"I don't know. If Cody's sick, I can't walk away."

"That doesn't sound good." Figures. He couldn't really blame her. It wasn't like he was asking her out. He thought she felt the same way. Maybe his judgmental attitude had made her like him less. "You can't be with him out of guilt."

"I can't leave him if he's sick."

He nodded. "Does that mean you still have feelings for me?" All he wanted was any sign she might still want a future with him.

She smiled, took his hand, and entangled her fingers in his. "You do what you have to do. It doesn't matter what I think or want, it's in God's hands."

"You're amazing sometimes." Instead of revealing her own desires she answered in the Godly way. He couldn't deny that in this case, he wished she would've been a little less Christ-like. It made him laugh.

"What?"

"Nothing." He gave her hand a squeeze and stood. "I've got to go."

* * *

Raven shut the door, leaned against it, and smiled. She couldn't believe he admitted to wanting more than a friendship. The smile left her face when she remembered his parents. Could she jeopardize his ministry if he wanted something more? *No. I won't risk it. And I won't leave Cody if he's sick again.*

The doorbell rang.

She peeked outside to see Cody. She took a deep breath and opened the door.

"I came to apologize." His hands stuck deep in his pockets.

Raven stood at the doorway, unsure if she should let him in.

His face softened. "I won't do anything, I promise. I'm sober. You can smell my breath."

She opened the door and motioned for him to come in.

"I saw Matthew was here."

"How do you know that?"

"I was waiting around the corner. Did he take my advice?"

She sat in the chair furthest from him, arms crossed. "What advice would that be?"

"Admitting his feelings to you." He shook his head. "I guess it's none of my business. When you were with him and his parents, it drove me crazy. Really nuts. I had a doctor's appointment. They told me I was out of remission. It's no excuse for my behavior, but I was angry that the cancer was back. On top of that, you were with Matthew, and I went a little nuts. I'm sorry."

Raven's anger melted and her heart sunk. "I'm so sorry you're sick again. What happens now?"

"Back to Mayo. Chemo, drugs. They're planning a stem cell transplant. The only thing I know is that the prognosis isn't as good as before."

"You know I'll be with you through it all."

"I don't want your sympathy. I never have."

"It's not sympathy."

He looked into her eyes. "But it's not love."

"Not like it used to be." Raven moved from the chair, sat next to him, and took his hand. "But I'll be there for you."

He squeezed her hand, gently raised it to his lips, and kissed it. "I'll take whatever I can get. You know I would've never hurt you. I laid in bed last night and kept replaying it in my head. I never meant to scare you like that."

"I know," she said.

"I love you so much."

"You're impossible." They sat in silence for the longest time. He was sick. He might die. Could she go through this again? It didn't seem to matter, she was going to, regardless of what she wanted. "You leave today?"

"As soon as I tell my mom, we'll pack and head out."

"And start chemo right away?"

"Yeah. They're going to try to get me back in remission before the transplant. They're searching for a donor now. When I'm in remission, they'll do the transplant and that should be it. I hope."

"You'll get through this. You've got a lot of people praying for you."

"I know."

She was frightened for him but didn't show it. Instead, she tried to let him feel love and hope. "Can I come over and help you pack?"

He grinned. "I'd like that. Give me about thirty minutes to tell my mom."

They stood. "Okay. See you in a bit."

Raven grabbed her cell phone and dialed Matthew's number. She paced the living room, waiting for him to pick up.

"Hey," he said.

"Um…" Tears filled her eyes. "It's Cody."

"He's sick again?"

She sniffed. "Yeah. I'm heading over there to help him pack. He's going to tell his mom." She grabbed a Kleenex and wiped her nose. "Do you think you can meet his mom over there in about an hour? I think she'll need some support."

"Sure. You okay?" he asked.

"Yeah, I think so."

"I'll see you over there."

"Matthew?" Her chest felt heavy.

"Yeah?"

"Thanks."

She sensed him smiling. "Anything for you," he said.

* * *

Raven peeked into the window on the door as she waited for someone to answer her knock. Cody opened the door. "Come on in."

"How's your mom?"

"Sad, angry, upset. She's packing."

Raven followed him into his room. "Can I come up with you? I'll drive. I've got nothing major pressing. School doesn't start for a few weeks."

He grabbed her hand and squeezed it. "Thanks, but no. Let them get me settled in and drugged up. When I'm in remission, you can come up…before they do the transplant." He dropped her hand and reached for his suitcase.

"How long do you think it'll be until you're back in remission?"

He threw a pillow at her. "Would you quit being such a downer? I'll call you. Hopefully not very long."

"I wish you'd let me come now."

"After the way I've acted, I don't know how you can be in the same room with me."

"It takes some trying." She smiled then sat. "You're sure taking this well. This is serious."

"Yeah, I took it real well. I was drunk and attacked you, remember?" He sat next to her, then lay back on the bed and stared at the ceiling. "You want me to tell you how scared I am? Okay, I'm so scared I feel like my insides are full of needles. I'm afraid of dying. There's so much more I want to do. I don't want heavy doses of chemo. I don't want to puke all day. I don't want to be so sick I beg God to let me die. I have to go through it, and I'd rather not think about it. Got it?"

She nodded and hit him with the pillow. He grabbed her and they wrestled. They were both laughing when he pinned her down. He was breathing hard as he held her arms. He looked at her, sat up, and became solemn. "I'm sorry."

She sat up next to him and put her arm around him. "Hey, it's no biggie. I'll be here for you. I'll come visit. You won't go through this alone."

Cody turned to her with tears in his eyes. He buried his face in her chest and began to cry. She held him.

His mother peeked in and Raven painfully smiled at her. Martha looked down and closed the door.

Raven kissed his head.

He looked up at her. "I'm sorry for being such a baby. Not very manly, is it?"

"You don't have to be macho around me. You forget. I know you too well."

"I suppose I'd be overstepping my boundaries if I asked you for a real kiss?"

Raven leaned toward him and kissed his cheek. "It's all I can give right now."

He nodded and pulled her into an embrace. "Thank you for not hating me."

They finished packing in silence. As they walked to the car, she saw Matthew pull up. She put her arm around Cody. "I asked him to come. He cares about you and your mother."

"That's fine. He's a good support for my mom." Cody turned to Raven and gave her a hug. "I'll call you."

"You better." Raven grinned.

Matthew met his mom at the car. She watched them say a few words, pray, and hug. Raven waved at Cody as their car pulled away. She walked to her car and got in.

Matthew leaned into the window. "Are you going to be all right?"

Raven nodded but refused to look at him. She was afraid if she talked, the tears would start and never stop. She stared straight ahead.

"I don't know," Matthew teased. "Last time I wasn't there for you, you…nothing. Do you want to go get some coffee?"

She started her car. "No, I'll be fine, really."

Matthew backed away from the car as she pulled out. When she got out on the road, she began to cry and pray selfishly. She asked God to save her friend's life once again.

Chapter 28

Cody lay in the dark room, isolated from the world. He imagined himself the center of a nuclear holocaust with cancer cells laughing as they swarmed to every crevice of his body. Heavy doses of combination chemotherapy were being simultaneously pumped into his veins, chasing the cancer cells, attaching to and killing them. Only downfall was the chemo couldn't decipher between good and bad cells, so it killed them all.

Nurses and doctors would appear and disappear wearing gowns, masks, and gloves. "Just keeping out the germs," they would say. "Don't want a secondary infection to deal with."

Like it could get any worse, Cody wanted to scream, but he couldn't muster up energy to speak.

His mom stood vigil as the war raged on. She would cry, pray, talk, and pray more. He saw her, but was never strong enough to respond.

Unwilling to endure any more pain, there were moments when he begged God to let him die. A split second later he'd beg God to let him live. Finally, he gave up and whispered, "Live or die. I don't care anymore." Only no one heard him.

* * *

Raven got to the hospital after visiting hours, but the nurses said she could see Cody anyway. She walked into the waiting room. Martha stood.

Raven took deep breaths trying to calm her pounding heart. "Thank you for calling."

Martha nodded. "I want you to be prepared for what you see. He's really sick and looks it. You'll need to wash and put on a gown and mask before you can go in. He's had high doses of chemo, and they can't risk an infection before the transplant."

"But he's not in remission. I thought they had to wait?"

Martha's voice shook, "He's too sick."

Raven knew it had to be bad since Martha called and told her to come. They hadn't spoken since the argument at the house. Raven's eyes widened as the hospital chaplain approached. She watched Martha and him embrace and whisper to each other. She felt sick to her stomach. She sat down and tried to collect her composure.

Martha walked to her. "Do you want to see him now?"

Raven nodded and followed Martha through the transplant wing. Nurses and doctors were everywhere. Martha pointed to the sink.

Raven mechanically scrubbed her hands and arms up to her elbows, then put on the gown and the mask. She opened the door to his room. Cody appeared to be sleeping. She raised her hand to her mouth in an attempt to hide her gasp. Nothing Martha said could've prepared her for what she saw.

Martha put her arm around her and squeezed her shoulder. "He looks worse than he is."

Raven nodded and stared. Cody looked like something out of a horror film. His skin was almost completely white and simply lay on his bones, making him appear as though he were over one hundred years old. His eyes were sunken with black circles around them. Raven fought the tears.

Martha whispered, "The nurses say this is normal. I know he looks bad."

Raven still couldn't speak. She knew if she tried she would lose it.

"You can get closer. Come on." Martha walked to him. She touched Cody's arm. "Cody, Raven's here."

Raven walked to his side.

274

Cody opened his eyes and looked up at the ceiling. He slowly turned his head toward her, and with what seemed like every ounce of energy he had, he turned one side of his mouth up in a smile.

Raven touched his arm. Tears rolled down her face. He turned away and closed his eyes. Martha tapped her arm and led her back to the waiting room. Both women sat down, and the chaplain asked them if they wanted to pray. Martha nodded. Raven dropped her head and closed her eyes. She didn't hear a word the chaplain said. She fought to keep the image of Cody out of her head. She felt Martha pat her leg and realized they must be done.

"Thanks for coming," Martha said. "Are you staying at the same hotel where you were last time?"

Raven nodded. "Call me if there is any change. I'll be back first thing in the morning."

Martha smiled. "I know he appreciates you being here."

Raven got to her hotel room and locked the door before she lost it. She paced, cried, and prayed. The ringing of her cell made her jump. She hoped it wasn't bad news from Martha. There was no way Cody would live through the night.

"Hello?" Her chest shuddered.

"Raven?" Matthew's voice usually brought her some comfort but not tonight. "How is he?"

She took a deep breath and fought the tears. "He looks dead. I'm so scared. The nurses say it's normal, but I don't see anything normal about it." She started to cry and every word she said shook with fear. "His face was like a skeleton and his eyes were sunken in. I think he's going to die."

If Matthew was scared, Raven didn't know it. He was Matthew, the minister. "But they say that's normal. He's going through a lot."

Raven took a deep breath. "I've never been so scared in my life. I don't know if he'll make it. I don't know what I'll do if I lose him."

"Do you want me to come up in the morning? I'd have to rearrange some stuff, but I will be there for you and for Cody."

"You'd do that?"

"Yeah."

"Thanks." She wiped her eyes. "I think I'll be all right."

"Are you sure?"

"No." The tears came fast.

"Remember, God's in control. He loves you. He loves Cody."

She took a deep breath. "I know. I'm okay."

"You sure?"

"Yeah. I'll call you tomorrow."

"We don't have to hang up. I'm here for you."

"No, I'm okay." Raven sniffed. "I'll be okay."

"All right. Call me if you need anything…anytime."

"Thanks, Matthew."

She hung up the phone and closed her eyes. Teresa stared at her. The blood was everywhere. The smell hung in the air. She stood and shook her head. "Stop," Raven shouted, but her father lay in the casket. "Please stop," she begged, pacing as she tried to get the images out of her mind. Cody's face came at her with a vengeance.

Vodka. It was the only thing that took the images away after Teresa died. Raven needed a drink. Just one. She pushed the thoughts of what taking that first drink might cause, grabbed her keys, and drove to the convenience store on the corner. Nothing mattered anymore. All she wanted was to numb the pain. She had to.

She paid for a soda, a bottle of vodka, and a large cup of ice, then went back to the hotel. Setting the vodka on the dresser next to the pop, she sat down on the bed and stared at it.

Drink it. Drink away the picture of Cody.

She shut her eyes and the images rushed back into her mind. Teresa, her father, then Cody—this time lying in a coffin.

Raven opened her eyes. Her heart pounded and her hands shook as she reached for the bottle. She held it. One drink. What could it hurt?

Drink it.

Resist the devil and he will flee from you.

One drink, no one will know.

Stand firm in your faith.

Raven set the bottle down and paced the room for what seemed like forever before collapsing on the bed. She stared at the ceiling. "I have to rely on God. He is my strength. He will not forsake me, ever," she said out loud and closed her eyes. Tears flooded them. She turned over, buried her face in the pillow, and sobbed. She wasn't sure how long she cried until she finally fell asleep.

The hotel phone rang and startled her. Raven opened her eyes and looked around, trying to focus. She was on the bed, still dressed. Her heart pounded harder with every ring, too scared to pick it up, convinced it was Martha calling to tell her Cody was dead.

Her head pounded and the ringing stopped. She moaned as she crawled out of bed and grabbed some Tylenol from her purse. As she swallowed them, the phone rang again. Her hands shook but this time, she mustered up the courage to pick it up. Clearing her voice she whispered, "Hello?"

"This is your wake-up call."

Raven sank on the bed with relief. "Thanks." It was eight. Visiting hours officially started at nine, but Martha said she could get in anytime. She lay on the bed and waited for the Tylenol to take effect.

After making coffee, she looked at the unopened bottle of vodka. She turned to the window, stared out it, and sipped on the coffee. She knew why she bought it, but Matthew would never understand.

She was going to get Matthew out of her head. She proved to herself last night what he had known all along. She would hurt his ministry. Cody would be her focus. He was her future.

She jumped into the shower and tried to wash off the images and the desires from the night before. She got ready then fell to her knees. "Lord, I'll do anything. Please don't let Cody die. I'll be there for him, no matter how scared I am or how much it hurts. Please, let him live."

Mayo didn't seem any busier during the day than it was in the middle of the night. Martha drank coffee in the lounge. Raven joined her. "How's Cody this morning?"

"He's hanging in there. I was worried about you last night."

"It was shocking, to say the least. I know you tried to prepare me, but I wasn't."

"No one is."

"Is he doing okay?"

Martha stood. "I'll let you go see for yourself."

Raven followed Martha to the outer room. She scrubbed, gowned, and masked up, then walked inside. Her heart pounded when she saw his eyes open. He still looked as horrible as he did the night before.

Martha walked behind her. "You can get closer. I'll be outside."

Raven nodded and walked to him. "Hi." She wanted to touch him or hold his hand but was too afraid.

Cody spoke slowly, as if it took every ounce of energy to talk. "Hi." He smiled.

Raven leaned in. "You're doing great. Keep fighting. I miss you."

He smiled, but his eyes closed.

She sat and waited. She was here for him, and she wanted him to know.

The nurse walked into the room. "You may want to wait in the lounge. We need to run some tests."

Raven nodded and left. She got some coffee and leafed through a magazine. She looked up when Martha came in. "They asked me to come in here."

Martha nodded. "They have to check counts, give him more meds, stuff like that."

"How are you surviving all of this?"

Martha sat next to her. "I'm taking one day at a time. I get bored sometimes. As you can imagine. There's not a whole lot of things to do here. I've read about everything there is on leukemia. Cody is only awake for short periods of time. His poor little body." She shook her head.

"He's going to be fine. He has to be."

"I know. I keep telling myself that." Martha paused. "They may take a while. Did you eat? If you didn't, we could go get something."

Raven set the magazine down. "I'm not really hungry."

Martha laughed. "Me neither." She rubbed her hands together. "Thank you for staying by his side. I know this hasn't been easy for you. He told me how he acted the other night and he's really sorry about that. He really loves you."

"I know." Raven avoided her eyes. "He's got to make it through this."

"He will. We need to have faith."

Raven nodded.

"I'm going to go check on things."

Martha disappeared. Raven picked up a magazine and waited for them to tell her she could see him. Cody only woke for short periods at a time, so most of the day was spent in the waiting room. She hated to admit it, but she was glad to get back to the hotel.

Chapter 29

Three days at Mayo seemed like months. Raven knew most of the nurses and almost all knew her. She leafed through the same magazine she'd read a thousand times as she waited for someone to tell her she could go back and see Cody.

The daily routine. Ten minutes with Cody and two hours to wait. Heavy footsteps echoed in the hall. Her heart skipped a beat when she saw Matthew. She stood and smiled from ear to ear. They hugged.

"I'm so glad you made it." She drew strength from him.

"You look like you need some rest. How's Cody?"

"Doing better. He's not awake very often, so this is where I've spent most of my time." She sat and replaced the magazine to its proper place on the table.

He sat next to her. "Can we go see him now?"

"No. The nurse will come get us. You have to wash up and wear a mask and gown. He's still very weak so he doesn't say much." She looked down. "He still looks deathly sick."

Martha came into the lounge and smiled at Matthew. She went to him and they hugged. "Matthew, so nice of you to come up. He's awake. You two can come back."

Raven stood. "You go ahead." She motioned toward Matthew. "I'll be there in a minute." Raven knew how fragile Cody's health was. The last thing she wanted to do was upset him. Seeing her and Matthew together might do that. She sat and out of habit, picked up the same magazine and leafed through it.

When Martha and Matthew come back into the waiting room she stood and headed to Cody's room.

She sat next to him. "So, you saw Matthew?"

Cody nodded. "Nicer…to…see…you." A faint smile lit his face and he slowly lifted his hand toward her.

She took it and squeezed it. "School starts next week. I'm thinking about waiting another semester."

"Not…for…me."

"Yes, for you." Her eyes filled with tears, like they always did when she talked to him. "You should be better by then."

"No." He took a deep breath, briefly closing his eyes. "Go…to…school."

Raven was torn and wiped the single tear that escaped. Part of her wasn't fond of sitting in the hospital waiting to spend a few minutes a day with Cody. The other part of her knew she had to do anything she could to help him.

"School…"

"Only if you promise to be home in a few weeks."

"I…promise." He smiled, then turned his head. She watched him close his eyes and knew he would sleep for a couple of hours.

She walked back into the waiting room. Matthew stood. Raven smiled at him. "Have you eaten?"

"No. I came straight here."

Raven turned to Martha. "Would you join us?"

Martha shook her head. "You two go ahead. I've eaten already."

Matthew and Raven sat in the restaurant and sipped coffee. Matthew stared out the window. "You were right. He doesn't look very good. He looks almost…"

"You should've seen him two days ago. He looks so much better than he did then." She briefly closed her eyes. The images of Cody still haunted her.

"How long will he sleep?" Matthew dropped an ice cube into his coffee.

Raven rubbed her forehead. The stress was wearing her down. "He usually sleeps for a couple of hours. I just don't know what to do about school. I want to go back, but I feel like I need to be here for Cody."

"You can't sit up here and see him for thirty minutes out of the day. He wouldn't want you to. He'll get through this and come home."

She nodded but avoided his eyes. She knew if one tear fell they'd never stop. "That's what he said. But if I can help him by staying, I will."

"It won't help him if he feels guilty about it. You can come up on weekends. Besides, I need you at the church. It's just not the same."

"Oh, please." Raven laughed for the first time in days. "You could live without me at the church." Her voice turned monotone again. "Martha said she hoped they could transfer him back to Des Moines in two or three weeks."

"He's got a long road ahead of him. I think you should stick to your plan. Martha will tell you if something changes. You can be up here in a few hours."

Raven looked down at her coffee. "I feel guilty leaving him."

"Why? It's not your fault he's sick."

"I know, but he loves me. I can't let him down. I can't let his mother down. I already did that with Teresa. I have to do whatever I can to help him."

"I understand you want to help him, but you can't carry the weight of his illness like you did with Teresa."

"I just can't walk out on him."

"Have your feelings for him changed?"

"Part of me loves him, but I just don't know."

"You can't love him out of guilt. You're twenty-one. You've got your whole life ahead of you."

"Twenty-one. I feel like I'm forty."

"You've gone through more than most people who are forty have."

She raised her cup for a refill. "You know, I realized something the other night. I don't think I'll ever truly get away from my past."

Matthew's forehead wrinkled. "Why would you say that?"

"I just don't understand why certain things are still tempting to me."

"What happened? Did you get drunk?"

"You're so blunt." She tapped her fingers on the table trying to decide how to answer. Hurt and anger collided. She wasn't sure which one would win.

"So, you got drunk?" He pursed his lips. The harshness in his voice cut through her.

Anger won. "That's the conclusion you immediately jump to." She looked at him. When his eyes met hers, she could see the tension in them. "Man, you are so judgmental."

"I'm sorry. I'm disappointed. I thought you were over all of this."

She laughed in a condescending sort of way. "You amaze me. I can't believe I ever thought we could be together. You were right, you know."

"About what?" He leaned back in the booth. "That you still have a long way to go before you're strong enough for me to date?"

His words cut like a knife. "I really hate you sometimes." She fought the tears. Her chest shuddered. She threw some money on the table. "Come on. I want to show you something."

They walked across the skywalk into the hotel. She unlocked the door to her room. "Go."

He stood.

She rolled her eyes, grabbed his arm, and led him inside. "Look at that." She pointed to the unopened bottle of vodka.

"That first night after I talked to you, I couldn't handle it." She paced as he sat on the chair. "I thought I'd go crazy thinking about Cody dying. I had flashbacks. Teresa. My dad. I'd see Cody again, in the hospital then in a coffin. I really thought I was losing it. I went to the store and bought this. I thought I had to have it." She held up the bottle. "I brought it back here and set it on the dresser. It's never been opened. You want to know what stopped me? Not you. Not anything you've said. Not your condescending eyes or judgmental words. My commitment to Christ stopped me. What I meant when I said you were right was that I *am* stronger than I thought I was."

Matthew opened his mouth, but she held her hand up. "I'm not through. Your mother told me I needed to confess something to you, and I think now might be the right time. Do you remember that drink at my dad's office?"

Matthew nodded.

"It was Hailey's—not mine. I couldn't throw that drink away because I was scared to touch it. I was afraid of the power it held over me." Tears filled her eyes as she held the bottle up. "I'm so proud of myself. I can touch this stuff and know I don't need it. So, whatever preconceived ideas you have of my sins, you can relax. I haven't had a drink since the first day I walked into your church."

She dropped the bottle into the trash and sat on the bed, her arms crossed, her face hot. Their eyes met.

"I'm sorry. I just don't know how to respond to you sometimes."

"You always assume the worst."

"No." He rubbed his forehead. "You made it sound like you went and got drunk. How am I supposed to react to that?"

She looked away from him. "I don't know. With love, maybe?"

He nodded. His eyes softened. "Back in your dad's office, why didn't you tell me that drink wasn't yours?"

"You wouldn't have believed me."

"Yes, I would've."

"No, you wouldn't have."

The left side of his mouth went up into a grin. "Okay, maybe I wouldn't have. So, you told my mom?"

"Yes. Don't even ask me how we got on that subject." She laughed. "You know, she believed me, and that was the first time I'd ever met her."

"She's more trusting than me," he said with a hint of humor. "I'm glad you told me about this."

"You know something? A month ago, I would've been too ashamed to tell you."

"Why's that?"

She shrugged her shoulders. "I don't know. Maybe because we really are just friends."

* * *

Matthew nodded. Just friends? Was Raven telling him there was no chance for them? He ran his hand through his hair. She was strong and she'd proved it. How much more did she have to prove before he'd follow his heart? It didn't matter. Even if he was ready to give her a chance, she'd never leave Cody, not while he was sick. She had already made that perfectly clear.

"We should go see Cody." He stood. "I still have to drive home."

They walked back through the skywalk to the hospital. As they traveled down the hallway toward Cody's room, Martha came out the door.

"Hey," Martha smiled. "He's awake and asking for you."

Raven grinned. "Oh, sorry."

"Not you, Raven." Martha looked at Matthew. "He said he'd like to talk to Matthew."

Matthew shrugged his shoulders. "Be right back."

He washed and put on the gown and mask before walking into the room. "Cody?" He sat. "How're you feeling?"

"Weak." He pushed the button to raise his head. "I need… a favor."

"Sure." Matthew moved closer to the bed. "Anything."

"Can you…track down my dad?"

"Didn't they try to find him when they were looking for a bone marrow match?"

"They didn't have to. There was a close enough one on the registry."

Matthew nodded. "Does your mom know where to start?"

"No. I don't want her…or Raven to know."

"Okay. Why the big secret?"

"He hurt…my mom…bad."

"What about Raven? She'd be happy to find him for you."

"When I'm well…I'm going to live with him. I need…to get away."

"And Raven?" Matthew frowned.

"I love Raven…" He swallowed, closed his eyes then opened them. "She doesn't love me…not in the way I want. She'll stay with me out of guilt…I can't stand that."

Matthew felt sorry for him. He wished things were different. He couldn't change it, even if he wanted to.

Cody closed his eyes.

Matthew touched his arm. "I should let you rest."

"Not yet." Cody opened his eyes. "You're her friend…"

"Yes."

"Then you'll be there for her… She'll be upset…but she'll get over it."

"When will you tell her?"

"When I'm back home."

Matthew nodded.

"You and Raven need to be together."

Matthew looked into Cody's eyes. They were different. Softer. Wiser. "I'm not sure if that will ever happen."

"Because you're too stupid…to see what's in front of you." Cody coughed and pointed to the water.

Matthew picked up the cup and held the straw to Cody's mouth. After he took a sip, he set it down.

"Last I knew my dad was in Florida. Write this down."

"Okay." Matthew reached over to the side table and grabbed the pen and pad of paper.

"George…James Anderson… He was working at a power plant or something…in Jacksonville."

Matthew wrote the info down. "Do you want me to call him when I find him?"

"No…I'll call him."

Matthew nodded. "Anything else?"

"Thank you…for being there for…my mom and for Raven."

"No problem."

Cody grabbed his arm as he stood. "Set aside…your pride…be with her."

Matthew patted his hand. "Can we pray?"

"I guess…it couldn't hurt."

Chapter 30

Raven stood outside Mercy Hospital waiting for the ambulance to arrive. It had been six weeks since the transplant.

Her heart raced when she saw it pull in. She walked out and grinned when the nurse helped Cody into the wheelchair. His peach-fuzz brown hair had begun to grow in. His face was fuller, and he had good color. Much better than the images that still haunted her.

He waved and grinned. "Raven."

She went to him. "You look great. Can I really touch you?"

"Yes."

She hugged him and kissed his cheek.

"Excuse me." A nurse pushed past her.

Raven felt like a school-girl that had been scolded. She followed behind them, then leaned against the wall outside Cody's hospital room, waiting for permission to go in.

The nurse finally walked out. "He's all yours."

"Thanks." Raven almost ran into the room. "You had to ride with *that* the whole way? You're stronger than I am."

Cody held out his hand. "She wasn't a whole lot of fun. Come here and let me touch you." He took her hand and ran his thumb over the top of it. "You don't know what it was like to know you were there, but not have the energy to even hold your hand?"

"You were too sick to care."

He pulled her to him and they hugged. "It's good to be back."

"I was so scared for you. You looked bad during the transplant."

"Mom said I looked like a creature from a zombie movie."

Raven nodded. "I didn't think you were going to make it. You look so much better now. You look good. So, remission?"

"Yep. This is the home stretch. A few more tests. They'll run blood work for a few more weeks, hopefully as an outpatient. I'm going to get outta here tomorrow or the next day."

"Thank God." She kissed his hand then leaned over to kiss him when a light tap on the door interrupted her. She straightened up and saw Matthew poke his head in.

"Welcome back." Matthew walked in and shook hands with Cody. "You look good."

"That's what Raven was just telling me." Cody winked at Raven. "Hey, can you go to the cafeteria and get me some pop?"

"Sure."

* * *

Matthew slid his hands into his pockets. "You talk to your dad?"

"Yeah." Cody smiled. "Mom is okay with it. After they release me from the hospital, they want me to wait a couple of weeks, then I can head out. The doctors said I can get my blood work done down in Florida. To make sure the cancer doesn't come back."

Matthew sat down. "When are you going to tell Raven?"

"You mean break up with her?" he said, with a cockiness that made Matthew's stomach turn.

"Yeah. I guess that's what you'd call it." Matthew tried to mask his relief.

"Probably after I get out of the hospital." Cody dropped his head on the pillow. "You gonna ask her out?"

"I don't know."

"You'd be dumb not to."

Matthew nodded as Raven walked back into the room. "Your Mountain Dew." She smiled, setting it and a cup of ice on the table.

"Thanks."

She sat on the bed next to him and took his hand. Cody grinned at Matthew.

Matthew pursed his lips together and stood. If Cody was trying to make him jealous, it was working. "Well, I'll let you two catch up." Matthew turned to Raven. "See you tonight?"

"Yeah, see ya." She tossed a quick smile his way before turning her attention back to Cody.

Matthew stared at them for a moment before he realized it, then quickly made his exit. Even if he was going to ask her out, it was apparent she had feelings for Cody. He couldn't blame her. She'd played the game so long she was bound to fall back in love with him. He wondered how she'd feel when Cody told her he was leaving.

* * *

"So, when did you and Matthew get to be so chummy?" Raven lay down next to Cody and rested her head on his chest.

"I don't know. He's a pretty good guy, even if he's in love with my best girl."

She laughed. "He's not in love with me."

"Yes, he is."

"No, he's not, and what would it matter? I'm with you." She grabbed his hand and held it.

He put her hand to his lips and kissed it. "What are you guys doing tonight?"

"His mom's in town. She's coming over for dinner."

Cody nodded. "That should be fun."

She leaned into him. "I'd rather be hanging with you."

Cody laughed. "No, you wouldn't. I can see you still like him."

She sat up. "What? How can you say that?"

"Just calling it as I see it."

She shook her head and held tight to his hand. She'd pushed the thoughts of Matthew—and what might have been—deep within her soul. They were friends, she would live with that.

"Well, I guess I should go." She leaned over to kiss him.

He gave her a peck on the cheek. "Have fun tonight."

"Are you sure you're all right?"

He nodded. "I'll see you tomorrow."

Odd. Why didn't he kiss her? Over the last few months, all he'd talked about was how much he loved her. She shook the thoughts out of her mind and headed home.

* * *

Matthew peeked through the blinds. His mom's rental car pulled up. He hurried out to meet her and opened the car door. "Hi. How did it go?"

"It was amazing." She took his outstretched hand and climbed out of the car. They hugged. "How are you?"

"I'm okay." He popped the trunk, grabbed her bag, and led her into the house.

She kicked off her pumps. "How much time before we go over to Raven's?"

"About an hour. Do you want to change?"

"Yes, point the way."

Matthew carried her suitcase into the spare bedroom that had a bed, a dresser, and boxes of things that weren't important enough to unpack. "Will this be okay?"

"Of course. I'll be right out."

Matthew got her an ice water and set it down on the coffee table. She emerged in a pair of dark jeans and semi-dressy white top. "This feels so much better."

"Was there a big crowd?" They both sat on the couch.

"Not too bad." She sipped on the water. "It was good. My speech was shorter than it should've been, but I signed a lot of books." She grabbed his hand. "What's bothering you? Something's going on."

He smiled. She knew him well. "I'm just confused."

"Is it Raven?"

"Yeah."

"What's going on, sweetie?"

He rested his arm on the back of the couch. "I'd like to ask her out."

Fran smiled deeply. "She's a beautiful woman. I liked her the moment I met her." She cocked her head. "What's the problem?"

"How much time do you have?" He rubbed his forehead.

She grinned. "About an hour."

"Ha-ha. You remember Cody, the boy with cancer? They used to date. She stood by his side through his sickness, and I'm afraid her feelings for me have changed."

"Have you asked her about Cody?"

"At first, she was with him more as a friend. She couldn't run out on him while he was sick, but I think it's gone deeper."

"I could understand her wanting to help him while he was sick." Fran set the glass down. "But I saw the way she looked at you a few months ago. A love like that doesn't just go away. It's admirable that she would want to help a boy she used to date. Cancer is a hard battle to fight alone, but if it's meant for you two to be together, you'll be together." She ran her hand through her hair. "I don't think Cody will be your problem. She doesn't feel like she's good enough for you."

"Why would you think that?"

"She mentioned it that night at the restaurant."

He nodded.

"What made you change your mind? I thought you told your father that you were afraid she would hurt your ministry."

He stood and paced, his hands deep in his pocket. "I knew from the first time I saw her I wanted to be with her, but I couldn't date her because she wasn't following Christ. After she turned her life back over to Him, I thought she wasn't strong enough."

"Because of the alcohol at her father's office you thought she drank?"

"Yeah, I can't believe she didn't tell me it wasn't hers. When she finally told me the truth…" He sat down next to her. "It was like God slapping me in the face. I decided that I'd better quit fighting God on this. I felt Him leading me to her all along, but my pride and judgmental attitude kept getting in the way. Now, I know being with her is the right thing to do except I'm afraid it's too late. I think I've pushed her away one too many times."

"Nonsense." She patted his leg. "Let's go over there. I'll be able to tell by the way she looks at you whether she still has feelings for you."

He laughed. "She seems to like you, Mom. Maybe you can put in a few good words for me."

"I can do that."

* * *

Raven opened the door. "It's so good to see you again."

Fran pulled her into a hug. "Thank you."

Raven glanced at Matthew. "Hey." She tucked her blonde hair behind her ears.

"Cody okay?" The left side of Matthew's mouth turned into a grin.

"Yeah, I guess." They walked into the living room. "He was acting a little weird, but I'm sure it's because he'd had a long day."

Matthew nodded and turned as Irene came out of the kitchen.

Raven turned to her. "Mom, this is Fran, Matthew's mom."

Irene extended her hand to Fran, but was pulled into a hug.

"Nice to meet you," Fran said. "I've heard so many wonderful things about you."

"Same here." Irene led them into the kitchen.

"Is there anything I can do to help with dinner?" Matthew asked.

"There is." Raven turned to the two women. "Why don't you two go sit out on the deck? Matthew and I will finish up."

Both nodded. She watched Fran smile deeply at Matthew and touch his arm. Matthew nodded back and grinned.

Raven waited until they both left. "What was that?"

"What?"

She smacked his arm. "That look between you and your mom."

He blushed. "Nothing."

"You're a mama's boy, aren't you?"

He leaned against the counter. "Nothing wrong with that. They say you can tell how a man will treat his wife by the way he treats his mom."

"Hmmm." She pulled out two knives. "That's nice to know."

She handed him one. "Let's get these veggies cut."

They both reached for the tomato. Raven pulled her hand back and laughed.

"You want the tomato?" Matthew held it gently.

"Oh, no, by all means, you can have it. I'll cut the cucumber." She laughed. Her heart raced. He was flirting with her.

Raven tried to shake it off. She'd hidden her feelings deep in her soul. Why were they trying to resurface?

* * *

His mother was right. She'd seen it in Raven's face, and he'd just felt it. Raven did have feelings for him. He would have to wait for Cody to talk to her before trying to convince her to go out with him, but there was hope.

He tossed the diced tomatoes into the bowl of lettuce as Raven added the cucumbers and placed the bowl on the table. She walked to the deck. "Salad's ready." Irene and Fran walked in. Raven opened the oven door and pulled out the casserole and placed it on the table.

They sat down, joined hands, and Matthew prayed.

Raven passed the salad. "Fran, how long are you going to be able to stay?"

"I'll be leaving in the morning, going to Kansas City. I'm speaking at a women's conference."

"Wow. Have you ever done that before?"

Fran smiled. "A few times, but it still makes me nervous."

"I can't imagine you nervous. You'll be great."

"Raven gave me one of the books you wrote." Irene cut into the casserole. "It was really good."

"Thanks. I love writing."

Matthew looked down at his cell phone. "Excuse me. I need to take this." He walked away from the table, pressing the phone to his ear.

He joined them back in the kitchen. "That was Josephine, Mrs. Tatum's daughter. They've admitted Mrs. Tatum and it doesn't look good. I need to go over there. Raven, can you run my mom home when you guys are done eating?"

"Of course."

"Is that all right, Mom?"

"Yes," Fran said.

Raven stood and walked with him to the door. "We'll pray for her and for you."

"Thanks." He leaned in and gave her a hug. "And thanks for taking my mom home. Sorry to have to bail."

"It's not your fault. You need to be there."

Matthew nodded and left.

* * *

Fran climbed out of Raven's car. "Why don't you come in and keep me company until Matthew gets back."

"Sure." Raven followed her inside.

"Can I get you coffee?" Fran opened cupboards. "Matthew should have some here."

"Okay."

When it was done, they took their cups, went into the living room, and sat. "So," Fran kicked her shoes off, "how's school?"

"It's good. I like it. Of course, I always liked school."

"Are you working?"

"Part time at a sports grill."

"And you and Cody?"

Raven sipped on the coffee and wondered why she was asking about her and Cody. Her heart wanted to think Matthew was ready to ask her out, but even if he did, could she just dump Cody? Could she forget what she might do to Matthew's ministry? No, this family was way outta her league. "Cody's doing good. We're hoping he gets to go home tomorrow. He's in remission."

"Good, but you didn't answer my question."

"I know." She half grinned. "I'm just wondering why you'd ask. I saw that look you gave Matthew earlier."

Fran smiled. "I thought when I saw you and Matthew together tonight you looked close."

"We are, we're friends. I told him about the drink not being mine."

"He told me." Fran sipped on the coffee. "He said he felt really bad about how he treated you."

"I know he does."

"There's nothing more between you two?"

"We're friends. We'll always be friends." A flash of light shone through the curtains. She set the cup on the table and stood. "I think Matthew's home." She turned to Fran. "I should go. Thanks for the coffee." They hugged.

Raven met Matthew at the door. "Your mom's inside. How's Mrs. Tatum?"

"Not good but hanging in there. Do you want to stay for a while?"

"No, your mom said she's tired. I should go."

They walked to Raven's car. "Thanks for bringing my mom home." He opened the car door for her.

"No problem." She looked up at him. He did appear to look at her differently, but she wasn't going to get lost in his eyes. She wouldn't. Cody was her future and that was that. "See you later." She left.

* * *

Matthew shut the front door. "Hey, Mom."

"Hi, how's Mrs. Tatum?"

"She's hanging in there. So, how was dinner?" He sat.

"You mean, did I find anything out for you?" Fran laughed.

"Well, that, too." Matthew rested his arm on the back of the couch.

"You saw the way she looked at you."

Heat filled his face. "You think she still has feelings for me?"

"Yes." Fran sipped the last of her coffee. "Be patient with her. It may take some convincing but if it's God's will, you know it will happen."

"I know, thanks, Mom."

Chapter 31

Cody sat on the bed in the hospital room waiting for Raven. Life was finally going to get back to its new normal, and he planned to enjoy it to the fullest. The hardest decision was to let Raven go, but he knew it was the right thing to do.

Raven walked into the room like a breath of warm spring air. She hugged him and gave him a kiss on the cheek. "Are you ready?" She cocked her head. "Aren't you excited about going home? You've waited a long time for this."

Cody hesitated a second to gather his courage, took a deep breath, and turned to face her. "I wanted to talk to you about something. I've made some decisions."

"Okay."

He rubbed his hands together. "I got in touch with my dad. He's in Jacksonville, Florida. As soon as the doctors say I can go, I'm going to move down there. I just gotta get out of here."

Her forehead wrinkled. "You're leaving?"

He began to shove things into his suitcase. He couldn't look at her. "I really appreciate all you've done for me. I still consider you one of my best friends, and I'll never forget what you've sacrificed for me, but…"

"You're breaking up with me?"

"You don't love me."

She grabbed his arm, making him turn toward her. "How can you say that?"

He saw Matthew open the door then stop. Their eyes met briefly before Matthew backed out.

Cody sat down next to her and took her hand. "Because I know who you're in love with."

"Was. There's no chance for Matthew and me. I've come to realize that."

"Either way, you don't love me, not in the way I want to be loved. I learned through this whole mess that I deserve more." He paused. His heart ached for her. He hated hurting her, but knew it was the right thing to do.

Tears filled her eyes. "How can you do this to us? I love you. I want to be with you."

"Do you know that's the first time you've said that you love me? What's that tell you?" Cody stared at her. "No, you don't really love me. It's better this way. Don't you understand? I love you so much I have to let you go."

Her face reddened. "Maybe if you loved me a little less, I'd be a lot happier. Fine, have it your way. I finally figured out that I want to be with you and I get shoved out of the way. I shouldn't have expected anything less from you."

"That's hardly fair," he barked. "I'm just stating the obvious."

"To whom? You and some fantasy in your head? Never mind." Raven laid down the black leather Bible. "I bought this for you." She tapped it. "Anyway, bye." She opened the door and ran into Matthew. She looked up at him, shook her head, and walked away without saying a word.

Matthew walked into the hospital room. Cody turned to finish packing. "How much did you hear?"

"Most of it."

"Go after her, Matthew. Do the right thing by her." Cody stared out the window, fighting the tears. He didn't turn back until he heard the door shut. He picked up the Bible and opened to the first page. She had it inscribed. *With all my heart, Raven.* It made him smile.

* * *

Matthew caught Raven still waiting for the elevator. He knew she was upset and now may not be the best time but he had to tell her how he felt. It's what he should've been done months ago.

He stood behind her and leaned in. "Do you want to talk?"

"No." She jabbed the down arrow a few more times. "I want to be left alone."

The elevator doors opened and she walked in. Matthew followed. They rode in silence, walked off the elevator and into the front entrance of the hospital.

"Let's go somewhere and talk," Matthew said.

She turned to him with a quivering chin, fists in balls, and white knuckles. "Listen, I'm trying to stay calm because I don't want to make a scene and tarnish your precious preacher status. I just got dumped, so leave me alone, please." She turned away.

His next statement might hurt her even more, but he also knew it would get her to stop and talk. The left side of his mouth went up into a grin. "Why, so you can go get drunk?"

She did what he'd hoped she would. Stopped, turned around, and walked back toward him, her neck red. She pointed at him, her voice raised and shaking. "That was uncalled for."

"Got you to stop and talk." He smiled. She was so beautiful, even when she wanted to hit him. His grin deepened. "I want to talk to you."

Her eyes narrowed. "I've got to go."

She turned and walked out to her car, but he followed with his hands deep in his pockets. He understood her anger, but somehow he had to get her to realize he was sincere.

"What do you want me to do? Beg?" Silence. Matthew opened his arms. "Raven, please come and have a cup of coffee with me."

"Hah. Not very becoming for a preacher." She turned and hurried to her car.

"Then come with me. Just some coffee, please." He began to yell. "I need to talk to you."

She pointed her keys at her car and unlocked it. He jogged to her and caught the car door as she opened it, then he slammed it shut before she could stop him.

"What is so important it can't wait?" she asked.

"Would you just listen to me for a moment?" Humor wasn't working. Maybe he should wait until she cooled off. He shook his head. He wasn't sure what to do.

She crossed her arms and leaned against the car. "I'm all ears. Make it fast. I've got to go to work."

"I'm sorry…" He looked into her cold eyes, her face hard. "Forget it." He moved out of her way. The funny thing was, he understood why she was angry. It wasn't her fault he couldn't face the truth. His stupidity had caused her all this pain. "I'll talk to you later." He backed farther away from her.

"Thank you." She climbed in her car and drove off.

* * *

Raven sat on the stool at the sports grill staring blankly at ESPN on one of the TVs. The two customers in her section had their food and were eating.

She drew small circles on the counter and wished she was more of a girl. Most women had lots of girlfriends to talk to about junk like this. She had no one. Maybe she could call Travis. No, he was too close to Matthew. Maybe she could call her sister. Then again, Hailey never was any good at giving relationship advice.

The front door opened and Matthew strolled in. He gave her a head nod and slid into one of her booths. She sighed. *Guess it's a free country.*

She walked over, set down an ice water, and handed him a menu. "See, I really did have to work. I'm not going to get drunk over Cody dumping me. I don't need a babysitter."

"That's not what I think." He took the menu. "I said I wanted to talk to you. You made me talk when we were in Minnesota, so I think you should at least do the same for me."

She pursed her lips together. He had a point. "Okay." She slid into the booth. "I guess that's fair. What do you want to talk about?"

Matthew rubbed his hands together. "How do you feel about me?"

She rolled her eyes. "I have other customers."

When she began to slide out, he grabbed her hand. He stared deep into her eyes. "How do you feel about me?"

"Cody just dumped me." She pulled her hand from his. "I can't believe you're asking me this now."

"You know I've had feelings for you and I have fought them. I thought I could push you out of my mind and out of my heart, but I can't. Cody saw it. That's why he broke up with you." He ran his fingers along the water glass. "He still loves you, you know. You could probably convince him to take you back, if that's what you really want."

She frowned. "I don't understand. He still loves me, but he broke up with me?"

"He believes you have feelings for me. Do you?"

She shook her head. "I did, but I thought I was falling in love with Cody again."

"But do you still have feelings for me?"

"I really don't know anymore. I've spent the last six months trying to forget you. I had finally accepted the fact that we'd never work."

She looked at him and her heart began to pound. She pushed the thoughts of him out of her head. She couldn't believe he was ready to throw out the idea of her hurting his ministry. But even if he threw it out, the fact remained—she *would* hurt his ministry.

"I'll be right back." She approached her two other tables, asked them if they needed anything, grabbed herself a Diet Coke and him a tea, and sat back down. "Sorry about that. I do have to work."

He smiled. "Thanks for the tea." He grabbed some sweetener and poured it in, stirred it, and took a drink. "I was wondering if you'd go out on a date with me."

"You what?"

"Tomorrow night. I'll pick you up around six?"

She shook her head. "Do you honestly think I can turn my emotions on and off like that? I can't."

Matthew's eyes widened. "You're turning me down?"

"Yes."

"I'm serious. I want to take you out. It's what we've both wanted but I've been too stupid to admit it."

Raven stared at Matthew, speechless. She'd dreamed of him saying those words, but it was too late. She wouldn't take the chance that she'd drag him down. Eventually, her faith would falter and his ministry would suffer.

"Well? Will you go out with me?" he asked.

"You have to think of your ministry. I wouldn't be good for it."

"What's your heart tell you?"

"I'm not concerned about my heart. It's been broken so many times it doesn't matter. I'm thinking about your future. I'm no good for you, at least not right now. I'm not strong enough. Two months ago I was buying vodka. How can you possibly even think about taking me out?"

"Do you plan on doing that again?"

"No, but I didn't plan it then."

"Well, if it happens again, I'll just dump you." He cracked a smile. "I believe we can build on each other's strengths. I don't believe you'll fall back into that lifestyle again. Now, back to my original question. Will you go out with me?"

Raven stared at him, her heart pounding. She fought the tears. "No, I can't. Did you want to order anything?"

He leaned back in the booth and stared at her. She blinked frantically, slid out, and stood. "If you want to order something, let me know."

She sat on the stool by the kitchen and glanced at him. He pulled his cell phone out, talked, and slid it back into his pocket. When he turned to look at her, she looked away.

Her manager came around the corner. "That guy gonna eat anything?"

"I'll go check." She walked back over to the table and pulled out her notepad. "You want anything to eat?"

"Not yet, I'm waiting for someone."

"Okay."

"Here he is now."

She turned to see Cody strut through the door. She looked back at his smiling face and rolled her eyes. "Whatever."

Raven left to grab a Mountain Dew from the kitchen and took it back to the table. "You guys ready to order?"

Cody smiled at her. "You know what I like."

She nodded, looked away from him and back at Matthew. "What can I get you?"

"Same."

She grabbed the menu from Matthew's hand and walked away from them fast, on the verge of tears. How could Cody break up with her one minute, and then come here with Matthew, who'd just asked her out? *Really? God, please help me hold it together.*

* * *

Matthew sipped his tea.

"She turned you down flat?" Cody sat tall, his shoulders back and chest thrust out.

"I don't know, maybe she really does love you," Matthew said.

"Oh, she loves me, just not the way she loves you. I get that. We just need to convince *her* of it."

"You'd do that?"

"Yeah. It's funny, when Raven dumped me before, she said it was because I reminded her of Teresa. I didn't buy it until now. I love that she stood by me with my cancer, but she reminds me of how close to death I was. I just want to forget about all of that." Cody laughed. "Guess I understand why my dad left now, too. Funny how things work out."

"God working all things together for good." Matthew grinned.

"I guess." Cody took a gulp of the drink. "Okay, we have to convince her she needs to go out with you."

"And how do we do that?"

Raven walked to the table with two mushroom burgers and onion rings. "You two need anything else?"

"Not right now." Cody grabbed the ketchup.

Matthew looked up at her and smiled before she walked away. It broke his heart to see her so upset, but Cody knew her well enough to know how to get her to admit the truth.

After a couple bites of the sandwich, Matthew pushed his plate away. "I need to go. I can't stand to see her like this. I think we're only making it worse."

"I'll stick around and talk to her."

"Okay." Matthew threw some cash on the table.

"I'll let you know."

Matthew nodded. He stood, looked at her, and gave her a faint smile. When she smiled back at him, it forced a tear out of her eye. She wiped it away and turned from him. He put his hands deep in his pockets and left.

* * *

Raven slid into the booth across from Cody.

"Are you dumbest person in the world?" Cody asked.

"Why, because I'd choose you over him?"

"There is no us."

She shook her head. "Last week you're telling me you couldn't live without me. Now you can just pack up and move to Florida?"

"Yeah, I have to." He took the last bite of his burger. "So, what about you and Matthew?"

"I don't want to be with Matthew, I want to be with you."

"No, you don't, not really. Why don't you admit it? What's really going on?"

Raven picked at the onion rings on Matthew's plate. "It's nothing."

"I think that man has loved you since the first day he met you. I've known it. You know it. He knows it."

"How can you claim to love me and push me to him?"

"It's because I love you that I push you to him. You two deserve each other. He's finally admitting it, and you're ignoring him."

"No," Raven corrected him. "I acknowledged his feelings—I'm just not going to return them. I just can't."

"Why?"

"All right, besides the fact I'd rather be with you…" She ignored his rolling eyes. "If I fall back into my old ways I couldn't live with what it would do to his ministry, it's his life. I can't handle his judgment, and most importantly, what if it doesn't work? I couldn't live with the rejection. Not after Teresa and my father, and not after almost losing you. I'm afraid I'd fall into a bottomless pit and never be able to get out. I can't risk it."

"Those are the dumbest reasons I've ever heard." He threw a cold onion ring at her.

She smiled.

"Do you plan on drinking again?" he asked.

"No, but I didn't plan on it that night in Minnesota either."

"Do you know how that makes me feel? You saw me sick and just about threw everything you've fought for away?"

"I'm sorry. It wasn't you. It was my lack of faith."

"And what if I would've died?" Cody cocked his head. "Would you have turned your back completely on your new life? You'd go back to being a drunk?"

"No. Why would you think that?"

"I don't, but that's what you're saying. Don't you think now would be a good time to start trusting in yourself and God? Not wait until you think you need a drink."

Raven shook her head. "I'm not going out with him." She raised her eyebrows. "What are you doing tomorrow night?"

"Are you asking me out?" Cody cocked his head.

"As a matter of fact, I am. Girls have been asking guys out for years now. I need to move into the twenty-first century. How about it, movie and dinner?"

Cody shook his head. "You'd choose me over Matthew?"

"Yes."

"But you don't mean it."

Raven got out of the booth and slid in next to him. "I can't turn my back on what we had."

"What we had was me loving you and you *trying* to love me."

His words wounded her even though they were true. "But I do love you."

Cody took her hand and gently kissed it. "You're sweet. I'm not angry with you. In fact, I'm grateful to you. You stood by me at the worst time of my life. I can never repay you for that, except to make you realize you never could love me like you love Matthew."

Raven looked into his eyes. She'd seen them hundreds of times but they were different—older, wiser. She lifted his hand that was still entangled in hers. "Now it's me trying to convince you to give us a chance?"

"There is no us."

"I don't understand. Is there something else you're not telling me?"

"Remember how you couldn't stand to be around me after Teresa? It's kinda like that. When you dumped me then, did you stop loving me?"

"No, but it changed. That's how you feel? I remind you of your sickness—of almost dying?"

He nodded.

"That, I can understand. It's a horrible feeling."

"I know." He leaned toward her. "I love you so much, but I just can't be around you, not like that. I want to be friends, though."

She nodded. "Okay."

Raven sat for a minute. She understood his feelings, but she also knew they wouldn't be there forever. She could give him the space he needed. She'd wait. "How about tomorrow night?"

"Okay, to a movie. Dutch, not a date."

"Friends." Raven smiled.

He nodded. "I'll meet you at the movie. Let's do the five, though. Dinner afterwards."

"All right, see you tomorrow."

"I still think you're making a big mistake."

"It's my mistake to make."

Chapter 32

Raven walked into the movie theater. Cody stood in the lobby, waving the tickets at her. "I thought you said it was Dutch." Raven said.

"It is. You buy popcorn and drinks, that'll make us even."

"Fair enough."

Raven bought the snacks and followed Cody into the theater. Cody motioned to a row. He winked at her as she started down the aisle. Cody came behind her. All of a sudden, she was staring down at Matthew. She turned back to Cody. "You set me up?"

Cody laughed. "Yeah, I did."

Matthew cleared his throat. "Raven. Cody. Nice to see you guys here."

"Um, hello." She sat, sandwiched between the two men. "There's nothing wrong with this," she mumbled. "It's no big deal. It's a movie."

Matthew leaned in. "Who're you trying to convince?"

Raven forced a smile as she sighed heavily and stuffed her mouth full of popcorn. She wasn't about to let him know she was nervous or happy to see him.

A cell phone rang. Cody answered it. "Yeah. Sure. Be right there." He leaned over her and looked at Matthew. "Man, I'm sorry but I gotta bail. That was my mom. She needs me."

"Hey," Matthew grinned. "I rode with you."

"Raven can take you home. She won't mind, will you, Raven?"

Raven rolled her eyes and refused to look at either of them. "Yeah, whatever."

Cody laughed. "Have fun."

She looked at Cody. "I'm going to kill you."

Matthew nudged her. The left side of his mouth rose in a grin. "It's that bad, huh? Spending an evening with me?"

"You know I didn't mean it that way. It's just that I can see a set-up, and this is one."

"Yep, and you fell for it." Matthew laughed.

They spent the next hour and a half fighting over the armrest, never speaking a word. As the credits rolled, Raven stood and stretched. "Come on, I'll take you home."

"What about dinner?"

"What about it?"

Matthew followed her out to the car. She opened the door and he shut it. "We're supposed to be having fun."

"We're not supposed to be here. You guys tricked me."

"Oh, come on. You are not mad about that, are you? Really?" He looked into her eyes.

Raven folded her arms. "No. I'm mad because you don't respect my feelings enough to take no for an answer."

"I respect your feelings, but I won't take *no* for an answer. We're going to dinner and talk about this. Now," he held his hand out, "give me the keys so I can drive."

Raven stared. He didn't budge. Sighing, she handed him the keys and got in the car.

"Thank you." He closed the door for her and drove them to the restaurant.

After the hostess seated them, the waitress came. Matthew looked over the menu. "I know what you like. I'll order."

Raven nodded. She felt angry and foolish.

"You're not going to make this easy, are you?"

"Nope."

"Okay, then I'll talk. Let's see, how's this week's edition of the student ministries paper coming?"

"Fine."

"And the high school lock-in. How are the plans on that?"

"Fine."

Matthew sighed. "All right, jokes over. You said you wanted to be friends, friends don't act like this."

"No, they don't."

"Man." He laughed and leaned back in his chair. "You're really mad."

"And the more you say that and laugh, the madder it makes me."

"Okay, how about this." He leaned. "I'm madly in love with you and don't know what'll happen if you don't go out with me."

"Ha-ha. Very funny."

"Have you ever known me to lie?" He raised an eyebrow.

She stared at him, trying to keep her face emotionless, but her heart pounded so hard he could probably hear it.

The left side of his mouth went into a smile. "Remember that first day you walked into the church? I knew then. You wore jeans and a white T-shirt with a black sweater over it. Your hair was pulled up tight in the back and pinned. The front was...I don't know...kinda poofy."

"Poofy?"

Matthew laughed. "Yeah. You also had on sandals, brown ones, and you wore that silver toe ring. That was the first day I knew, but I wouldn't admit it."

"You remember all of that?"

"Yes. Now, why won't you go out with me?"

Raven sipped on her water. "I thought we talked about this already. I don't want to go out with you. I can't."

"Which is it? You don't want to, or you can't?" he asked.

"I can't."

"Give me another reason besides the drinking thing. We've already resolved that one, remember? You drink, I dump."

"Here's the deal. I've had two stable men in my life. One is dead. And there's you. I can't lose you. I don't think I'd survive."

"I'm flattered, but you're saying if we dated and things didn't work out, you'd what? Give up on Christ?"

"No, but how could I sit in church? How could you be my preacher? How could we be friends? I'm scared it might not work out."

"Well, we'll just have to make it work." He smiled, sipped on his pop, and pushed the queso closer to her. "Aren't you eating any?"

Raven couldn't believe what he had just said. Had she heard him right? Was he kidding? Did he really want to date her? He seemed serious. *Lord, what am I supposed to do?*

I am able to do immeasurably more than you ask or imagine.

"You honestly want to try, you and me?" she asked.

"That's what I've been saying. I will lay down some ground rules, though. No drinking, that's obvious—"

"I'm serious. I'm not strong enough."

"Put every excuse aside and tell me how you feel. Do you want to go out with me?"

"It's not that simple," she said.

"I believe it is. I've been using excuses to not date you for months. Let me tell you what God has shown me. First, He showed me we all sin. A sin is a sin in God's eyes, and we are all forgiven. Your sins are no greater than mine. Second, He showed me you are a virgin."

Raven blushed.

Matthew smiled. "I always believed I'd marry a virgin because I am one. When you said you were one, it was like God said, "Here, I told you so.""

"Lastly, God has shown me that this ministry of mine—the one I'm so afraid of losing—it's not mine. It's His." He paused for a moment. "I'm not asking you to marry me, but you know I never date anyone I wouldn't marry, so that's a plus." He winked at her. "I've fought God on this for months and if you want to be the one to tell God no, fine. Better you than me. I know that I'm finally doing His will."

Raven took the fork and pushed her food around on her plate without ever taking a bite. "I can't believe the way God works. You wondered about my virginity, so God allowed Cody to attack me, so you could find out the answer. You could've just asked me."

"Yeah, right. Hey, Raven, you got that article done for the student news? Oh, by the way, are you a virgin?"

Raven couldn't stifle a giggle.

Matthew smiled. "Am I finally making some headway?"

"I didn't say that." Raven stared at him, her heart racing. "I've always been the one to insist we get it all out in the open, so here it is. I'm scared of disappointing you. I've never dated anyone like you. I wouldn't know how to act."

"You act just like you are right now."

"You're going to have an answer for everything, aren't you?"

"Pretty much. So, what do you think?"

Raven laid her fork down and stared at him. She took a deep breath, unable to fathom what she was about to do, but her mind told her it was the right thing. She waved the waiter over. "Could I get a box?"

"What're you doing?"

Raven scraped her food into the Styrofoam to-go box, pulled a twenty from her purse, and set in on the table. "My answer is still no. I need to go."

Outside, Matthew followed her, squeezed between the rows of parked cars. He grabbed her arm. "Wait a minute. You can't…"

Raven held her hand up, tears filling her eyes. "You're right, I can't."

Matthew stared into her eyes. He placed his hand on the back of her neck and pulled her to him and gave her a gentle kiss on the lips. "You can't tell me you don't love me."

The darkness tried to engulf them, but a small glimmer of light from a distant street light allowed her to stare into his eyes. She tried not to get lost in them. "I do love you," she whispered. "But it won't work."

Matthew held her with both hands cupped on either side of her head. He pulled her close and kissed her again.

A shudder ran through her. She fought the urge to kiss him back but failed. He tucked her hair behind her ear and smiled. "It will work."

"You're smashing my food."

He looked down at the Styrofoam box. "Sorry."

"We need to go."

She turned from him, walked to the car, and got in. He stood, shaking his head before walking to the car and getting into the passenger side. She drove to his house in silence.

"This is your decision? It's really what you want?"

Tears fell from her eyes. "Yes." She didn't look at him. She couldn't. It was plain to her—she would fail him. Maybe not today or tomorrow but someday. They were from two different worlds and the two would eventually collide.

Chapter 33

It took every ounce of Raven's energy to get up and go to church. She knew the awkwardness she'd feel around Matthew would be unavoidable. She sat in the same pew. Her heart pounded as she glanced around. No Matthew.

She sighed and gave her head a gentle shake as Cody slid down the pew and stopped next to her. "I heard you gave Matthew the brush-off."

"Yes, and I don't want to hear a lecture from you. Why are you here anyway? I figured you'd be packed and headed out of town to start your *new life*."

"Matthew asked me to come." Cody put his arm around her and gave her shoulder a rub. "I think you're making the biggest mistake of your life. That man loves you."

"You of all people know why I can't date him. If he ever knew half the stuff we did...I just can't." There were things about her past she was still ashamed of. Things Matthew knew nothing about. Things he would never know, if she could help it. Raven looked down at her Bible and folded her hands. Cody took the hint and left her alone.

Irene slid into the pew on her other side. "I just made a lunch date, so I won't need a ride home."

"Okay. Who're you going to lunch with?"

"Someone from class."

The music minister began the song service. Matthew walked in and sat down. Her stomach flipped when he stood and walked to the front of the church. He looked directly at her, bowed his head, and began to pray for the service.

* * *

After church, Matthew sat across from Irene. She had ordered a salad but he couldn't eat so he ordered coffee. His stomach was in knots. He couldn't figure out why God would lead him down this road only to find it blocked. "I just don't understand. I've told her over and over again that her past doesn't matter to me. Why is she shutting me out?"

Irene cut the lettuce with her knife while she spoke. "I think she's scared more than anything."

"Of what?"

"Of disappointing you."

Matthew rubbed his forehead. "I don't understand."

Irene chewed the food in her mouth before talking. "Her father was a gentle man, but he was never one to praise the girls. If they did something wrong, he was first to point it out. When they did something right, he never acknowledged it. Hailey just went about doing her own thing, not caring what Russ thought. Raven was different. She wanted Russ's approval, and I don't think she ever felt like she got it."

Matthew sipped on his coffee. "But why would that keep her from following her heart? She told me she loved me, but *can't* date me."

"She's had a rough life, even though it didn't have to be that way. She chose a path and now regrets it."

"But I know all about that, and I don't care. I've told her that over and over again." Matthew rubbed his forehead. How else could he assure her? How do you show someone that you don't care about their past? He scratched his head. Maybe he was wrong to tell her if she got drunk, he'd dump her.

Irene's voice drew him out of his thoughts. "I think all you can do is be patient with her and don't give up. She'll come around. She loves you. Why not come over for dinner and try again?"

Matthew hesitated. "I don't know if I should push it."

* * *

Raven couldn't go home. She had to think and the park had always brought her solitude and answers. Going straight to the swings, Raven sat down, kicked off, and pumped her legs hard, making the swing go higher and higher. Leaning back, she stared up at the sky. Her hair flew freely. When she was little, her father would swing her so high she thought she'd touch the clouds. She longed for those days—without a care in the world.

She slowed down and came to a stop. She hung her head low and stared at the gravel. The cold metal chains made blisters on her hands, but she didn't care. They couldn't hurt as bad as her heart. She pushed her feet on the gravel and got her momentum up again, and began pumping her legs, this time with a fury. *You're making the worst mistake of your life.* Was Cody right?

Raven stopped working the swing and relaxed into each glide, back and forth. Memories of the past flooded her mind. Countless parties. Being so drunk, she couldn't remember how she got home. So many people she had hurt, but she couldn't get past what she'd done to Teresa. She had stood by, watching everyone else turn their backs on her friend. Teresa called her just a week before she died, begging for help. Raven could've done something—*but she didn't.*

Grieving with Teresa's mother. Taking the compact that meant so much to Teresa. *Teresa would want you to have it,* Martha had said. Raven knew Teresa wouldn't want her to have anything. But she took the compact, and stood by Teresa's mom at the funeral. She even played hostess at the house afterwards.

She thought of Matthew. Pure, wholesome Matthew. He didn't realize her mind was so full of filth that it made her sick to her stomach. Yes, she was a virgin, but it didn't mean she was a saint.

God, why would any Christian man ever want me, let alone a minister? She sighed. *The pity party needs to end.*

But if her decision to push Matthew away was the right one, why did she still doubt? She brushed her hair back out of her face and tucked it behind her ears as she looked up. She jumped. "You scared me."

Matthew leaned against the pole of the swing set, chewing on his thumb nail.

"How long have you been there?" she asked.

"Not long. I thought you might come here. Can we talk?"

Raven avoided his eyes. "Sure." She grabbed the chains on the swing and pulled herself out to follow him to the picnic table. They both sat down facing each other.

"I had lunch with your mom today."

"You were the friend from class, huh?" Raven rested her elbows on the table. "She didn't mention it was you."

Matthew turned to her and pulled one leg up on the bench. "Listen, this is crazy. I know how you feel and you know how I feel. Why are you doing this?"

She shook her head and looked straight ahead.

He cupped his hand under her chin, forcing her to look at him. He held it there. "Tell me you don't love me."

"It's not that. You don't know who I once was."

"I don't care who you were. I care about who you are right now, and what you're going to become."

Raven pulled his hand away and stood. "I can't begin to explain the crud my mind has been filled with. Do you want to know what we used to do for fun? We would search the school for anybody who never drank. We'd take them out and get them drunk at some party and leave them."

Matthew's face showed no shock or emotion.

"Did you know I've been arrested? That I went to court?"

"Yes, when you were fourteen. Your father told me."

Raven tilted her head. "What? My father? When?"

"Right after you got hurt. He overheard something I prayed over you at the hospital—about my feelings. We got together and he tried to do what you're doing right now, shock me into changing my mind. It didn't work then, and it's not going to work now."

Raven placed her hands in her pockets. "Matthew, it's not just that. I don't think I can live with the pressure. You want me to be something I'm not. I can't be pure and innocent. I can't promise to live a sinless life, but that's what you expect. Okay, so I won't go get drunk, but what happens when I lose my temper and say something I'm not supposed to?"

Matthew shook his head. "I owe you an apology."

"An apology? For what?"

"For putting conditions on our relationship. I was wrong to do that." He took her hands and pulled her to him. "I should've never said that I would dump you if you ever got drunk. If something happens to pull you down, I will stand by you and help you back up. I treated you so bad after your father died. I thought you were doing something I despised, and I didn't deal with it right. I should've been there for you."

Tears filled Raven's eyes. Had he finally realized that she couldn't be perfect? She sat next to him. "I don't want to let you down."

"You won't." He held tightly to her hands. "Man, the things you've allowed God to accomplish in your life are amazing. I'm anxious to see what God has in store for you."

Raven pulled her hands from his and wiped the tears that escaped and now ran down her face. "You're too easily impressed."

"No, I'm not. I'm very judgmental. It's a problem I'm working on." He smiled. "So, how about it? Will you go out with me?"

Her heart pounded. "I'm still worried about backsliding. I don't plan on it, but it would be devastating to your ministry."

"God's ministry."

"Are you really sure about this?"

Matthew nodded. His eyes glistened in the sunlight and she thought she'd melt.

Raven squeezed his hand. "Okay."

"What did you say?"

She stared deep into his eyes and got lost in them. "I said, yes."

Matthew hugged her. "Man, you have made me so happy." He pulled away from her, holding her head in his hands. "You won't be sorry. How about tomorrow night?"

"Okay."

He took her hand and they walked to her car. Matthew grabbed the car door but didn't open it, instead he turned back to her. "Are you sure? You're saying you'll go out with me?"

"Yes, I'll go out with you."

He brushed his knuckles along her cheek until his hands cradled the back of her neck. She lifted her eyes to meet his and he kissed her. He raised an eyebrow. "Tomorrow night, a date? Six o'clock?"

"Yes." She giggled and pulled him into another kiss.

"I'll see you tomorrow." He opened the door for her. After she got in, he tapped on the roof of the car. "Yes!" she heard him exclaim before shutting the door.

Chapter 34

Raven stared out the window of Matthew's car, chewing on her thumbnail. *This is so dumb. Why am I nervous? We've been out many times. She sighed. This is different…this is a date.*

"You seem uneasy." His voice drew her to him.

"It shows?" She watched him darting glances at her, as if he couldn't keep his eyes on the road. It made her heart race. "I spent hours trying to decide what to wear."

Matthew touched her hand. "Quit making such a big deal out of this. It's dinner."

"I know. I'm being silly."

Matthew pulled into the restaurant lot and parked. He walked around and opened the door. He grabbed her hand, led her inside, and they followed the hostess to a table.

After ordering, she clutched her hands together in a praying position. "I'm sorry for acting so stupid. I've pictured this moment so many times, I just can't believe it's happening. Now that it is, I don't know how to act."

"Act like you always do. That's what I like about you."

"I told you we shouldn't do this." Raven laughed and tucked her hair behind her ears. "I just want everything to be perfect."

"It is." He moved his glass of water so the waitress could put their plates down. He pointed. "Why don't you try and eat something? You know how I hate paying for that expensive popcorn at the show." After they prayed, Matthew's phone rang. He looked at the caller ID. "I need to get this."

"Sure." She forced herself to take a bite of the food.

"Okay." He hugged the phone close to his ear. "I'm so sorry. I'll be right there." He slid the phone in his pocket. "That was about Mrs. Tatum. They don't think she'll make it through the night. I've got to head over to the hospital. Would you like to come? I'm not sure how long I'll be there, though. Maybe I should take you home."

"I'll tag along, if that's okay."

"Did you get enough to eat?" He pointed to her food. "We could get it to go."

Raven scooted the plate away, thankful for an excuse. Her stomach was still in knots. "No, I'm good."

"We'd better go."

When they got to the hospital, Raven stopped in the room to say hello to the Tatum family. She squeezed Mrs. Tatum's lifeless hand, leaned in, and said her own silent goodbye. It brought back a flood of memories of her father. She wished she had been able to say goodbye to him.

"Can I get anybody anything? More coffee?" Raven asked.

"Coffee would be great," one of the family members said.

"I'll be right back." She gave Matthew a nod and left. When she returned, she passed out the cups and noticed a little girl sitting in the corner, playing quietly. Raven knelt down next to her. "I'm Raven. What's your name?"

The little girl looked up at her. "Sara."

"Hi, Sara. Would you like to take your things in the other room with me? We'll have more room to play in there, if you want."

Sara nodded.

"Let's ask your mommy." Raven stood, unsure of which woman was her mother, but the confirming nod of one of them told her it was okay. Raven and Sara made their way to the waiting room. They read books, played games, and played with her Barbie. Sara climbed up on Raven's lap and laid her head down. Raven sang to Sara as she dozed off. She stroked Sara's auburn hair and watched her sleep. It wasn't a perfect first date but it was a memorable one.

Matthew walked into the waiting room. Raven put her finger to her mouth, motioning for him to be quiet. Matthew squatted next to her and whispered, "I'm going to need to stay here. Why don't you take my car? I can have someone drop me off later."

"No, I'm fine. Sara just fell asleep and it'll be better for her mother if she doesn't have to worry about her."

"Are you sure? It could be all night."

"We're fine. Tell her mom not to worry."

"Do you want to call Irene?"

"No, she's knows I'm out with you. What possible trouble could a preacher get into?"

"You never know." Matthew raised his eyebrows.

"I'll text her."

"Thanks for sticking around." He stopped at the door and turned back at her. She looked up at him. He gave her a wink and disappeared.

Raven dozed off and woke when Sara moved. Sara looked up at Raven and rubbed her eyes. "How's my grandma? Did she go to heaven yet?"

Raven rearranged Sara on her lap. "I don't know, but heaven's a great place. My dad's there. He'll show your grandma the ropes."

"He is?" Sara picked up a piece of Raven's hair and twirled it around her little finger. "When did he go there?"

Raven moved Sara's hair out of her eyes. "Not very long ago."

"Was he old like my grandma?"

"No."

Sara stared at Raven. "Why did he go to heaven?"

"I guess Jesus needed him more than we did."

"Jesus must need my grandma, too."

Raven kissed the top of her head. "I'm sure He does."

Sara's mom slipped into the lounge next to Raven. Sara saw her, jumped off of Raven's lap, and ran to her. "Mommy, is Grandma with Jesus?"

She began to cry. "Yes, honey." She looked at Raven. "I can't thank you enough for watching her."

Raven stood. "She's great. We had fun, didn't we, Sara?"

"Yes." Sara patted her mother's face. "Raven's daddy is in Heaven with Jesus, too."

Her mother hugged Sara.

Matthew came out of the room with the last of the Tatum children. They talked for a moment before he turned to Raven. "I can take you home now."

Raven nodded and they walked into the elevator.

"I'm sorry about this evening." Matthew touched her back.

"It was nice, really. I enjoyed spending time with Sara."

"You were a big help. I know the Tatum family appreciated it. I've got to head over there in a few hours." He pulled into her driveway and looked at his watch. "It's after four. I hope your mom's not upset."

"She won't be," Raven said, as they walked to the front door.

"I'll call you later."

"Okay."

He leaned down and gave her a kiss.

Chapter 35

Raven sat in the bleachers half watching Matthew play a basketball game in a men's league. She'd watch him for a few minutes, then work on her homework. She looked up from the college English book to see Lisa walk through the door. Her eyes narrowed, but she forced a smile when Lisa gave her a wave, walked up the bleachers, and sat down next to her.

"I didn't know you were coming." Raven turned to Matthew, who glanced up, gave his head a gentle shake, and got back into the game.

"I'm just passing through on my way back home. My dad asked me to stop by."

"You spending the night?" Raven chewed on the cap of the pen.

"The Greens are letting me stay with them. I hope that's not a problem." Lisa looked over at her. "So, are you and Matthew dating?"

"Yes."

"I figured you guys would."

"We never intended…he wasn't unfaithful to you ever."

Lisa's nod was unconvincing. Raven let it go. "What brings you here?"

"There's a revival at my dad's church in a couple of weeks. The preacher he brought in can't preach one of the nights and they asked Matthew to fill in."

"They did? That's neat. So, why did you have to come?"

"For some reason Matthew hasn't given an answer. My dad asked me to come by and personally ask him."

Raven closed the book and looked over at her. "Why wouldn't he preach? Sounds like a great opportunity."

"Oh, it will be. There'll be a couple thousand people. It would really give him exposure. You know he's destined to preach like his dad. He's good enough, just has to get out there."

"I know." She looked back at the court and at Matthew. He glanced up at her and smiled. She wondered why he wouldn't jump at the chance to preach to a crowd that size.

"Will it bother you if I talk to him?" Lisa asked.

"Of course not."

The final buzzer blew. They won. Matthew grabbed his towel and wiped the sweat off of his forehead. He smiled at Raven while being bombarded by players shaking his hand.

Matthew walked up to where they were sitting. "Hey, Lisa, what brings you to town?"

"I need to talk to you. I wondered if we could grab a bite to eat."

"Raven and I had plans."

"That's okay." Raven tucked her hair behind her ears. "You guys can go."

Matthew smiled at Raven before turning to Lisa. "Why don't you join us?"

"That'd be okay, if it's okay with Raven."

Raven nodded.

"I'm going to take a quick shower. Be right back."

When Matthew disappeared into the locker room, Lisa gave a small laugh.

"What's that for?" Raven slid her books into her backpack.

"Just wondered why he doesn't want to be alone with me." She turned to Raven, a smug grin on her face.

"I'm not the jealous type so you don't have to try. If he doesn't want to be alone with you, I doubt it's because he's still attracted to you."

The smile left Lisa's face and her eyes narrowed. "Doesn't it make you wonder why he won't go preach at my dad's church in front of thousands of people?"

"Maybe he doesn't want to."

"Why? It's his dream." Lisa stood. "Maybe there's another reason that doesn't have anything to do with him."

That stung. Raven followed her down the bleachers. "You think it's because of me?"

Lisa shrugged her shoulders. "I don't know. You've got a past."

"So what? That's my past. It doesn't have anything to do with his decision."

"If you say so." Lisa leaned against the wall.

Raven crossed her arms. She really wasn't the jealous type, but Lisa sure found out fast that her weakness was self-confidence.

Matthew emerged dressed in khaki pants and a white shirt. Raven grabbed Matthew's extended hand. "You sure you're okay with this?" he asked her.

"Yeah," Raven said.

He turned to Lisa. "We'll have to make it quick. I've got to study for my sermon tomorrow."

"I haven't forgotten."

"You can follow us." Matthew and Raven got in his car and left. "I'm sorry, I didn't know she was coming."

"It's all right."

"You okay? You're not jealous, are you?" he teased as he pulled the car into the restaurant lot. He threw the car into park and killed the engine. He grabbed Raven's hand and pulled her to him. "You've got nothing to be jealous about." He kissed her.

"I'm not jealous."

They heard Lisa tap on the window. Matthew playfully rolled his eyes and climbed out of the car, walked around to Raven's side, and opened the door for her.

The three of them walked into the deli, ordered their sandwiches, and sat.

"How's work?" Matthew asked Lisa.

"It's going good. Dad wanted me to stop by and ask about the revival." She stared at him. "I can't believe you didn't jump at the opportunity."

"I just haven't decided."

"I thought this was your dream, to preach like your dad?"

"I don't know anymore." He shrugged his shoulders. "All I know is that I'm doing what God wants me to do right now, and I just have to wait and see where He leads me."

"That doesn't sound like you. You've talked about a chance like this since as far back as I've known you." Lisa glanced at Raven.

If Lisa was trying to make her feel guilty, it was working. Lisa didn't seem like the type of person to be vindictive. Maybe she felt guilty because Lisa was right. She could be the reason Matthew wasn't preaching. Was he ashamed or worried about her past?

She sat quietly. If Matthew hadn't discussed it with her before, she doubted he wanted her input now, especially in front of Lisa.

Matthew ran the napkin over his mouth and moved his almost empty plate to the center of the table. "It's a great opportunity, I won't deny that, but I don't know. I don't feel like I've gotten a confirmation that it's what God wants me to do right now."

"And if you don't get this confirmation, do you think if you preached God wouldn't bless it? Come on, Matthew." Lisa sipped on her water. "I know you better than that. This is a chance for you to really get the Word out there, in front of thousands. There's another reason. What is it?"

Raven finished her last bite and waited. If it was because of her past, he wouldn't admit to it in front of Lisa.

When he said nothing. Lisa rolled her eyes. "I think it'd be pretty stupid of you not to preach, but I guess it's your choice."

"I told your dad I'd have an answer for him tomorrow. I'll call him after church."

They stood and walked to the parking lot. "You're staying at the Greens?" Matthew asked.

"Yes, after church I'm heading home. I have to teach on Monday." Lisa opened her car door. "See you in the morning."

"Goodbye." Raven climbed into the car.

As Matthew drove her home, she looked over at him and watched him closely. "Why didn't you tell me you were asked to preach there?"

He shrugged his shoulders and pulled the car into her driveway. "Didn't think it was that big of a deal." He climbed out of the car and walked her to the front porch.

"You didn't think that was a big deal? You'd be preaching in front of thousands of people. Isn't that your dream?"

He grabbed her hand and pulled her onto the porch swing next to him. "It's a few weeks away and I just haven't decided." He caressed her hand as he kicked off, swinging the swing.

"But why wouldn't you mention it? I don't have to go or anything, but *you* should go."

"If I preached, why wouldn't you go?" His smile deepened. "Don't tell me you think I'm not sure because of you?"

"Well, I do have a past. It can't look good."

"A past is good. It shows people how Christ has changed your life." He put his arm around her. "My decision to preach at his church has nothing to do with you."

"Then what on earth would stop you from going after your dream?"

"I don't know. I just haven't felt led by God to say yes."

That made her pull away from him. "I don't understand. If your dream is to preach before thousands and the opportunity comes up, how could you not think that was God handing it to you?"

"It's kinda hard to explain, unless you've felt it. You ever hear a tiny voice inside your head or heart that tells you something and you're like, where'd that come from?"

She laughed. "Yeah, I've heard that."

"Most of the time, that's the Spirit. You have to test it against the Scripture, because sometimes your 'self' gets involved. I haven't felt that yet with this. I've asked God to confirm it and haven't gotten confirmation, so I wait."

"Wouldn't Lisa coming here be a confirmation? Or me telling you that you should go?"

His grin deepened. "It probably is. I'll know when I pray more about it."

She shook her head. "How can you possibly think we should be together? I'm so stupid about this stuff."

"It's refreshing. I love seeing you learn new things about the Lord."

"You're too easily impressed."

He laughed, stood, and grabbed her hand. "I really need to study."

"Okay."

Matthew held the front door open for her. Raven's mother sat on the chair, her hands folded, her face pale. "Hi, Mom, everything okay?"

"I need to talk to you about something."

"Sure, I'll be right there."

"Everything okay?" Matthew asked.

Raven shrugged her shoulders. He leaned over and gave her a quick kiss.

"See you in the morning." He looked over at Irene. "Goodnight Irene."

"Goodnight."

Raven shut the door. "What'd you need?"

"I received a call tonight from Mr. Thompson. Mr. Frank Thompson."

Raven's eyes widened. "Isn't that the man who killed Daddy?"

Irene nodded. Her hands began to shake.

"He's got a lot of nerve calling here," Raven almost shouted. "What does he want?"

Irene shifted her weight. "He'd like to meet with us tomorrow. I spoke to Hailey and she's willing to go with me. I'd like you to come also."

Raven shook her head and backed up to the stairs. "No. No way. That man killed Daddy and almost killed you. I wouldn't give him the time of day and I don't understand how you can even consider going to see him."

"Raven…"

"I'm not going." Raven ran up the stairs.

She shut the door to her room and lay on the bed staring up at the ceiling. When everything was going so well, why would this man want to drag up all these old feelings? She heard her cell phone ring and saw on the caller ID it was Matthew. She sat up and answered it. "Hi."

"Is everything all right? Your mom didn't seem like herself."

"Mom got a call tonight from the man that hit them and killed Daddy. It seems he wants to meet with us. Mom and Hailey are going and they want me to go, too. I just can't believe they would give that man the time of day." Raven paced the small room, her anger building with every step.

"Maybe he wants to apologize."

"And that would make it all better? I'm not going give him the satisfaction of easing his conscience. He almost killed my mom and he did kill my dad."

"Boy, do you have a temper." She could hear an easiness in his voice. He was Matthew the boyfriend, not Matthew the minister. "You know, he didn't hit them on purpose. He dozed off at the wheel. Maybe you should sleep on it, pray about it. I think you need to forgive him. Christ forgave the people who killed Him."

"Christ is perfect; unfortunately, I am not."

"There's that nasty temper again."

Raven slowly let out her breath. "I've got to go."

"Hey, don't get mad at me."

Raven closed her eyes. It wasn't Matthew she was angry with, it was this man. This stranger who in a moment changed her life forever. It was this man who was stirring up pain she thought had been dealt with. "I'm not mad at you. I don't want to talk about it."

"Pray about it. Promise me?"

"I will. I'll see you tomorrow. Are you going to be able to stay for the youth meeting after church? They're serving food."

"I'll be there for part of the time. I'll see you then and remember to pray about meeting that man, what was his name?"

"Mr. Thompson." She sighed and rolled her eyes. Yes, she should want to pray about it, but the idea made her stomach hurt. "I will, but I just don't think I can meet with him, let alone try to forgive him."

"I'll pray about it, too."

"Goodnight."

Raven stared at the ceiling and wondered how God could even ask her to face this man. He killed her father. He changed her life forever. There was no way she could forgive him.

Chapter 36

Raven walked into Matthew's office after the youth meeting. He looked up from his papers. "You look tired."

"I am. I didn't get much sleep last night."

Raven sat, prepared for any argument he would throw at her about Mr. Thompson. "You decide about preaching at the revival?" she asked.

"Yeah, I'm going to do it and I want you to come."

She smiled. "Okay."

"We'll need to leave around noon. Can you miss classes?"

"Yeah, no problem."

"Are you going with your mom and Hailey today?"

"No. I was up half the night praying, thinking, and trying to find forgiveness, but I just don't think I can be in the same room with him, not after what he's done."

"I really think it will help you as much as it would help him."

"I know, and I'm sure you're right. But I can't, at least not right now. Someday…maybe. I know you're disappointed." She looked down at the floor, avoiding his eyes. "I don't want to fight with you about this. I know I should go. I know I should forgive him, and I know what Jesus would do, but I can't."

"You won't even try?"

She stood. "I need to go."

"When are they going?"

"They're probably there right now."

Matthew walked around her desk, grabbed her hand, and pulled her to him. "I'll go with you, if you'd like. You don't have to do this alone."

She nodded. "I know you would, but I don't have it in me right now."

He walked her to the car. "Are you going to be okay?"

"You mean am I going to get drunk?" she snapped and rolled her eyes. "I thought we were past this."

"That's not what I meant." He held his arms up defensively. "I just asked if you're going to be okay. I want you to rely on Jesus, not on me, but I want to be there for you."

"I'll be just fine, thanks for the vote of confidence." She turned.

Matthew grabbed her arm and made her look at him.

Raven fought the tears. "I'm hurt you would think that low of me. Wasn't it you that said my slate was clean? And now it's you who's dragging up my past."

"I didn't mean it like that. I'm sorry."

Raven pulled away from him. "I've gotta go."

"Look at me."

She sighed and brought her eyes to meet his. He gently rubbed the side of her face. "I wasn't there for you when your dad was killed and I feel bad about it. I want to be here for you now. I trust you, I really do. Don't go off half-cocked and angry with me, please."

She clasped her hand on his outstretched arm, squeezed it, and forced herself to smile. "I'm not angry with you. I'm angry at myself because I know you're right, but I can't make myself go over there."

"You want to go get some coffee? Food? Go to a movie? I've got the whole afternoon."

She took his hand. "No. I think I'll just go home." Her anger was subsiding and melancholy was setting in.

"I'll see you for dinner tonight?"

"Of course."

Matthew pulled her into a hug. "It's going to be okay."

"I know." She stretched up and gave him a kiss.

Raven got in her car and looked down at the piece of paper with Mr. Thompson's address. She had placed it in her Bible that morning, just in case she changed her mind.

Hailey and her mother had already gone, offered their forgiveness, and were probably home by now. Should she go? Why was she even thinking about it? Something was changing inside of her. Her own words echoed back in her head, and she knew what she had to do. She'd forgive him. Or at least she had to try.

She took off to the Thompsons. The numbers grew smaller until she finally found the house, parked the car, and watched. A woman came out with a small child. They played on the grass. Raven noticed the ramp going up the sidewalk into the house. She hoped to catch a glimpse of the man who killed her father.

Her heart raced. The woman had seen her and was now approaching the car. Raven got out and walked around to the sidewalk.

The woman smiled. "Are you having car trouble?"

Raven shook her head. "I don't really know what I'm doing here. I guess I'm here to see your husband, Frank Thompson."

The woman bounced the child that rested on her hip. "And you are?"

. "Raven Pennington."

The woman's eyes widened. "Yes. He's inside. Your mother and sister left a little while ago. Please come in."

As they approached the house, Raven began to feel uneasy. She stopped when she saw the front door open and a man come out in a wheelchair. She watched the little girl leap from her mother's arms and run to him.

Raven felt sick to her stomach. "I'm sorry. I can't..." She turned around and hurried to her car. The woman yelled something, but Raven ignored her.

She pulled into the drive at Matthew's. Her chest shuddered as she knocked.

Matthew opened the door with a grin. "Hey."

"Can I talk to you?"

Matthew nodded and motioned for her to come in.

"Can we sit outside?"

"Sure."

They sat on the porch steps. Ashamed, Raven stared straight ahead, unable to look into his eyes. Her hands shook. "I went over to the Thompson house. I tried, but I just couldn't do it. I saw him come out of the house in a wheelchair and I got so angry. Something came over me, and I just couldn't do it."

"At least you tried." Matthew put his arm around her.

Raven dropped her head and let it rest on her knees. "Why can't I get over it? I'm just so mad." She looked back up at him and hugged her knees tightly to her chest. "Mom and Hailey have. Why can't I?"

"There's nothing wrong with being angry. His recklessness killed your father. I'd be ticked, too." Matthew's compassion began to put her at ease. "What you have to do is try to forgive him. The anger will pass."

"I don't know how." She stood, looked down at him, and wiped the tears that rolled down her cheek. "I can't describe how I felt when I saw him with his family after he destroyed mine. Why did he fall asleep at the wheel?"

"You're asking the wrong person." He stood and took her hand, gently kissing it. "Come on, let's go ask Mr. Thompson. I'll drive you."

She stood firm, unable to move. "I don't think I can go back there." She stared at him. "You'll come with?"

"Of course."

"Okay."

They pulled up to the house and she began to shake. Mrs. Thompson picked up her daughter and walked to the car. Matthew got out, reached out his hand, and shook hers. Raven watched them talk. Matthew came back to the car, opened the door, and squatted down. "He's inside. We can go in whenever you're ready."

Raven hesitated, but got out. She grabbed Matthew's hand like it was her lifeline. Mrs. Thompson opened the front door. After taking a deep breath, Raven walked in with Matthew.

The house smelled of mulberries and things were built low to accommodate the wheelchair, she guessed. She stared at the crucifix that hung right in front of her and thought of the irony. *I got the message, God. I'm here.*

Frank Thompson sat in a wheelchair in what looked like the living room. It was small and in desperate need of updating. As she approached him, he smiled at her and held out his hand.

Raven sat down. She wasn't ready to shake the hand of the man who killed her father.

Matthew took the extended hand and shook it before sitting down next to her. "Matthew Stewart. I'm a close friend of Raven's and I'm also her minister."

"Nice to meet you."

Raven had a thousand questions, but couldn't seem to bring herself to ask any of them.

Matthew whispered to her, "Do you want me to leave?"

Raven quickly grabbed Matthew's arm. "No."

"I'd like to talk to her alone." Frank's eyes moved from Matthew's to Raven's. "If that's all right."

Matthew patted her arm. "Maybe it'd be better if I waited outside."

Raven clung to him.

Matthew looked into her eyes. "I'll stay if that's what you want, but I think it'll be easier for you to talk if I'm not here. I'll be right outside."

"Okay." Raven released her grip on Matthew's arm. Matthew was right. It'd be better if he wasn't there so if she said anything she shouldn't, he wouldn't hear. She'd only have to apologize to God.

Matthew excused himself and left Raven alone with Frank.

Frank wheeled closer to her. "I'm glad you came back. Your mom is a nice woman."

"Yes, she is. It's a shame she has to live the rest of her life alone…without her husband." Her eyes narrowed.

Frank lowered his head. "I'm so sorry. I can't tell you how bad I feel about what happened."

"You mean when you killed my dad?" She wanted her words to cut through him, for him to feel the pain she felt.

He looked away. "Yes, and hurting your mother. My attorney says I'm stupid for talking to you guys. Says you could hit me up with a lawsuit, but as you can see, I haven't got much for you to take. I'm sorry that I killed your dad. If I could change what happened that night, I would. It haunts me every minute of every day. It's ruined my life, too, you know."

Raven stared at him. She could feel the heat creeping up her neck. "How can you say that? You're still alive. You'll be able to see your daughter grow up, know your grandchildren. My father will never have any of that."

"Why did you come here? I can tell you're not interested in hearing anything I have to say."

"What did you expect? How would *you* act?"

"Probably the same way." He began to chew on his fingernail.

Raven pursed her lips. "Are you in that wheelchair because of the accident?"

"Yes." He turned the chair and moved it toward the table. He picked up a picture of himself and handed it to Raven. "That was me...before."

Raven looked at the picture. The man looked twenty years younger, sat on a bike with his daughter in a yellow seat attached to the back. He appeared happy. The man sitting in front of her was empty, almost pathetic. Raven replaced the picture on the table and began pacing the room. "How could you do it? How could you fall asleep like that?"

"I didn't think I was that tired. It was only nine-thirty." Frank followed her with his head. "You can't imagine what I live with every day. I have to look in the mirror, knowing that because of my stupidity, I killed a man. A man you loved. Your father. A husband. Look what I did to my own family. My wife will never have a real husband again. And my daughter, she'll never have a brother or a sister and she has a cripple for a father." He lowered his head in defeat. "I'm so sorry." He cupped his hands over his face and began to cry. "If I could trade my life for his, I'd do it in a second."

Raven could see his pain but quickly hardened her heart. How could she possibly feel sorry for him? He killed her father. "What do you want from me? Forgiveness?"

Frank looked up at her through his tears. "Oh, no. I don't ever expect you to forgive me. I just wanted you to know that I was sorry."

She fought the urge to cry. She sat on the couch, resting her head in her hands. How could she claim to be a Christian and not forgive him?

"I'm sorry I asked you to come." Frank wheeled to the door. "My wife can show you to the door."

Mrs. Thompson came into the room. "Your friend is waiting outside."

Tears filled Raven's eyes as she nodded and stood. She walked to the door, and paused before turning back. "I miss my father very much."

"I know. I'm so sorry." Frank patted his wife's hand which rested on his shoulder. "My own life is worthless now."

Raven chest shuddered. "I'd hate for your little girl to grow up with you thinking that. You're not worthless." She took a deep breath and slowly let it out. "I don't believe you meant to kill my dad. I hoped that I could come here and forgive you. I think, in time, I can."

Raven looked at Mrs. Thompson. "I'm sorry we've all had to go through this. What was your name?"

"Nancy."

Raven held out her hand. "Do you know Jesus?"

Nancy nodded, tears overflowing. "Yes, I do."

Raven looked back at Frank. "And you do, too?"

"I've seen His power today," he said.

Raven knelt next to him. "I can only forgive you through His power. You have to forgive yourself. Let Him help you. Thank you for apologizing to me and my family. I believe that's rare in our world today. I have to go." She turned and walked out. She could barely see the car through her tears.

"Miss Pennington?"

Raven stopped and turned back.

"Thank you." Nancy wiped her eyes. "I can't begin to explain how much this will help him."

Raven nodded, crossed her arms, and held her stomach tight as she stumbled blindly toward the car.

Matthew drove them back to his place. He opened her car door and took her hand as she climbed out. Her heart raced, and she desperately tried to stop the tears. "I need to go."

"Why don't we talk?"

"No. I want to be alone."

Matthew backed away.

As she drove to the cemetery she glanced in her rearview mirror and smiled. Matthew was following her. She parked her car and got out the same time Matthew did.

"You'd never make a good cop." She grabbed his hand. "Come on."

They climbed a small hill to a tombstone that stood six feet tall. It was dark gray with the etched letters reading Russell Dwayne Pennington II, husband, father and friend. Raven fell to her knees, dropped her head, and quietly cried.

Matthew knelt next to her and rubbed her back.

Raven wiped her eyes and stood. She took Matthew's hand and pulled him up. "I want to show you something."

A few steps and they stood before the small tombstone that read Teresa Marie Anderson. She pulled the small compact out that held the suicide note and also took out a lighter. Taking the note from the compact, she lit it and the note caught fire. She kissed the compact before placing it on the tombstone.

Matthew pulled her close. "Are you okay?"

"Yeah. For the first time in over a year, I think I am."

Matthew led her to the small bench that sat by her father's grave. "You want to know something?"

"What?"

Matthew turned to her, his grin deep. "I love you. I mean, I really love you."

Her heart raced and her eyes flooded with tears of joy. "I love you, too."

He brushed her hair aside and touched her cheek. He took a deep breath, reached into his pocket, and pulled out a small black velvet box.

Her heart pounded as her eyes widened.

He opened it and pulled out what she guessed was a one-carat diamond solitaire. "I've been carrying this around for about a month." His grin deepened. "Raven, I would be honored if you would be my wife." He slowly slid the ring on her finger and looked up at her.

Staring into his loving eyes, she whispered, "I'd love to."

DANA K. RAY has been writing gutsy, true to life Christian stories since she became a teenager. A full-time children's minister in her church, she and her husband reside in the Midwest with their four children and four dogs. *A Second Chance* is her first published novel.

56210637R00211

Made in the USA
Charleston, SC
16 May 2016